Washington Irving, Pierre Munroe Irving

The Life and Letters of Washington Irving

Vol. I

Washington Irving, Pierre Munroe Irving

The Life and Letters of Washington Irving
Vol. I

ISBN/EAN: 9783337249502

Printed in Europe, USA, Canada, Australia, Japan

Cover: Foto ©Raphael Reischuk / pixelio.de

More available books at **www.hansebooks.com**

THE

LIFE AND LETTERS

OF

WASHINGTON IRVING

BY HIS NEPHEW
PIERRE M. IRVING

IN THREE VOLS.
VOL. I

NEW YORK
G. P. PUTNAM'S SONS
27 & 29 WEST 23D STREET
1883

Press of
G. P. Putnam's Sons
New York

iv

PREFACE.

HE work, of which I now offer the first volume to the public with the most unfeigned diffidence, has been mainly compiled from papers committed to me by Mr. Irving, with the understanding that I was to construct a biography from them, should it be my fate to survive him. " Somebody will be writing my life when I am gone," said he to me some years before his death, and after having resisted repeated applications for an autobiography, " and I wish you to do it. You must promise me that you will."

Though deeply sensible of the confidence implied in such a request, my first impulse was to decline an office so responsible, and for which I felt myself so little qualified ; but the request was repeated with an earnestness which showed the subject had seriously engaged his thoughts, and with the assurance that he would be able to place in my keeping materials which he would only confide to a relative, and which would of themselves go far to furnish a picture of his life from his first launch in the world. I yielded my scruples to this assurance ; and not long after, he placed in my possession a mass of material, consisting of journals, note-books, diaries at scattered intervals, and a large collection of family letters, with files of others from various correspondents, which, as he said, he had neither time nor spirit to examine or arrange. He afterward procured for me his numerous letters to his friend, Henry Brevoort, which were furnished through the kindness of his son, J. Carson Brevoort, Esq.; and shortly before his death, indicated to me others, both in this country and in Europe, which, if still in existence, might be of interest in a narrative of the shifting scenes of his life. Of these I have been able to obtain, since his death, the originals or copies of such as had been preserved; and to them have been added numerous letters, both of his early and later life, which have been contributed by various friends, to whom I here offer my acknowledgments.

In the delicate office of sifting, selecting, and arranging these different materials, extending through a period of nearly sixty years, it has been my aim to make the author, in every stage of his career, as far as possible, his own biographer, conscious that I shall in this way best fulfil the duty devolved upon me, and give to the world the truest picture of his life and character.

CONTENTS.

CHAPTER I.

CHAPTER VII.

CHAPTER VIII.

CHAPTER IX.

CHAPTER X.

CHAPTER XI.

CHAPTER XII.

CHAPTER XIII.

LIST OF ILLUSTRATIONS.

LIFE AND LETTERS

OF

WASHINGTON IRVING.

CHAPTER I.

Birth, Parentage, and Ancestry.—William De Irwin.—Curious Tracing of the Descent.—Settlement in New York.—Flight to Rahway.—A Prisoner's Certificate.—Home of the Author's Boyhood.—His Domestic Training.—His Baptism.—Early Introduction to his Namesake.

ASHINGTON IRVING was born in the city of New York, April 3, 1783. He was the eighth son of William and Sarah Irving and the youngest of eleven children, three of whom died in infancy. He had four brothers and three sisters who lived to mature age, and whom, as I shall have occasion to speak of them in the course of my narrative, I here name in the order of birth : William, Ann, Peter, Catharine, Ebenezer, John, Sarah.

The parents of Washington came from the opposite ends of Great Britain : his father from the Orkneys; his mother from Cornwall. The father was the son of Magnus Irving and Catharine Williamson, and his ancestors bore on their seals the three holly leaves, which are the arms of the Irvines of Drum, one of the oldest and most respectable families of Scotland, which dates its origin from the days of Robert Bruce.

According to a received tradition, in his secret and precipitate flight for Scotland from the court of Edward I., Bruce sought shelter in the tower of Woodhouse, the dwelling of an Irving of Bonshaw, who was chief of the name. Here he was harbored for some time, and on leaving, he took with him the eldest son of his host, whom he made his secretary and armor-bearer. The son accompanied him through all his varying fortunes, was with him when he was surprised and routed at Methven, in June, 1306, shared all his subsequent dangers and hardships, and was one of seven who lay concealed with him in a copse of holly when his pursuers passed by. In memory of his escape in this extremity of peril, Bruce assumed the holly as a device, and afterward gave it to his faithful secretary, with the motto, *Sub sole sub umbra virens.* The motto and the evergreen leaves, both having relation to his unchanging fidelity to his king in prosperity and adversity, in sunshine and in shade, have been the arms of the family ever since. Sir William Irvine, as he is styled in Nisbet's " Heraldry,"[1] was subsequently Master of the Rolls, and the charter is still extant, dated 4th October, 1324, by which the king conveyed to his faithful and beloved William de Irwyn, in free barony, the lands of Drum, a hunting-seat of the kings of Scotland, situated on the north bank of the river Dee, about ten miles from Aberdeen. The tower of Drum, with its walls of solid masonry, still stands as sound and unimpaired as when the estate was conveyed, and is still occupied by the Irvings, and lays claim to the distinction of being the oldest inhabited dwelling in Scotland.

William De Irwyn married Mariota, the daughter of Sir Robert Keith, Great Mareschal of Scotland, who led the horse at Bannockburn, and was killed at the battle of Duplin in 1332.

---

[1] The name is written in ancient deeds and parchments in a great variety of ways, as Irvin, Erwyne, De Irwin, etc. Dr. Christopher Irvine, one of the stock, in 1660, says : "Some of the foolish write themselves Irving." The present family of Drum spells the name Irvine.

Of this family, says Dr. Christopher Irvine, historiographer of Charles II., in an ancient document quoted in Playfair's "British Family Antiquity," are the Irvines of Orkney. But at what time his branch of the family was transplanted to that locality, the author had no information other than a family tradition, that it was during some troubles in Scotland prior to the reign of Charles II. A few years previous to his death, some legal controversy arising in England on the subject of the copyright of his works, a London publisher was led to apply to Kirkwall for documentary proof of his father's place of birth. In making the necessary researches, the Clerk of the Records was induced to trace his descent as far back as possible, and it is a curious fact that he was enabled to do it through four centuries, from a facility afforded by the ancient "Udal" laws of that region, which required that lands, on the death of the owner, should be divided equally among the sons and daughters; a peculiarity which led in the partition, to the mention of the names and relationships of all the parties who were to draw a share. The result of these researches showed that "William De Erwin," the first Orkney Irvine and earliest cadet of Drum, was an inhabitant of Kirkwall, the metropolis of the island group, in 1369, the same year in which Thomas, the eldest son and successor of the armor-bearer, is mentioned among the barons of the Scottish Parliament; that the Irvings held landed possessions in Pomona, the island in which Kirkwall is situated, up to 1597, when Magnus, eldest son of James, the "Lawman" or chief judge of the Orkneys, sold his share of his father's property in the neighborhood of Kirkwall to a younger brother, and removed to the contiguous island of Shapinsha, where, in 1731, was born William, the father of the author.

On the death of his mother, who had always opposed his wishes on this point, William yielded to the long-cherished desire of his boyhood, and went to sea. During the war between France and England he engaged on board of an armed packet-ship of his British Majesty plying between Falmouth and New York, and was a petty officer in this service when he met with Sarah Sanders, the only child of John and Anna Sanders, and granddaughter of an English curate whose name was Kent.   Their marriage took place on the 18th of May, 1761, and two years thereafter, on the return of peace, the youthful pair embarked for New York, where they landed on the 18th of July, 1763, having buried their first child on the shores of England.

Mr. Irving took up his residence in the city not far from " The old Walton House," as it now proclaims itself with boastful longevity, then recently erected, which with the Middle Dutch Church, still resisting at that time the language of England in spite of a century of British domination, now shorn of its honors and transformed into a post-office, are almost the only relics left of the contracted and half-rural city of that day.

On settling in New York, the father of the author entered into mercantile business.   He was getting on successfully, when the Revolution broke out ; and he found his quiet dwelling under the guns of one of the English ships in the harbor at the time when, in consequence of General Lee's measures, it was apprehended they would fire upon the town.   A general panic prevailed ; many of the inhabitants fled to the country, and among the number Mr. Irving and his little flock, with whom he took refuge at Rahway in New Jersey.   Here he was not much better off: business was at an end ; his children suffered from fever and ague, and finally, when the British made an incursion into the Jerseys, he returned to New York, after an absence of nearly two years, during which almost half of the city had been destroyed by fire.

Throughout the revolutionary contest, he and his wife exerted themselves without ceasing in alleviating the sufferings of American prisoners.   The mother of the author, who possessed a character of rare generosity and benevolence, was especially zealous in this charitable ministry.   Prisoners were supplied with food from her own table ; and she often went in person to visit them when ill, furnishing them with clothes, blankets, and other necessaries. Cunningham, so noted for his brutality, always softened at her appearance.   " I 'd rather you 'd send them a rope, Mrs. Irving," he would say ; but her charity was invariably permitted to reach its object.

Mr. Irving was particularly concerned in administering to some patriot clergymen of his denomination, who were imprisoned. From one of these, as the time approached for the British to evacuate New York and the American troops to take possession, he received the following quaint certificate, evidently given under an impression that his residence in the city during the war might subject his loyalty to doubt, and expose him to the risk of harsh and proscriptive treatment.

" These may certify whom it may concern, whether civil or military officers, that Deacon William Irving, merchant in this city, appeared to be friendly inclined to the liberties of the United States, and greatly lamented the egregious barbarities practiced by her enemies on the unhappy sons of liberty, that unhappily fell in their power—contributed largely to my relief (who was a prisoner in this city as early in the war as June, 1779), and was probably an instrument under God of the preservation of my life—and by credible accounts I have had from other prisoners, both in the city and country, has been the means of the preservation of theirs also."

This document is signed " Blackleach Burritt, Minister of the Gospel in the Presbyterian Church," and bears date November 15, 1783, ten days before Washington and his army entered the city.

It was some months previous, as we have seen, that his infant namesake first saw the light. The two-story dwelling in which he was born, No. 131 William Street, about half-way between Fulton and John, was long ago pulled down. Within a year after his birth, the family moved across the way to No. 128. A deed from the executors of Samuel Prince, bearing date in the August succeeding his birth, conveys to " William Irving, Merchant," the house and lot, " 25 feet front by 156 feet deep," for the " consideration of two thousand pounds current money of the State of New York." This was then, or had lately been, occupied by a British commissary, and after some alterations and additions it became the family residence, and was the homestead in which the author grew up, and around which were gathered the recollections of his infancy and boyhood.

It was a triple structure, composed of a front and rear edifice of two stories, with a narrow central building, forming a passage between them, and connecting the two; its roof descending to an attic window in each division. It was my fortune to accompany the author when he visited the old homestead in 1849, on the eve of its demolition, and I remember with what a half-giddy feeling, as we stood in the yard, he pointed out the rear building from which, a venturesome urchin, he would climb to this sloping roof, steal along its dizzy edge to the higher window of the front garret, mount thence to the roof of one of the adjoining buildings, drop a stone down the chimney, and then clamber back to his hiding-place, chuckling over the imagined wonder and perplexity he had created.

This was but one instance of a mischievous vivacity of spirits, which showed itself in a great variety of pranks; though the system of domestic government under which he grew up was little calculated to foster a lively disposition. The father, a sedate, conscientious, God-fearing man, with much of the strictness of the old Scotch Covenanter in his composition, had small sympathy with the amusements of his children, and lost no opportunity of giving their thoughts a serious turn. That he was somewhat overstrict in his discipline there can be little doubt—at least his children, with a high respect for his character, always retained that impression of him. When I was young, I have heard Washington say, " I was led to think that, somehow or other, every thing that was pleasant was wicked." Notwithstanding the paternal strictness, however, they were a merry household, finding diversion in every thing; and though sometimes their frolics partook of mischief, and they were tempted to steal away, as they grew older, to some fascinating, the more so because forbidden, place of amusement, the foundation laid resulted throughout in characters of rare uprightness, combined with a more than ordinary degree of the intellectual and imaginative. Among his contemporaries, the father was held in the highest regard. " You come of a gude stock," said a worthy Scot of his acquaintance to the writer of this memoir, waiving a proffered security; " I 'll trust you."

It is a little curious, considering the form of faith in which the author was reared, that he should have been conducted to the chapel of St. George in Beekman Street, to receive his baptismal name. This was soon after Washington and his army had entered the city. But the rite was performed by a Presbyterian, though in an Episcopal sanctuary, an anomaly growing out of the circumstance that the churches of that denomination had been dismantled during the Revolution, and were now being refitted with pulpit and pews ; during which interval their Episcopal brethren gave the returning congregations the use of their precincts for half the Sabbath.

His name of Washington was the means of procuring him an early introduction to that illustrious personage, when he came back to New York, then the seat of government, as President of the United States. A young Scotch maid-servant of the family, struck with the enthusiasm which everywhere greeted his arrival, determined to present the child to his distinguished namesake. Accordingly, she followed him one morning into a shop, and pointing to the lad who had scarcely outgrown his virgin trousers : " Please your honor," said she, " here's a bairn was named after you." In the estimation of Lizzie, for so she was called, few claims of kindred could be stronger than this. Washington did not disdain the delicate affinity, and placing his hand on the head of her little charge, gave him his blessing.

CHAPTER II.

N his fourth year, Washington was sent to a school in Ann Street, between William and Gold, kept by a Mrs. Ann Kilmaster. Here he continued upward of two years, making very little progress beyond the alphabet.

From Mrs. Kilmaster's he was transferred, toward the close of 1789, to a school for both sexes kept by Benjamin Romaine, at 198 Fulton, then 37 Partition Street. Romaine had been a soldier in the Revolution, and was a thorough disciplinarian. He was a man of good sense and sound judgment, but of moderate scholarship. At this school the author remained until he was fourteen years of age. He soon became a favorite with the quondam soldier, who had a way of designating his preference by calling him "General," though his partiality seems to have arisen at first, not so much from any indications of talent in his pupil as from the fact that, though constantly in mischief, he never sought to shelter himself by prevarication when called up to be questioned, but always confessed the truth.

Another trait which was mentioned by a female school-mate in after-life, was his unwillingness to witness the chastisement of the

8

other boys. The standing punishment inflicted on truants was horsing, or hoisting, so called, and as the culprits had to be untrussed, it was always administered after school when the girls had been dismissed. But little Irving, she said, could not endure the spectacle ; the sight of the unlucky urchin shrinking under the rod was too much for his nerves, and he finally insisted on leaving with the girls, and was permitted.

Though he had little inclination for dry study, his taste for reading was early developed. In his tenth year, he fell in with Hoole's translation of the " Orlando Furioso," then just published, and I have heard him recur with delight to the exciting interest of its pages, and dwell with evident complacency upon his achievements in parodying the feats of arms of which he had been reading ; sallying forth into the yard of his father's house, the grand theatre of his youthful exploits, with wooden sabre to encounter some little playmate, fired like himself with noble zeal to prove himself a true knight, and rushing to the onset with his favorite motto :—

> " Where'er my footsteps go, my deeds proclaim,
> War is my sport, and Rodomont my name."

At the age of eleven, books of voyages and travels became his passion. This feeling was first awakened by the perusal of " Robinson Crusoe " and " Sindbad the Sailor." Afterward he met with " The World Displayed," a collection of voyages and travels, selected from the writers of all nations, in twenty small duodecimo volumes, embellished with cuts, and this was an inexhaustible treasure. He was not permitted to read at home after retiring to his bed, but such was their fascination that he used to secrete candles to enable him to do so. These volumes he would also take to school, and snatch hasty moments of reading under the shelter of his desk. One day, Romaine saw him busily intent on one of them, and creeping up slyly behind him, thrust his hand down, and seizing the forbidden book, ordered him to remain after school to answer for the offence. The result, however, was very different from what he had anticipated ; for his instructor, perceiving in what the reading consisted, gave him credit for the taste he showed in the selec-

tion, and only cautioned him that he could not permit him to cultivate the propensity to the neglect of the regular exercises of the
school.

This continual reading of travels and voyages begot in time a
great desire to go to sea. " How wistfully," says he, in the introduction to the " Sketch-Book," " would I wander about the pier-
heads in fine weather, and watch the parting ships bound to distant
climes—with what longing eyes would I gaze after the lessening
sails, and waft myself in imagination to the ends of the earth ! "

A performance, which indicates an early literary tendency, and
which may be referred to the age of thirteen, was the writing of a
play, which was represented at a friend's house in the presence of
Mrs. Melmoth, a well-known actress of that day. He had first attended the theatre with James K. Paulding, his early literary associate, who had left his home in Westchester County for the city, where
he was then living with William Irving, who had married his
sister. Paulding was four and a half years his senior. The performance was " Speculation," a comedy in which Jefferson was the
chief attraction. He was delighted with the acting of this comedian,
and from this time he conceived great fondness for the theatre. It
was at this period that he was delivered of his play, of which, however, not a fragment, not even the title, lingered in his memory. It
is fair to presume it had great dramatic demerit.

The anecdote is of use only as serving to display an early scribbling propensity. He had been remarked at school for the ease
and fluency of his pen, and would frequently effect an exchange of
tasks with the other boys, and write their compositions, while they
in turn would work out his sums ; for arithmetic was the most
tedious of all his studies.

His education was completed before he had attained his sixteenth
year ; at least from this period he assumed the direction of his own
studies. His brothers, Peter and John, had been sent to Columbia
College, and why he did not receive the same advantage he could
never satisfactorily explain, except that he was more alive to the
drudgery than the advantage of a course of academic training. He
never failed, however, to regret the omission in after-life.

At the age of sixteen he entered the law-office of Henry Masterton, a respectable practitioner with whom his brother John was also serving an apprenticeship to a distasteful vocation ; for though this brother afterward attained to the dignity of the bench, his early preference inclined him to the ministry.

Whatever may have determined the choice of Washington to the thorny paths of the law, it is certain he could not have been prompted to it by his father, for the profession never enjoyed his good opinion. At an earlier period, when Peter had decided to embrace it, he interposed his authority to prevent him, and he thereupon turned his attention to medicine, a pursuit always uncongenial to him, and speedily abandoned ; though the title of " Doctor " remained with him for life. Washington spent an interval of two years in the office of Mr. Masterton, which was marked by considerable proficiency in belles-lettres, but very slender advancement in the dry technicalities of the practice.

It was at this period of still happy boyhood, that he made his first voyage up the Hudson, the extraordinary beauty of which, says Bryant, he was the first to describe. His eldest sister, Ann, in 1788, at the early age of seventeen, had married Richard Dodge, of Dutchess County, who, previous to their marriage, while employed as surveyor on the Mohawk, had been tempted to try his fortunes in this, at that time, frontier world. He had persuaded William Irving, the elder brother, then just twenty-one, to accompany him. They established themselves on the river about forty miles west of Albany, that country being then filled with Indians, with whom the trade in furs was extremely profitable. William remained there four years, when he wearied of the frontier life, and in 1791 returned to the city to engage in commercial business, and Mr. Dodge removed to Johnstown, a colonial town founded by Sir William Johnson, and having something of historic interest as the scene where, at his stately mansion, " The Hall," this agent of the British Government ruled for years over the neighboring tribes of Indians with sovereign sway. His second sister, Catharine, some years later had married Daniel Paris, a young lawyer of that region, with whom she had become acquainted at New York, while in college with her brother Peter, and who afterward removed to the same place, which, from the character of its early settlement and its proximity to Schenectady and Albany, still boasted at that time quite a gay and cultivated society. To gratify his restless desire to see more of " the vast globe " he inhabited, his parents had consented to his making an excursion to visit these two married sisters. He had before passed a holiday in Westchester County, during the fever of 1798, and explored the recesses of Sleepy Hollow with his gun, but his migrations had extended no farther. The Highlands and all beyond were still, to his eager imagination, a realm of wonder and enchantment. From the moment, therefore, the expedition was mentioned, he thought and dreamed of nothing else.

I transcribe from his papers some reminiscences of this early voyage, which was made in 1800. They form part of an unfinished article commenced in June, 1851, for " The Home Book of the Picturesque," and afterward thrown aside to give place to " The Kaatskill Mountains," the title of the contribution from his pen which appears in its pages. The reader familiar with that sketch will detect here and there a passage which has been retained from the rejected fragment, but with this exception the extract is new, and affords a curious picture of some of the features of the river travel of bygone days.

My first voyage up the Hudson was made in early boyhood, in the good old times before steamboats and railroads had annihilated time and space, and driven all poetry and romance out of travel. A voyage to Albany then was equal to a voyage to Europe at present, and took almost as much time. We enjoyed the beauties of the river in those days ; the features of nature were not all jumbled together, nor the towns and villages huddled one into the other by railroad speed as they are now.

I was to make the voyage under the protection of a relative of mature age—one experienced in the river. His first care was to look out for a favorite sloop and captain, in which there was great choice.

The constant voyaging in the river craft by the best families of New York and Albany, made the merits of captains and sloops matters of notoriety and discussion in both cities. The captains were mediums of communication between separated friends and families. On the arrival of one of them at either place he had messages to deliver and commissions to execute which took him from house to house. Some of the ladies of the family had, peradventure, made a voyage on board of his sloop, and experienced from him that protecting care which is always remembered with gratitude by female passengers. In this way the captains of Albany sloops were personages of more note in the community than captains of European packets or steamships at the present day. A sloop was at length chosen; but she had yet to complete her freight and secure a sufficient number of passengers. Days were consumed in "drumming up" a cargo. This was a tormenting delay to me who was about to make my first voyage, and who, boy-like, had packed up my trunk on the first mention of the expedition. How often that trunk had to be unpacked and repacked before we sailed!

. . . . At length the sloop actually got under way. As she worked slowly out of the dock into the stream, there was a great exchange of last words between friends on board and friends on shore, and much waving of handkerchiefs when the sloop was out of hearing.

Our captain was a worthy man, native of Albany, of one of the old Dutch stocks. His crew was composed of blacks, reared in the family and belonging to him, for negro slavery still existed in the State. All his communications with them were in Dutch. They were obedient to his orders; though they occasionally had much previous discussion of the wisdom of them, and were sometimes positive in maintaining an opposite opinion. This was especially the case with an old gray-headed negro, who had sailed with the captain's father when the captain was a mere boy, and who was very crabbed and conceited on points of seamanship. I observed that the captain generally let him have his own way.

. . . . What a time of intense delight was that first sail through the Highlands! I sat on the deck as we slowly tided along at the foot of those stern mountains, and gazed with wonder and admiration at cliffs impending far above me, crowned with forests, with eagles sailing and screaming around them; or listened to the unseen stream dashing down precipices; or beheld rock, and tree, and cloud, and sky reflected in the glassy stream of the river. And then how solemn and thrilling the scene as we anchored at night at the foot of these mountains, clothed with overhanging forests; and every thing grew dark and mysterious; and I heard the plaintive note of the whip-poor-will from the mountain-side, or was startled now and then by the sudden leap and heavy splash of the sturgeon.

. . . . But of all the scenery of the Hudson, the Kaatskill Mountains had the most witching effect on my boyish imagination. Never shall I forget the effect upon me of the first view of them predominating over a wide extent of country, part wild, woody, and rugged; part softened away into all the graces of cultivation. As we slowly floated along, I lay on the deck and watched them through a long summer's day, undergoing a thousand mutations under the magical effects of atmosphere; sometimes seeming to approach, at other times to recede; now almost melting into hazy distance, now burnished by the setting sun, until, in the evening, they printed themselves against the glowing sky in the deep purple of an Italian landscape.

In the foregoing pages I have given the reader my first voyaging amid Hudson scenery. It has been my lot, in the course of a somewhat wandering life, to behold some of the rivers of the Old World most renowned in history and song, yet none has been able to efface or dim the pictures of my native stream thus early stamped upon my memory. My heart would ever revert to them with a filial feeling, and a recurrence of the joyous associations of boyhood; and such recollections are, in fact, the true fountains of youth which keep the heart from growing old.

To me the Hudson is full of storied associations, connected as it is with some of the happiest portions of my life. Each striking feature brings to mind some early adventure or enjoyment; some favorite companion who shared it with me; some fair object, perchance, of youthful admiration, who, like a star, may have beamed her allotted time and passed away.

CHAPTER III.

IN the summer of 1801, Mr. Irving left Masterton, and entered the office of Brockholst Livingston; and when that eminent lawyer was called to the Bench of the Supreme Court of the State, in January, 1802, he continued his clerkship with Josiah Ogden Hoffman, a distinguished advocate of the city, who took a fancy to him, though, as he says himself, a very heedless student. The house of Hoffman soon became another home to him.

The family of Mr. Hoffman consisted of a second wife, whom he had lately married, a Miss Fenno of Philadelphia, much younger than himself, a daughter of the Federal editor of that name, and five children by a former marriage—four daughters, the two eldest, Ann and Matilda, of the ages of fourteen and twelve, and a son, quite a child, Ogden Hoffman, afterward distinguished at the bar and on the floor of Congress for his silver-tongued oratory. With Mrs. Hoffman, a most amiable and interesting woman, the young student formed an intimacy which continued till her death, and to her many of his letters are addressed. "She was like a sister to me," is the language in which he once wrote of her.

Soon after his admission to this little circle, he made a second visit to Johnstown. The following letter, dated from that old colonial town, is the earliest which has come into my possession, and is of interest chiefly as showing his delicate state of health at this period, and the indications of that consumptive tendency which subsequently led to his first visit to Europe.

JOHNSTOWN, July 2, 1802.

MY DEAR PARENTS:—

We had a very quick passage to Albany, where we arrived at three o'clock on Thursday morning. I was unwell almost the whole time, and could not sleep either night. We left Albany about an hour after we arrived there, in a wagon, and reached Johnstown between ten and eleven in the evening. The roads were fine, being turnpike almost the whole way; but I was so weak that it was several days before I got over the fatigue. I have had a little better appetite since I have been up here, though I have been troubled with the pain in my breast almost constantly, and still have a cough at night. I am unable to take any exercise worth mentioning, and doze away my time pretty much as I did in New York; however, I hope soon to get in a better trim.

From Johnstown he accompanied his brother-in-law, Daniel Paris, to Ballston Springs. His cough would seem to have been very aggravated. "Was that young Irving," asked Judge Kent of Mr. Paris, "who slept in the next room to me, and kept up such an incessant cough during the night?" "It was," was the reply. "He is not long for this world," rejoined the foreboding querist. The Judge, afterward the distinguished Chancellor, lived to preside at a public dinner given thirty years later to the consumptive invalid.

Though his health was still drooping, we find him a few months after his return commencing a series of humorous contributions to the *Morning Chronicle*, under the signature of Jonathan Oldstyle. This was a daily paper, of which his brother Peter was proprietor and editor, and which was established in October, 1802. The first of these articles appeared in the middle of November, when the writer was nineteen years of age. In these juvenile essays we may see traces of the same play of humor which marked his pen in after-years; and though of local and temporary interest, it is singular to what degree, in that barren period of our literature, they attracted attention, being generally copied, as I have been informed, into the newspapers of the day. They also procured him a visit from Charles Brockden Brown, who had given to the world a series of remarkable novels, and was the first in our country to make a profession of literature. Brown sought, but without success, to enlist his pen in the service of the *Literary Magazine and American*

Register, a periodical he had just undertaken in Philadelphia. In 1823, when Mr. Irving was abroad, and had become something of a literary lion in Europe, the Oldstyle papers were given anew to the world without his knowledge or consent, and a good deal to his regret, though he subsequently thought of including four of them in his collected writings.

In the summer of 1803, Irving was invited by Mr. Hoffman to accompany him on an expedition to Ogdensburg, Montreal, and Quebec, and gladly availed himself of the opportunity to extend the range of his travels. In this progressive age, when we can be whirled the entire distance in less than twenty-four hours, a journey from New York to Ogdensburg would promise little of incident or adventure; but it was a formidable undertaking at that early day, and involved difficulties, discomforts, and trials of patience, of which the modern tourist can have no idea. Indeed, could the travellers themselves have foreseen the fatigues and hardships they would have to encounter, it is certain their enterprise would not have been equal to the trial. Without, however, any just knowledge or appreciation of its labors or privations, the party of seven, Mr. and Mrs. Hoffman, Mr. and Mrs. Ludlow Ogden, Miss Eliza Ogden, Miss Ann Hoffman, and himself, found themselves, on the 31st of July, 1803, on board of a sloop bound for Albany. From that place they proceeded to Ballston and Saratoga Springs, and thence, Irving making a flying visit to Johnstown by the way, to the modern city of Utica, then a village unconscious of the sound of "church-going bell." From this point they were to diverge to Ogdensburg, or Oswegatchie, as it was then called, on the St. Lawrence, where Hoffman and Ogden owned some wild land and purposed to lay out a town.

Irving kept a journal of the expedition from New York to Ogdensburg, which was struck off in the midst of hurry and fatigue, and of course is very carelessly written; but it has an interest independent of any literary value, as a picture of travel in those early days of our country.

On Monday, August 9th, they set off from Utica for the High Falls, on Black River, in two wagons, having despatched another with the principal part of their baggage. The roads were bad, and lay either through thick woods, or by fields disfigured with burnt stumps and fallen bodies of trees. The next day they grew worse, and the travellers were frequently obliged to get out of the wagon and walk. At High Falls they embarked in a scow on Black River, so called from the dark color of its waters; but soon the rain began to descend in torrents, and they sailed the whole afternoon and evening under repeated showers, from which they were but partially screened by sheets stretched on hoop poles. About twenty-five miles below the Falls they went ashore, and found lodgings for the night at a log-house, on beds spread on the floor. The next morning it cleared off beautifully, and they set out again in their boat. On turning a point in the river, they were surprised by loud shouts which proceeded from two or three canoes in full pursuit of a deer which was swimming in the water. A gun was soon after fired, and they rowed with all their might to get in at the death. "The deer made for our shore," says the journal. "We pushed ashore immediately, and as it passed, Mr. Ogden fired and wounded it. It had been wounded before. I threw off my coat, and prepared to swim after it. As it came near, a man rushed through the bushes, sprang into the water, and made a grasp at the animal. He missed his aim, and I jumped after, fell on his back, and sunk him under water. At the same time I caught the deer by one ear, and Mr. Ogden seized it by a leg. The submerged gentleman, who had risen above water, got hold of another. We drew it ashore, when the man immediately despatched it with a knife. We claimed a haunch for our share, permitting him to keep all the rest. . . . . In the evening we arrived at B——'s at the head of the Long Falls. A dirtier house was never seen. We dubbed it 'The Temple of Dirt'; but we contrived to have our venison cooked in a cleanly manner by Mr. Ogden's servant, and it made very fine steaks, which after two days' living on crackers and gingerbread were highly acceptable.

"*Friday, 13th.*—We prepared to leave the Temple of Dirt, and set out about sixty miles through the woods to Oswegatchie.

We ate an uncomfortable breakfast, for indeed it was impossible to relish any thing in a house so completely filthy. The landlady herself was perfectly in character with the house : a little squat French woman, with a red face, a black wool hat stuck upon her head, her hair greasy and uncombed, hanging about her ears, and the rest of her dress and person in similar style. We were heartily glad to make an escape."

The journal omits to mention, that just before they started, the young traveller took out his pencil, and scribbled over the fire-place the following memorial :—

> " Here Sovereign Dirt erects her sable throne,
> The house, the host, the hostess, all her own."

In a subsequent year, when Mr. Hoffman was passing the same way with Judge Cooper, the father of the distinguished novelist, James Fenimore Cooper, he pointed out this memento of his student, still undetected and uneffaced ; whereupon the Judge, whose longer experience in frontier travel had probably raised him above the qualms of over-nicety, immediately wrote under it this doggerel inculcation :

> " Learn hence, young man, and teach it to your sons,
> The wisest way 's to take it as it comes."

They set off again " in caravan style," two wagons for them-selves, and another, drawn by oxen, for the luggage. They found the road dreadfully rugged and miry. The horses could not go off a walk in any part. The road had not been made above a year, and the stumps and roots of trees stood in every direction. At night they put up at a small hut consisting of but one room, which, however, the hostess, by the sagacious expedient of stretching a long blanket across, managed to divide into two. " On one side," says the journal, " we spread our mattress for the ladies, and great-coats, blankets, etc., for ourselves. The other side was left for the drivers, etc."

The next day the wagon in which Irving and some of the ladies were riding stuck fast, and one of the horses lay down, and refused to move. They had therefore to get out and travel after the other wagon, into which the ladies mounted; but soon that also mired, and there was no alternative but for them to take to their feet. " The rain by this time," proceeds the journal, "descended in torrents. In several parts of the road I had been up to my middle in mud and water, and it was equally bad, if not worse, to attempt to walk in the woods on either side.

" We helped the ladies to a little shed of bark laid on crotches, about large enough to hold three, where they sat down. It had been a night's shelter to some hunter, but in this case it afforded no protection. One-half of it fell down as we were creeping under it, and though we spread great-coats over the other, they might as well have been in the open air. The rain now fell in the greatest quantity I had ever seen.

" The wind blew a perfect hurricane. The trees around shook and bent in the most alarming manner, and threatened every moment to fall and crush us. . . . . The ladies were in the highest state of alarm, and entreated that we should walk to a house which we were told was about half a mile distant."

They therefore dragged along, and after a most painful walk arrived at the hut, which consisted of one room about eighteen by sixteen feet. In this small apartment, fifteen people were to pass the night; for besides the owner, they found here two men who were driving an ox-team through to Oswegatchie, both noisy and boisterous, and one of them stigmatized in the journal as " the most impudent, chattering, forward scoundrel" the writer had ever known. There was much noisy greeting between these and the drivers, and, to add to the confusion of the scene, they soon seated themselves in a corner and " began to play cards for liquor"; an amusement from which they retired after a while almost intoxicated, and stretched themselves on the floor to sleep. " I never," says the journal, "passed so dreary a night in my life. The rain poured down incessantly, and I was frequently obliged to hold up an umbrella to prevent its beating through the roof on the ladies as they slept. I was awake almost all night, and several times heard the crash of the falling trees, and two or three times the long dreary howl of a wolf."

On resuming their route the next day, they found it impossible to travel the road with horses, and they were therefore compelled to engage the men to take their baggage through in their ox-cart, while the ladies rode in the ox-wagon which had hitherto held their luggage, and the gentlemen proceeded on foot.

Two days more of the same forlorn travel, through deep mudholes, over stumps and stones, obliged at times to cut their way through fallen trees, and resting at night in the same wretched hovels, brought them at last in sight of Oswegatchie. The journal says: "The prospect that opened upon us was delightful. After riding through thick woods for several days, ... the sight of a beautiful and extensive tract of country is inconceivably enlivening. Close beside the bank on which we rode, the Oswegatchie wound along, about twenty feet below us. After running for some distance, it entered into the St. Lawrence, forming a long point of land on which stood a few houses called the 'Garrison,' which had formerly been a fortified place built by the French to keep the Indians in awe. They were now tumbling in ruins, excepting two or three, which were still kept in tolerable order by Judge Ford, who resided in one of them, and used the others as stores and outhouses. We recrossed the Oswegatchie River to the Garrison, as we intended to reside with Judge Ford for some time."

The interval spent by the young traveller on the St. Lawrence was divided between Oswegatchie, Lisbon, one of Mr. Hoffman's townships, ten or twelve miles farther down the river, and Madrid, at a still greater distance, where lay the lands of Mr. Ogden. His sports would seem to have been fishing and shooting, while in the last entry but one of his journal, which breaks off at this point, we have this hint of recreation of another kind :—

"*August 29th.*—Hired a horse to take me to Lisbon, where Mr. Hoffman was. Arrived about one o'clock, and found him surrounded by tenants, and hard at work. *Amused* myself the rest of the day writing bonds and deeds."

It was at Lisbon that he encountered his first rude experience of savage life. I give the anecdote as I have heard it from himself. He was staying at the house of Mr. Turner, Mr. Hoffman's agent, with whose son he had rowed to a small island to hire a bateau to take the travellers down the river.   At the wigwam where they expected to engage the boat, they found a number of persons of both sexes, but the Indian of whom they were in quest was absent selling furs.   He soon came home, however, rather tipsy, accompanied by his wife, a pretty-looking squaw, whose potations also had been somewhat liberal.   The latter seated herself beside Irving, and, either attracted by his personal appearance, or hoping to cajole from him a fresh draught of the fiery beverage, began to show him much flattering attention.   The husband, a tall, strapping Hercules, sat scowling at them with his blanket drawn up to his chin and his face between his hands, while his elbows rested on his knees.   In this posture he watched the pair for some time, until at length the continued assiduities of his wife becoming too much for his patience, he suddenly rushed upon Irving, calling him a " damned Yankee," and with a blow levelled him to the floor.   Taken by surprise, and utterly unconscious of offence, the young traveller jumped up, and asked the meaning of this strange salutation.   " He is jealous," hinted one of the company.   Perceiving that he was feeling for his knife, Irving, retreating, requested the men to hold the savage, evidently maddened by drink, and young Turner immediately went up to him, when a sudden revulsion of feeling ensued.   He and the Indian had exchanged names, and were therefore sworn friends. The savage hugged him in his arms, called him " good fellow " and other endearing names ; " but he," said he, glaring again with eyes of ominous ferocity at his companion, " he—damned Yankee." Apprehending further violence, Turner intimated to Irving that he had better escape to the boat, and he would follow—which he was glad enough to do.

This adventure was a capital joke for Hoffman, who was never weary of quizzing his student on the subject of his delicate attentions to the squaw.

Proceeding in their bateau to Montreal, the party stopped at Caughnawaga, where they were received in great state by the Indians.   Here Hoffman, in a spirit of frolic, persuaded them to go through the ceremonial of exchanging names with Irving, or of giving him a name—to the great annoyance of the former, and the infinite diversion of the ladies, who stood at the door enjoying the scene with undisguised unction. The ceremony was novel, and to the object of it extremely embarrassing, as one of the chiefs or principal Indians took him by the hand, led him out into the middle of the room, then commenced a sort of Indian waltz, turning slowly round with him to a low chant, while the others would look gravely on, and every now and then strike in with a monosyllabic chorus, " Ugh! ugh!" The solemn gravity of the Indians and the merriment of the lookers-on formed quite a ludicrous contrast. The chant concluded, the chief made him a formal and deferential speech, and gave him his name, which was Vomonte, meaning, as interpreted to him, Good to Everybody.

It was now Irving's turn to have his fun, and as soon as the Indian had concluded, he told him he had made a great mistake in conferring this distinction on him ; that he was but an insignificant individual to be so highly honored ; but that the other, pointing to Hoffman, had been Attorney-General of the State of New York, and was much more worthy of this great distinction than himself ; that he would feel it an abatement of his dignity if they honored an obscure stripling in this way, and passed by so illustrious a personage.

Nothing would do, therefore, but they must march Hoffman out, and go through the same parade with him, to the great amusement of the ladies, and the irrepressible glee of Irving, who had felt too keenly the rueful dignity of the situation in his own case, not to enjoy it with the highest relish when the tables were turned. Hoffman's name was Citrovani, or Shining Man.

At Montreal, which was the great emporium of the fur trade, the party was fêted in genial style by some of the partners of the Northwest Fur Company. " At their hospitable board," says Mr. Irving, in his introduction to " Astoria," including in his allusion two later visits, " I occasionally met partners and clerks and hardy fur traders from the interior posts ; men who had passed years remote from civilized society, among distant and savage tribes, and who had wonders to recount of their wide and wild peregrinations, their hunting exploits, and their perilous adventures and hair-breadth escapes among the Indians. I was at an age when the imagination lends its coloring to every thing, and the stories of these Sindbads of the wilderness made the life of a trapper and fur trader perfect romance to me."

Here he made the acquaintance of his life-long friend, Henry Brevoort, a native and resident of New York, but then on a visit of business or pleasure to Montreal.

It was not until the lapse of fifty years that Mr. Irving made a second visit to Oswegatchie, now Ogdensburg ; and I cannot resist the temptation to take from its place the letter which gives the touching contrast. On a return from a tour by the Lakes to Niagara, he writes to a niece at Paris (Mrs. Storrow):—

September 19, 1853.

One of the most interesting circumstances of my tour was the sojourn of a day at Ogdensburg, at the mouth of the Oswegatchie River, where it empties into the St. Lawrence. I had not been there since I visited it fifty years since, in 1803, when I was but twenty years of age ; when I made an expedition through the Black River country to Canada in company with Mr. and Mrs. Hoffman, and Ann Hoffman, Mr. and Mrs. Ludlow Ogden, and Miss Eliza Ogden. Mr. Hoffman and Mr. Ogden were visiting their wild lands on the St. Lawrence. All the country then was a wilderness ; we floated down the Black River in a scow ; we toiled through forests in wagons drawn by oxen ; we slept in hunters' cabins, and were once four-and-twenty hours without food : but all was romance to me.

Arrived on the banks of the St. Lawrence, we put up with Mr. Ogden's agent, who was quartered in some rude buildings belonging to a ruined French fort at the mouth of the Oswegatchie. What happy days I passed there! rambling about the woods with the young ladies ; or paddling with them in Indian canoes on the limpid waters of the St. Lawrence ; or fishing about the rapids and visiting the Indians, who still lived on islands in the river. Every thing was so grand and so silent and solitary. I don't think any scene in life made a more delightful impression upon me.

Well—here I was again after a lapse of fifty years. I found a populous city occupying both banks of the Oswegatchie, connected by bridges. It was the Ogdensburg, of which a village plot had been planned at the time of our visit. I sought the old French fort, where we had been quartered —not a trace of it was left. I sat under a tree on the site and looked round upon what I had known as a wilderness—now teeming with life—crowded with habitations—the Oswegatchie River dammed up and encumbered by vast stone-mills—the broad St. Lawrence ploughed by immense steamers.

I walked to the point, where, with the two girls, I used to launch forth in the canoe, while the rest of the party would wave handkerchiefs, and cheer us from shore; it was now a bustling landing-place for steamers. There were still some rocks where I used to sit of an evening and accompany with my flute one of the ladies who sang. I sat for a long time on the rocks, summoning recollections of bygone days, and of the happy beings by whom I was then surrounded; all had passed away—all were dead and gone; of that young and joyous party I was the sole survivor; they had all lived quietly at home out of the reach of mischance, yet had gone down to their graves; while I, who had been wandering about the world, exposed to all hazards by sea and land, was yet alive. It seemed almost marvellous. I have often, in my shifting about the world, come upon the traces of former existence; but I do not think any thing has made a stronger impression on me than this second visit to the banks of the Oswegatchie.

CHAPTER IV.

ASHINGTON IRVING came of age on the third of April, 1804.

The delicate state of his health at this time began to awaken the solicitude of his family, and the father, now paralytic, having retired from business with a moderate independence, his brothers, animated by a common spirit, determined to send him on a voyage to Europe.

"It is with delight," writes his brother William to him soon after his departure, " we share the world with you; and one of our greatest sources of happiness is that fortune is daily putting it in our power thus to add to the comfort and enjoyment of one so very near to us all."

William was the third child of his parents, and the oldest who lived to grow up. He was nearly seventeen years the senior of Washington, and there was something of the father mingled with the strong fraternal affection with which he regarded him. Of this brother, Washington remarks in one of his letters, "He was the man I most loved on earth;" and his conversation would often turn on his rich mellow humor, his range of anecdote, his quick sensibility, and fine colloquial flow.

On the 19th of May, he was helped up the side of the vessel, in which he had engaged his passage for Bordeaux. The captain (Shaler) eyed him with a foreboding glance as he stepped upon the deck, and as he afterward told him, said to himself, " There 's a chap who will go overboard before we get across." Mr. Irving himself seems also at times to have had his fears that he was sinking by slow degrees to the grave. His emotions on leaving are described in a letter from Bordeaux to Alexander Beebee, one of his young friends :—

I felt heavy-hearted on leaving the city, as you may suppose ; but the severest moments of my departure were when I lost sight of the boat in which were my brothers who had accompanied me on board, and when the steeples of the city faded from my view. It seemed as if I had left the world behind me, and was cast among strangers without a friend, sick and solitary. I looked around me, saw none but strange faces, heard nothing but a language I could not understand, and felt "alone amidst a crowd." I passed a melancholy, lonesome day, turned into my berth at night sick at heart, and lay for hours thinking of the friends I had left behind.

. . . . Had this unhappy mood held possession of me long, I do not know if I should not have been a meal for the sharks before I had made half the passage, but thanks to "the Fountain of health and good spirits," He has given me enough of the latter to brighten up my dullest moments. My home-sickness wore off by degrees ; I again looked forward with enthusiasm to the classic scenes I was to enjoy, the land of romance and inspiration I was to tread, and though New York and its inhabitants often occupied my thoughts, and constantly my dreams, yet there was no longer anything painful in the ideas they awakened.

On the 25th of June his vessel was quarantined at the mouth of the Gironde. From shipboard he writes to his brother William the next day :—

My health is much better than when I left New York. I was but slightly sea-sick for about a day and a half on first coming out. The rest of the voyage I was tolerably well, except fevers that often troubled me at night. We were seventeen in the cabin besides the master and mates, and as I cannot speak very highly of the cleanliness of some of my fellow-passengers, you may suppose our nights were not over-comfortable. I have often passed the greatest part of the night walking the deck.

Our passage was what the sailors term "a lady's voyage," gentle and mild. We were tantalized, however, with baffling winds, particularly after entering the Bay of Biscay, where the wind came directly ahead. The first land we made, therefore, was Cape Penas, on the coast of Spain (on the 20th of the month). I cannot express the sensations I felt on first catching a glimpse of European land.

In a postscript he adds :—

The only news I have yet heard is, that Bonaparte is declared Emperor of the Gauls—Moreau is banished two years to his estate in the country— Georges is shot—Pichegru has hung himself in prison, and preparations are still making for the invasion.

In a letter a few days later to the same brother, he writes from Bordeaux :—

On yesterday morning [Saturday, the 30th June] we arrived and disembarked at this port, after having been exactly six weeks on shipboard. I had begun to be considerably of a sailor before I left the ship. My round jacket and loose trousers were extremely convenient. I was quite expert at climbing to the mast-head and going out on the main topsail yard.

. . . . Every thing is novel and interesting to me—the heavy Gothic-looking buildings—the ancient churches—the manners of the people,—it really looks like another world.

In this city, where the young traveller remained six weeks to improve himself in the language, he commenced a copious journal, which he continued with some intermissions until his arrival in Paris in the following year. His plan in regard to it was to minute down notes in pencil in a small book, and extend them whenever he could seize a moment of leisure. This journal, his notes in pencil when the journal was suspended, and his letters to the family which are preserved, will enable us to accompany him in his journeyings. I shall have but partial recourse to the journal, however, and confine myself mainly to such selections from his letters as may serve to illustrate his life and personal adventures, and give his character a chance to unfold itself ; omitting altogether, or retrenching largely from, the descriptions of scenery and places with which they abound, and other particulars which

would be minute or tedious ; and adding here and there such anecdotes worthy of note as do not appear in either, but have been
gathered from his own lips.

On the 5th of August, Irving set out in the diligence from
Bordeaux. The company presented a curious "jumble of
character"—a little opera-singer, with her father and mother, who
were returning to Toulouse after a short visit to Bordeaux ; a
young officer, not much older than himself, going to see his mother
in Languedoc ; and a French gentleman, who had some knowledge of English, and had just returned from a voyage round the
world. But the most amusing personage was a little American
doctor, full of whim and eccentricity, who had taken passage in the
cabriolet, a seat in front of the diligence, and who is thus introduced in the journal, which records the fact, that after breakfast
on the morning of the 6th, the writer exchanged places with a
Frenchman who was seated in the cabriolet, to obtain a better
view of the luxuriant and enchanting country through which he
was passing.

In this place [says the journal], I found a singular little genius, quite
an original—his name was Henry, a doctor of medicine, originally of
Lancaster, in Pennsylvania ; by his talk he appears to have been for a long
time a citizen of the world. He is about five feet four inches high, and
thick-set ; talks French fluently, and has an eternal tongue. He knew
everybody of consequence—ambassadors, consuls, etc., were Tom-Dick-
and-Harry, intimate acquaintances. The Abbé Winkleman had given him
a breast-pin ; Lavater had made him a present of a snuff-box ; and several
authors had sent him their works to read and criticise.

Whenever the diligence stopped in any of the towns to change
horses, etc. [he writes in a letter to his brother William], we generally
strolled through the streets talking to every one we met. We found the
women very frequently seated at the doors at work, and they were always
ready to enter into conversation. The lower class throughout this part of
France speak a villainous jargon, termed *patois*, composed of a jumble of
Italian, French, and Spanish, so that I found it difficult to understand
them, though I can make them understand me very readily. In one of
our strolls in the town of Tonneins, we entered a house where a number
of girls were quilting. They gave me a needle, and set me to work. My
bad French seemed to give them much amusement, as I talked contin-

ually. They asked me several questions; as I could not understand them,
I made them any answer that came into my head, which caused a great
deal of laughter amongst them. At last the little doctor told them that
I was an *English prisoner*, whom the young French officer (who was with
us) had in custody. Their merriment immediately gave place to pity.
"Ah! le pauvre garçon," said one to another; "he is merry, however, in
all his trouble." "And what will they do with him?" said a young
woman to the voyageur. "Oh, nothing of consequence," replied he; "perhaps shoot him, or cut off his head." The honest souls seemed quite
distressed for me, and when I mentioned that I was thirsty, a bottle of
wine was immediately placed before me, nor could I prevail on them to
take a recompense. In short, I departed, loaded with their good wishes
and benedictions, and I suppose furnished a theme of conversation
throughout the village.

The kind-hearted creatures not only brought him wine, but
obliged him to fill his pockets with fruit. Some of them got
round the young officer to intercede in his behalf, and to charge
him to be kind to him.

The incident here related seems to have left so durable an
impression on the fancy of the pretended prisoner, that long years
afterward, in 1845, when Minister to Spain and on his way from
Madrid to Paris, we find him diverging from his route expressly
to revisit this scene of his youthful travel.

In a letter to his sister, Mrs. Paris, dated Paris, November 1,
1845, he writes:—

My visit to Tonneins, and the banks of the Garonne, was induced by
recollections of my youthful days. On my first visit to Europe, when I
was but about twenty-one years of age, my first journey was up along the
banks of this river on my way to Montpellier; and the scenery of it
remained in my memory with all the magic effects of first impressions.

Then after recounting the incident as given in his early letter,
and adding, "it was a shame to leave them with such painful
impressions," he proceeds:—

The recollections of this incident induced me to shape my course so as
to strike the river just at this little town. A beautiful place it is; situated
on a high *côte*, commanding a wide view of the Garonne and the magnificent
and fertile region through which it flows. I found all my early impres-

sions of the beauty of the scenery fully justified, and almost felt a kindling of the youthful romance with which I once gazed upon it. As my carriage rattled through the quiet streets of Tonneins, and the postilion smacked his whip with the French love of racket, I looked out for the house where, forty years before, I had seen the quilting party. I believe I recognized the house ; and I saw two or three old women, who might once have formed part of the merry group of girls ; but I doubt whether they recognized in the stout elderly gentleman, thus rattling in his carriage through their streets, the pale young English prisoner of forty years since.

The little doctor had an incessant flow of spirits, and was continually creating whimsical scenes and incidents throughout the journey.

In another town [says a further extract from the letter to his brother William], he took the landlady aside, told her I was a young Mameluke of distinction, travelling *incog.*, and that he was my interpreter ; asked her to bring me a large chair that I might sit cross-legged, after the manner of my country, and desired a long pipe for me that I might smoke perfumes. The good woman believed every word, said she had no large chair, but she could place two chairs for me ; and as to a pipe, she had none longer than was generally used by the country people. The doctor said that would not do, and since she could not furnish the articles, she might bring a bottle of her best wine with good bread and cheese and we would eat breakfast.

The doctor, who was " a continual fund of amusement to him," he also found an " excellent hand," as an old traveller, in protecting him from imposition, so that when any unreasonable demand " was made upon me," he writes, " I pretended not to understand, and turned them over to him ; by this means I escaped much trouble, and the doctor was highly pleased with his employment."

At Meze, " a small town beautifully situated on the sea-shore," he parted with this eccentric genius, who, in bidding him good-by, told him when next they met he might probably find him a conjurer or High German doctor.

It was not long before he missed the services of his amusing companion, for he had no sooner stopped at Montpellier than he was assailed by a regiment of porters, two of whom seized his trunk and brought it to his room.

One of them [says the journal], I paid amply; the other insisted on a gratuity, and was so clamorous, that I had to bundle him head and heels out of the door and slammed it to, telling him to go and divide the *spoils* with his brother vagabond.

This summary method of settling with the persistent porter affords a characteristic illustration of the traveller's nervous impetuosity under annoyance. "You have a *little* of the family impatience," says an admonitory passage in one of his brother William's letters. It was a peculiarity which all the children inherited in greater or less degree from the mother.

But his protector is soon back again. On returning at night from the theatre to the inn, says a letter to his brother, " I was surprised to find the little doctor at the hotel. He had despatched his business at Cette and intends going on to Nice. I shall travel in company with him, and by that means be protected from extortion. I find he is a more important character than I at first supposed."

On the 16th, early in the morning, he set off in a *voiture* with the doctor for Nismes, and arrived in the evening. Here, where his curiosity and admiration were strongly excited by the Roman antiquities of the place, he began to have misgivings about the sufficiency of his passport.

By some conversation [says the journal] I had with Dr. Henry, I had got quite out of conceit of my American protection; it was in writing from the mayor in New York, and he said it was a chance if any of the French officers of police would be able to read it, or would know whether to give credence to the signature of the mayor or not. My French passport also gave a very poor description of me; and as I was continually mistaken on the road for an Englishman, I began to apprehend I might get into some disagreeable situation with the police, before I could reach Marseilles. I was much startled, therefore, while sitting at supper with several others in the hotel, at the entry of two or three officers of the police with a file of soldiers. They only came, however, to examine our passports, and they passed over mine very lightly.

The traveller would seem to have had two passports from the city of Bordeaux, one from the Police, the other from the Chancellerie. A comparison of the description given of him in each, discloses some discrepancies, especially as to the color of his eyes, which is described as blue in one and gray in the other. Their actual color was sometimes a moot point among his friends. " Nose long," " nose middling," " forehead high," " forehead middling," mark a further disagreement, though more easily reconciled.[1]

At Nismes he parted once more with the little doctor, who was so unwell that he determined to return to Montpellier, and endeavor to proceed from Cette by water.

After staying two days at Nismes [says a letter to his brother William], I set off for Avignon, full of enthusiasm at the thoughts of visiting the tomb of Laura, and of wandering amid the wild retreats and romantic solitudes of Vaucluse.

The sun was setting when he caught his first view of the city of classic immortality, and the next morning he rose early, and, to resume with the letter,—

Inquired for the Church of Cordeliers that contained the tomb of the belle Laura. Judge my surprise, my disappointment, and my indignation, when I was told that the church, tomb, and all, were utterly demolished in the time of the Revolution. Never did the Revolution, its authors and its consequences, receive a more hearty and sincere execration than at that moment. Throughout the whole of my journey I had found reason to exclaim against it for depriving me of some valuable curiosity or celebrated monument, but this was the severest disappointment it had yet occasioned. . . . . I had calculated much upon visiting Vaucluse, but had most reluctantly to abandon the idea. It would have taken me two days to go there and return to Avignon. My passport mentioned that I was to go *directly* to Marseilles, which I was told was something particular. I had been continually mistaken on the road for an Englishman, and there were one or two spies of the police keeping a strict watch on me while at Avignon. To have set off for Vaucluse might therefore have occasioned an arrest; and as I could not understand the patois which is spoken throughout these parts, I might have been involved in vexatious difficulties, so that I had to deny myself the gratification. One of the spies paid me a visit, *incog.;* I however discovered him by a ribbon he wore under his

---

[1] I give the entire passports in translation :—

Chancellerie.—Hair chestnut—eyebrows do.—eyes gray—nose long—mouth middling—chin large—forehead middling—face oblong—height 5 feet 7 inches.

Police.—Hair and eyebrows chestnut—eyes blue—nose middling—mouth middling—chin round—forehead high—face oval.

coat, and as I was not in the best of humors, I gave him a reception so dry and ungracious, that I believe he was glad to make his *congé*.

He spoke a little English, and introduced himself by asking, in a careless manner, if I was from England. I said I was from America. " From what part of America, if he might take the liberty to ask?" " From *North* America." The dry, laconic manner in which this was given rather disconcerted him—he soon recovered. " Perhaps Monsieur experienced some vexations in travelling, from resembling so much an Anglois?" " No—not much—though I was sometimes subjected to impertinent intrusions!" " Hem—hah—Monsieur, *sans doute*, took care always to be provided with good passports?"—no answer. " Because, Monsieur must know, the police was very strict in the interior, and had a sharp look-out on every stranger." " Yes, Monsieur," said I, turning pretty short upon him, " I know very well the strictness of your police, the constant watch they keep on the actions of strangers, and the spies with which an unfortunate devil of a traveller is continually surrounded. Above all despicable scoundrels I despise a spy most superlatively—a wretch that intrudes himself into the company of an unwary traveller, endeavors to pry into his affairs, and gain his confidence only to betray him; such creatures should be flogged out of society, and their employers meet with the contempt they merit for using such ungenerous means." The poor chap shrugged his shoulders, bit his nails, shifted his seat, and when I had finished, replied that all I had said was very true; the police were very wrong, their regulations very vexatious; that he had thought proper, as I was a stranger, to give me a hint or two; hoped I might have a good journey, and wished me a good-day. I heard him *diable*-ing to himself all the way down stairs, and meeting the master of the hotel at the foot he exclaimed in a half-loud tone, "*Je crois il est véritablement un Anglois.*" In the evening the master of the hotel required my passport to show to the police; it was returned to me without any further trouble, and I was permitted to resume my journey without interruption.

At Marseilles, where he spent three weeks, the ubiquitous doctor turns up again, and on the 10th of September they left Marseilles together, having engaged a carriage to take them to Nice. The inns on the road are described in the journal as miserable. " Dirt, noise, and insolence reigned without control. The custom of piling manure up against their houses, which was used to fertilize the country, was destructive to comfort." In a letter to his brother William, he remarks :—

Fortunately for me, I am seasoned, in some degree, to the disagreeables from my Canada journey of last summer. When I enter one of these inns, to put up for the night, I have but to draw a comparison between it and some of the log hovels into which my fellow-travellers and myself were huddled, after a fatiguing day's journey through the woods, and the inn appears a palace. For my part, I endeavor to take things as they come, with cheerfulness, and when I cannot get a dinner to suit my taste, I endeavor to get a taste to suit my dinner.

And he adds :—

There is nothing I dread more than to be taken for one of the Smell-fungi of this world. I therefore endeavor to be pleased with every thing about me, and with the masters, mistresses, and servants of the inns, particularly when I perceive they have " all the dispositions in the world " to serve me ; as Sterne says, " It is enough for heaven and ought to be enough for me."

On the evening of the 13th September, the travellers arrived at Nice.

Thus [says he in the letter before quoted], having happily accomplished my journey through the South of France, I felicitated myself with the idea that nothing remained but to step into a felucca and be gently wafted to the classic shore of Italy ! Little did I think of being *persuaded* by the police to defer my departure and take time to enjoy the climate and prospects of Nice. The next morning I waited on the municipality to deliver my passport and request another for Genoa. Monsieur le Secretaire-General perused my passport, and told me it was not in his power to grant me permission to depart—that my passport was such as is given to suspected persons, and that I must rest here contented until a better passport was sent on, or a permission from the Grand Judge at Paris authorizing my departure. This speech absolutely struck me dumb. The doctor, however, who was with me and could speak French far more fluently than I, took up my cause. He represented to the Secretary-General my situation : young, inexperienced, for the first time separated from my family, in a foreign land and ignorant of the language, a vile passport had been given to me, and I, ignorant of the forms of the police, had taken it as one of the same kind that was generally given to my countrymen. That now I would be detained among strangers, not understanding their language, out of health, solitary (as his affairs obliged him to set off immediately for Italy). In short, I cannot repeat one-half of the distresses, the calamities, and the bug-bears that the doctor summoned to his assistance to render his harangue as moving as possible. The Secretary-General assured him that he felt for my situation, but it was absolutely out of his power to allow me to proceed—that he was amenable to superior authority, and dared not indulge his inclination, and that *something suspicious* in my deportment or affairs must certainly have occasioned this precaution in the municipality of Bordeaux. The doctor assured him that it was a mistake. He had travelled with me all along, and would swear, would pledge his person, his property, his all, for my being a citizen of the United States, and that nothing had occurred either in my deportment or conversation that merited suspicion. In short, he manifested the most friendly zeal and earnestness in my cause, and said every thing he could think of to obtain my passport. It was all in vain. The Secretary repeated it was out of his power to grant it, or he would with the sincerest pleasure, but that he would write to the Commissary-General of Police at Marseilles, inclosing my passport, and requesting another that should enable me to proceed; in the meantime he would give me a letter of surety that granted me the liberty of the place without being subject to molestation from police officers. Having received this we withdrew, thanking him for the politeness he had shown. By the doctor's advice I immediately wrote to Mr. Schwartz and our consul at Marseilles, requesting them to represent my case to the Com.-General and endeavor to have a good passport sent on immediately, or if there was no other way, to reclaim me as an American citizen. I have written to Dr. Ellison and our consul, Mr. Lee, at Bordeaux, requesting them to take the same measures there; and as Dr. Henry was to depart from here for Genoa in two days, I wrote by him to Hall Storm to get our consul there to reclaim me. Dr. Henry has promised to do all in his power to forward the business in that quarter, so I think it will be hard if there does not come relief from one quarter or another.

Hall Storm, here mentioned, was a native of New York, established in business at Genoa, and then acting as vice-consul. He had been an early playmate of Mr. Irving, though somewhat his senior.

CHAPTER V.

Continued Detention.—Friendly Offices of Dr. Henry.—Liberation.—Takes Felucca for Genoa.—A Whistling Shot.—Loiter at Genoa.—Agreeable Acquaintances.—Determines to Visit Sicily.—Allusion to Duel of Hamilton and Burr.

I CONTINUE my extracts from the letter last quoted, to his brother William.

The next day [15th September], I was lying down after dinner, when I was suddenly awakened by the noise of some persons entering my chamber, and found an officer of the police and the doctor standing before me. He had come to demand my papers to carry before the mayor, for particular reasons. The doctor told me not to disturb myself, that he would accompany the man and learn what was the cause of this visit. In about half an hour I heard him coming up stairs humming a tune in a voice something like that of Tom Pipes—between *a screech and a whistle.* He entered my room with a furious countenance, flung himself into a chair, and stopping all at once in the middle of his tune, began to curse the police in the most voluble manner, nor could I get a word of intelligence out of him until he had consigned them all to purgatory. He then let me know that we had been dogged about by some scoundrel of a spy who had denounced me as an Englishman, which had occasioned the demand of my papers. He told me he had been before the Adjoint of the mayor, who spoke English and was very polite; that he had represented my situation to him, and had told him that he would bring me before him, and if he did not at once see by my countenance that I was an honest man, incapable of deceit, he would himself pledge both his property and his person that I would prove so in the end. I accordingly accompanied the doctor before the Adjoint. The latter received me very politely; as he spoke English I simply stated the circumstances of my case, but he told me that it was unnecessary; he was convinced of the folly of the suspicions that had been indulged against me, and assured me that while I remained in Nice my tranquillity should not be again disturbed. Having received my papers we withdrew. On the 17th, the doctor set off in a felucca for Genoa, and though I was sorry to part with a man whose company was so amusing and who had proved himself sincerely my friend, yet I could not

37

but be pleased on one account, as it would facilitate my own departure, for I look chiefly to Genoa for effectual assistance.

Sept. 26*th.*—I have just received two or three letters; to express to you the revolution of feelings they occasioned is impossible. They were put into my hands by the maitre d' hôtel just as I returned from one of my solitary morning rambles on the sea-shore, where I had been wistfully contemplating the ocean, and wishing myself on its bosom in full sail to Italy. The first packet was from my indefatigable friend, Dr. Henry. inclosing a letter from Hall Storm, and a reclamation from our consul, and all within twenty-four hours after his arrival. As to the letter from Storm, it breathes all the warmth and openness of heart that distinguishes that worthy fellow.

.   .   .   .   I have also received a packet from our consul at Marseilles, inclosing a letter to the Préfet of Nice, representing my case and urging him to give me a passport for Italy. Thus you see the prospect is opened. I have but to go to the municipality, get a passport, etc., and then away to Italy and Hall Storm!

Evening.—Such were the enlivening ideas of this morning, and with a light heart I danced attendance on the Secretary-General five or six times in the course of the day. At last I had the good fortune to have my paper carried either before him or the Préfet by one of the head clerks, and after waiting in sanguine expectation of a passport being ordered me, I was greeted with the cheering intelligence that I must rest here still for four or five days, till they received an answer to a letter that had been written to the Commissary-General of Marseilles. What this answer is, or of what importance it is, I neither know nor care; it is sufficient for me to know that I am in their power, and that it is needless to complain—*patience par force* is my motto. [The journal says, " I never wanted a knowledge of the language so much as when the clerk brought this answer; I fairly gasped for words. As it was, I gave him my sentiments pretty roundly in the best French I could muster."]

The letter continues :—

I was promised that I should be forwarded with pleasure when a reclamation arrived from Genoa, and now that I have a reclamation supported by a letter from our consul at Marseilles, I am still detained; and shall be obliged to dance attendance on these scoundrels, I do not know how much longer; I have felt what it is to have to deal with *Dogs in office,* and can say with Swift :—

> " Ye Gods! if there 's a man I ought to hate,
> *Attendance* and dependence be his fate."

October 14th.—Upwards of two weeks have elapsed since the above was written; the time in that interval has dragged on without any thing particular to vary its monotony. I have been made the sport of promises and evasions by the police, who pretend that they are unable to give me a passport, notwithstanding the reclamation, etc.; that they must have authority from Paris, though they have not taken the trouble to write to Paris. Fortunately, however, I wrote to Mr. Lee, our consul at Bordeaux, when I was first detained; he immediately wrote to our minister at Paris, in my favor, in consequence of which I received a very polite letter from Robert L. Livingston, Esq., son-in-law of the minister, informing me that the minister had received the account of my situation from Mr. Lee, and immediately had sent a passport to the Grand Judge for his signature, and that it would most probably come on by the same mail, at furthest by the mail ensuing.

The promised passport arrived on the 16th, and the next morning, after a tedious detention of five weeks, he set sail in a felucca for Genoa, coasting along near the land, for fear of the privateers that infested the Mediterranean, and in the evening putting into the town to pass the night. At one place near Alberga the felucca had receded beyond her usual distance from the shore, when a small vessel that lay under an island fired a gun ahead of them on suspicion of her being a privateer.

"Our padrone," says the journal, "immediately displayed the Genoese flag, and hailed the vessel. Either they did not see or hear him, or their suspicions were very strong, for they fired another shot at us, which whistled just over our heads. Toward evening the breeze died away, and the men had to take to their oars. It was a bright moonlight, and the sound of a convent bell from among the mountains would now and then salute their ears, and immediately the rowers would rest on their oars, pull off their caps, and offer up their prayers."

They passed the night at Savona, and the next day entered the harbor of Genoa, where he met with a most cordial and open-hearted reception from his friend Storm, with whom he took up his quarters in the wing of an old palace. The pleasure of this meeting was no doubt wonderfully heightened by his long and friendless solitude at Nice. In a letter to his young friend, John

Furman, dated Genoa, October 24, 1804, he is almost at a loss to express his sense of the happiness of this meeting with an old comrade from New York.

> You [he says] who have never been from home in a land of strangers, and for some time without friends, cannot conceive the joy, the rapture of meeting with a favorite companion in a distant part of the world.

Time passed rapidly and pleasantly with the young traveller at Genoa.

> I have now been in Genoa six weeks [he writes to William, November 30th], and, so far from being tired of it, I every day feel more and more delighted with my situation, and unwilling to part. I can not speak with sufficient warmth of the reception I have met with from Storm. We have scarcely been out of each other's sight all the time I have been here, and he has introduced me to the first society in Genoa, from whom I have received the most flattering attentions.

Some weeks later we find him in the following letter still at Genoa, preparing to tear himself away from the friendly circle of acquaintance he had formed, and mingle again among strangers.

[*To William Irving.*]

GENOA, December 20, 1804.

DEAR BROTHER :—

I yesterday received your letter, and return you a thousand thanks for the length and minuteness of it. You cannot imagine how enlivening it was to me, and with what a greedy eye I read every line three or four times. . . . . Part of your letter was written on the 25th of October, which was *five days after I arrived in Genoa*, and here it found me still. It is a most fortunate thing that I received your letters before my departure, as they will influence me much in my route. You will be pleased to hear that your wish that I should visit Sicily will be fully gratified, and in a manner most convenient and agreeable to myself. I set sail to-morrow in the ship *Matilda*, of Philadelphia, bound for Messina in Sicily, where she takes in a cargo of wines for America. The ship was formerly a Charleston packet, and has excellent accommodations. The captain is an honest, worthy old gentleman, of the name of Strong. He is highly delighted with the thoughts of my going, has laid in excellent stores, prepared the best berth, and says he intends to make my passage as comfortable as possible. Had not this opportunity offered, I would have been obliged to make a long roundabout tour by the way of Milan, Bologna, Ancona, etc., etc., to Rome, as all Tuscany is surrounded by cordons (lines of soldiers) where I should be detained, quarantined, smoked, and vinegared, and perhaps, after all, not have been suffered to pass.

I have been to-day to bid farewell to my Genoese friends, and a painful task it was I assure you. The very particular attentions I have received here have rendered my stay delightful. I really felt as if at home, surrounded by my friends. Though my acquaintances were very numerous, I particularly confined my visits to three places, Lady Shaftesbury's, Madame Gabriac's, and Mrs. Bird's. From Lady Shaftesbury I have experienced the most unreserved and cordial friendship. I visited her house every night, dined there frequently, and supped whenever I chose. . . . .

Madame Gabriac's was another favorite visiting place. She is a lady of the first rank, and speaks English extremely well. We were always sure of a merry evening in her company, when she would discuss the fashionable intelligence of Genoa with a whim and humor peculiar to herself. She expressed the greatest regret at my departure, and furnishes me with a letter of introduction to her friend, the Marchesa Miranda at Florence, a lady of whom I have heard much, both for beauty and understanding.

I dined to-day at Mrs. Bird's at Sestri, to bid her family farewell. I believe I have spoken before to you of this charming woman and her lovely daughters. We have spent several delightful days in their company at Sestri, and received the most hospitable attentions. . . . .

I had nearly forgotten to mention to you that I was presented to the Doge on his levee night by his nephew, Signor Lerra, and had a very polite reception. . . . .

It is with the greatest uneasiness that I hear of the continued precariousness of sister Nancy's health. I wish to heaven I had her with me in these mild climates, where her feeble frame would soon recruit. The rude shocks of the western winters she has to encounter are too violent for a delicate constitution that is at the mercy of every breeze. For myself I am another being. Health has new strung my limbs, and endowed me with an elasticity of spirits that gilds every scene with sunshine and heightens every enjoyment.

It was at Genoa that the traveller received a letter from his brother William, enclosing an official account of the sad duel in which Hamilton fell by the hand of Burr, and exhibiting a distressing picture of the political excitement which was then at its height in his native city.   His reply gives, incidentally, an insight into his early political preferences ; while he regrets the rancorous height party animosity was attaining in the country, he speaks of himself as " an admirer of General Hamilton, and a partisan with him in politics."   " My fellow-countrymen do not know the blessings they enjoy," he adds ; " they are trifling with their felicity, and are, in fact, themselves their worst enemies.   I sicken when I think of our political broils, slanders, and enmities, and I think, when I again find myself in New York, I shall never meddle any more in politics."

I close this chapter with his last lines from Genoa, in a letter to his brother William, already quoted in part.

I am finishing this letter in the morning; the wind is fair, the day lovely, and every thing appears to befriend me.   I have to haste and pack up my trunk, so that I must tear myself away from the pleasure of writing to you.   In a little while I shall be once more on the ocean.   I am a friend to that element, for it has hitherto used me well, and I shall feel quite at home on shipboard.

You see I set off in high glee, though I expect to have a serious heartache when I lose sight of Genoa.

Heaven bless you, my dear brother.

W. I.

CHAPTER VI.

*From Genoa to Messina.—Christmas at Sea.—Adventure with Pirates.—
Quarantine.—High Converse with Captain Strong.*

[*To William Irving.*]

SHIP "MATILDA," December 25, 1804.

MY DEAR BROTHER :—

IN my last letter from Genoa, I mentioned that I was on the point of embarking with a fine wind and charming weather. I was disappointed in the expectation. The wind blew too strong for the vessel to warp out of the harbor, and we were detained till the 23d, when we set sail at two o'clock with a brisk gale, and soon left *sweet Genoa* and all its friendly inhabitants behind us. [I remained (says the journal) alternately gazing upon Sestri and Genoa, till they faded in the distance, and evening veiled them even from the sight of the telescope.] The wind died away before evening, and the next day it sprung up ahead, where it has continued ever since, keeping us baffling about opposite Leghorn.

. . . . I began this letter on Christmas-day—it is now the evening of the twenty-eighth; all this while have we been beating about in nearly the same place, among some small islands that lie between Corsica and the Tuscan shore. There are three other passengers, Genoese captains of vessels, who speak French very well; they sleep in the steerage, and leave me the cabin to myself. The captain is an honest, worthy old soul of a religious turn (though he never talks of religion), and violently smitten with an affection for lunar observations. The old gentleman has likewise an invincible propensity to *familiarize* the names of people; it

43

is always *Tom* Truxton, *Kit* Columbus, and *Jack* Styles with him, and he cannot tell you the name of the author of a book without *Jacking* or *Gilling* him. He is extremely obliging and good humored, and strives to render my situation as agreeable as possible.

29th.—We have at length, to our great satisfaction, cleared the island of Elba, and are now passing between it and the island of Planosa. The latter is a place of shelter and ambuscade for small privateers that infest these parts, and lie in wait here to sally out on vessels as they pass. These little privateers are of the kind that seamen term *pickaroons.* They are unprincipled in their depredations, plundering from any nation. One of the Genoese captains assured me that they were worse than the Algerines or Tripolitans, as the latter nations only capture and make prisoners, whereas these villains often accompany their depredations with cruelty and murder, and have even been known to plunder the ship, sink her, and kill the crew to prevent discovery and punishment. They may be termed the *banditti of the ocean,* having very seldom any commission or authority.

30th.—I was sitting in the cabin yesterday writing very tranquilly, when word was brought that a sail was seen coming off toward us from the island. The Genoese captain, after regarding it through a spy-glass, turned pale, and said it was one of those privateers of which he had been speaking to me. A moment after she fired a gun, upon which we hoisted the American flag. Another gun was fired, the ball of which passed between the main and fore masts, and we immediately brought to. We went to work directly to conceal any trifling articles of value that we had. As to myself, I put my letters of credit in my inside coat-pocket, and gave two Spanish doubloons (which was all the cash I had), one to the cabin-boy, and the other to a little Genoese lad, to take care of for me, as it was not very probable that they would be searched. By this time the privateer had come within hail. She was quite small, about the size of one of our Staten Island ferry-boats, with lateen-sails, and two small guns in the bow. (As for us, we had not even a pistol on board.) They were under French colors, and, hailing us, ordered the captain to come on board with his papers. He accordingly went, and after some time returned, accompanied by several of the privateersmen. One of them appeared to have command over the rest ; he was a tall, stout fellow, shabbily dressed, without any coat, and his shirt sleeves rolled up to his elbows, displaying a formidably muscular pair of arms. His crew would have shamed Falstaff's ragged regiment in their habiliments, while their countenances displayed the strongest lines of villainy and rapacity. They carried rusty cutlasses in their hands, and pistols and stilettos were stuck in their belts and waistbands. After the leader had given orders to shorten sail, he demanded the passports and bills of health of the passengers, etc., and made several inquiries concerning the cargo. These we answered by means of one of his men, who spoke a little English, and another who spoke French, and to whom I translated our replies. He then told the captain and myself that we must go on board of the privateer, as the commander wanted to make some inquiries, and that I could act as interpreter. As we were going over the side, the Genoese captain stopped me privately, and with tears in his eyes entreated me not to leave the ship, as he believed they only intended to separate us all, that they might cut our throats the more easily. I represented to him how useless and impolitic it would be to dispute their orders, as it would only enrage them; that we were completely in their power, and they could as easily despatch us on board the ship as in the privateer, we having no arms to defend ourselves. The poor man shook his head, and said he hoped the Virgin would protect me. When we arrived on board the privateer, I own my heart almost failed me; a more villainous-looking crew I never beheld. The dark complexions, rough beards, and fierce black eyes scowling under enormous bushy eyebrows, gave a character of the greatest ferocity to their countenances. They were as rudely accoutred as their comrades that had boarded us, and, like them, armed with cutlasses, stilettos, and pistols. They seemed to regard us with the most malignant looks, and I thought I could perceive a sinister smile upon their countenances, as if triumphing over us who had fallen so easily into their hands. Their captain, after reading over our papers and asking us several questions about the vessel and cargo, said he only stopped us to know if we had the regular bills of health, telling us some confused contradictory story of his being employed by the health office of Leghorn. After a while he gave us permission to return on board, with which we cheerfully complied, but our pleasure was damped when we found that he retained our papers. On arriving on board we understood that they had been rummaging the ship, and had ordered them to stand for the shore that the vessel might be brought to anchor. When our sails were almost in, a signal was given, upon which the privateer fired a gun, gave three cheers, and hoisted English colors. The captain or leader then turned round with a grin, and said that we were a good prize. We told him to recollect we were Americans. He said it was all one; every thing was a good prize that came from Genoa, as the port was blockaded. We replied that there had been no English frigates off the port for six months past, consequently they could not pretend but that the blockade had ceased. He said we would find the contrary when we arrived at Malta, where he intended to carry us. We thought it most advisable to be silent, confident that if we were carried to Malta they could do nothing with us. The Genoese captain said he was convinced from their behavior that they had no idea of carrying us there, but that they were merely a band of pirates without commission, and bent upon plundering.

They then commenced overhauling the ship in hopes of finding money. The leader, and one of his comrades who spoke a little English, began with the cabin, ordering the others to remain on deck to keep guard. They first came across my portmanteau, which I opened for them, and the captain rummaged it completely without finding any money, which appeared to be his main object. The one who spoke English was employed in reading my papers, perhaps hoping to find bills of exchange; but as they were chiefly letters of introduction he soon grew tired, and turning to his companion said it was an unprofitable business, that I had letters for all Italy and France, but they were nothing but recommendations.

Eh bien, replied the other, we may as well let his things alone for the present—*c'est un homme qui court tout le monde.* ('Tis a man who is rambling over all the world.) Among other letters of introduction they came across two for Malta, one to Sir Isaac Ball, the governor, and another to a principal English merchant ; after this they treated me with much more respect, and the captain told me I might put up my things again in the portmanteau. I huddled them in carelessly, as I expected never again to have the use of them, and locking the trunk offered the key to the captain ; he, however, told me to keep it myself, as he had no present occasion for it. By this time his myrmidons on deck had lost all patience, and came crowding into the cabin demanding permission to search the vessel. The leader spoke something to them, and immediately they went to work, ravenous as wolves, ransacking every hole and corner. They were extremely disappointed at finding so little aboard to pillage. The vessel having an intention of loading with wine at Messina had no cargo on board but five or six pipes of brandy, some few tons of paper, a little verdigris, and two boxes of quicksilver. The latter they hoisted out of the run with triumph, thinking them filled with money, but were highly chagrined at discovering their real contents.

After several hours spent in this manner, the *commander-in-chief* came off from the island in a boat. This fellow, I believe, was *commodore* of the squadron, for I learned that there were two more small privateers in a harbor of the island. He was as ragged as the rest, though rather a good-looking fellow in the countenance. After looking over our papers and consulting with his comrades, I suppose they found out that it was impolitic to be very hard upon us, as we had not sufficient on board to encourage them in running any risk, and they well knew they could not justify themselves in taking an American vessel. They therefore returned our papers, and told us that though the ship was a lawful prize, yet they would be *generous* and permit us to proceed; that they did not wish to use any *force*, but would be much obliged to us for some provisions, as they were almost out. We of course had to comply with their *request*, and they took about half the provisions that we had on board.

They likewise took some articles of ship furniture, and one of the under vagabonds stole a watch and some clothes out of the trunks of the Genoese passengers. It is impossible to describe the chagrin and rage of the common fellows at being restrained from plundering; they swore the ship was a *good prize*, and I almost expected to see them rise against their leaders for contradicting them. The captains then gave us a *receipt* for what they had taken, requesting the British consul at Messina to pay for the same; and about sunset, to our great joy, they bade us adieu, having been on board since eleven o'clock in the morning. For my own part, they did not take the least article from me. The wind was fair, and we spread every sail in hopes of leaving this nest of pirates behind us; but the wind fell before dark, and we lay becalmed all night. You may imagine how unpleasant was our situation, under strong apprehension that some of the gang, inflamed with the liquor they had taken from us, might come off in the night, unknown to the leaders, and commit their depredations without fear or restraint. In spite of my uneasiness, I was so fatigued that I lay down in my clothes, and soon fell asleep; but my rest was broken and disturbed by horrid dreams. The assassin-like figures of the ruffians were continually before me, and two or three times I started out of my bed, with the horrid idea that their stilettos were raised against my bosom.

Happily for us, a favorable wind sprung up early this morning, and we had the satisfaction of leaving the island far behind us before sunrise.

January 5th.—At daybreak this morning we found ourselves within a few miles of the Strait of Messina, and near to the Calabrian coast. The sunrise presented to us one of the most charming scenes I ever beheld. To our left extended the Calabrian mountains, their summits still partially enveloped in the mists of morning, the sun having just risen from behind them, and breaking in full splendor from among the clouds. Immediately before us was the celebrated strait immortal in history and song; to the right Sicily gradually swept up into verdant mountains, skirted with delightful little plains. The whole country was lovely and blooming as if in the midst of spring; and villages, towns, and cottages heightened the beauty of the prospect. . . . .

On arriving at Messina the vessel had to undergo quarantine, " one of the torments of these seas," he pronounces, " infinitely more hideous than Pelorus, Scylla, and Charybdis with all their terrors."

January 10*th*.—We are safely moored at Quarantine [he continues] in front of the Lazaretto, which is built on the promontory facing the town. They have doomed us to this species of imprisonment for twenty-one days, notwithstanding we come from a healthy port, are all hearty, and have scarcely any cargo on board. Our quarantine is longer than it other- wise would have been, in consequence of our having been boarded by the pirates off Planosa. . . . .

The Genoese captain had advised Strong to suppress the fact of their having been boarded by the pirates, if he wished to escape quarantine. " If the question is put to me," said the honest captain, " I must tell the truth." I have heard the author relate, with marked satisfaction, another instance of the scrupulous probity of the captain. The pirates took half a cask of brandy. There were five on board, one of which belonged to Strong. " That's from my cask," said the captain, as he noted the depredation. " Tut, captain," rejoined the mate, " don't you know the proverb, ' cap- tains' fowls never die.' " " No, no," said the captain. " I marked it—it *is* my cask."

I resume with the letter :—

 . . . . The same day that we arrived, there entered also the United States schooner *Nautilus* from Syracuse. I have already become quite intimate with the officers, and have had several conversations with them. As we are an *infectious* vessel, we are not allowed to communi- cate with them, except at a proper distance. Dent (the captain) is a Philadelphian, and appears to be a very clever gentleman-like fellow. He expects to return to Syracuse in a few days, and has invited me to take a passage with him, which I, of course, shall do. . . . . At Syracuse there are several of our vessels, so that I shall be quite among my fellow- countrymen, and most probably find some old acquaintances. . . . .

His long quarantine had proved an intolerable species of im- prisonment to the traveller ; though what with the study of Italian, the reading of books on Sicily, procured from shore, and ranging the harbor in the yawl of the ship, which he had fitted up with sails, he managed to pass away the time. This last amusement, however, was attended with the drawback of having a guard from the health office constantly with him. He also found a fund of entertainment in frequent discourses with the captain.

Our conversation [he writes] is whimsical enough, and we alternately discuss the New Testament and the Nautical Almanac, and talk indiscriminately of *Joe* Pilmore, *Jack* Hamilton More, *Tom* Truxton, *Kit* Columbus, and *Jack* Wesley. Methodism and lunar observations preside by turns, and you may judge how well calculated I am to shine at either. The poor old gentleman thinks he is among a set of barbarians, who are *groping in ignorance*, and "stumbling upon the dark mountains." He groans whenever the bells ring for mass, abominates the herds of priests and monks that crowd this place, and has plainly demonstrated to me, that the Roman Church is the great beast with seven horns, and the pope is no more and no less than the whore of Babylon.

Poor Strong! on his next voyage his vessel was found a floating wreck, but he always lingered in the mind of his young companion in loving remembrance; and one of the last allusions to his early years that he ever made to me recalled the worthy commander.

CHAPTER VII.

Scylla and Charybdis.—Nelson's Fleet.—Passage to Syracuse.—Ear of Dionysius.—The Listening Chamber Explored.—Catania.—Partial Ascent of Ætna.—To Palermo.—Dismal Accommodations.—A Night Alarm.—A Chance Entertainment.

MESSINA was at this time but the shadow of what it had been, not having yet recovered from the paralyzing effects of the earthquake of 1783, the marks of which were everywhere discernible in heaps of ruins. His stay in it was short, and was rendered unpleasant by an unfortunate rencontre in the streets at night between one of the officers of the *Nautilus* and the mate of an English transport, in which the latter was killed. This occasioned much stir among the English at Messina, who insisted upon the governor's demanding the officer from the captain of the schooner. Captain Dent refused to give him up, but pledged his word of honor that he should be delivered into the hands of the commodore at Syracuse, with a full statement of the affair. With this the governor was satisfied, though the English were strenuous that he should use forcible measures, urging him to have the forts manned, and the *Nautilus* stopped from leaving the port until the officer was surrendered. Mr. Irving, who had, as soon as he was released from Quarantine, taken up his quarters on board of the *Nautilus*, where he was treated quite like an old friend by Captain Dent, in consequence of this unfortunate affair avoided mingling much in company at Messina, especially as the society to which his letters introduced him was chiefly English, and a circumstance of this nature must necessarily throw a constraint over that intercourse. "When so far from home," he remarks, in alluding to the affair, " it is impossible to avoid being extremely national."

On the morning of the 29th of January they set sail for Syracuse, in company with an English schooner, with timber for repairing the mast of the *President.* Losing sight of their convoy the next morning, and supposing that she had put back to Messina, they veered about, and ran before the wind for that port. "We passed through Charybdis," says the journal, "which made a heavy broken sea. After all that has been said and sung of this celebrated place, it would make but a contemptible appearance aside of our pass called Hell-gate; and is nothing to compare to it either in real or apparent danger."

They found the city in a state of alarm. News had been brought that a fleet had been seen off the strait, and the inhabitants feared that it was the French or English coming to take possession of the place. The richer part began to push off into the country with their money and valuables.

The next morning, to resume with the journal :

Two ships of the line were seen entering the strait. The whole town was immediately in an uproar; the Marino was crowded with spectators; couriers passing and repassing from the city to the Faro, and troops marching about to man the forts. Several more ships made their appearance, and it was ascertained to be the English fleet. In a short time Lord Nelson's ship, the *Victory,* hove in sight. They all advanced most majestically up the strait. The people seemed to wait in fearful expectation. The fleet, however, soon relieved their apprehensions; they continued on without entering the harbor. We immediately got under way, making a signal for the English schooner to do the same, as we wished to have a good view of them. The English schooner was a long time in coming out, which gave us a fine opportunity by standing back again to examine the fleet. It consisted of eleven sail of the line, three frigates, and two brigs, all in prime order, and most noble vessels. We had understood, before we left Messina, that Nelson was in search of the French fleet which had lately got out of Toulon. They continued in sight all day. It was very pleasing to observe with what promptness and dexterity the signals were made, answered, and obeyed. It seemed as a body of men under perfect discipline. Every ship appeared to know its station immediately, and to change position agreeably to command, with the utmost precision. Nelson has brought them to perfect discipline; he has kept them at sea a long time with very little expense, they seldom having more than three sails set all the while they were off Toulon. He takes great pride in them, and says there is not a vessel among them that he would wish out of the fleet.

In less than a year, Nelson's young admirer, who chronicled this animating spectacle, was one of thronging thousands that pressed to behold his remains as they lay in state at Greenwich, wrapped in the flag that now floated so proudly above him.

The passage to Syracuse was short and agreeable. The society of the officers made a lively wardroom. "Good-humor reigned among them, and they had always a joke or a good story at hand to make the time pass away gayly." He found at Syracuse several of the American ships that had been sent out against Tripoli—the frigates *President, Essex, Constellation,* and *Congress,* and the brig *Vixen,* and was introduced to the officers.

Arrived at Syracuse, " I was impatient to land," says the journal, "and view the interior of a city once so celebrated for arts and arms. But, heavens! what a change! Streets gloomy and ill-built, and poverty, filth, and misery on every side ; no countenance displaying the honest traits of ease and independence; all is servility, indigence, and discontent."

In this once magnificent and populous city, now so reduced, there was still much to interest the imagination and gratify the curiosity of the young traveller: the singularly picturesque and beautiful garden of the Latomie, that needed only the hand of taste to make another Eden; the classic fountain of Arethusa, whose gushing waters were now the resort of " half-naked nymphs busily employed in washing"; the remains of its ancient theatre, aqueduct, and temples, which spoke of the days of its highest splendor ; and the vast catacombs that extended to an unknown distance under ground—the silent abodes of a mighty population passed away.

His journal contains descriptions of these and other interesting curiosities, which it does not fall within my plan to extract. I give only, as partaking of adventure and presenting some features of novelty, his exploration of the secret chamber of Dionysius, which Brydone, in his tour in Sicily, describes as "totally inaccessible." To make proof of its mysteries, therefore, was something of a notable exploit.

February 4th.—This morning I walked out of town to visit the celebrated Ear of Dionysius the Tyrant. I was accompanied by Dr.

Baker of the *President*, Davis, a midshipman, and Tootle, purser of the *Nautilus*.

The approach to the Ear is through a vast quarry, one of those from whence the stone for the edifices of ancient Syracuse was procured. The bottom of this quarry is cultivated in many places, and being entirely open overhead to the sun and sheltered on every side from the wind by high precipices, it is very fertile.

Travellers have generally been very careless in their account of the *Ear*. Some one originally started the observation that it was cut in the form of a human ear, and every one who has since given a description of it has followed in the same track and made the same remark. Brydone, among the rest, joins in it. . . . .

The Ear is a vast serpentine cavern, something in the form of the letter S reversed; its greatest width is at the bottom, from whence it narrows with an inflection to the top, something like the external shape of an ass's ear. Its height is about eighty or ninety feet, and its length about one hundred and twenty. It is the same height and dimensions from the entrance to the extremity, where it ends abruptly. The marks of the tools are still perfectly visible on the walls of the cavern.

The rock is brought to a regular surface the whole extent, without any projection or curvatures as in the human ear. About half-way in the cavern is a small square recess or chamber cut in one side of the wall even with the ground, and at the interior extremity there appears to be a small recess at the top, but it is at present inaccessible. A poor man who lives in the neighborhood attended us with torches of straw, by which we had a very good view of the interior of the Ear. Holes are discernible near the interior end of the cave, which are made in the wall at regular distances and ascend up in an inclined direction. They are about an inch in diameter. Some of the company were of opinion that they have formerly contributed to the support of a stairs or ladder, but there is no visible place where a stairs could lead to, and the holes do not go above half the height of the cavern.

There are several parts of the Ear in which the discharge of a pistol makes a prodigious report. heightened by the echoes and reverberations of the cavern. One of the company had a fowling-piece which he discharged, and it made a noise almost equal to the discharge of artillery, though not so sharp a report. A pistol also produced a report similar to a volley of musketry. The best place to stand to hear the echoes to advantage is in the mouth of the cavern. A piece of paper torn in this place makes an echo as if some person had struck the wall violently with a stick in the back of the cave.

This singular cavern is called the Ear of Dionysius, from the purpose for which it is said to have been destined by that tyrant. Conscious of the disaffection of his subjects, and the hatred and enmity his tyrannical government had produced, he became suspicious and distrustful even of his courtiers that surrounded him. He is said to have had this cavern made for the confinement of those persons of whom he had the strongest suspicions. It was so constructed that any thing said in it, in ever so low a murmur, would be conveyed to a small aperture that opened into a little chamber where he used to station himself and listen. This chamber is still shown. It is on the outside of the Ear, just above the entrance, and communicates with the interior. Some of the officers of our navy had been in it last summer; they were lowered down to it by ropes, and mention that sounds are conveyed to it from the cavern with amazing distinctness. I wished very much [continues the journal] to get to it, and the man who attended us brought me a cord for the purpose, but my companions protested they would not assist in lowering me down, and finally persuaded me that it was too hazardous, as the cord was small and might be chafed through in rubbing against the rock, in which case I would run a risk of being dashed to pieces. I therefore abandoned the project for the present. [He resumed it, however, in two days.]

6th.—This morning [says the journal], Lieuts. Murray and Gardner, and Capt. Hall, of the ship *President*, Capt. Dent of the *Nautilus*, and myself, set off to pay another visit to the Ear of Dionysius. We despatched beforehand a midshipman and four sailors with a spar and a couple of halyards. On arriving there, we went to the top of the precipice immediately over the mouth of the cave. Here we fastened ourselves to one of the halyards, and were lowered successively over the edge of the precipice (having previously disposed the spar along the edge of the rock so as to keep the halyard from chafing) into a small hole over the entrance of the Ear, and about fifteen feet from the summit of the precipice. The persons lowered were Murray, Hall, the midshipman, and myself, the others swearing they would not risk their necks to gratify their curiosity.

The cavern narrows as it approaches the top, until it ends in a narrow channel that runs the whole extent, and terminates in this small chamber. A passage from this hole or chamber appears to have been commenced to be cut to run into the interior of the rock, but was never carried more than ten or fifteen feet. We then began to make experiments to prove if sound was communicated from below to this spot in an extraordinary degree. Gardner fired a pistol repeatedly, but it did not appear to make a greater noise than when we were below in the mouth of the cavern. We then tried the conveyance of voices; in this we were more successful. One of the company stationed himself at the interior extremity of the Ear, and applying his mouth close to the wall, spoke to me just above a whisper. I was then stationed with my ear to the wall in the little chamber on high and about two hundred and fifty feet distant, and could hear him very distinctly. We conversed with one another in this manner for some time. We then moved to other parts of the cavern, and I could hear him with equal facility, his voice seeming to be just behind me. When, however, he applied his voice to the opposite side of the cave, it was by no means so distinct. This is easily accounted for, as one side of the channel is broken away at the mouth of the cavern, which injures the conveyance of the sound. After all, I doubt very much whether the cave was ever intended for the purpose ascribed to it. The fact is, that when more than one person speaks at a time, it creates such a confusion of sound between their voices and the echoes, that it is impossible to distinguish what they say. This we tried repeatedly, and found to be invariably the case.

But the antiquities of Syracuse did not engage the exclusive attention of the traveller. He found a romantic interest in visiting the convents, and endeavoring to get "a sly peep" at the nuns. The following extract from his journal shows him seeking amusement in another scene.

10*th*.—In the evening I went to a masquerade at the theatre.

I had dressed myself in the character of an old physician which was the only dress I could procure, and had a vast deal of amusement among the officers. I spoke to them in broken English, mingling Italian and French with it, so that they thought I was a Sicilian. As I knew many anecdotes of almost all of them, I teazed them the whole evening, till at length one of them discovered me by my voice, which I happened not to disguise at the moment.

In the further prosecution of his tour in Sicily, Mr. Irving found it impossible to continue the accustomed minuteness of his journal. His correspondence also was suspended. He was so constantly in motion, and objects presented themselves so rapidly and in such variety that he had scarcely a moment to write, and was obliged to content himself with a few hurried notes in pencil, and to forego altogether his usual mode of scribbling a little every day or two to his brother William, treating of objects and incidents as they occurred.

About two o'clock of the second day they arrived at Catania. The letter proceeds :—

Our stay in Catania was rendered extremely agreeable by the attentions of the Chevalier Landolini, a knight of Malta, to whom we had brought letters. He introduced us to several of the nobility, by whom we were received with great politeness and attention, and invited to all the parties that took place during our stay. The situation of Catania is very beautiful; behind it the mountain rears its awful head, vomiting smoke, often enveloped in clouds; in front is the ocean forming a vast bay, and to the right is the extensive plain of Catania with the river Giuretta wandering through it. We ascended about half-way up the mountain, but were prevented from attaining the summit by the vast quantity of snow in which it was enveloped. No guide would venture up it, and the attempt we were told would be hazardous in the extreme, and certainly fruitless. We mounted to the top of several of the small mountains thrown up on the sides of the great one by different eruptions, particularly Monte Rosso (red mountain), from which issued the last stream of lava that destroyed Catania. The view from hence was superb, and almost unbounded, and we could trace the enormous flood of lava till it lost itself in the sea, about ten miles distant.

. . . . At Catania our company divided. Wynn and Wadsworth returned to Syracuse, and Captain Hall and myself set out to cross the island to Palermo. We were mounted as before on mules, armed ourselves well with pistols and swords, and had a servant with us, a courageous fellow, with at least half a dozen pistols stuck in his pockets and girdle.

I give a few reminiscences of this part of his tour, gathered from the lips of Mr. Irving.

The evening after their departure from Catania, for lack of better accommodations, they were forced to accept an offer to sleep in a chapel, much to the discomfort of their servant Louis, who, though willing to submit to any privation, professed that he did not quite fancy " le bon Dieu " for a " Maitre d' Hôtel." The next day, at dusk, they reached the village of Guadarara, consisting of a few wretched cabins. The muleteer stopped at a solitary house, where he told them they must pass the night. It was the only inn in the place, but the landlord was absent, and it was without master or mistress, or attendant of any kind. They did not at all like the looks of the house or the place ; every thing had an appearance the most deplorable and forlorn. Their sleeping-room was a long dismal-looking apartment, to the door of which the ascent was by outside stairs, and underneath it was a shed for horses. It was almost bare of furniture. In one part were a few chairs, and in the corner farthest from the door was a large mattress which a man from the village had brought for the night, and spreading a blanket over it, had left. They purchased some fowls from the village, which Louis cooked for supper; and after a tolerably comfortable meal they fastened the door as securely as possible, and prepared to retire for the night. There was a small room near the door in which the servant slept. Hall chose the mattress in the farther corner of the room, nothing daunted by the swarming fleas which had driven his companion from it on turning down the blanket; while the latter spread a mattress brought with them on some chairs near the door, and wrapped in his great-coat, and with his pistols and portmanteau under his head, prepared to resign himself to sleep. He was far, however, from feeling at ease in his forlorn lodgings ; the wild and solitary situation of the house, the abject poverty of the inhabitants, combined with the constant rumors of robbers, were enough to produce disagreeable sensations. In spite, however, of his uneasy reflections, he soon fell asleep. It was not long before he was awakened by Louis calling in Italian, " Who 's there ? " Mr. Irving asked him what was the matter, and he answered that he heard some one at the door. The latter laid his hand on his pistol, prepared to fire if the door opened. He heard nothing, however, and telling Louis his imagination had been playing him a trick, soon fell asleep again. Again, however, was he roused by the sudden, sharp cry of Louis, " Who 's there ? " and on listening, he now heard with painful distinctness a sound as of some one slyly attempting the door. Louis could endure the suspense no longer, but resolved to confront the danger at once, and in a few brief words whispered his determination to get to the door, and throw it suddenly open, hoping the surprise might frighten the intruders, or thinking that at all events they could be better kept

at bay on the stairs, where one could be encountered at a time.
Mr. Irving assented to the plan, and grasping a pistol firmly in each
hand, stood ready for the fray.   Louis seized his dirk, and groping
his way with a light tread to the door, threw it suddenly open, and
in bolted—a half-starved and inoffensive dog.   The denouement
was prosaic enough.   The poor animal had been attracted by the
smell of some bones which had fallen from the supper-table just
inside of the door, and was trying in vain to reach them with
his paws under the crevice.   The feeling of relief which followed
this discovery may readily be imagined.   Mr. Irving had a hearty
laugh at the adventure, and soon fell again into a sound sleep, from
which he awoke the next morning, as he said to me, " perfectly
satisfied to be neither robbed nor murdered."

Two days more brought them again to the sea-side, and they
pursued the road along the coast to Termini, a town of some three
thousand inhabitants, delightfully situated on the side of a hill, and
commanding from its higher parts a fine view of the Mediterranean
and of the Sicilian coasts.   Here they arrived after dark.   Irving
was much fatigued, and on reaching the inn, threw himself on a bed
in a corner of the large room into which they were shown, and fell
asleep.   He was roused from his slumbers by the sound of voices
in conversation at the other end of the apartment, and listening,
perceived the language was English.   Hall, observing that he was
awake, immediately turned to him, and told him there was to be a
ball that evening, it being the season of the carnival, and that the
gentleman with whom he was conversing, and who was in the mask
of a Turk, had promised them admittance ;   and being ever ready for
a frolic, he proposed that they should go.   His fellow-traveller made
some demur on the score of fatigue, and the trouble of unpacking
his trunk to dress, but finally consented to appear in one of Hall's
uniform coats, as a Captain of Marines.   The stranger then took
leave, promising to return after supper, and conduct them to the
place.   At the appointed hour he came, dressed as a Turk, and
masked as before, and the two set out with him, supposing they
were going to a public entertainment.   They were somewhat staggered, however, when they found themselves ascending the stairs

of a stately mansion, through rows of servants in livery, and a brilliant array of lights, and the feeling was not dissipated when they were ushered into a spacious saloon adorned with taste and magnificence; and casting a startling glance upon the numerous company, they saw in their conductor the only mask in the room. Before they had recovered from their surprise, the Turk marshalled them to the part of the saloon where stood the master of the entertainment and his daughters, in waiting to receive their guests. Pointing to his companions as they drew near, then crossing his arms and making a low salaam, without a word of explanation or introduction, he stood as mute as a statue. It was an awkward situation for the two guests, and the idea flashed across their minds that they had been decoyed into what could not but seem a graceless intrusion upon the hospitality of a stranger. With much confusion, therefore, and in the best Italian he could muster, Mr. Irving announced their names, and attempted an explanation of the apparent indecorum, by stating their impression that they were coming to a public entertainment. Their host replied very graciously, that they were at the house of the Baron Palmeria, and asked the name of their conductor. Here was a new embarrassment, for they could not give it. " Whoever he is," he rejoined, " I am indebted to him for introducing to my house gentlemen whose uniform is a sufficient passport anywhere." Upon this the Turk whispered a rapid explanation of his interview with the strangers, and the baron turning to them with a smile, informed them that their unknown conductor was a teacher in his family, who was engaged in instructing his daughters in English. Confiding in the general popularity of strangers in Sicily, and the special attraction to his pupils of two who could converse with them in the language they were acquiring, it turned out that he had assumed the responsibility of contriving what he had little doubt would prove to both parties an agreeable surprise. Renewing his welcome with genuine hospitality, the baron now commenced a conversation with the spurious captain, in the midst of which the folding-doors were suddenly thrown open, and a *corps de ballet* made its appearance to commence the ball. After this the rest of the company prepared to join in the dance; the two strangers, on being urged, excused themselves on the plea of ignorance of the figures. Perceiving, however, the dance to be a country dance with which they were familiar, they were induced to change their minds, and Mr. Irving having been introduced to a daughter of the baron, and his companion to one of the belles of the place, they soon entered with zest into the spirit of the scene. Other dances followed in which they took part, and before they had finished the evening, their spirits had risen to so high a point, and they abandoned themselves with so little constraint to the animation of the scene, that they heard a Sicilian whisper, as they raced by him in the dance, " Son diavoli ! "

When the assembly broke up, the master of the house expressed great regret at parting with them, and pressed them to remain some days at Termini, tendering to them the hospitality of his mansion, and offering to send for an American in Palermo to keep them company. This was Mr. Nathaniel Amory, of Boston, whose brother was an officer in the fleet, and to whom the author had a letter of introduction. The invitation, however, was declined. The baron then despatched a servant with them, with torches to light them to their lodgings, and bade them farewell.

There was a strangeness and a spice of romance about this adventure that gave it a wonderful zest to the young traveller, and separated it in his after-recollections from all his commonplace experiences. Twenty years later he records in his note-book a meeting with a cousin of his " chance acquaintance, the Baron Palmeria."

CHAPTER VIII.

Palermo.—Passage to Naples.—Ascent of Vesuvius.—Farewell to Naples.—Rome.—Allston the Painter.—Proposes to Irving to Try the Brush.—Suspense of the Latter.—Torlonia the Banker.—His Flattering Attentions.—Its Ludicrous Solution.—Baron Von Humboldt.—Madame De Staël.

Peter Stuyvesant

COPY from a letter to his brother William, dated Rome, April 4, 1805.

We arrived at Palermo about the 24th of February, and passed several days there very agreeably. We had brought letters to Mr. Gibbs, American agent there, and to the Princess Camporeale from her sister at Catania. We, therefore, soon found acquaintance among the nobility; and as it was the latter part of carnival, the gayest season of the year, our time was completely occupied by amusements. As the time for my departure from Palermo approached, I began to feel extremely uneasy. The packet that sails constantly between that city and Naples, and is always well armed, was unfortunately undergoing repairs at Naples. No alternative offered than to venture across in one of the small vessels that carry fruit to the continent. Reports were in circulation of two or three Tripolitan cruisers hovering about the Italian coast, and that they had taken two American ships; besides these the Sicilian vessels are subject to capture from the cruisers of every Barbary power.

He determines to risk the fruit boat, which started after dark, as was usual, to escape any lurking cruiser near the land, and in the morning was almost out of sight of Sicily, when the wind turned ahead, and the captain, without more ado, put back to a small bay, about ten miles from Palermo, where he remained two days waiting for a favorable wind.

All that time [the letter continues] I passed on shore in a wretched hovel, where I had scarce any thing to eat, and where I had to sleep in my clothes and great-coat at night, for want of other covering. After these two days of suffering, we made out to get to Palermo. There I passed another day of uneasiness of mind till a favorable wind sprung up. We hoisted sail and weighed anchor at night; the next morning we were out of sight of Sicily, had a fine run all day, and in the course of the next night entered the Bay of Naples, where, to my great comfort, I saw the flaming summit of Vesuvius, which was a joyful token that we were out of danger. I have been several times congratulated on my good fortune, for three or four days after two Neapolitan vessels were taken by Barbary cruisers, as they were crossing from Sicily. [His travelling notes give a little more minuteness to the picture.] I had lain down [he says] on deck and fallen asleep, and on waking after dark, the first thing that struck my eyes was Mount Vesuvius afar off making a most luminous appearance. It has been in a state of eruption for several months. I could plainly perceive the red-hot lava running out of one side of the crater, and flashes at intervals from its mouth. I was up the greater part of the night, contemplating this interesting object.

March 7th.—This morning early I arose, and found that we were within the Bay of Naples. Mount Vesuvius still continued luminous; by degrees the day broke; the objects were gradually lighted up. I remained earnestly gazing around, endeavoring to trace places that I had often read descriptions of. At length the heavens were brilliantly illuminated. The sun appeared diffusing the richest rays among the clouds, and gilding every feature of the prospect. Then it was that I had a full view of this lovely bay: the classic retreats of Baiæ, Pozzuoli, the superb city of Naples, the delightful towns of Portici, etc., that skirt Mount Vesuvius; the mountain itself emitting an immense column of smoke, with the coast that terminates the bay beyond the mountain, affording the most picturesque scenery. The view of Naples from the sea is truly magnificent and imposing.

His stay at Naples was rendered particularly agreeable by the acquaintance of Mr. Joseph C. Cabell and Colonel John Mercer, " two gentlemen of Virginia, of superior talents and information." The latter was one of the Commissioners of Claims sent out to

France. " We examined all the curiosities of the place together," he writes, " and mounted Vesuvius at night, when we had a tremendous view of the crater, a stream of red-hot lava, etc. We approached near enough to the latter to thrust our sticks into it."

The journal gives a full account of this night ascent, but I will not fatigue the reader with the description of a scene so familiar. I give only this little item of personal experience :—

We were toiling up the crater, nearly in a parallel line with this object [a hillock in the lava, out of which sulphurous flames issued with a violent hissing noise], when the wind set directly from it and overwhelmed us with dense torrents of the most noxious smoke. I endeavored to hold my breath as long as possible, in hopes another flaw of wind would carry it off, but at length I was obliged to draw it in, and inhale a draught of the poisonous vapor that almost overcame me. Fortunately for us the wind shifted, or I sincerely believe that in a little time we should have shared the fate of Pliny, and died the martyrs of imprudent curiosity. Col. Mercer, as soon as he saw the smoke coming, turned about and made a precipitate retreat, and did not make a second attempt to ascend the crater. As to Cabell and myself, we were so exhausted and bewildered that we could not stir from the spot, but should have fallen a certain sacrifice.

On the 24th of March, Irving and Cabell bade adieu to Naples. Colonel Mercer had sailed a few days before for Marseilles. " I have been in no city," says the journal, " where the population is so crowded and the bustle so great as at Naples, and I shall be heartily glad to bid it adieu, and repose myself in the silent retreats of Rome." If all was hurry and bustle at Naples, he had ample time for revery and reflection on the road. "There is no country," he writes, " where the prospects so much interest my mind, and awaken such a variety of ideas as in Italy. Every mountain, every valley, every plain, tells some striking story. . . . . I am lost in astonishment at the magnificence of their works, at their sublime ideas of architecture, and their enormous public undertakings." At half-past one o'clock on the 27th they entered Rome by the Lateran gate, " and we made our way," says the journal,

" ' 'Mid fanes, and wrecks, and tumbling towers,'

to our hotel, which is situated in the modern part. To describe the emotions of the mind and the crowd of ideas that arise on entering this ' mistress of the world,' is impossible; all is confusion and agitation. The eye roves rapidly from side to side, eager to grasp every object, but continually diverted by some new scene; all is wonder, restlessness, unsatisfied curiosity, eagerness, and impatience.

" On arriving at the hotel we determined to rest ourselves for the day, collect our scattered ideas, and prepare to examine things deliberately and satisfactorily. We heard that there were three American gentlemen at Rome on their travels, namely, Mr. Allston of Carolina, Mr. Wells of Boston, and Mr. Maxwell. As Mr. Cabell was acquainted with two of them we called on them. Mr. Allston only was at home. He is a young gentleman of much taste and a good education. He has adopted the profession of painter through inclination, and intends to remain in Rome two years to improve himself in the art."

Such is the brief allusion to his first meeting with our distinguished painter, Washington Allston, then unknown to fame. Allston was about three years his senior. In a few evenings he returned the call, and his society is pronounced to be " peculiarly agreeable." In more mature years he writes : " I do not think I have ever been more completely captivated on a first acquaintance. He was of a light and graceful form, with large blue eyes and black silken hair, waving and curling round a pale, expressive countenance. Every thing about him bespoke the man of intellect and refinement. His conversation was copious, animated, and highly graphic, warmed by a genial sensibility and benevolence, and enlivened by a chaste and gentle humor."

The third of April (Irving's birthday) was spent by him and Allston in visiting a variety of paintings. " We visited together," says the former, in a communication to Duyckinck's " Cyclopedia of American Literature," " some of the finest collections of paintings, and he taught me how to visit them to the most advantage, guiding me always to the masterpieces, and passing by the others without notice. ' Never attempt to enjoy every picture in a great

collection,' he would say, 'unless you have a year to bestow upon it. You may as well attempt to enjoy every dish in a lord mayor's feast. Both mind and palate get confounded by a great variety and rapid succession, even of delicacies. The mind can only take in a certain number of images and impressions distinctly; by multiplying the number you weaken each and render the whole confused and vague. Study the choice pieces in each collection ; look upon none else, and you will afterward find them hanging up in your memory.' "

I give a further extract from the communication here quoted, which brings the author before us seriously revolving a project of remaining at Rome and becoming a painter.

We had delightful rambles together about Rome and its environs, one of which came near changing my whole course of life. We had been visiting a stately villa, with its gallery of paintings, its marble halls, its terraced gardens set out with statues and fountains, and were returning to Rome about sunset. The blandness of the air, the serenity of the sky, the transparent purity of the atmosphere, and that nameless charm which hangs about an Italian landscape, had derived additional effect from being enjoyed in company with Allston, and pointed out by him with the enthusiasm of an artist. As I listened to him, and gazed upon the landscape, I drew in my mind a contrast between our different pursuits and prospects. He was to reside among these delightful scenes, surrounded by masterpieces of art, by classic and historic monuments, by men of congenial minds and tastes, engaged like him in the constant study of the sublime and beautiful. I was to return home to the dry study of the law, for which I had no relish, and, as I feared, little talent.

Suddenly the thought presented itself,—"Why might I not remain here, and turn painter." I had taken lessons in drawing before leaving America, and had been thought to have some aptness, as I certainly had a strong inclination for it. I mentioned the idea to Allston, and he caught at it with eagerness. Nothing could be more feasible. We would take an apartment together. He would give me all the instruction and assistance in his power, and was sure I would succeed.

For two or three days the idea took full possession of my mind, but I believe it owed its main force to the lovely evening ramble in which I first conceived it, and to the romantic friendship I had formed with Allston. Whenever it recurred to mind, it was always connected with beautiful Italian scenery, palaces and statues and fountains and terraced gardens, and Allston as the companion of my studio. I promised myself a world of enjoyment in his society, and in the society of several artists with whom he had made me acquainted, and pictured forth a scheme of life all tinted with the rainbow hues of youthful promise.

My lot in life, however, was differently cast. Doubts and fears gradually clouded over my prospect ; the rainbow tints faded away ; I began to apprehend a sterile reality, so I gave up the transient but delightful prospect of remaining in Rome with Allston and turning painter.

Whether he had any peculiar gifts for such a vocation, I am unable to say ; but he once remarked to me that he thought he might have succeeded in landscape-painting, for which he had a great passion. One qualification he certainly possessed, an eye for color ; and no painting could long please him, whatever might be its other merits, if its tints were cold and raw. " I should get the rheumatism," said he once to Leslie, " if I were compelled to live in a room surrounded with such landscapes."

Mr. Irving had brought a letter to Torlonia, the banker, which his travelling companion advised him not to deliver. " It will procure you no attention," said he. " I have been here before and have tried it." His reception, however, was very flattering. He gave him a general invitation to conversaziones, that were held twice a week at his house, offered to introduce him to a conversazione of nobility on the following night, and through his stay continued to treat him with marked politeness and civility, to the no small surprise of Cabell, who was at a loss to account for the difference. Irving jocularly ascribed it to the superior discrimination of Torlonia. The joke was turned, however, when he came to make his adieus, and Torlonia, calling him aside, said, " *Dites moi, Monsieur, êtes vous parent de General Washington ?* " [Tell me, sir, are you a kinsman of General Washington ?] It was to the name of " Washington " and the supposed relationship it indicated to him that he was indebted for his extra attention.

As a set-off to this, I may mention an anecdote of a conversation overheard by Carter, author of " Letters from Europe," and by him communicated to an intelligent female friend, who told it to me. Not long after Mr. Irving had attained celebrity in Great

Britain by his writings, an English lady and her daughter were passing along some gallery in Italy and paused before a bust of Washington. After gazing at it for a few moments, the daughter turned to her mother with the question: " Mother, who was Washington?" " Why, my dear, don't you know?" was the reply ; "he wrote the ' Sketch-Book.' "

The journal records that he was present the evening of April 7th, " at a crowded assembly that filled four rooms, consisting of the first nobility of Rome, and several foreigners of distinction."

In this conversazione he accompanied the Baron de Humboldt, Minister of Prussia to the Court of Rome, and brother of the celebrated traveller, to whom he had brought a letter of introduction from Naples. On a previous evening, at the house of this gentleman, he had met Madame de Staël. The literary reputation of this gifted woman had not yet reached the height to which it was carried by the publication of her " Corinne " (in 1807), and " Delphine " was the only one of her productions which Mr. Irving had then read. " We found there," says he, in recording the visit, " Madame de Staël, the celebrated authoress of ' Delphine.' She is a woman of great strength of mind and understanding, by all accounts. We were in company with her but a few minutes." He afterward dined with her at the table of the minister, and would seem, by what he once stated to me, to have been somewhat astounded at the amazing flow of her conversation, and the question upon question with which she plied him.

CHAPTER IX.

AFTER remaining in Rome long enough to witness the ceremonies of the Holy Week, which were rendered less imposing than usual by the absence of the Pope, the young traveller proceeded on his journey, accompanied by Mr. Cabell.

As the two fellow-travellers drew near to Bologna, they found the road thronged with French soldiers on their way to Castiglione, to form a camp for the purpose of celebrating the approaching coronation of Bonaparte as King of Lombardy. " Each had his knapsack on his back, his gun on his shoulder, and a loaf of brown bread slung on one side, and was trudging along through mud and mire, with all the cheerfulness and flow of spirits of a Frenchman."

They arrived at Bologna about sunset, and put up at the Albergo del Pelegrino, " glad," says the journal, " to be emancipated from the miserable carriage in which we had been jolted along for nine days successively." They lingered a few days in Bologna, and then set out for Milan, after some difficulty in getting their passports signed, orders having been issued enjoining the greatest strictness in respect to passports, in consequence of the approaching coronation. They reached Milan by way of Modena, Parma, Piacenza, and Lodi. Between this last place and Milan the country was very much infested with robbers, and they were cautioned against travelling either before sunrise or after dark. They had sufficient proof that the caution was well founded, in the number of crosses they passed nailed to trees, to mark the spot where travellers had been robbed and murdered. " In one place

five crosses were nailed on one tree, in another place two." The road, however, was rendered perfectly safe at the time they passed by the number of peasants going to their labor in the fields.

They arrived at Milan on the 29th of April, and remained three days, but they were so fatigued in body, and their imaginations were so sated with the profusion of masterpieces they had seen, that they could not prevail upon themselves to visit any of the productions of art to be found in this city.

If Mr. Irving's admiration of the paintings and sculpture of Italy had become somewhat sated, his fondness for its music would seem to have grown by what it fed on. When he first attended one of its operas, he had been inclined to think the frantic bravos and bravissimos with which the Italians gave vent to their feelings "a ridiculous affectation. I allowed the Italians," he says, " the highest musical disposition, but thought they carried their applause beyond their real approbation. In a little while, however, by frequenting the operas and accustoming myself to the novelty of their music, I began to find a fondness for it stealing on myself, and I now hurry to an opera with as much eagerness as an Italian." This was a passion which knew no decline ; throughout life he was devotedly fond of this entertainment.

They left Milan on the 2d of May, and the same day arrived at the little village of Sesto, where they procured a bark to transport them across the Lago Maggiore to Magadino at the other end. The remainder of their journey, upon which I cannot detain the reader, lay over Mount St. Gothard to Altorf, from Altorf along the Lake of the Four Cantons to Lucerne, from Lucerne to Zurich, from Zurich to Basle, and from Basle through Franche Comté, Alsace, and Champagne to Paris, which they reached on the 24th of May.

The distant view of this capital, when they first came in sight, was very fine. " To us," says the journal, " it was a most interesting sight, and, like mariners after a long voyage, we hailed with joy our haven of repose."

His residence at Paris extended through four months, during which time he kept no journal, and would seem, also, from the few letters that remain, to have remitted his usual punctuality to the family. The only record he has left behind of his mode of life in the gay metropolis during this sojourn, consists of some brief and hasty memoranda, continued through a few weeks, which I give in part below.

May 24th.—Arrived in Paris this afternoon. Put up at the Hôtel de Richelieu, Rue de la Loi.

25th.—Had a levee of tailors, shirt-makers, boot-makers, etc., to rig me out *à la mode de Paris.* . . . .

In the evening went to the Théâtre Montansier in the Palais Royal. Acting humorous and rather gross; scenery tolerable. After theatre took a stroll in the garden of the Palais Royal; accosted by a *fille de joie,* who begged me to purchase a bouquet for her. I saw it was a mere scheme of the poor girl to get a few sous to buy herself some bread for the next day; it was evident she and the old woman who sold bouquets acted in concert. I pitied her, and paid double price for the bouquet. My head is as yet completely confused with the noise and bustle of Paris.

29th.—Get my protection from the police. In the evening to the Théâtre Français—Tragedy of the Templars—Talma, La Fond, and Mademoiselle Georges—Talma fine figure—great powers.

31st.—'Tended lectures on botany; evening, opera—music sublime—costume and scenery fine and appropriate.

June 2d.—Walking in the garden of the Tuileries, encountered young French officer with whom I had travelled in diligence last summer from Bordeaux to Toulouse. He had passed all the winter at his mother's in Languedoc, and had come to Paris in hopes of getting a commission to go over to England in the flotilla—warm in praise of the Emperor—said the army universally loved him, and would carry him even in their hands.

The young officer here mentioned was the one whom the compassionate damsels of Tonneins besought to be kind to his prisoner. As the quondam prisoner was passing by without seeing him, he suddenly broke from a group of companions, and rushing toward him, threw his arms around him, and kissed him *à la Française* on both cheeks before he had time to scan his features or know to whom he was indebted for such an affectionate salutation.

4th.—Left Hôtel de Richelieu and took room the other side of the Seine. Hôtel d' Angleterre, Rue de Colombier, Faubourg St. Martin, at 60 livres per month—room pleasantly situated on ground-floor, well furnished, looks out on a handsome little garden—hotel genteel and extensive—in the neighborhood of Vanderlyn.

6th.—Dined with Vanderlyn at a Swiss restaurateur's in Louvre—cheap. In evening went to little theatre of Jeunes Artistes—garden des Capuchins—boys acting plays—sing the fine airs that are produced at the great theatres.

8th.—Went with Vanderlyn to theatre of Porte St. Martin—built in thirty days in time of revolution—intended for an opera—superb theatre.

13th.—Went to a 15-sous ball in Palais Royal with Vanderlyn.

The following letter, among other particulars, makes further mention of Vanderlyn :—

[*To Peter Irving.*]

PARIS, July 15, 1805.

MY DEAR BROTHER:—

. . . . In consequence of my acquaintance at the Minister's, I have the reading of all the American papers which he receives, so that I have continually opportunities of informing myself how matters go on at home. . . . . I am very agreeably situated in respect to lodgings. I have taken handsome apartments in company with Mr. Bankhead, late secretary to Mr. Monroe. They are in a genteel hotel in the Faubourg St. Germain, near the Seine. Though retired from the gay, noisy part of the city, we have but to cross the Pont des Arts, and we are immediately among the amusements. This part of Paris is tranquil and reasonable, and almost all the Americans of my acquaintance reside here.

One of my most intimate acquaintances is Vanderlyn; he lives in my neighborhood. By the bye, I wish you would interest yourself with the Academy about this worthy young fellow. He has been sent out here by the Academy to collect casts, etc., and has executed his commission with faithfulness, but he is extremely in want of money. The Academy gave him a credit on Leghorn, in the name of Wm. M. Seton, but the death of that gentleman has rendered the letter useless. He has written repeatedly to the Academy, but has received no answer. His object was to go on to Italy, and he has been detained here merely for want of the means. Mr. McClure, one of our commissioners, has generously patronized him, and advanced him money for the journey; he will therefore set off in about a fortnight. I trust the Academy will evince a spirit of generosity toward a young artist, whose talents and character do credit to our country. They are in a manner responsible, having already taken such marked notice of him. I beg you to attend to this request, and to write Vanderlyn word as *soon as possible*, of the disposition and intentions of the Academy toward him. The poor fellow seems to be quite low-spirited, and to think that the Academy has forgotten him!

By the papers I find that the Emperor is at Fontainebleau, having travelled *incog.* from Genoa to that place in eighty hours! This is an instance of that promptness, decision, and rapidity that characterize his movements. You may well suppose I am impatient to see this wonderful man, whose life has been a continued series of actions, any one of which would be sufficient to immortalize him.

You expect, most probably, that I will say something of Paris, but I must beg you to excuse me. I have neither time nor inclination to begin so endless a subject. I should be at a loss how to commence, and I am almost afraid to own that I have not taken a single note since I have been in this metropolis. This, however, I find to be the case with all my acquaintances, so that I plead for some degree of indulgence on that score. The city is rapidly beautifying under the auspices of the Emperor; the Louvre, Tuileries, etc., are undergoing alterations and repairs. The people seem all gay and happy, and *vive la bagatelle !* is again the burden of their song.

Of all the places that I have seen in Europe Paris is the most fascinating, and I am well satisfied that for pleasure and amusement it must leave London far behind. The favorableness of the climate, the brilliancy of the theatres, operas, etc., the beauty of the public walks, the gayety, good-humor, and universal politeness of the people, the perfect liberty of private conduct, are calculated to enchant a stranger, and to render him contented and happy with every thing about him. You will smile to see that Paris has obtained complete possession of my head, but I assure you that America has still the stronghold of my heart.

I am busily employed in studying the French language, and I hope before I leave France to have a pretty satisfactory acquaintance with it. I shall remain in Paris as late in the fall as possible, as there is no place where I can both amuse and instruct myself at less expense, and more effectually. . . . .

When you see Mr. Hoffman present him my warmest remembrances, and tell him I long for the time when I shall be once more numbered among his disciples.

You will excuse the shortness and hastiness of this letter, for which I can only plead as an excuse that I am a *young man* and in *Paris.*

Your affectionate brother,

W. I.

In what proportion the "young man in Paris" managed to combine amusement and instruction, pleasure and study, it would not be easy to determine. That he did not make complete default in his plans of improvement may be inferred from some entries in his expense book, by which I find he paid for two months' tuition in French, and bought a Botanical Dictionary. In the same memorandum-book, under date of August 12th, occurs an entry of payment to " Vanderlyn for Portrait." This was a crayon sketch taken of him by the painter, and represents his hair as falling over his forehead, a peculiarity not observable in any later likenesses.

The letter which follows will enable us to accompany him to London.

[*To Peter Irving.*]

LONDON, October 20, 1805.

MY DEAR BROTHER :—

By the date of this letter, you will perceive that I am safely arrived in the land of our forefathers, and have become an inhabitant of the famous and foggy city of London. Thus you see I shift from city to city, and lay countries aside like books, after giving them a hasty perusal. Thank heaven my ramblings are nearly at an end, and in a little while I shall once more return to my friends, and sink again into tranquil domestic life! It may seem strange to you, who have never wandered far from home, but I assure you it is true, that in a short time one gets tired of travelling, even in the gay and polished countries of Europe. Curiosity cannot be kept ever on the stretch: like the sensual appetites it in time becomes sated, and no longer enjoys the food it formerly searched after with avidity. On entering a strange place at present, I feel no more that interest which prompted me on first arriving in Europe to be perpetually on the hunt for curiosities and beauties. In fact, the duty imposed upon me as a traveller to do so, is often irksome.

On arriving at Naples, I became acquainted with an American gentleman of talents, who had made the tour of Italy. I was much diverted with the manner in which he addressed his *valet de place* one morning, as we were going out in search of curiosities. " Now, my friend," said he, " recollect, I am tired of churches, convents, palaces, galleries of paintings, subterraneous passages, and great men—if you have any thing else to show me, *allons !*" At present I could almost feel inclined to make a similar speech myself. I own, notwithstanding, that London is extremely interesting to me, as it offers, both in buildings and inhabitants, such a contrast to the cities on the continent, and then it is so completely familiarized to me from having heard and read so much about it since my infancy, that every square, street, and lane appears like an old acquaintance.

I left Paris on the 22d of September, in company with Mr. Gorham, of Boston, and Mr. Massie, of Virginia, and after a pleasing tour through the Netherlands, by the way of Brussels and Maestricht, we arrived at Rotterdam on the 30th. We had made a stop of two days at Brussels, which is one of the most beautiful cities I have seen in Europe. We stayed another day at Maestricht, in order to visit a remarkable cavern in its neighborhood, but I will not fatigue you with a description of it. I was much interested by the change that I continually observed as I proceeded from the carelessly cultivated plains of France to those of the Netherlands, where the hand of labor appears to be never idle in the improvement of the soil; from the dirty, comfortless habitations of the French peasantry, to those of Holland, where cleanliness is almost a vice: in fine, from the light skip and gay, thoughtless air of the Frenchman, to the heavy tread and phlegmatic features of the Dutchman. How astonishing is it that a trifling space—a mere ideal line—should occasion such vast difference between two nations, that neither the people, houses, manners, language, tastes, should resemble each other! The Italian and the Turk are more similar than the Parisian and the Hollander.

I had intended making a hasty tour in Holland, but on arriving at Rotterdam I found an excellent packet about sailing for Gravesend. The passing and repassing of these packets is connived at by the French general who commands at Rotterdam, as he pockets a part of the passage money of each passenger. The vessel clears out for Embden under the Prussian flag. On my arrival at Rotterdam, I heard a report that Prussia either had declared, or was about to declare, in favor of France, in consequence of which, the owners were fearful of sending any more packets to England under Prussian colors. As I dreaded any accidental detention in the phlegmatic cities of Holland, I determined on availing myself of the packet that was about sailing, as did likewise my companions. Indeed, I did not regret much my not being able to see more of Holland, as the little I had already seen, I was told, was a faithful specimen of the rest—a monotonous uniformity prevailing over the whole country.

Leaving, therefore, the gentle Mynheers to smoke their pipes in peace, we embarked on the evening of the third of October, and on the morning of the fourth sailed from the mouth of the Meuse. The next morning on *turning out*, I had the first glimpse of old England; we were just opposite Margate, within four or five miles of the shore. We anchored the same evening in the Thames, opposite Gravesend. As we were direct from an enemy's country, we were not permitted to land till permits should arrive from the alien office at London. I did not receive mine till the morning of the eighth (suffering a detention of three days), when I went immediately on shore, took a post-chaise, and arrived in the afternoon at London. Such is a concise sketch of my journey. . . . .

In this city, as in Paris, he was a frequent attendant upon the theatres, and his impressions of John Kemble, Cooke, and Mrs. Siddons, are thus given in a letter to his brother William :—

Kemble appears to me to be a very studied actor. His performances throughout evince deep study and application, joined to amazingly judicious conception. They are correct and highly finished paintings, but much labored. Thus, therefore, when witnessing the exertion of his powers, though my head is satisfied and even astonished, yet my heart is seldom affected. I am not led away to forget that it is Kemble the actor, not Othello the Moor. Once I must own, however, I was completely overpowered by his acting. It was in the part of Zanga. He was great throughout, but his last scene with Alonzo was truly sublime. I then, in very truth, forgot that it was a mere mimic scene before me—indeed Kemble seemed to have forgotten himself, and for the moment to have fancied himself Zanga. When the delusion ceased I was enraptured. I was surprised at what had been my emotions. I could not have believed that tragic representation could so far deceive the senses and the judgment. I felt willing to allow Kemble all the laurels that had been awarded him. The next time I saw him, however, I was less satisfied. It was in the character of Othello. Here his performance was very unequal. In many parts he was cold and labored ; in the tender scenes he wanted *mellowness* (I think him very often wanting in this quality); it was only in particular scenes that he seemed to collect all his powers, and exert them with effect. His speech to the Senate was lofty and admirable ; indeed, in declamation he is excellent. The last time I saw him was in the part of Jaffier, and I again remarked that it was but in certain passages that he was strikingly fine, though his correct and unceasing attention to the character was visible throughout. Kemble treads the stage with peculiar grace and dignity ; his figure is tall and imposing, much such a one as Fennell's. His countenance is noble and expressive ; in a word, he has a most *majestic presence.* I must not forget to observe that the *Pierre* to Kemble's Jaffier was acted by Mr. Hargrave, and a *noisy swaggering bully* did he make of him. I would have given any thing to have had Cooper or Fennell in the character ; so you see a principal character may be miserably performed even on a London stage. Kemble's grand disadvantage is his voice; it wants the deep, rich, bass tones, and has not sufficient extent. Constant exercise has doubtless done a vast deal for it, and given it a degree of flexibility and softness which it had not naturally. Some of its tones are touching and pathetic, but when violent exclamation is necessary, it is evident from the movements of his head, and mouth, and chest, that he is obliged to use great exertions. This circumstance was at first a considerable drawback on the pleasure I received from his performances. I begin now to get reconciled to it, and not to notice it so much, which confirms me in the opinion I originally entertained, that it is necessary to become in some degree accustomed to Kemble's manner before you can perfectly enjoy his acting. To give you, if possible, a fuller idea of my general opinion of Kemble, I shall only say that though at present I decidedly give him the preference, yet were Cooper to be equally studious and pay equal attention to his profession, I would transfer it to him without hesitation. It would be a long time, however, before Cooper would be equally *correct* in his performances. Perhaps he would never be so; his style is different, and, with a little correction, its warmth and richness would make up for the want of Kemble's correctness and precision. Actors are like painters—they seldom combine all these qualities, but excel in different styles.

Cooke is the next to Kemble in the tragic department, or rather his equal, taking them in their different lines. Cooke's range is rather confined; the artful designing hypocrite is his *forte*, and in Iago he is admirable. I never was more completely satisfied with a performance. His Richard, I am told, is equally good, but I have not seen it. In Sir Pertinax MacSycophant, also, he is every thing that could be desired, and gives the Scotch accent with peculiar richness. Nothwithstanding that he has disgusted the audience several times in consequence of his bacchanalian festivities, he is a vast favorite, and is always hailed with the warmest applause. Indeed, I am told he performs with peculiar spirit when inspired by the grape; he must at any rate be *mellow* on such occasions.

Were I to indulge without reserve in my praises of Mrs. Siddons, I am afraid you would think them hyperbolical. What a wonderful woman! The very first time I saw her perform I was struck with admiration. It was in the part of Calista. Her looks, her voice, her gestures, delighted me. She penetrated in a moment to my heart. She froze and melted it by turns; a glance of her eye, a start, an exclamation, thrilled through my whole frame. The more I see her, the more I admire her. I hardly breathe while she is on the stage. She works up my feelings till I am like a mere child. And yet this woman is old, and has lost all elegance of figure; think then what must be her powers that she can delight and astonish even in the characters of Calista and Belvidera. In person Mrs. Siddons is not unlike her sister, Mrs. Whitlock, for she has latterly out-grown in size the limits even of *embonpoint.* I even think there is some similiarity in their countenances, though that of Mrs. Siddons is infinitely superior. It is in fact the very index of her mind; and in its mutable transitions may be read those nice gradations of passion that language is inadequate to express. In dignity and grace she is no way inferior to Kemble, and they never appear to better advantage that when acting together. What Mrs. Siddons may have been when she had the advantages of youth and form I cannot say, but it appears to me that her performance at present leaves room to wish for nothing more. Age has planted no visible wrinkles on her brow, and it is only by the practice and experience of years that she has been enabled to attain her present consummate excellence. . . . .

The enthusiam here expressed for the great actress leads me to step aside from the regular order of events to give an anecdote of a later date, for which I shall not find a more appropriate introduction.

Not long after the " Sketch-Book " had been published in London, and made its author remarked among its literary circles, he met Mrs. Siddons in some fashionable assemblage, and was brought up to be introduced. The Queen of Tragedy had then long left the stage, but her manner and tones to the last partook of its measured stateliness. The interview was characteristic. As he approached and was introduced, she looked at him for a moment, and then, in her clear and deep-toned voice, she slowly enunciated : "You've made me weep." Nothing could have been finer than such a compliment from such a source, but the " accost " was so abrupt, and the manner so peculiar, that never was modest man so completely disconcerted and put out of countenance. The appropriate response would have been obvious enough at a more collected moment, but taken entirely by surprise, Geoffrey had not a word to say for himself, and very soon took occasion to retreat and join a group of talkers that were near. After the appearance of his "Bracebridge Hall" he met her in company again, and was asked by a friend to be presented. He told him he had before gone through that ceremony, but he had been so abashed by her address, and acquitted himself so shabbily, that he was afraid to claim acquaintance. " Come then with me," said his friend, "and I will stand by you"; so he went forward, and singularly enough was met with an address of the self-same fashion : "You 've made me weep again." But now he was prepared, and immediately replied with a complimentary allusion to the melting effect of her own pathos, as realized by himself at the period we have been tracing.

In the following letter we have an allusion to Nelson's victory and death. The traveller was at the theatre when the thrilling tidings were announced from the stage, and was witness to the deep and mingled emotions with which it was received.

[*To Peter Irving.*]

LONDON, November 7, 1805.

MY DEAR BROTHER :—

By the papers you will perceive that England is all alive with the news of Nelson's victory. It could not have happened more opportunely, for the disastrous accounts from the continent had made poor John Bull quite heart-sick—nothing was heard from him but execrations of Mack's conduct as cowardly and treacherous, and desponding anticipations of the future. It is the prevalent opinion here that Mack has been bribed, and they are vociferous in their abuse both of him and his purchasers.

Poor John, however, was so completely down-hearted and humble, that I began really to pity him, when suddenly the news of Nelson's triumph arrived, and the old fellow reared his broad rosy countenance higher than ever. To his honor, however, let me say, that I have universally remarked, that whenever speaking of the affair, his first mention was of " poor Nelson's death," with a tribute of feeling to his memory; but John, as I have before testified, is a " kind-hearted old soul " at bottom. Notwithstanding the brilliancy of this victory and its importance at so alarming a crisis, yet I can scarcely say which is greatest : joy at its achievement, or sorrow for Nelson's fall. Last evening the chief streets and buildings were illuminated, but the illumination was not universal. The song of triumph is repressed—among the lowest of the mob I can hear Nelson's eulogium passed from mouth to mouth; every one yields his voice to the national tribute of gratitude and affection.

Mr. Irving had anticipated on his arrival in London a number of introductory letters from home, that would have procured him an agreeable and advantageous acquaintance ; but these letters unfortunately miscarried, and the disappointment prevented him from fully enjoying the pleasures of a city in which every thing bore to him an air of business, and in which he had, for a while, to find his entertainment in rambling about the streets. The only letter which he brought with him was one from Mrs. Johnson, of the Park Theatre, to Miss De Camp, of Covent Garden, which proved, in the dearth of others, a valuable resource. He had a most friendly reception from her, and I have heard him speak with interest of a dinner at her house, in which he met for the first time with Charles Kemble, whom she afterward married.

Left still more solitary by the departure of his companions from Paris, the young traveller began to turn his thoughts toward home, without going to Scotland, as his brother had desired. As in Paris, so in London, he kept no journal, but it appears by a small memorandum-book, among his papers, that he set out, on the 14th of December, on a short tour to Oxford, Bath, and Bristol, with a Mr. Mumford from New York as a travelling companion ; and that the two left London, January 17th, in a post-chaise for Gravesend, where they embarked the next day in the ship *Remittance*, Captain Law, for New York. They had a stormy passage of sixty-four days, and for twenty-four hours were in imminent danger of going ashore in a snow-storm off Long Island. "The passengers," said Mr. Irving, in speaking of this voyage, " cracked their jokes on each other in great good-humor at first, while Mumford sat like an owl, and said nothing ; but, before we landed, he became the greatest favorite of all. The familiarity of the others led to quarrels, and the jokes we had cracked on each other soured on our stomachs."

CHAPTER X.

A Literary Antiquary (Bracebridge).

THE traveller had felt a growing impatience to return home before he embarked.

"Already," he writes in one of his letters prior to his departure from Europe, "I begin to feel the truth of the line in Voltaire,—

"'Il est doux de rentrer dans sa chère patrie.'"

There was much to gladden his return. He came back with health renewed and invigorated. The reputation achieved by his scribblings before he left had made him an object of attention and civility, and at that "home-keeping" era to have visited foreign parts was of itself quite a title to consideration.

New York was a more "handy" city in those days, to borrow a descriptive epithet of the author, and offered much greater facility of intercourse. No man could hide his light under a bushel. Everybody knew everybody, and there was more of good-fellowship and careless ease of manners than distinguish the social circles of either sex in these more formal times. The literati and men of wit and intellect entered more into society, and gave to it something of their own tone and character. If the dinners were less costly than now, they were more merry, and there was greater heartiness of enjoyment. Singing—sentimental and bacchanalian— was quite a feature in the entertainment. Conviviality, however, it must be confessed, was sometimes pushed to an extreme ; it was almost treason against good-fellowship not to get tipsy, and the senseless custom of compelling guests to drink bumpers, not unfrequently laid many under the table who never would have been led willingly to such excess.

Mr. Irving used to relate a piece of pleasantry of one of his early friends, Henry Ogden, illustrative of this feature of the dinners of those times. Ogden had been at one of those festive meetings on the evening before, and had left with a brain half bewildered by the number of bumpers he had been compelled to drink. He told Irving the next day that in going home he had fallen through a grating, which had been carelessly left open, into a vault beneath. The solitude, he said, was rather dismal at first, but several other of the guests fell in, in the course of the evening, and they had on the whole quite a pleasant night of it.

Among Mr. Irving's associates at this time, few of whom now survive, were Peter and Gouverneur Kemble, Henry Brevoort, Henry Ogden, just named, and James K. Paulding, who, with himself, his brother Peter, and a few others, made up a small circle of intimates designated by Peter as "the nine worthies," though Washington in his correspondence more frequently alludes to them as "the lads of Kilkenny."

One of their favorite resorts was an old family mansion—old, at least, according to the American calendar of antiquity—which had descended to Gouverneur Kemble from a deceased uncle. It was on the banks of the Passaic, about a mile from Newark, and has been shadowed forth in "Salmagundi" as Cockloft Hall. It was full of antique furniture, and the walls were adorned with old family portraits. The place was in charge of an old man, his wife, and a negro boy, who were its sole occupants except when "the nine," under the lead, and confident in the hospitality of the Patroon, as they styled its possessor, would sally forth from New York and enliven its solitude by their madcap pranks and juvenile orgies. "Who would have thought," said Mr. Irving to Gouverneur Kemble, in alluding to these scenes of high jollity, at the age of sixty-six, "that we should ever have lived to be two such respectable old gentlemen!"

Some of the letters preserved by Mr. Irving contain pleasant allusions to the Hall, and show how fondly this scene of youthful frolic was remembered by the little circle in the separation of after-years. "Cockloft Hall is still mine," writes Gouverneur Kemble to his long-absent friend in 1824. "I still look forward to the time when you, Paulding, Brevoort, the Doctor [Peter Irving], and myself shall assemble there, recount the stories of our various lives, and have another game at leap frog."

"Your mention of James Paulding and Gouverneur Kemble," writes Peter to him in 1832, "brings to my memory some of the pleasant scenes in the Hall near Newark, and among the rest the procession in the Chinese saloon, in which we made poor Dick McCall a knight, and I, as the senior of our order, dubbed him by some fatality on the seat of honor instead of the shoulder." And in a still later letter he writes: "I often call to mind our Sundays at the Hall, when we sported on the lawn until fatigued, and sometimes fell sociably into a general nap in the drawing-room in the dusk of the evening."

One of the rendezvous of the little coterie in the city was Dyde's, a genteel public-house in Park Row near the theatre, in which they held convivial suppers, and sometimes regaled their friends from Philadelphia, who, for the time, became "true lads of Kilkenny."

"To riot at Dyde's on imperial champagne,
    And then scour our city—the peace to maintain,"

is a distinction of "SAD DOGS" in the rhymes of "Salmagundi." There was another place of less note and cheaper prices, a porter-house at the corner of John Street and Nassau, to which they occasionally repaired for festivity and refreshment when their purses were low, and where they probably had equal merriment, though these entertainments they characterized with humorous disparagement as their "blackguard suppers." Paulding has an allusion to them in a letter to Washington of 1824, recalling old times, in which he indulges in whimsical lament over the degenerate transformation which their host had since undergone. " When I mentioned a jollification just now," he writes, " do you know that the word conjured up the idea of poor B——? Alas for this topsy-turvy world! He who whilom wore a long coat, in the pockets whereof he jingled two bushels of sixpenny pieces, and whose daughter played the piano to the savory accompaniment of broiling oysters, hath sunk into a measurer of tape at the foot of Vesey Street."

In July Mr. Irving concludes an epistle to his young friend, Henry Ogden, who had recently sailed for China, as follows :—

I am so completely engrossed with law at present that I have no time to go about and pick up intelligence. Examination comes on in about three weeks, and I begin to feel the fever incident to occasions of the kind. I wish, while in Canton, you would pick me up two or three queer little pretty things, that would cost nothing, and be acceptable to the girls ; but above all do not forget the Mandarin's dress. If you can conveniently, get two or three drawings of the most superlative tea put up in a little quizzical box for me, and packed up with mighty care and importance. I will have some fun with it.

The Mandarin's dress and the tea evidently point to some whimsical project, but whether any " high fun " came of it I cannot say, though there is a hint in his correspondence of Ogden's return, " laden with the riches of the East, some of which were intended for him," and of a supper at the Kembles' which followed, " in true Chinese style, in which none were permitted to eat except with chopsticks."

Though Mr. Irving would seem to have been preparing for an examination in August by the preceding extract, he must have deferred it until the autumn, for it was on the 21st of November, 1806, that he went through the ordeal and was admitted to the bar. The termination of his clerkship, however, found him still sadly deficient in legal lore. His studies, previous to his departure for Europe, as we have seen, had amounted to little ; his almost two years of absence, though computed in the period of clerkship, could not have enlarged the sphere of his legal knowledge, and the few months of his return previous to his admisssion, did not add much to the stock.

Soon after his admission, I find him sharing the office of his brother John, at No. 3 Wall Street, and invoking the influence of Mr. Hoffman with the Council of Appointment, for some professional office which he might turn to the advantage of both, evidently reposing for success in the discharge of its duties, should his application prevail, more on the superior legal competency and assiduous business habits of his brother John than upon his own qualifications. I give the letter, which is addressed to Mr. Hoffman at Albany.

New York, February 2, 1807.

DEAR SIR :—

I am writing this letter from your parlor, and have the pleasure of informing you that the family, at this moment, are perfectly well : the girls all out in the sunshine ; Mrs. H. sewing like a good housewife ; little Charles sleeping up-stairs ; and *little old fashion* by my side, most studiously turning over the leaves of a family Bible. The only occurrences of *importance* that have taken place in the family since Mrs. Hoffman wrote last, are, that Mr. Edgar has sent to know if you took the house for the ensuing year, and Mrs. Hoffman has answered in the affirmative. Louis has received *sailing orders*, and I have beaten the old lady most deplorably at cribbage. . . . .

Having given you all the domestic intelligence that I am master of, I hope you will not think it impertinent if I speak a little of myself.

I learn with pleasure, that the Council of Appointment are decidedly Lewisite. As there will, doubtless, be a liberal dispensation of loaves and fishes on the occasion, I would humbly put up my feeble voice in the general application. Will you be kind enough to speak "a word in season" for me? There will, doubtless, be numerous applicants of superior claims to myself, but none to whom a "crumb from the table" would be more acceptable. I can plead no services that I have rendered, for I have rather shunned than sought political notoriety. . . . . I know that there are few offices to which I am eligible, either from age or legal information. My brother, John T. Irving, is much older than myself, and from his knowledge of the law is capacitated to fill offices to which I cannot pretend; our interests are the same, as we shall share whatever falls to either of our lots. . . . . I do not intend that you should give yourself any trouble on my account ; your good word is all I solicit, should any thing present which you should think suitable to me. . . . .

So little, however, does he seem intent at this time upon professional employment, that we find him concerting with James K. Paulding the project of "Salmagundi," the first number of which appeared only two months after the date of his license, and prior by a few days to this unfruitful appeal to Mr. Hoffman. Paulding was then a clerk in the Loan Office, living under the same roof with his brother-in-law, William Irving, and used to amuse his leisure by scribbling satirical strictures for the newspapers. Washington proposed to him to drop that and join with him in the plan of a work which should be mainly characterized by a spirit of fun and sarcastic drollery, and should come out in numbers, and at such intervals as should suit their pleasure and convenience. Paulding readily fell in with the idea. They were afterward joined by Washington's eldest brother, William, who made up the trio, Launcelot Langstaff, Anthony Evergreen, and William Wizard. Peter, no longer editor of the *Morning Chronicle*, in which Paulding and Washington had first tried their wings, would in all probability have formed a fourth if he had been in the city, but he had departed on a tour in Europe, just previous to the appearance of the first number.

The work was undertaken purely for their own amusement ; to please themselves, and with no expectation of pecuniary profit. If they covered the expense of paper and printing it was all they cared for, and the publisher, David Longworth, "dusky Davie," as they called him from a song of the period, was made to profess "the same sublime contempt for money with the authors."

The work ran through twenty numbers, and was continued one year.

The first number appeared on the 24th of January, 1807, and the opening article, the joint product of Washington and Paulding, breathes a dashing, buoyant audacity, well calculated to disturb the sobriety of Gotham. The second article—"From the Elbow-chair of Launcelot Langstaff, Esq."—came from the pen of

Paulding, and the two which followed, " On Theatrics," and " The New York Assembly," were written by Washington.

The success of the first number was decisive. The sensation produced by it in the New York circles was intense, and great was the curiosity and speculation to know who were the mysterious trio who, with such unquestioning confidence, had undertaken to amuse, edify, and castigate the town.

The second number appeared on the 4th of February, of which the first article was by Washington, the second and third by Paulding, the poetry, signed Pindar Cockloft, by William Irving, and the concluding advertisement by Washington. There is a trivial anecdote connected with this last article, which illustrates the free and daring humor in which the work was conceived. The manuscript had characterized their satirical pleasantries as " good-natured raillery," which last word, by an expressive blunder, the printer converted into " villainy." Whether the blunder was felicitous or not, there was something waggishly descriptive in the epithet which hit the humor of Washington, and he resolved at once to retain it. The adopted misprint, " good-natured villainy," has stood from that day to this to characterize the merry mischief of their labors.

The third number appeared on the 13th of February, containing, among other papers, the first of the series of letters from Mustapha Rub-a-dub Keli Khan, which was written by Paulding, with the exception of the paragraph giving the account of the Tripolitan's reception on landing, which was thrown in by Washington.

In the preface to the "Salmagundi" in Harper's uniform edition of his works, Paulding remarks : " The thoughts of the authors were so mingled together in these essays, and they were so literally joint productions, that it would be difficult as well as useless to assign to each his exact share." The indication I have here given of their joint property in this oriental paper will elucidate the remark, though it would be pressing it beyond its intent and meaning to confound all the essays in a joint indeterminate authorship. Many of the articles were exclusively from the pen of Paulding ; Washington stood alone in the authorship of others, while William's participation in the work was confined to the poetry and the letters of Mustapha in Nos. V. and XIV., though to these last Washington contributed some additional touches. All the remaining letters of Mustapha came exclusively from the pen of Washington, with the exception of that in No. XVIII., which is to be ascribed to Paulding. I speak with the more confidence in this matter, that I have Paulding's own authority for these special assignments, who claims but two of the nine letters of Mustapha, and distinguishes the authorship of the others as I have indicated. His share in the work, however, though it could not be accurately discriminated, was quite equal to that of Washington.

The fourth number of " Salmagundi " appeared on the 24th of February, making four numbers in a month. The sensation increased with every issue, and eight hundred copies were once disposed of in a day. They were also circulated in other cities of the Union, where imitations sprung up, went through a few numbers, and died. The authors were astonished at their own success, and finding that the work was yielding a large profit to the publisher, began to doubt whether some share of the advantage should not accrue to themselves. Washington, in particular, who, as we have seen, had but recently taken his license, was by no means raised above the necessity of turning the unexpected success of the papers to account. " What arrangements have you made with the Dusky for the profits?" he writes to Paulding from Virginia, in a letter to be hereafter given in full; " I shall stand much in need of a little sum of money on my return."

Some months prior to the date of this extract, Longworth had taken out the copyright of " Salmagundi " before Paulding or Irving was aware of its value, and all they ever received from him was a hundred dollars apiece, although at the time the original copyright expired, in 1822, Paulding conjectures, in a letter to Ebenezer Irving, that he had made by all accounts ten or perhaps fifteen thousand dollars out of it; probably an extravagant estimate. Longworth had at first suggested a copyright to them, but they did not think it worth while, and he thereupon took it out himself.

Not long after the appearance of the fourth number of "Salmagundi," Mr. Irving visited Philadelphia, and went the rounds of fashion and gayety. I give some specimens of his correspondence at this period.

The letter which follows is addressed to Miss Mary Fairlie, a belle famed for her wit and vivacity, who was afterward the wife of the eminent tragedian, Thomas A. Cooper. The " fascinating Fairlie," as she is styled in a letter of Mr. Irving, was the " Sophy Sparkle," of " Salmagundi." I am indebted to the politeness of her daughter, Mrs. Robert Tyler, for this and other letters which will be given to the same address.

[*To Miss Mary Fairlie.*]

PHILADELPHIA, March 17, 1807.

Your charming letter has just reached me, and the post shall not depart without an answer, if it is only to testify my gratitude for the exquisite entertainment you have furnished me. I should have written you a second letter without waiting for a reply to my first; but really, I have been reduced to such an extremity of nervous affliction, that I dared not run the hazard of being stupid. Oh, my friend, how dreadfully I have been maltreated in this most facetious city ! The good folk of this place have a most wicked determination of being all thought wits and *beaux esprits*, and they are not content with being thought so by themselves, but they insist that everybody else should be of the same opinion, and it has produced a most violent attack of puns upon my nervous system. The Philadelphians do absolutely " live and move, and have a being," entirely upon puns, and their wits are absolutely cut up into sixpenny-bits, and dealt out in small change. I cannot speak two sentences but that I see a pun gathering in the faces of my hearers. I absolutely shudder with horror—think what miseries I suffer—me to whom a pun is an abomination ; is there any thing in the whole volume of the " miseries of human life " to equal it ? I experienced the first attack of this forlorn wit on entering Philadelphia ; it was equal to a twinge of the gout, or a *stitch in the side*. I found it was repeated at every step. I could not turn a corner, but that a pun was hurled at my head ; till, to complete my annoyance, two young devils of punsters, who began just to crow in the art like young bantams, penned me up in a corner at a tea-party, and did so *bepun* me, that I was reduced to absolute stupidity. I hastened home prodigiously indisposed, took to my bed, and was only roused therefrom by the sound of the breakfast-bell. I have suffered more or less ever since ; but, thank heaven, it is a complaint of which few die, otherwise I should be under no small apprehension. Your message to the elegant —— shall be faithfully remembered. —— —— has sent him a handkerchief of yours, which she happened accidentally to have with her. I expect to see him wearing it in his bosom, or on his hat, or perhaps as a nightcap. He still retains a spark of faithful recollection, and was particular in his inquiries of Brevoort, whether you were not in low spirits. He called on me two or three times, and I on him, but we could not find each other at home ; by good fortune, however, I overtook him yesterday, as he was treating his legs to an airing in Market Street. As I hold those ponderous supporters of his body in no inconsiderable estimation, I was particular in noticing their appearance, and am happy to say they are in a state of tolerable prosperity, though they have rather a pensive aspect, owing, I suppose, to the weight of misery and carcass they have to *undergo* (meaning a villainous pun, for which God forgive me). The dear dog was very loving in his salutation, and made several kinds of *pulse-feeling* questions. Were there not several ladies coming on from New York? No! The reply was like a guillotine ; it chopped off his hopes and his question at one stroke, and the unhappy —— relapsed into stupidity, and thought of the moon ! As I have no such thing as malice in my composition, and do love dearly to make everybody happy, I advised him to make New York a visit. He expressed a wish to do so. I begged him to go with me ; he wanted to know how soon I should go ; this I could not tell ; as my stay depends entirely on my whim and my pocket ; he seemed to listen to the proposition with complacency, and it shall go hard, but you will have him puffing and lumbering about your parlor in the course of a week or two. . . . .

I have been introduced to Mrs. D—— by her husband. I won't speak all that I think of her ; you would accuse me of hyperbole ; but, to say that I admire her would be too cold, too feeble. I think she would be a belle in heaven itself. I cannot refrain from gazing on her continually whenever I meet her, and were I an Eastern visionary, I should bow down and do her homage, as one of the Houris destined to perfect the bliss of true believers. This is all honest, sober fact, whatever you may think of it. . . . .

You need not be under any apprehensions of my forgetting New York while you are in it (very like a compliment); but I have so many engagements on hand, am so intolerably admired, and have still so much money in my pocket, that I really can fix no time when I shall return to my New York insignificance.

I fear I shall miss the post, so, though I have a world of matter more to communicate, I must hastily conclude with my warmest remembrance to your family, and a fervent request for an immediate *answer.*

P. S.—As your mamma is so kindly solicitous about my health, do not let her know of my being so violently indisposed with this *pun* fever, particularly as I feel myself on the recovery ever since I have read that estimable work entitled " God's Revenge against Punning."

In her reply of March 19th, this lady begs him to try to come back by the next assembly, which was that day week and was to be the last.

It seems that he must have returned, for a female correspondent at Philadelphia (March 30th), gives, with playful extravagance, the following picture of the impression he had left behind. " As for me, my consequence lessens every day ; indeed I begin to think seriously of leaving this terrestrial paradise. Half the people exist but in the idea that *you* will one day return. When will pleasure return to these wretched beings ? They have no philosophy, and ages will not reconcile them to the loss of your society."

It was on this visit to Philadelphia that Mr. Irving made the acquaintance of Joseph Dennie, then in high repute as the author of the " Lay Preacher" and conductor of the *Portfolio,* and, next to Charles Brockden Brown, the first American writer who made a profession of literature.

CHAPTER XI.

Letter to Miss Fairlie.—Mingles in an Election.—Passage of a Letter from Miss Fairlie.—His Likeness.—Attends the Trial of Burr.—Letter to Mrs. Hoffman.—General James Wilkinson.—Letter to James K. Paulding.—Striking Account of the First Encounter of Burr and Wilkinson.—Strictures on No. 10 of "Salmagundi" by himself.—Thomas A. Cooper, the Tragedian.—Letter to Miss Fairlie.—Last Interview with Burr.—Death of his Father.

IMMEDIATELY after his return from Philadelphia, his lively correspondent, Miss Fairlie, paid a visit to Boston. In the following fragment of a letter, addressed to her at that place, we have an amusing sketch of himself and other juvenile patriots at the polls :—

[*To Miss Mary Fairlie.*]
NEW YORK, May 2, 1807.

I thank you a thousand times for the wish you express that I should write to you . . . . Well . . . . We have toiled through the purgatory of an election, and may the day stand for aye accursed on the Kalendar, for never were poor devils more intolerably beaten and discomfited than my forlorn brethren, the Federalists. What makes me the more outrageous is, that I got fairly drawn into the vortex, and before the third day was expired, I was as deep in mud and politics as ever a moderate gentleman would wish to be ; and I drank beer with the multitude ; and I talked handbill-fashion with the demagogues, and I shook hands with the mob—whom my heart abhorreth. 'T is true for the two first days I maintained my coolness and indifference. The first day I merely hunted for whim, character, and absurdity, according to my usual custom; the second day being rainy, I sat in the barroom at the Seventh Ward, and read a volume of Galatea, which I found on a shelf; but before I had got through a hundred pages, I had three or four good Feds, sprawling around me on the floor, and another, with his eyes half shut, leaning on my shoulder in the most affectionate manner, and spelling a page of the book as if it had been an electioneering handbill. But the third day—ah! then came the tug-of-war. My patriotism all at once blazed forth, and I determined to save my country! Oh, my friend, I have been in such holes and corners; such filthy nooks and filthy corners, sweep offices and oyster cellars! "I have been sworn brother to a leash of drawers, and can drink with any tinker in his own language during my life"—faugh! I shall not be able to bear the smell of small beer or tobacco for a month to come! . . . .

Truly this saving one's country is a nauseous piece of business, and if patriotism is such a dirty virtue—prythee, no more of it. I was almost the whole time at the Seventh Ward—as you know, that is the most fertile ward in mob, riot, and incident, and I do assure you the scene was exquisitely ludicrous. Such haranguing and puffing and strutting among all the little great men of the day. Such shoals of unfledged heroes from the lower wards, who had broke away from their mammas, and run to electioneer with a slice of bread-and-butter in their hands. Every carriage that drove up disgorged a whole nursery of these pigmy wonders, who all seemed to put on the brow of thought, the air of bustle and business, and the big talk of general committee men. . . . .

I extract from the lady's reply; reminding the reader that, in the number of "Salmagundi" issued a few weeks before, there was a queer likeness of Launcelot Langstaff with a preposterous length of nose.

BOSTON, 11th May.

How my heart joyed to hear of your defeat! never did I receive a letter which gave me so much pleasure. I cannot say, however, that it was unexpected, as I am too good a Republican to have thought of leaving New York without being perfectly sure of our victory.

You are all blown. A *cute* young man, an author of the "Anthology," dined with us to-day. After having (by the way of entertaining me) been catechized by him on all points, he asked me the usual question of who was the author of "Salmagundi"? I told him that it was not absolutely *known*, but that you were shrewdly *suspected;* he said he thought so; that he had seen you in Italy; that the instant he saw the likeness of Launcelot in No. VIII., he perceived it bore a strong likeness to you, indeed very striking; it had your nose and the whole contour of your face exactly; to be sure, he added, it was a little caricatured! I forthwith determined to have it set in pearl, and shall evermore wear it next my heart, in token of the great love and kindness I bear the original!

Mr. Irving had made a sudden departure from New York before the date of this extract, having received an informal retainer from one of the friends of Colonel Burr, whose trial was expected to take place in Richmond. His client had little belief in his legal erudition, and did not look for any approach to a professional debut, but thought he might in some way or other be of service with his pen. He himself felt that the movements and deportment of Burr were likely to be highly interesting in his present circumstances, and seems eagerly to have embraced the opportunity of mingling in the excitements of the trial. Enveloped as had been the proceedings of Burr in doubt and mystery, he did not at this time share in the prevalent belief of his treason, and he writes to Mrs. Hoffman, " though opposed to him in political principles, yet I consider him as a man so fallen, so shorn of the power to do national injury, that I feel no sensation remaining but compassion for him."

In the following letter to the same lady, we find him in attendance on the trial.

[*To Mrs. Hoffman.*]

RICHMOND, June 4, 1807.

. . . . You expected that the trial was over at the time you were writing; but you can little conceive the talents for procrastination that have been exhibited in this affair. Day after day have we been disappointed by the non-arrival of the magnanimous Wilkinson; day after day have fresh murmurs and complaints been uttered; and day after day are we told that the next mail will probably bring his noble self, or at least some accounts when he may be expected. We are now enjoying a kind of suspension of hostilities; the grand jury having been dismissed the day before yesterday for five or six days, that they might go home, see their wives, get their clothes washed, and flog their negroes. As yet we are not even on the threshold of a trial; and, if the great hero of the South does not arrive, it is a chance if we have any trial this term. I am told the Attorney-General talks of moving the Court next Tuesday, for a continuance and a special Court, by which means the present grand jury (the most enlightened, perhaps, that was ever assembled in this country) will be discharged; the witnesses will be dismissed; many of whom live such a distance off that it is a chance if half of them will ever be again collected. The Government will be again subjected to immense expense, and Colonel Burr, besides being harassed and detained for an additional space of time, will have to repeat the enormous expenditures which this trial has already caused him. I am very much mistaken, if the most underhand and ungenerous measures have not been observed toward him. He, however, retains his serenity and self-possession unshaken, and wears the same aspect in all times and situations. I am impatient for the arrival of this Wilkinson, that the whole matter may be put to rest; and I never was more mistaken in my calculations, if the whole will not have a most farcical termination as it respects the charges against Colonel Burr. . . . .

To understand the force of this allusion to General James Wilkinson, then at the head of the army, and Governor of the Territory of Louisiana, it will be necessary to remember that he was supposed at the time to be in some way implicated in the schemes of Burr. He had known him in the Revolution, and the intimacy had continued through a long course of years. Not a great while prior to the arrest of Burr, when he was wandering in the West, they had corresponded in mysterious characters, as if the subject of their communications required concealment, and though he had finally taken an active part in baffling his schemes and bringing him to trial, doubts were still entertained whether— if clear of actual participation in the designs of his former friend— he had not at least pursued a temporizing policy, until he saw the impending explosion. Certain it is that Burr claimed him as an associate, and charged him with perfidy.

On the 24th of June the grand jury, of which the celebrated John Randolph was foreman, came in with charges of treason and misdemeanor against Burr. Two days before, Mr. Irving had written a letter to James K. Paulding, which, among other matters of interest, contains a striking account of the first encounter of Burr and Wilkinson. I give the letter.

RICHMOND, June 22, 1807.

DEAR JAMES:—

I have been expecting a few lines from you for some time past, and am sorry to find you stand upon ceremony. Had I the same leisure that

I had when in New York, you should not want for scrawls as often as you choose, but here I have but a few moments that are not occupied in attending the trial, and observing the character and company assembled here. I wish to know all the news about our work, and any literary intelligence that may be in circulation. I am much disappointed at your having concluded the first volume at No. 10. Besides making an insignificant baby-house volume, it ends so weakly at one of the weakest numbers of the whole. At least it is a number which is not highly satisfactory to me, perhaps because I wrote the greatest part of it myself, and that at hurried moments. I had intended concluding it in style, and commencing Vol. II. with some eclat : " but let that pass." I have no doubt you had *three special reasons* for what you have done, and am content. What arrangement have you made with the Dusky for the profits? I shall stand much in need of a little sum of money on my return. I shall endeavor to send you more matter for another number, as soon as I can find time and humor to write it in ; at present I have neither.

I can appoint no certain time for my return, as it depends entirely upon the trial. Wilkinson, you will observe, has arrived ; the bets were against Burr that he would abscond, should W. come to Richmond ; but he still maintains his ground, and still enters the court every morning with the same serene and placid air that he would show were he brought there to plead another man's case, and not his own.

The lawyers are continually entangling each other in law points, motions, and authorities, and have been so crusty to each other, that there is a constant sparring going on. Wilkinson is now before the grand jury, and has such a mighty mass of *words* to deliver himself of, that he claims at least two days more to discharge the wondrous cargo. The jury are tired enough of his verbosity. The first interview between him and Burr was highly interesting, and I secured a good place to witness it. Burr was seated with his back to the entrance, facing the judge, and conversing with one of his counsel. Wilkinson strutted into the court, and took a stand in a parallel line with Burr on his right hand. Here he stood for a moment swelling like a turkey-cock, and bracing himself up for the encounter of Burr's eye. The latter did not take any notice of him until the judge directed the clerk to swear General Wilkinson ; at the mention of the name Burr turned his head, looked him full in the face with one of his piercing regards, swept his eye over his whole person from head to foot, as if to scan its dimensions, and then coolly resumed his former position, and went on conversing with his counsel as tranquilly as ever. The whole look was over in an instant ; but it was an admirable one. There was no appearance of study or constraint in it ; no affectation of

disdain or defiance; a slight expression of contempt played over his countenance, such as you would show on regarding any person to whom you
were indifferent, but whom you considered mean and contemptible.
Wilkinson did not remain in court many minutes.

Do write me immediately. Answer me the questions I have already
asked, and give me all the news you hear.

Love to Pindar and family.

Yours truly,

W. I.

"Pindar" was his brother William, who wrote the poetical
pieces of "Salmagundi" under the signature of Pindar Cockloft.
The hurried article to which he objects as having been written by
himself, was styled "The Stranger in Philadelphia." It was made
up of satirical observations on men and manners in that city, but
did not satisfy him, and was not retained in subsequent editions.

Mr. Irving was still absent at Richmond, when the number
which succeeded this appeared, containing a letter from Mustapha
by himself, and "Mine Uncle John," which is exclusively from the
pen of Paulding. Of this finished and delightful sketch he used
always to speak in terms of warm admiration. He appreciated it
the more, no doubt, from having known the original, a veritable
uncle of the writer.

Though his attendance at the trial turned out a professional
sinecure, Mr. Irving contrived to pass two months in Richmond
very agreeably. "I have been treated," he writes some time
before he left, "in the most polite and hospitable manner by the
most distinguished persons of the place—those friendly to Colonel
Burr and those opposed to him, and have intimate acquaintances
among his bitterest enemies. I am absolutely enchanted with
Richmond, and like it more and more every day. The society is
polished, sociable, and extremely hospitable, and there is a great
variety of distinguished characters assembled on this occasion,
which gives a strong degree of interest to passing incidents."

One occurrence which befell him there illustrates somewhat
comically a romantic phase of his character.

Cooper, the actor, had been playing a round of characters at
Richmond during the trial, and was requested to give the part of

Beverly in the " Gamester," but he lacked the necessary equipment of small clothes. Whereupon Mr. Irving lent him a pair for the occasion—breeches being all the vogue in those days,—which Cooper afterward carried off to Baltimore. Here he discovered in the pocket a mysterious locket of hair in the shape of a heart, and he thereupon dispatched a humorous half-poetical epistle to Irving to relieve the anxiety he presumed he might feel on account of its supposed loss. The whole lines need not be quoted, but after sundry inquiries as to :—

> " Where was the sylph when his fingers entwined
>   The dear lock,"

he adds,—

> " Receive these inquiries, dear friend, in good part,
>   And since you have locked the fair hair in your heart,
>   Ne'er trust, of the girl who your fancy bewitches,
>   Such an emblem of love in another man's breeches."

The history of this "emblem of love" is curious. During his romantic sojourn at Genoa, Mr. Irving was very much taken with the beauty of a young Italian lady, the wife of a Frenchman. He had met her frequently in the social circles of Genoa, but had never been introduced to her, and was content to worship the lovely vision afar off. At a party which he attended just prior to his leaving, she dropped her handkerchief, which he, observing, picked up, and with more gallantry than honesty transferred to his own pocket as a secret but precious keepsake. At Catania he had the misfortune to be robbed of this handkerchief. He had gone one evening to the cathedral of St. Agatha to be present at a fête in honor of the saint. The church was brilliantly lighted and densely filled. After moving about among the crowd for a while, he and his naval companions, whose uniform denoted them to be strangers, were ushered very politely into the chapel of St. Agatha, separated from the rest of the church by a grating of gilt iron, and from hence, heretics as they were, they were admitted into an inner chapel where the bust of the saint was deposited, and which was generally sacred from profane intrusion. It was an unusual stretch of civility toward heretics, and here it was—in these sacred precincts—as if as a set-off to the unwonted courtesy, that his pocket was picked of its stolen treasure.

A history of the whole affair was dispatched to his friend Storm at Genoa, lamenting his misfortune. The latter, through some fair medium, communicated it to the lovely Bianca, for that was her name, who thereupon sent him a lock of her hair, with a request that he would come to see her on his return to Genoa. He did not return that way, as we have seen, though such had been his intention, but the hair was enclosed in a locket and worn round his neck, a cherished memorial of a radiant vision which had once crossed his path and been seen no more. It was this locket which had been left in the borrowed breeches, and gave occasion to Cooper's witty *jeu d' esprit.*

On his way home from Richmond, he writes the following letter to his charming correspondent, Miss Fairlie, which, among other things, gives an interesting account of his last interview with Burr, who seems to have exercised over his youthful fancy that peculiar fascination for which he was so remarkable.

[*To Miss Mary Fairlie.*]

WASHINGTON CITY, July 7, 1807.

The interval that has elapsed, since last I wrote to you, certainly requires some apology ; but apologies I always consider as implying some restraint, or ceremony, or control ; and, as I wish our correspondence to be perfectly free, pleasant, independent, voluntary, unconstrained, unshackled, etc., etc., I am determined, though I have some half a dozen excellent apologies at the end of my pen, yet they shall be passed over in silence, or taken for granted, as best suits your humor. I feel the more indebted to you for the letters I have received, inasmuch as they must have interfered with a thousand of those splendid enjoyments by which you, as a declared belle, must be necessarily engrossed. Trust me, it is grateful to my feelings, and not a little flattering to my vanity, the proud idea, that, when surrounded like the grand Lama, or the immortal Josh, by a crowd of humble adorers, you can still think upon such an insignificant personage as myself, and even steal away from the shrine at which you are worshipped, to bestow on me an hour's conversation. Inspired by such thoughts, I open your letters with a kind of triumph ; I consider them as testimonies of those brilliant moments which I have rescued from the buzzards that surround you; moments, perhaps, for which some hapless Damon sighed, of which he counted the tedious seconds by a stop watch; fancied them puffed up into half hours or any other portly dimensions, and cursed the *giant minutes* as they passed! Vain-glorious mortal that I am! perhaps these same epistles on which I so much value myself are merely the effusions of some vacant hour, some interval between dressing and dinner, or dinner and a ball; perhaps the mere method by which you *delassitude* yourself after the fatigues of an evening's campaign, like the illustrious Jefferson, who, after toiling all day in deciding the fates of a nation, retires to his closet and amuses himself with impaling a tadpole; but let them be written when, where, or how they will, be assured they will ever be received with delight, and read with avidity.

I am now scribbling in the parlor of Mr. Van Ness, at whose house I am on a visit; having, as you plainly perceive, torn myself from Richmond. I own the parting was painful, for I had been treated there with the utmost kindness, and having become a kind of old inhabitant of the place, was permitted to consult my own whims, inclinations, and caprices, just as I chose; a privilege which a stranger has to surrender on first arriving in a place. By some unlucky means or other, when I first made my appearance in Richmond, I got the character, among three or four novel-reading damsels, of being an *interesting young man ;* now of all characters in the world, believe me, this is the most intolerable for any young man who has a will of his own to support; particularly in warm weather. The tender-hearted fair ones think you absolutely at their command; they conclude, that you must, of course, be fond of moonlight walks, and rides at daybreak, and red-hot strolls in the middle of the day (Fahrenheit's thermom. 98½ in the shade), "and melting-hot—hissing-hot" tea-parties, and what is worse, they expect you to talk sentiment and act Romeo, and Sir Charles, and King Pepin all the while. 'T was too much for me; had I been in love with any one of them, I believe I could have played the dying swain as eloquently and foolishly as most men; but not having the good luck to be inspired by the tender passion, I found the slavery insupportable; so I forthwith set about ruining my character as speedily as possible. I forgot to go to tea-parties; I overslept myself of a morning; I protested against the moon, and derided that blessed planet most villainously. In a word, I was soon given up as a young man of most preposterous and incorrigible opinions, and was left to do e'en just as I pleased. Yet, believe me, I did, notwithstanding, admire the fair damsels of Richmond exceedingly; and, to be candid at once, the character of the whole sex, though it has ever ranked high in my estimation, is still more exalted than ever. I have seen traits of female goodness while at Richmond, that have sunk deeply in my heart—not displayed in one or two individual instances, but frequently and generally manifested; I allude to the case of Colonel Burr. Whatever may be his innocence or guilt, in respect to the charges alleged against him (and God knows I do not pretend to decide thereon), his situation is such as should appeal eloquently to the feelings of every generous bosom. Sorry am I to say, the reverse has been the fact—fallen, proscribed, prejudged, the cup of bitterness has been administered to him with an unsparing hand. It has almost been considered as culpable to evince toward him the least sympathy or support; and many a hollow-hearted caitiff have I seen, who basked in the sunshine of his bounty, when in power, who now skulked from his side, and even mingled among the most clamorous of his enemies. The ladies alone have felt, or at least had candor and independence sufficient to express, those feelings which do honor to humanity. They have been uniform in their expressions of compassion for his misfortunes, and a hope for his acquittal; not a lady, I believe, in Richmond, whatever may be her husband's sentiments on the subject, who would not rejoice on seeing Colonel Burr at liberty. It may be said that Colonel Burr has ever been a favorite with the sex; but I am not inclined to account for it in so illiberal a manner; it results from that merciful, that heavenly disposition, implanted in the female bosom, which ever inclines in favor of the accused and the unfortunate. You will smile at the high strain in which I have indulged; believe me, it is because I feel it; and I love your sex ten times better than ever. The last time I saw Burr was the day before I left Richmond. He was then in the Penitentiary, a kind of State prison. The only reason given for immuring him in this abode of thieves, cut-throats, and incendiaries, was that it would save the United States a couple of hundred dollars (the charge of guarding him at his lodgings), and it would insure the security of his person. This building stands about a mile and a half from town, situated in a solitary place among the hills. It will prevent his counsel from being as much with him as they deemed necessary. I found great difficulty in gaining admission to him for a few moments. The keeper had orders to admit none but his counsel and his witnesses—strange measures these! That it is not sufficient that a man against whom no certainty of crime is proved, should be confined by bolts and bars and massy walls in a criminal prison; but he is likewise to be cut off from all intercourse with society, deprived of all the offices of friendship, and made to suffer all the penalties and deprivations of a condemned criminal. I was permitted to enter for a few moments, as a special favor, contrary to orders. Burr seemed in lower spirits than formerly; he was composed

and collected as usual; but there was not the same cheerfulness that I have hitherto remarked. He said it was with difficulty his very servant was allowed occasionally to see him; he had a bad cold, which I suppose was occasioned by the dampness of his chamber, which had lately been whitewashed. I bid him farewell with a heavy heart, and he expressed with peculiar warmth and feeling his sense of the interest I had taken in his fate. I never felt in a more melancholy mood than when I rode from his solitary prison. Such is the last interview I had with poor Burr, and I shall never forget it. I have written myself into a sorrowful kind of a mood, so I will at once desist, begging you to receive this letter with indulgence, and regard, with an eye of Christian charity, its many imperfections.

Believe me, truly and affectionately,

Your friend,

WASHINGTON IRVING.

In the autumn of this year Mr. Irving lost his father, who had long been suffering from paralysis. He died October 25, 1807, at the age of seventy-six, having sustained through life a character for undeviating rectitude and the most sincere piety. Washington continued for some time to reside with his mother, who was left in independent circumstances.[1]

---

[1] The dwelling in which the father died, and which the widow continued to occupy, was one which he had purchased, and to which he had removed in 1802. It stood, but stands no longer, at the northwest corner of William and Ann streets.

CHAPTER XII.

Discontinuance of " Salmagundi."—Disparaging Estimate of the Work by Irving.—Paulding's Allusion to it.—Remarks on the Subject by Duyckinck and Bryant.—Reprinted in London in 1811.—Reviewed.— " Knickerbocker " Commenced.—Peter Embarks for Europe.—Change in the Plan of " Knickerbocker."—Matilda Hoffman.—Her Death.

THE twentieth number of " Salmagundi," in which the writers take leave of the public, appeared on the 25th of January, 1808. It was an unexpected and abrupt discontinuance. I have heard the youngest of the trio say the work was given up just when his mind was kindling with new conceits, and he had designed, among other plans in embryo, a marriage of William Wizard with one of the Miss Cocklofts, and had amused himself in idea with a description of their queer nuptials. Paulding also intimates in the opening article of the number, which is written by him, that it was not " for want of subjects " they did not keep on, but gives no glimmering of the true cause, which, in fact, grew out of a difficulty between themselves and their publisher, who had put the price at a shilling, and was disposed to limit somewhat dictatorially for these novices in authorship the quantity of matter for each number.

The reader of " Salmagundi " at the present day must bear in mind that it was given to the world when our city scarce numbered more than eighty thousand inhabitants, and that its pages are impressed with the local images and humors of that epoch. "Take it altogether," says a critic in the *North American Review*, in looking back upon it, " it was certainly a production of extraordinary merit." Whatever its merit, however, in other eyes, Mr. Irving never valued himself much upon his share of it in his riper years. Paulding has an allusion to this in one of his letters to him, in which he says : " I know you consider old Sal. as a sort of saucy,

flippant trollop, belonging to nobody, and not worth fathering."
" The work was pardonable as a juvenile production," writes
Washington to Brevoort, in 1819, " but it is full of errors, puerilities,
and imperfections. I was in hopes it would gradually have gone
down into oblivion." But this is the rigorous and over-sensitive
estimate of his maturer years. Mr. Evert A. Duyckinck, in his
preface to the recent volume of " Salmagundi," printed from the
original edition with notes, gracefully remarks, in allusion to Mr.
Irving's too slighting appreciation of the work : " We cannot
suppose him insensible to the many excellencies which the work
undoubtedly possesses ; charms of manner and of thought spring-
ing from the fresh, joyous period of youth, and lending their grace
to the brightest pages of his matured labors. ' Salmagundi ' is the
literary parent not only of the ' Sketch-Book' and the ' Alhambra,'
but of all the intermediate and subsequent productions of Irving,
even of some slight ornaments of the graver offspring of the
' Columbus ' and ' Washington.' There is, for instance, in one of
the later numbers, a chapter of ' The Chronicles of the Renowned
and Ancient City of Gotham,' which anticipates the humor of
' Knickerbocker' ; there are traits of tenderness and pathos sugges-
tive of the plaintive sentiment of the ' Sketch-Book'; and the
kindly humors of the Cockloft mansion are an American ' Bracebridge Hall.'" Bryant, too, in his genial and very beautiful commemorative address, remarks of " Salmagundi" : " Its gayety is
its own ; its style of humor is not that of Addison or Goldsmith,
though it has all the genial spirit of theirs ; nor is it borrowed from
any other writer. It is far more frolicsome and joyous, yet
tempered by a native gracefulness. ' Salmagundi ' was manifestly
written without the fear of criticism before the eyes of the authors,
and to this sense of perfect freedom in the exercise of their genius,
the charm is probably owing, which makes us still read it with so
much delight. Irving never seemed to place much value on the
part he contributed to this work, yet I doubt whether he ever
excelled some of those papers in ' Salmagundi ' which bear the
most evident marks of his style ; and Paulding, though he has since
acquired a reputation by his other writings, can hardly be said to

have written any thing better than the best of those which are ascribed to his pen." [1]

" Salmagundi" was reprinted in London in 1811, and critically noticed in the *Monthly Review*. " I don't know whether I mentioned to you " [writes Washington to his brother William], "that ' Salmagundi' has been reviewed in the London *Monthly Review*, and much more favorably than I had expected. The faults they point out are such as I had long been sensible of, and they seem particularly to attack the quotations and the Latin inter-woven in the poetry, which certainly does halt most abominably in the reading. On the whole, however, I think we came off very handsomely, and I only hope the other critics may be as merciful."

It was not long after the completion of " Salmagundi " that Mr. Irving resumed his literary labors. Peter had returned from a year's absence in Europe, just before the appearance of the last number, and in conjunction, as the younger informs us in the account of its composition, the two brothers commenced the " History of New York." The first idea of the work was a mere *jeu d' esprit* in burlesque of Dr. Samuel Mitchell's " Picture of New York," then just published, and with this view they took a vast quantity of notes, in emulation of the erudition displayed in the commencement of that work, which began with an account of the Aborigines. They started, therefore, with the creation of the world. The author has informed us how this idea expanded into a different conception, after the departure of his brother a second time for Europe ; but it would seem that the original plan of the work must have been near its fulfilment, as early as April 30, 1808, as I find a letter of that date from his brother Peter to him, in which he says : " I presume you must be aware *esta obra* " (the language used to designate it—being the Spanish for " that work ") " must terminate for the present at the point at which I left it. It should, therefore, be completed without loss of time, and I entreat you either to whip your imagination into a gallop, or to leave it for

---

[1] *A Discourse on the Life, Character, and Genius of Washington Irving*, delivered before the New York Historical Society, at the Academy of Music, in New York, on the 3d of April, 1860, by William Cullen Bryant.

an uncomplying jade, and saddle your judgment. If you do not, I shall have to give the thing such a hasty finish as circumstances may permit, immediately on my return—for my pocket calls aloud and will not brook delay." At the date of this letter the writer was at Schenectady, on his way to Johnstown, to visit a sick sister (Mrs. Dodge). The next day he met very unexpectedly, at the same place, the party to whom it was addressed, Washington having left New York on the 28th, on a sudden mission to Montreal, and having diverged at Albany to Schenectady. Here he prevailed on Peter to defer his visit to Johnstown, and accompany him to Montreal ; and the two brothers, partners in pleasure as in purse, proceeded together to that place.

On his return, Washington hears, at Saratoga Springs, of his sister's death.

The following letter was written the next day, at Albany :—

[*To Mrs. Hoffman.*]

ALBANY, June 2, 1808.

MY DEAR FRIEND :—

I have just arrived in Albany, and found two letters from you and Mr. Hoffman, so kind and so affectionate that I cannot express to you how grateful they were to my feelings. My journey has been tedious and unpleasant, but it is so far over, and past fatigues are soon forgotten.

On the road, as I was travelling in high spirits with the idea of home to inspire me, I had the shock of reading an account of my dear sister's death, and never was a blow struck so near my heart before. Five years have nearly elapsed since I have seen her, and though such an absence might lessen the pang of eternal separation, still it is dreadfully severe. One more heart lies still and cold that ever beat toward me with the warmest affection, for she was the tenderest, best of sisters, and a woman of whom a brother might be proud. . . . .

To-morrow morning early I set off for Johnstown. Would to heaven that I had gone there a month ago. . . . .

On returning to Albany from Johnstown, he had the novel luxury of descending the Hudson by steamboat ; leaving, as his record testifies, June 8th, at 8 A.M., and arriving in New York the next evening.

In December of this year Mr. Irving made a second trip to Montreal, on business for a commercial house in New York. It was a sad disappointment to him, upon his return, to find that his brother Peter had sailed again for Europe. He had gone out to Liverpool, about the 1st of January, on pressing business for his brother William's house, Irving & Smith, leaving Washington to proceed with the "History of New York." It was then that the latter changed the whole plan of the work, and, discarding what had reference to a later period than the Dutch dynasty, and grappling with the other mass of notes, undertook to frame a work according to his new conception. I have heard him say he had hard work to condense into its present shape the ponderous mass of notes which had been taken for the first book, as a burlesque of erudition and pedantry ; that he managed, with infinite labor, to compress it into five introductory chapters, and in subsequent editions would have been glad to compress these into one, but was deterred from undertaking it by the labor it would cost. The residue of the book was exclusively his, and I cannot but regard it as a fortunate circumstance, that it was not completed in conjunction, for Peter had not the rich comic vein of Washington ; and though his taste was pure and classic, it was a little too nice and fastidious not to have sometimes operated as a drawback upon the genial play of his brother's exuberant humor.

The "History of New York" was far advanced toward its completion, when Mr. Irving was called to encounter a blow which left him for a while little heart for his work, and probably gave a color to his whole future existence. For some months past, the partiality with which he had regarded the second daughter of Mr. Hoffman had deepened into a serious passion, and the point to which all his hopes were turning lay in a union with her. He was not one, however, to have been easily instigated to the imprudence of involving another in his own lot without some "sober certainty" of income. "I think," he writes in one of his later letters, "these early and improvident marriages are too apt to break down the spirit and energy of a young man, and make him a hard-working, half-starving, repining animal all his days." Sometimes his sense

of the imprudence of early matrimony, where the lover is without the means of maintaining a wife, would appear in a playful illustration. " Young men in our country," he would say, " think it a great extravagance to set up a horse and carriage without adequate means, but they make no account of setting up a wife and family, which is far more expensive." But in proportion as he felt the improvidence of such a step, in the same degree did he feel his own precarious prospects, and the necessity of bettering his condition. His letters to Peter, of this period, are unfortunately lost, but the replies of the latter have been preserved, and show what uncongenial plans he was sometimes revolving to advance his fortunes. " I am averse," says this brother, in a letter dated Liverpool, March 9, 1809, " to any supercargoship, or any thing that may bear you to distant or unfriendly climates. I would not take one of those cursed India voyages—hardly—for a young fortune." Other letters contain intimations of his repining at being unemployed in some means of steady livelihood ; and of plans and purposes which were passing through his mind, evidently pointing to some advantage which might place him in a condition to link another's fortunes with his own. In the midst of these came the blow, by which the dearest hope of his life was forever overthrown.

Matilda Hoffman, the intended sharer of his lot in life, closed her brief existence in the city of New York on the 26th of April, 1809, in the eighteenth year of her age. Though not a dazzling beauty, she is described as lovely in person and mind, of the most gentle and engaging manners, and with a sensibility that mingled gracefully with a delicate and playful humor. In a letter to Washington, written just after the tidings of her death had reached him, Peter has this allusion to her: " May her gentle spirit have found that heaven to which it ever seemed to appertain! She was too spotless for this contaminated world." It is an indication of the depth of the author's feeling on this subject, that he never alluded to this part of his history, or mentioned the name of Matilda even to his most intimate friends ; but after his death, in a repository of which he always kept the key, a package was found, marked on the outside " Private Mems."; from which he would seem to have once unbosomed himself. This memorial was a fragment, of which the beginning and end were missing. The ink was faded, and it was without address, but it has since appeared, from the testimony of a daughter, that it was addressed to Mrs. Amelia Foster, an English lady whom, as will be seen hereafter, he met at Dresden at the close of 1822, and with whose family, during his sojourn in that city, he became extremely intimate. The daughter says : " It was left with us under a sacred promise that it should be returned to him ; that no copy should be taken ; and that no other eyes but ours should ever rest upon it. The promise was faithfully kept "—which will account for its remaining among his papers. The communication was evidently the result of inquiries about his early history, and how it happened he had never married, for toward its close, after recounting the story of his youthful love and its sad termination, he says : "You wonder why I am not married. I have shown you why I was not long since. . . . . My time has now gone by, and I have growing claims upon my thoughts, and my means, slender and precarious as they are."

With these private memoranda was found a miniature of great beauty, enclosed in a case, and in it a braid of fair hair, and a slip of paper, on which was written, in his own handwriting, " Matilda Hoffman."

The two months succeeding the death of Matilda were spent in the retirement of the country, at the house of his friend, Judge William P. Van Ness, at Kinderhook, afterward the residence of President Van Buren.

It is a striking evidence how little Mr. Irving was ever disposed to cultivate or encourage sadness, or suffer his " melancholy to sit on brood," that he should be engaged during this period of sorrow and seclusion, in revising and giving additional touches to his " History of New York." In the private communication before mentioned, in alluding to this period, he says : " When I became more calm and collected, I applied myself, by way of occupation, to the finishing of my work. I brought it to a close, as well as I could, and published it ; but the time and circumstances in which it was produced, rendered me always unable to look upon it with satisfaction."

Although the poignancy of his grief had worn away when he returned to the city, his countenance long retained the trace of melancholy feelings. A portrait by Jarvis, taken some months afterward, and conceded, without dissent at that time, to be a faithful and admirable likeness, is remarkable for its expression of pensive refinement. Mr. Irving never alluded to this event of his life, nor did any of his relatives ever venture, in his presence, to introduce the name of Matilda. I have heard of but one instance in which it was ever obtruded upon him, and that was by her father, Mr. Hoffman, nearly thirty years after her death, and at his own house. A granddaughter had been requested to play for him some favorite piece on the piano, and in extracting her music from the drawer, had accidentally brought forth a piece of embroidery with it. "Washington," said Mr. Hoffman, picking up the faded relic, "this is a piece of poor Matilda's workmanship." The effect was electric. He had been conversing in the sprightliest mood before, and he sank at once into utter silence, and in a few moments got up and left the house.

It is an evidence with what romantic tenderness Mr. Irving cherished the memory of this early love, that he kept by him, through life, the Bible and Prayer-book of Matilda. He lay with them under his pillow, in the first days of keen and vivid anguish that followed her loss ; and they were ever afterward, in all changes of climate and country, his inseparable companions.

Perhaps the following anecdote may be regarded as of kindred significance. But two or three years before his death, in the course of an interesting conversation with a niece, who was visiting him, he was led to descant upon the solitude of a life of celibacy ; and then, as if suddenly struck with the incongruity of his own practice, he remarked to her in a half-playful, half-mournful way, " You know I was never intended for a bachelor." She did not, of course, intrude upon the sacredness of his recollections to inquire how it happened he had never married ; but a few hours afterward, as if furnishing his own solution to the enigma, he handed her a piece of poetry, with the remark, " There's an autograph for you." She took it, and casting her eye upon the paper, perceived it to be a copy of those noble lines of Campbell, " What's hallowed ground?" It was in his own handwriting, and bore the marks of having been transcribed years before.   I quote some of the stanzas :—

> " That 's hallowed ground, where, mourned and miss'd,
>   The lips repose our love has kiss'd :—
>   But where 's their memory's mansion ?   Is 't
>   Yon churchyard's bowers ?
>   No ! in ourselves their souls exist,
>   A part of ours.
>
> " A kiss can consecrate the ground
>   Where mated hearts are mutual bound ;
>   The spot where love's first links were wound,
>   That ne'er are riven,
>   Is hallowed down to earth's profound,
>   And up to heaven.
>
> " For time makes all but true love old;
>   The burning thoughts that then were told
>   Run molten still in memory's mold,
>   And will not cool
>   Until the heart itself be cold
>   In Lethe's pool."

It is in the light of this event of Mr. Irving's history, that we must interpret portions of his article on " Rural Funerals " in the " Sketch-Book," and also that solemn passage in " St. Mark's Eve," in " Bracebridge Hall," beginning, " There are departed beings that I have loved as I never shall love again in this world—that have loved me as I never again shall be loved."   To this sacred recollection also, I ascribe this brief record, in a note-book of 1822, kept only for his own eye : " She died in the beauty of her youth, and in my memory she will ever be young and beautiful."

CHAPTER XIII.

Jacob Van Tassel (Wolfert's Roost).

THE first letter I find, after his return from Kinderhook, is addressed to his brother Peter, from which I make the following extract :—

. . . . I am really at a loss what to write to you about. I have been so little abroad in the world since my return from Van Ness' that I know nothing how matters are going on. . . . . My health has been feeble and my spirits depressed, so that I have found company very irksome, and have shunned it almost entirely. I propose setting out on an expedition to Canada with Brevoort on Saturday next, to be absent sixteen days. There is a steamboat on the lake which makes the journey sure and pleasant. I trust the jaunt will perfectly renovate me. On my return I shall go to Mr. Hoffman's retreat at Hellgate, and prepare *esta obra* for a launch. . . . .

We are all well. Irving & Smith are highly satisfied with your assiduity. I refer you to Hal and Sally for family particulars.

The "Hal and Sally" here mentioned were Henry Van Wart and wife, the youngest sister of Mr. Irving. Mr. Van Wart had engaged in business in England, just after his marriage in 1806, in connection with the house of Irving & Smith in New York ; he had returned to this country in 1808, under an appre-

111

hension of impending war between the United States and Great Britain, and was now about to go back, to find in England his permanent home.

The country retreat spoken of, in which Mr. Irving was to prepare his " History of New York " for publication, was delightfully situated at Ravenswood, near Hellgate.   He passed much of his time here in August and September, and had a boat at command belonging to his friend Brevoort, called *The Tinker*, in which he used to ply between the city and this summer residence of the Hoffmans.

In the November succeeding, Mr. Irving repaired to Philadelphia, to superintend the publication of his " History of New York." He adopted the expedient of putting it to press in that rather than his native city, to prevent, as far as possible, any idea of the real character of the work from getting wind in advance of its appearance.   At the same time curiosity was awakened in New York, by a series of preparatory advertisements, foreshadowing its appearance, without betraying its grotesque and mock-heroic qualities.   These were afterward collected by me at his request, and inserted by him after " The Author's Apology," in the introduction to his revised edition of " Knickerbocker " in 1848.

The first of these notices appeared in the *Evening Post* about six weeks prior to the publication, and was as follows :—

DISTRESSING.

Left his lodgings some time since, and has not since been heard of, a small elderly gentleman, dressed in an old black coat and cocked hat, by the name of KNICKERBOCKER.   As there are some reasons for believing he is not entirely in his right mind, and as great anxiety is entertained about him, any information concerning him, left either at the Columbian Hotel, Mulberry Street, or at the office of this paper, will be *thankfully* received.

P. S.—Printers of newspapers would be aiding the cause of humanity in giving an insertion to the above.—*Oct.* 25.

In less than a fortnight this was followed by another :—

To the Editor of the " Evening Post ":—

SIR :—Having read in your paper of the 26th October last a paragraph respecting an old gentleman by the name of *Knickerbocker*, who was missing from his lodgings; if it would be any relief to his friends, or furnish them with any clue to discover where he is, you may inform them that a person answering the description was seen by the passengers of the Albany stage early in the morning about four or five weeks since, resting himself by the side of the road, a little above Kingsbridge. He had in his hands a small bundle tied in a red bandana handkerchief; he appeared to be travelling northward, and was very much fatigued and exhausted.

Nov. 6, 1809.   A TRAVELLER.

To this succeeded, in ten days, a letter signed by Seth Handaside, landlord of the Independent Columbian Hotel, Mulberry Street :—

SIR :—You have been good enough to publish in your paper a paragraph about Mr. Diedrich Knickerbocker, who was missing so strangely from his lodgings some time since. Nothing satisfactory has been heard of the old gentleman since ; but a *very curious kind of a written book* has been found in his room in his own handwriting. Now I wish you to notice him, if he is still alive, that if he does not return and pay off his bill for board and lodging, I shall have to dispose of his Book, to satisfy me for the same.

This device to call attention to the appearance of the forthcoming work was sufficiently ingenious and original, and it is an amusing incident, in this connection, that one of the city authorities found his sympathies so much enlisted by the appeal, as to call on the author's brother, John T. Irving, and consult him on the propriety of offering a reward for the discovery of the missing Diedrich.

Though the author had carried the manuscript in a complete state to Philadelphia, yet he afterward made some additions, as was not unusual with him, as the work was going through the press. It was here that he wrote the voyage of Peter Stuyvesant up the Hudson, and the enumeration of the army. Coming home late one night, and finding himself locked out of his lodgings, he repaired to the quarters of a bachelor friend, but could not sleep after obtaining admittance. It was then that the idea of that journey flashed through his mind ; and so rapidly did the images crowd upon him, that he rose from the bed to strike a light, and write them down— but he could not find the candle, and after stumbling about for awhile, to the annoyance of his sleepy but wondering companion, he managed to get hold of a piece of paper, and jot down some of his impressions in pencil in the dark. The next morning he stopped the press, until he had finished his picture and secured its admission.

On the 6th of December, 1809, appeared the advertisement of its actual publication, in these words :—

IS THIS DAY PUBLISHED,

BY INSKEEP AND BRADFORD, NO. 128 BROADWAY,

A HISTORY OF NEW YORK.

In 2 vols. duodecimo—price 3 dollars.

Containing an account of its discovery and settlement, with its internal policy, manners, customs, wars, etc., etc., under the Dutch government, furnishing many curious and interesting particulars never before published, and which are gathered from various manuscripts and other authenticated sources, the whole being interspersed with philosophical speculations and moral precepts.

This work was found in the chamber of Mr. Diedrich Knickerbocker, the old gentleman whose sudden and mysterious disappearance has been noticed. It is published in order to discharge certain debts he has left behind.

This advertisement, it will be seen, is unpromising enough, and awakens no expectation but of a sober matter-of-fact history of our Dutch progenitors—an impression which the covert humor of its dedication, " To the New York Historical Society," " as a humble and unworthy testimony of the profound veneration and exalted esteem of the Society's sincere well-wisher and devoted servant, Diedrich Knickerbocker," would no doubt help to confirm. It is easy, therefore, to imagine the astonishment of many, on taking up the work, to find that the author had seized upon " the events which compose the history of the three Dutch governors of New York, merely as a vehicle to convey a world of satire, whim, and ludicrous description."

I give a contemporaneous notice of the work from the *Monthly Anthology and Boston Review*, the precursor of the *North American*. The notice begins with a short sketch of the original possession of the country by a few Dutch colonists, and its erection into an English province in 1664, and proceeds :—

The meagre annals of this short-lived Dutch colony have afforded the groundwork for this amusing book, which is certainly the wittiest our press has ever produced. To examine it seriously in an historical point of view would be ridiculous ; though the few important events of the period to which it relates are, we presume, recorded with accuracy as to their dates and consequences.

These materials, which would hardly have sufficed to fill a dry journal of a few pages, are here extended to two volumes. They only compose the coarse net-work texture of the cloth, in which the author has embroidered a rich collection of wit and humor. The account of these honest Dutch governors has been made subservient to a lively flow of good-natured satire on the follies and blunders of the present day, and the perplexities they have caused.

The great merit, and indeed almost the only one, which the varied labors of former times have left to the literature of the present day, aptness and fertility of allusion, will be found almost to satiety in these pages. Those who have a relish for light humor, and are pleased with that ridicule which is caused by trifling, and, to the mass of the world, unobserved relations and accidents of persons and situations, will be often gratified. They will soon perceive that the writer is one of those privileged beings, who, in his pilgrimage through the lanes and streets, the roads and avenues of this uneven world, refreshes himself with many a secret smile at occurrences that excite no observation from the dull, trudging mass of mortals. "The little Frenchmen, skipping from the Battery to avoid a shower, with their hats covered with their handkerchiefs"; the distress of "the worthy Dutch family" annoyed by the vicinage of "a French boarding-house," with all its attendant circumstances, even down to "the little pug-nose dogs that penetrated into their best room," are examples, among many others, of this disposition. The people of New England are the subjects of many humorous remarks, but, we are glad to observe, made with so much good-nature and mingled compliment and satire, that they themselves must laugh.

Many of the descendants of the original colonists, however, looked at it with a less indulgent eye. This irreverent handling of their Dutch ancestors, and conversion of the field of sober history into a region of comic romance, was not to their taste. "Your good friend, the old lady," writes Mrs. Hoffman to him, at Philadelphia, on its first appearance, "came home in a great stew this evening. Such a scandalous story had got about town—a book had come out, called a 'History of New York'; nothing but a satire and ridicule of the old Dutch people—and they said you was the author ; but from this foul slander, I 'll venture to say, she has defended you. She was quite in a heat about it."   The old lady here alluded to was the mother of Josiah Ogden Hoffman.

If some of the Dutch were nettled, others perceived that the work was written in pure wantonness of fun, without a particle of malevolence, and were willing to laugh, with the rest of the community, over pages of which a correspondent of a Baltimore paper wrote at the time : " If it be true, as Sterne says, that a man draws a nail out of his coffin every time he laughs, after reading Irving's book your coffin will certainly fall to pieces."

Walter Scott was the first transatlantic author to bear witness to the merit of " Knickerbocker."   In the following letter to Henry Brevoort, who had presented him with a copy of the second edition in 1813, he writes :—

MY DEAR SIR :—

I beg you to accept my best thanks for the uncommon degree of entertainment which I have received from the most excellently jocose history of New York. I am sensible that, as a stranger to American parties and politics, I must lose much of the concealed satire of the piece, but I must own that, looking at the simple and obvious meaning only, I have never read any thing so closely resembling the style of Dean Swift, as the annals of Diedrich Knickerbocker. I have been employed these few evenings in reading them aloud to Mrs. S. and two ladies who are our guests, and our sides have been absolutely sore with laughing. I think, too, there are passages which indicate that the author possesses powers of a different kind, and has some touches which remind me much of Sterne. I beg you will have the kindness to let me know when Mr. Irving takes pen in hand again, for assuredly I shall expect a very great treat which I may chance never to hear of but through your kindness.

Believe me, dear sir,

Your obliged humble servant,

WALTER SCOTT.

ABBOTSFORD, April 23, 1813.

It was some years after the date of this letter, that his friend, Gulian C. Verplanck, in an anniversary discourse, delivered before the New York Historical Society, December 7, 1818, when the author was in Europe, took occasion to allude to this burlesque history in a spirit of regret, at the injustice done by it to the Dutch character. " It is painful," he says, " to see a mind as admirable for its exquisite perception of the beautiful, as it is for its quick sense of the ridiculous, wasting the riches of its fancy on an ungrateful theme, and its exuberant humor in a coarse caricature."

This censure was much softened by the complimentary remarks which followed, which nevertheless did not prevent his brother Ebenezer, who feared its effect upon a new edition of the work which had just been put to press in Philadelphia, from giving vent to some vexation on the subject in a letter to Washington. The latter writes, in reply :—

I have seen what Verplanck said of my work. He did me more than justice in what he said of my mental qualifications ; and he said nothing of my work that I have not long thought of it myself. . . . . He is one of the honestest men I know of, in speaking his opinion. There is a determined candor about him, which will not allow him to be blinded by passion. I am sure he wishes me well, and his own talents and acquirements are too great to suffer him to entertain jealousy; but were I his bitterest enemy, such an opinion have I of his integrity of mind, that I would refer any one to him for an honest account of me, sooner than to almost any one else.

To Brevoort, to whom he had just transmitted across the Atlantic the first number of the " Sketch-Book," which included the story of " Rip Van Winkle," he alludes to these critical strictures in a more playful vein. After a high compliment to the oration of Verplanck, he adds :—

I hope he will not put our old Dutch burghers into the notion that they must feel affronted with poor Diedrich Knickerbocker, just as he is about creeping out in a new edition. I could not help laughing at this burst of filial feeling in Verplanck, on the jokes put upon his ancestors ; though I honor the feeling, and admire the manner in which it is expressed. It met my eyes just as I had finished the little story of " Rip Van Winkle," and I could not help noticing it in the introduction to that bagatelle. I hope Verplanck will not think the article is written in defiance of his vituperation. Remember me heartily to him, and tell him I mean to grow wiser, and better, and older, every day, and to lay the castigation he has given seriously to heart.

The avails of the first edition of "Knickerbocker," I have heard Mr. Irving say, amounted to about three thousand dollars.

Soon after its publication he was urged by his friends to offer himself at Albany as a candidate for a clerkship in one of the courts in New York. He could plead no party services, for he had shunned rather than sought political notoriety, but his brother-in-law, Daniel Paris, was a member of the Council of Appointment, and ready to forward his interest, and this presented an opportunity to provide for his maintenance and give him leisure for literary pursuit, which it was urged he ought not to lose. He failed to get the post, however, mainly through the counterworking of some candidates for other offices, who sought, by such manœuvre, to compel the support of Paris to their claims. The integrity of Paris, however, was of too stubborn a mold for such a game.

The following letter was written after he had renounced all hopes of success, and gives an amusing picture of his reception at the headquarters of Dutch domination, and his success in mollifying the wrath of some of the older families who had felt themselves aggrieved in the liberties taken with their ancestors.

[*To Mrs. Hoffman.*]

ALBANY, Feb. 26, 1810.

MY DEAR FRIEND:—

I have just left Mr. Hoffman, who is suffering under a severe attack of the sick headache, and groaning in his bed most piteously. Since last I wrote you, I have relinquished all cares and thoughts about an appointment, and am now merely remaining in Albany to witness the interesting scenes of intrigue and iniquity that are passing under my eye—to inform myself of the manner of transacting legislative business, with which I was before but little acquainted—to make myself acquainted with the great and little men of the State whom I find collected here, and lastly to enjoy the amusements and society of this great metropolis. I think I have most bountiful variety of occupation. You will smile, perhaps, when I tell you, that in spite of all my former prejudices and prepossessions, I like this queer little old-fashioned place more and more, the longer I remain in it. I have somehow or another formed acquaintance with some of the good people, and several of the little Yffrouws, and have even made my way and intrenched myself strongly in the parlors of several genuine Dutch families who had declared utter hostility to me. Several good old ladies, who had almost condemned my book to the flames, have taken me into high favor, and I have even had the hardihood to invade the territories of Mynheer Hans ———, and lay siege to his beauteous daughter, albeit that the high blood of all the burghers of the ——— family was boiling against me and threatening me with utter annihilation.

So passes away the time. I shall remain here some days longer, and then go to Kinderhook. What time I shall return to New York I cannot tell. I have no prospect ahead, nor scheme, nor air castle to engage my mind withal; so that it matters but little where I am, and perhaps I cannot be more agreeably or profitably employed than in Van Ness' library. I shall return to New York poorer than I set out, both in pocket and hopes, but rich in a great store of valuable and pleasing knowledge which I have acquired of the wickedness of my fellow-creatures. That, I believe, is the only kind of wealth I am doomed to acquire in the world, but it is a kind of which I am but little covetous. . . . .

Though he was very much fêted and caressed at Albany before he left, yet many at first were very slow to extend any civility to him. One lady was pointedly indignant against him, and in an outburst of wrath vowed, if she were a man, she would horsewhip him. The historian was wonderfully amused on hearing this, and with a degree of modest impudence quite foreign to his natural character, forthwith determined to seek an introduction. He accordingly prevailed on a friend to take him to her house. She received him very stiffly at first, but before the end of the interview he had succeeded in making himself so agreeable that she relaxed entirely from her hauteur, and they became very good friends.

She was satisfied, I presume, that he had taken the old Dutch names at random, without intending personal allusion, which was the case, as he has himself told me. "It was a confounded impudent thing in such a youngster as I was," said he to me in his latter years, "to be meddling in this way with old family names; but I did not dream of offence."

CHAPTER XIV.

Letter to Mr. Hoffman.—To Mrs. Hoffman.—Biographical Sketch of Campbell.—Longings for Independence.—Partnership Proposal.—Embraces it.

THE following account of a journey to Philadelphia, in which Mr. Irving acted as escort to Mrs. Hoffman and her three infant children, is not without interest, as an example of the jocose extravagance in which he sometimes indulged in scribbling to Mr. Hoffman.

[*To Mr. Hoffman.*]

PHILADELPHIA, June 5, 1810.

DEAR SIR:—

We arrived safe in Philadelphia this morning, between eight and nine o'clock, and took the city by surprise, the inhabitants not having expected us until evening. All this is in consequence of my unparalleled generalship, which already begins to be talked of with great admiration throughout the country. I took a light coachee from Brighton to Brunswick where we breakfasted, and finding it impossible to procure a four-horse carriage there, I changed carriage and horses and pushed on to Trenton, where, while the Philistines were dining, I engaged a fresh carriage and horses for Philadelphia, and made out to reach Homesburgh (about ten miles from Philadelphia) between seven and eight in the evening. I was anxious to get as far as possible, lest the weather might change, or the children get unwell. The journey has been infinitely more comfortable and pleasant than I had anticipated. Yesterday was a fine day for travelling, and I never knew children to travel so well. Charles has behaved like a very good boy, and George is one of the sprightliest little travellers I ever knew; he has furnished amusement during the whole ride, and what is still better, has gained unto himself a very rare and curious stock of knowledge; for besides the unknown tongue in which he usually converses, and which none but Mammy Caty (who you know is at least one-half witch) can understand, he has picked up a considerable smattering of high Dutch since he entered the State of Pennsylvania, so that I regretted

exceedingly, and that more than once during my travels, that the immortal Psalmanazar was not present to discourse with him.

Little Julia has had an astonishing variety of complaints since our leaving New York ; has had two doctors to attend her, has taken threescore and ten doses of medicine, not to mention anise-seed tea and peppermint cordial, and what is passing strange, is still alive, fat, and hearty ; a case only to be paralleled by that of the famous Spinster of Ratcliff Highway, who was cured of nineteen diseases in a fortnight, and every one of them mortal !

You cannot conceive what speculation our appearance made among the yeomanry of Jersey and Pennsylvania. Many of the excellent old Dutch farmers mistook us for a family of Yankee squatters, and were terribly alarmed, and the little community of Bustletown (who are very apt to be thrown into a panic) were in utter dismay at our approach, insomuch that when we entered one end of the town, I saw several old women in Pompadour and Bird's-eye gowns, with bandboxes under their arms, making their escape out of the other. However, I contrived to pacify them by letting them know it was the family of the Recorder of New York, who, being an orthodox Bible man, always travelled into foreign lands, as did the patriarchs of yore—that is to say, with his wife, and his sons, and his daughters, his men-servants and his maid-servants, and his cattle, and the stranger that is within his gates, and every thing that is his, whereat they were exceeding glad and glorified God.

We are all comfortably situated at Ann's,[1] who lives in a little palace. . . . . Mary is much improved in her looks, and appears to be a great favorite with the family. Ann has taken her under her care, and is making her a hard student. She has already read seven pages in Rollin, and the whole history of Camilla and Cecilia, not to mention a considerable attack which she has made upon " The Castle of Inchvalley ; a tale, alas, too true !"

In the hurry of my writing the above (for I write as fast as we travelled) I forgot to mention to you that having safely arrived within the suburbs of Philadelphia, the old carriage in which we came from Trenton sank beneath its burden and gave up the ghost !

In other words, we broke down just after entering the city ; but as it was merely a spring had given way, the whole party, man, woman, and child, were dug out of the ruins without any other mishap than that of overturning the medicine chest, and spilling fifteen phials, which were as

---

[1] Ann was the eldest daughter of Mr. Hoffman, married, the year before, to Charles Nicholas, of Philadelphia. Mary was a younger sister by the first marriage, afterward Mrs. Philip Rhinelander.

full of plagues as those mentioned in the Revelation. I immediately perceived a change in little Julia for the better, and I make bold to conjecture that had a dozen more been demolished, she would have been the heartiest child in Philadelphia at this present writing. You cannot imagine the astonishment of all Philadelphia at seeing so many living beings extracted out of one little carriage.

Farewell, my good sir. Remember me to the remnants and rags of your household that remain behind. Keep all marauders from breaking into my room and disturbing the pictures of my venerable ancestors, and believe me

Ever your friend,   W. I.

A letter to Mrs. Hoffman at Philadelphia, after his return to New York, shows him to be domesticated at a cottage on the east bank of the Hudson, within a few miles of the city, which Mr. Hoffman had hired for a summer retreat. At its close he says :—

Tell Charles I will be able to write to him about the beginning of the week, as Mr. Campbell is to spend part of to-morrow with me. . . . .

The Campbell here mentioned was a brother of the Bard of Hope. He was a resident of New York, and had lately applied to Mr. Irving for his good offices in procuring the publication of " O'Connor's Child," and a new edition of " Gertrude of Wyoming," the manuscript of which the poet had sent out to him, with a view to a pecuniary remuneration on this side of the water. Mr. Irving proposed the publication to Charles I. Nicholas and his partner, booksellers in Philadelphia, who agreed to take the work for a stipulated sum, provided he would preface it with a biographical sketch of the poet. To this he assented ; and having obtained some meagre particulars from the brother, worked them up into a brief biography, which was received with approbation by the public, though it gave little satisfaction to the author himself. He once told me it was written against the vein, and was, as he expressed it, " uphill work."

The biographical sketch of Campbell was the only thing which came from his pen this year, and his literary pursuits would seem now to have been brought to a stand. The success of "Knickerbocker" had been far beyond his expectations, but it did not quicken his zeal for literature as a profession. He liked the exercise of his pen as an amusement, or a source of occasional profit, but to be tied down to a literary career as his destiny, to be under bonds to write for a livelihood, this presented no enviable prospect to him. Indeed, his whole soul recoiled from the idea of a dependence upon literature for his daily bread. Such a career was beset with too many trials and vexations, was too precarious, too fitful, too much exposed to caprice, vicissitude, and failure. His happiness was at stake in obtaining some employment that would insure a steady income ; and disappointed, as we have seen, in some hopes of an office, for which his friends had urged his claims, and shut out apparently from every other avenue to a modest competence—he seems at this period to have pondered the future with a boding heart. Brevoort, to whom he confided his doubts and misgivings, used playfully to rally him on his dread of the almshouse ; but his brother Peter, with a deeper insight into his nature, read the traces of these feelings in his letters in a different vein. He knew well, that though never inclined to take trouble upon interest, he was not so constituted that he could live for the moment without casting anxious glances ahead, dreading, of all things, to have his spirit clouded by an uncertain future.

As there had been a sort of literary alliance in regard to "Knickerbocker," so whatever either did at this time was for the benefit of both. Peter's letters abound in allusions to a sort of compact or partnership, by which they held all things in common. His main anxiety abroad seems to have aimed at rendering his expedition useful to Washington as well as to himself.

I have already authorized you [he writes] to appropriate the proceeds of my expedition in any way that may seem for our mutual benefit. I need not repeat that I consider your attention to *esta obra* as amply per- forming your part in our little partnership. In truth, I only require you to be cheerful and not to repine at being unemployed, and I shall be happy. My only fear is that you may indulge different feelings, and so acquire a temper of mind unfavorable to happiness. Be assured that if nothing of further profit grows out of my present occupation, we will, on my return, devise other plans of advantage.

And again :—

I need not say how deeply essential your health and happiness are to my own enjoyment. I have the apprehension that you allow yourself to be dispirited by the idea that you are prevented by want of opportunity from playing an active part in our little partnership. Be assured that I am sincere in the expression of my opinion that the state of compelled inactivity is much the more irksome than that of active employment. On my honor, I consider yours the more difficult situation of the two. I shall only regret that you should view it differently, yet that I trust cannot be. We certainly understand each other too well to have any consideration for the laws of *meum* and *tuum* between us, or for either of us to care on which side the opportunity of profitable exertion lies.

These passages give an interesting picture of the character of Peter, but it is doubtful whether they would have been effectual to repress the impatient longing of Washington for some active pursuit, if they had not been followed speedily by a letter from his brother, of a very different description, which seemed to open the long-coveted prospect to independence.

I have just received [writes Peter from London, May 31, 1810] a proposal from brother Ebenezer to form a connection in business, and have written to him that it will be a pleasure to me, if it will be agreeable to him, to form a third with you and myself. He will explain the plan contemplated. . . . .

It has never been my idea that you should become engaged in commerce, except so slightly as not to interfere with your other habits and pursuits. Nor would I have it. The drudgery of regular business I would not undertake for any reasonable consideration. Those who have been educated for it, and practised in it, I have no doubt find it pleasant ; to me and to you it would be excessively irksome.

My own plan here is to give it close attention at the necessary periods of purchase and shipment, and to be a man of leisure during the intervals. I have no doubt that we shall in a short time realize enough to establish a little castle of our own, in which we may assemble the good fellows we esteem.

Washington grasped readily at this proposal, especially as the business was not likely to be attended with any trouble to himself, while it allowed long intervals of leisure to his brother Peter, and

afforded to Ebenezer a sphere of activity in which he took delight.
The firm took the name of P. & E. Irving & Co., in New York,
and P. Irving & Co., in England. Peter made the purchases and
shipments at Liverpool, while Ebenezer conducted the sales at New
York. By the terms of the partnership, the profits were to be
divided into fifths, the two active partners to receive each two
fifths and Washington one ; but if he should marry or become an
active partner, the profits were then to be divided into equal thirds.
It was not expected by his brothers, however, that he would pay
any attention to the business ; their object in giving him an interest
in their concern being mainly to provide for his subsistence, and
leave him at liberty to cultivate his general talents and devote himself to literature.

CHAPTER XV.

THE winter which succeeded his partnership was one of great anxiety to the merchants. Their interests were likely to be seriously affected by the measures of Congress ; and his brothers, William and Ebenezer, thought it advisable to have an agent at the seat of government to watch the moving of the waters, and give the earliest intimations of coming danger. This business was confided to Washington ; who, nothing loth, accordingly started for his destination on the 21st of December, 1810, and reached it on the 9th of January, 1811—a degree of speed not calculated to encourage the hope of his proving a very alert channel of intelligence.

In a letter to his brother Ebenezer, dated Washington, January 9, 1811, he writes :—

I arrived here this evening, after literally struggling through the mud and mire all the way from Baltimore. I must confess I am not one of the most expeditious travellers in the world ; but it was impossible to withstand the extremely friendly and hospitable attentions of the good people of Philadelphia and Baltimore, at any rate, I am a mere mortal on these occasions, and yield myself up, like a lamb to the slaughter.

Congress had been sitting with closed doors for two or three days, engaged, as it is supposed, in the Florida business. I have not been able to learn any thing of matters as yet, but I mean to be as deep in the mysteries of the Cabinet as that " entire chrysolite " of wisdom, ... notwithstanding that he rode post, as I am well informed, from New York to Washington, with his finger beside his nose, and nodding and winking all the way to every man, woman, and child he saw.

In a letter which follows to Brevoort, who had accompanied him to Philadelphia, we have, among other things, an allusion to a French translation of "Knickerbocker," to Jarvis the painter, and to Mrs. Madison.

CITY OF WASHINGTON, Jan. 13, 1811.

DEAR BREVOORT :—

I have been constantly intending to write to you ; but you know the hurry and confusion of the life I at present lead, and the distraction of thought which it occasions, and which is totally hostile to letter-writing. The letter, however, which you have been so good as to write me, demands a return of one kind or another ; and so I answer it, partly through a sense of duty, and partly in hopes of inducing you to write another.

My journey to Baltimore was terrible and sublime—as full of adventurous matter and direful peril as one of Walter Scott's pantomimic, melo-dramatic, romantic tales. I was three days on the road, and slept one night in a log-house. Yet, somehow or another, I lived through it all ; and lived merrily into the bargain, for which I thank a large stock of good-humor, which I put up before my departure from New York, as travelling stores to last me throughout my expedition. In a word, I left home determined to be pleased with every thing, or if not pleased, to be amused, if I may be allowed the distinction, and I have hitherto kept to my determination.

I remained two days in Baltimore, where I was very well treated, and was just getting into a very agreeable society, when the desire to get to Washington induced me to set off abruptly, deferring all enjoyment of Baltimore until my return. While there I dined with Coale [the bookseller]. At this table I found Jarvis, who is in great vogue in Baltimore, painting all the people of note and fashion, and universally passing for a great wit, a fellow of infinite jest ; in short, "the agreeable rattle." I was likewise waited on by Mr. Tezier, the French gentleman who has translated my history of New York. He is a very pleasant, gentlemanly fellow, and we were very civil to each other, as you may suppose. He tells me he has sent his translation to Paris, where I suspect they will understand and relish it about as much as they would a Scotch haggis and a singed sheep's-head.

The ride from Baltimore to Washington was still worse than the former one ; but I had two or three odd geniuses for fellow-passengers, and made out to amuse myself very well. I arrived at the inn about dusk ; and understanding that Mrs. Madison was to have her levee or drawing-room that very evening, I swore by all my gods I would be there.

But how? was the question. I had got away down into Georgetown, and the persons to whom my letters of introduction were directed lived all upon Capitol Hill, about three miles off, while the President's house was exactly half-way.   Here was a non-plus enough to startle any man of less enterprising spirit ; but I had sworn to be there, and I determined to keep my oath, and, like Caleb Quotem, to "have a place at the Review."   So I mounted with a stout heart to my room ; resolved to put on my pease blossoms and silk stockings; gird up my loins; sally forth on my expedition ; and, like a vagabond knight-errant, trust to Providence for success and whole bones.   Just as I descended from my attic chamber, full of this valorous spirit, I was met by my landlord, with whom, and the head waiter, by the bye, I had held a private cabinet council on the subject.   Bully Rook informed me that there was a party of gentlemen just going from the house, and one of whom, Mr. Fontaine Maury of New York, had offered his services to introduce me to " the Sublime Porte."   I cut one of my best opera flourishes, skipped into the dressing-room, popped my head into the hands of a sanguinary Jacobinical barber, who carried havoc and desolation into the lower regions of my face, mowed down all the beard on one of my cheeks, and laid the other in blood like a conquered province ; and thus, like a second Banquo, with " twenty mortal murthers on my head," in a few minutes I emerged from dirt and darkness into the blazing splendor of Mr. Madison's drawing-room.   Here I was most graciously received ; found a crowded collection of great and little men, of ugly old women and beautiful young ones, and in ten minutes was hand and glove with half the people in the assemblage.   Mrs. Madison is a fine, portly, buxom dame, who has a smile and a pleasant word for every-body. . . . .

Since that memorable evening I have been in a constant round of banqueting, revelling, and dancing.   The Congress has been sitting with closed doors, so that I have not seen much of the wisdom of the nation ; but I have had enough matter for observation and entertainment to last me a handful of months.   I only want a chosen fellow like yourself to help me wonder, admire, and laugh—as it is, I must endeavor to do these things as well as I can by myself.

I am delightfully moored " head and stern " in the family of John P. Van Ness, brother of William P.   He is an old friend of mine, and insisted on my coming to his house the morning after my arrival.   The family is very agreeable.

The other evening, at the City Assembly, I was suddenly introduced to my cousin, the Congressman from Scaghticoke, and we forthwith became two most loving friends.

—— —— is here, and "my brother George" into the bargain. —— is endeavoring to obtain a deposit in the Mechanics' Bank, in case the U. S. Bank does not obtain a charter. He is as deep as usual; shakes his head, and winks through his spectacles at everybody he meets. He swore to me the other day, that he had not told anybody what his opinion was, whether the bank *ought* to have a charter or not; nobody in Washington knew what his opinion was—not one—nobody—he defied any one to say what it was—"any body—damn the one—no, sir—nobody knows" —and, if he had added nobody cares, I believe honest —— would have been exactly in the right. Then there's his brother —— "damn that fellow—knows eight or nine languages—yes, sir—nine languages—Arabic, Spanish, Greek, Ital—and there's his wife now—she and Mrs. Madison are always together. Mrs. Madison has taken a great fancy to her little daughter; only think, sir, that child is only six years old, and talks the Italian like a book, by God—little devil learned it all from an Italian servant—damned clever fellow—lived with my brother—ten years—says he would not part with him for all Tripoli," etc., etc., etc.

A letter to Mrs. Hoffman, from Washington, at this time, concludes with the following message to Mrs. Renwick:—

When you see my good friend Mrs. Renwick, tell her I feel great compunction at having deprived her of her tartan plaiddie all the winter; but if it will be any gratification to her, she may be assured it has been of signal comfort to me, and has occasionally served as a mantle to some of the prettiest girls in Washington.

This lady, whose name will be held in honor as the heroine of "The Blue-eyed Lassie" of Burns, was the daughter of the Rev. Andrew Jeffrey, of Lochmaben, in Dumfriesshire, Scotland. She was early transplanted to these shores, and passed the greater part of her life in the city of New York, where her house was a cherished resort of Mr. Irving. A brief and well-written memoir of her, by Mrs. Balmanno, printed privately for her family and friends, speaks of her as follows: "Up to the advanced age of seventy-seven, she adorned a high social position with all those qualities of heart and mind, all those sweet and captivating ameni- ties of manner, which had, in her youth, when joined to great personal attractions, rendered her one of the most fascinating maidens of Annandale." She often met the Scottish poet at her father's fireside, and beside " The Blue-eyed Lassie," he made her the subject of another song, " When First I Saw my Jeanie's Face," which is contained in the memoir above mentioned. As this effusion has never appeared in any collection of the works of the immortal bard, I am tempted to quote the fine compliment of the concluding stanza :—

> " But sair, I doubt some happier swain
>   Has gained my Jeanie's favor,
> If sae, may every bliss be hers,
>   Tho' I can never have her.

> " But gang she east, or gang she west,
>   'Twixt Nith and Tweed all over,
> While men have eyes, or ears, or taste,
>   She 'll always find a lover."

It was to the subject of this poetic effusion that the author of the " Sketch-Book " was indebted for the slip of ivy from Melrose, which she planted with her own hands, and lived to see running in rich luxuriance over the walls of Sunnyside.

I give some further letters of this period.

To make intelligible the following interesting portion of a reply to a letter of his brother William, it is necessary to premise, that his name had been suggested as Secretary of Legation to France, under Joel Barlow as Minister. The author of the " Columbiad," however, had somehow or other associated him with some strictures on his epic of which he was innocent, and would not be likely to incline to such a secretary.

[To William Irving.]

WASHINGTON, Feb. 9, 1811.

MY DEAR BROTHER:—

I am very much obliged to you for your kind letter of the 5th. I had begun to feel quite impatient at not hearing from home, and to think that the news I occasionally scribbled from here might be of little importance. . . . .

Your opinion with respect to the matter I hinted at has decided me, should any thing of the kind be proposed. I have heard, however, nothing further on the subject, and do not suffer it to occupy my thoughts much.

I should only look upon it as an advantageous opportunity of acquiring information and materials for literary purposes, as I do not feel much ambition or talents for political life. Should I not be placed in the situation alluded to, I shall pursue a plan I had some time since contemplated, of studying for a while, and then travelling about the country for the purpose of observing the manners and characters of the various parts of it, with a view to writing a work, which, if I have any acquaintance with my own talents, will be far more profitable and reputable than any thing I have yet written. Of this, however, you will not speak to others. But whatever I may write in future I am determined on one thing—to dismiss from my mind all party prejudice and feeling as much as possible, and to endeavor to contemplate every subject with a candid and good-natured eye.

Whether the author ever finished the contemplated plan of study here alluded to, does not appear ; but certain it is, that the literary promise of this letter was never fulfilled. The work, of the nature and design of which we have only this imperfect intimation, was not even commenced.

In the letter which follows, we have, with other matters, further allusion to the appointment.

[*To William Irving.*]

WASHINGTON, Feb. 16, 1811.

. . . . The discussion of the Bank question is going on vigorously in the Senate. Giles made a very ingenious speech both for and against it. He was opposed to the Bank, but the enemies of the Bank thought he had done their cause more harm than any that had spoken on the opposite side. It seems Giles was compelled to take the side he did by the instructions of his constituents, but like an elephant he trampled down his own army. I was very much pleased with his speaking ; he is a close reasoner and very perspicuous. Clay, from Kentucky, spoke against the Bank. He is one of the finest fellows I have seen here, and one of the finest orators in the Senate, though I believe the youngest man in it. The galleries, however, were so much crowded with ladies and gentlemen, and such expectations had been expressed concerning his speech, that he was completely frightened and acquitted himself very little to his own satisfaction. When his speech is printed, I will send it to you ; he is a man I have great personal regard for. . . . .

As to the appointment of which I spoke to you, I do not indulge any sanguine hopes about it, and don't trouble myself on that score. I find that it has been the custom to leave the choice to the minister himself, in which case I have no chance. The Secretary of State was the first person who suggested the idea, and he is very solicitous for it ; indeed, I have experienced great civility from him while here. The President, on its being mentioned to him, said some very handsome things of me, and I make no doubt will express a wish in my favor on the subject, more especially as Mrs. Madison is a sworn friend of mine, and indeed all the ladies of the household and myself great cronies. I shall let the thing take its chance. I have made no application, neither shall I make any; and if I go away from Washington with nothing but the great good-will that has been expressed and manifested toward me, I shall thank God for all his mercies, and think I have made a very advantageous visit.

[*To Henry Brevoort.*]

PHILADELPHIA, March 16, 1811.

MY DEAR FELLOW :—

I arrived in this city the day before yesterday, and was delighted to find a letter from you, waiting for me on Charles' mantel-piece. I thank you for this mark of attention, and for the budget of amusing and interesting news you have furnished me with. I stopped but four days at Baltimore on my return; one of which I was confined at home by indisposition. The people of Baltimore are exceedingly social and very hospitable to strangers ; and I saw that if I let myself once get into the stream, I should not be able to get out again under a fortnight at least ; so being resolved to push homeward as expeditiously as was reasonably possible, I resisted the world, the flesh, and the devil at Baltimore; and after three days and nights' stout carousal, and a fourth's sickness, sorrow, and repentance, I hurried off from that sensual city. By the bye, that little "hydra and chimera dire," Jarvis, is in prodigious great circulation at Baltimore. The gentlemen have all voted him a rare wag and most brilliant wit ; and the ladies pronounce him one of the queerest, ugliest, most agreeable little creatures in the world. The consequence is that there is not a ball, tea-party, concert, supper, or any other private regale, but that Jarvis is the most conspicuous personage ; and as to a dinner, they can no more do without him than they could without Friar John at the roystering revels of the renowned Pantagruel. He is overwhelmed with business and pleasure, his pictures admired and extolled to the skies, and his jokes industriously repeated and laughed at. . . . .

Jack Randolph was at Baltimore for a day or two after my arrival. He sat to Jarvis for a likeness for one of the Ridgeleys, and consented that I should have a copy. I am in hopes of receiving it before I leave Philadelphia, and of bringing it home with me. . . . .

I was out visiting with Ann yesterday, and met that little assemblage of smiles and fascinations, Mary Jackson. She was bounding with youth, health, and innocence, and good-humor. She had a pretty straw hat tied under her chin with a pink ribbon, and looked like some little woodland nymph, just lured out by spring and fine weather. God bless her light heart, and grant that it may never know care or sorrow! It's enough to cure spleen and melancholy only to look at her.

Your familiar pictures of home make me extremely desirous again to be there. It will be impossible, however, to get away from the kind attentions of our friends in this city, until some time next week, perhaps toward the latter end, when I shall once more return to sober life, satisfied with having secured three months of sunshine in this valley of shadows and darkness. . . . .

I rejoice to hear of the approaching nuptials of our redoubtable Highland chieftain, and hope you are preparing a grand epithalamium for the joyful occasion. Remember me affectionately to the Hoffmans, Kembles, etc. Yours ever,

W. IRVING.

March 18th he writes to Brevoort:—

I shall be with you in a few days, and then we will look out for Gouv, and prepare for the captain's hymeneals.

He had hardly reached New York, however, before he found himself constrained to return to Washington—apparently on some mission of commercial necessity.

In the following letter to Brevoort from Philadelphia, on his return, we have an allusion to George Frederick Cooke, the great actor, who had come the year previous to this country, in which he died in 1812.

PHILADELPHIA, April 11, 1811.

DEAR BREVOORT :—

I have neglected answering your letter from an expectation that I should have been home before this; but I have suffered day after day to slip by, and here I still am, in much the same mood as you are when in bed of a fine genial morning, endeavoring to prolong the indolent enjoyment, to indulge in another doze, and renew those delicious half-waking dreams that give one an idea of a Mussulman's paradise.

I have for a few months past led such a pleasant life, that I almost shrink from awaking from it into the commonplace round of regular existence; "but this eternal blazon must not be" (Shakespeare), so in two or three days I'll take staff in hand and return to the land of my fathers.

To tell the truth, I have been induced to stay a day or two longer than I otherwise would have done, to have the gratification of seeing Cooke in Kitely and Lear; the first he plays to-night, the other on Wednesday. The old fellow is in great repute here, and draws excellent houses. I stopped in accidentally at the theatre a few evenings since, when he was playing Macbeth; not expecting to receive any pleasure, for you recollect he performed it very indifferently in New York. I entered just at the time when he was meditating the murder, and I remained to the end of the play in a state of admiration and delight. The old boy absolutely out-did himself: his dagger scene, his entrance to Duncan's chamber, and his horror after the commission of the deed, completed a dramatic action that I shall never forget as long as I live; it was sublime. I place the performance of that evening among the highest pieces of acting I have ever witnessed. You know I had before considered Cooper as much superior to him in Macbeth, but on this occasion the character made more impression on me than when played by Cooper, or even Kemble. The more I see of Cooke, the more I admire his style of acting; he is very unequal, from his irregular habits and nervous affections; but when he is in proper mood, there is a truth, and, of course, a simplicity in his performance, that throws all rant, stage-trick, and stage-effect completely in the background. Were he to remain here a sufficient time for the public to perceive and dwell upon his merits and the true character of his playing, he would produce a new taste in acting. One of his best performances may be compared to a masterpiece of ancient statuary, where you have the human figure, destitute of idle ornament, depending upon the truth of anatomical proportion and arrangement, the accuracy of character and gracefulness of composition; in short, a simple display of nature. Such a production requires the eye of taste and knowledge to perceive its eminent excellences; whereas, a vulgar spectator will turn from it to be enraptured with some bungling workmanship, loaded with finery and drapery and all the garish ornaments in which unskilfulness takes refuge.

Sully has finished a very fine and careful portrait of Cooke, and has begun a full-length picture of him in the character of Richard. This he is to receive three hundred dollars for from the gentlemen of Philadelphia who opened a subscription for the purpose, which was filled up in an hour. The picture is to be placed in the Academy of Arts. . . . .

Walsh's 2d number will be out in two or three days; I have seen it, but not had time to read more than a few pages of a masterly review of Hamilton's works. I think the number will do him great credit.

Give my love to all who love me, and remember me kindly to the rest.

Yours truly,   W. I.

I know not how soon it was after his return to New York, that he witnessed a performance of Cooke, of another sort, which I have heard him describe.   It was at his benefit at the Park Theatre, and he was to play Shylock and Sir Archy MacSarcasm.   Mr. Irving was in a stage box.   He went through Shylock admirably, but had primed himself with drink to such a degree, before the commencement of the afterpiece, that he was not himself.   His condition was so apparent that they hurried through the piece, and skipped, and curtailed, to have the curtain fall, when lo! as it was descending, Cooke stepped out from under it and presented himself before the foot-lights, to make a speech.   Instantly there were shouts from the pit :   " Go home—Cooke—go home—you 're drunk."   Cooke kept his ground.   " Did n't I please you in Shylock ? "   " Yes—yes—you played that nobly."   " Well, then, the man who played Shylock well could n't be drunk."   " You were n't drunk then, but you 're drunk now," was the rejoinder, and they continued to roar :   " Go home—go home—go to bed."   Cooke, indignant, tapped the handle of his sword emphatically :   " 'T is but a foil " ; then extending his right arm to the audience, and shaking his finger at them—" 't is well for you it is," and marched off amid roars of laughter.   It was a rich scene.

CHAPTER XVI.

Change of Quarters.—Literary Relaxation.—Passages of a Letter to Brevoort.—Breaking out of the War.—Letter of James K. Paulding.— Visit to Washington.—Letter to James Renwick.—Letter to Peter Irving.—To Brevoort.

IN the spring of 1811, Washington, who had hitherto resided with his mother, took up his quarters with Brevoort, at Mrs. Ryckman's, in Broadway, near the Bowling Green. Here they had a parlor in common, with bedrooms off, and Brevoort had a large and well-selected library, which was always at the command of his companion. This would seem to have been a situation propitious to literary labor, yet, with the exception of a revised edition of the " History of New York," the two years spent here were barren of literary fruit. He had at first intended a pretty thorough dedication of his time and talents to these congenial pursuits, but this purpose, however sincerely entertained, soon lost its sway over him. The spur of necessity was needed to quicken and invigorate his literary ambition, which gradually wore off under the temptations to ease and indolence which his circumstances offered, until at last he settled down into a sort of gentleman of leisure ; not neglectful of mental cultivation, it is true, yet mainly intent upon the pleasures and amusements of the passing hour. Not without a share of self-upbraiding, however, did he surrender himself to the indulgence of such entire literary relaxation. His conscience often smote him during this interval, I have heard him say, that he did not devote himself more closely to his pen ; but his compunction was not sufficiently keen to break the spell which held his faculties in bondage.

In March of the following year Brevoort sailed for Europe, leaving Irving at Mrs. Ryckman's, in possession of his library, but sadly missing his intellectual sympathy and companionship, and earnestly longing for his return from an absence which was unexpectedly lengthened to twenty months. "I have not been very well since your departure," he writes to him, March 17th, "and am completely out of spirits. I do miss you terribly. I dined yesterday at a small party at Mrs. Renwick's, and was at a tea-party in the evening ; and yet passed one of the heaviest days I have toiled through this long time." Brevoort, too, seems to have felt the separation, and writes : " I long to fill the vacant chair on the opposite side of the well-recollected table in our private sanctuary. Ah! how often has that friendly table sustained your incumbent head of a winter's evening! What treasures of moral precepts and good-humored sallies has that table witnessed! enough to reform a guilty world, but alas! forever lost to an admiring posterity."

In a letter to Brevoort, of March 29, 1812, we have this allusion to the revised edition of " Knickerbocker," upon which he had been engaged :—

I have been so much occupied of late, partly by a severe indisposition of my good old mother (who has, however, recovered), and partly by my History, that I have not had time to write you a letter worth reading. I will atone for it hereafter. I have concluded my bargain with Inskeep and am about publishing. I receive $1,200 at six months for an edition of 1,500 copies. He takes all the expense of printing, etc., on himself.

In this edition he dropped the dedication to the New York Historical Society.

The war between Great Britain and the United States, which broke out in June, 1812, presented no very comfortable prospect to the merchant, and Mr. Irving seems to have entertained the most serious forebodings of its effect upon the commercial interests. It was probably this circumstance that turned his thoughts once more into the channel of literature, and induced him to harbor a project of a joint undertaking with Paulding, which is alluded to at the close of the following extract from a letter of the latter. The letter transmits a copy of Paulding's " Diverting History of John Bull and Brother Jonathan," and is addressed to Washington at the residence of Captain Phillips, that favorite rendezvous in the Highlands, to which he had gone in August :—

September 5, 1812.

DEAR WASHINGTON :—

I send you a copy of " John Bull," who has made some talk here, but I believe don't sell very well ; for what reason I leave you to judge, it being such an excellent work.   There has been an advertisement in the papers for a week past, noticing the intended publication of a work, called " The Beauties of Brother Bullus, by his Sister Miss Bull — a."   The title, I think, is not very promising ; and I have discovered that it is written against my Bull.   Inskeep says it is the joint production of Parson Mason and his Polygraph Bristed, so you see what Goliaths are coming forth against me.   If this piece should be illiberal toward me, and I can once fasten it upon these jockeys, I think there will be a little sport, particularly if you should be here and inclined to lend a hand.   I have finished the draft of one essay and am at work with another ; so you see I don't forget the main object of our lives ; nor do I mean to suffer myself to be involved in any controversy that will interfere with our contemplated undertaking.

What this contemplated undertaking was does not appear.   It was never carried out, very possibly from Mr. Irving's being soon after induced to listen to a proposition to assume the conduct of a periodical magazine, the *Select Reviews*, in which Paulding also found scope for his pen.

In the autumn of 1812, Mr. Irving was selected to form one of a Committee of Merchants, deputed by the commercial community to repair to the seat of government, to obtain a remission of their bonds.   This kept him for six weeks at Washington.   During this period he addressed several letters to James Renwick, then at the early age of nineteen filling gratuitously the chair of Natural Philosophy in Columbia College, made vacant by the death of his relative, Dr. Kemp.   I have space only for the last, which treats of the *Select Reviews* he had undertaken to edit, and makes allusion to a matrimonial report, out of which, no doubt, his friends were having a little fun at his expense.

[*To James Renwick.*]

WASHINGTON, Dec. 18, 1812.

DEAR JAMES :—

In one of your letters you desired to know when I would be in Philadelphia, and you proposed passing the holidays there.   I forgot to answer the question, nor would I have been able to have done it with certainty. I now expect to leave this city to-morrow. Our business is yet undecided, and will probably linger through several days more ; but I consider the battle as won, and as there are enough here without me to take care of our interests, and as it is very important I should be elsewhere, I have made up my mind to depart. I may possibly stop a day in Baltimore, as I shall meet Governor Kemble there, and I wish to give him a farewell cheering; I shall then make the best of my way to Philadelphia, where I shall probably pass some days ; but, if possible, I will pass *my* holidays in New York. I never wish to spend the merry Christmas and jolly New Year elsewhere than in the gamesome city of the Manhattoes.

My dear fellow, you cannot imagine how I long to be once more at home, to doff this burden of care and business, and resume what the *Portfolio* calls my "elegant leisure." By the bye, I have been "stayed with flagons and comforted with apples" by these editors and newspaper writers, until I am sick of puffing. This *Select Review* has drawn upon me such an abundance of worthless compliments, that I really stagger under the trash. Add to this, my publisher . . . . has been advertising, every day or two, some new addition and improvement to be made to the *Select Reviews*, of which I have known nothing until I saw the advertisements. At one time there is to be a series of portraits of our naval commanders, with biographical sketches. At another, a history of the events of our maritime war, etc., on the plan of—the British Naval chronicle! and here am I—poor I—while absent here, tied by the leg to the footstool of Congress, most wickedly made the editor of a vile farrago, a congregation of heterogeneous articles that have no possible affinity to one another.

I have written to Philadelphia that I would not consent to have such a fool's cap put on my head; and if they intended to interfere in the conduct of the work, I should decline having any thing to do with it. I think Job was a little out when he wished that his enemy had written a book; had he wished him to be obliged to print one, he would have wished him a curse indeed ! . . . .

Tell your good lady mother that Mrs. Madison has been much indisposed, and at last Wednesday evening's drawing-room Mrs. Gallatin presided in her place ; I was not present, but those who were, assure me she filled Mrs. Madison's chair to a miracle. You may likewise tell her that she may call in her report about Madame —— and myself as soon as she pleases, for it is all over with me in that quarter ; I was last evening to have been introduced to her, and to have gone on a little *moonlight* party to Mason's Island ; you may suppose what a favorable opportunity it was for sentiment and romance. As my unlucky stars would have it, I dined with a choice party at the Speaker's, drank wine, got gay, went home, fell asleep by the fireside, and forgot all about Madame —— until this morning. Do beg your mother, for God's sake, to look out for some other lady for me. I am not particular about her being a princess, provided she has plenty of money, a pretty face, and no understanding.

God bless you,

W. I.

Not long after the date of this extract he had returned to "the gamesome city of the Manhattoes," whence he addressed the following letters :—

[*To Peter Irving at Liverpool.*]

NEW YORK, Dec. 30, 1812.

. . . . I mentioned in former letters that I had undertaken to conduct the *Select Reviews* at a salary of fifteen hundred dollars. It is an amusing occupation, without any mental responsibility of consequence. I felt very much the want of some such task in my idle hours ; there is nothing so irksome as having nothing to do. You will, in future, send the periodical publications to me, and from time to time send an account of cost and charges, that I may settle with my bookseller. I wish you also to forward, as soon as they can be procured, copies of new works that appear, that are not of a local or too expensive nature, fit for republication in this country. I suppose you can make arrangements with the principal booksellers to this effect, who would be attentive to so regular a customer. Any periodical work, besides those at present sent, which you may think of importance, I wish you to subscribe to.

We are all alive, at present, in consequence of our naval victories. God knows they were well-timed to save the national spirit from being depressed and humiliated by the paltry war on the frontiers. The impolicy of depending on militia and volunteers is now made glaringly apparent, particularly for offensive war, and the nation is incensed at having its character for bravery jeoparded by such short-sighted measures and such miserable military quacks as have been bolstered into command. Should this war continue, resort will be had to regular forces ; a larger army will be raised by means of increased bounty and pay ; and from the evidences given by our regular troops whenever they have had an opportunity to grapple with the foe, I make no doubt that they will sustain the national character as gallantly on land as it has been on the ocean. . . . .

The day before yesterday a public dinner was given in honor of Hull, Jones, and Decatur. It was the most splendid entertainment of the kind I ever witnessed. The City Assembly Room was decorated in a very tasteful manner with the colors and flags of the *Macedonian*. Five rows of tables were laid out lengthways in the room, and a table across the top of the room, elevated above the rest, where the gallant heroes were seated, in company with several of our highest civil and military officers. Upward of four hundred citizens of both parties sat down to the dinner, which was really sumptuous. The room was decorated with transparencies representing the battles, etc. The tables were ornamented with various naval trophies, and the whole entertainment went off with a soul and spirit which I never before witnessed. I never in my life before felt the national feeling so strongly aroused, for I never before saw in this country so true a cause for national triumph.

P. S.—I had almost forgot to mention that Dunlap has nearly finished a biography of Cooke. He wishes to send a copy of the MSS. out to you and get you to dispose of it advantageously for him. He will write to you particularly on the subject, and, as he is an old friend and a very worthy man, I make no doubt you will do every thing in your power to benefit him. . . . .

[*To Henry Brevoort.*]

NEW YORK, Jan. 2, 1813.

. . . . I am now once more at my old quarters, and am at this moment writing at my usual corner of the table before the fire, which honest John has just trimmed and replenished; would to heaven, my dear fellow, you were, as formerly, seated opposite to me! I cannot tell you, my good Hal, how very much I miss you. I feel just as I did after the departure of my brother Peter, whose place you had, in a manner, grown into and supplied. The worthy Patroon, also, has departed for Spain, to reside at Cadiz, and, though I rejoice in his good prospects, yet I cannot but deplore his departure. So we get scattered over this troubled world —this making of fortunes is the very bane of social life; but, I trust, when they are made, we shall all gather together again and pass the rest of our lives with one another.

When you return we must determine on some new mode of living, for I am heartily tired of this boarding-house system. Perhaps it will be better to get a handsome set of apartments and furnish them. But of this we will talk further when we meet. I was at your father's two or three days since. The old gentleman is highly tickled with the success of our navy. He was so powerfully excited by the capture of the *Macedo-*

nian, that he actually performed a journey to the Brothers, above Hell-gate, where the frigates lay, wind-bound ; and he brought away a piece of the *Macedonian*, which he seemed to treasure up with as much devotion as a pious Catholic does a piece of the true cross. Your mother is well, and is looking forward with the utmost impatience for your return.

A few days since we had a superb dinner given to the naval heroes, at which all the great caters and drinkers of the city were present. It was the noblest entertainment of the kind I ever witnessed. On New Year's eve a grand ball was likewise given, where there was a vast display of great and little people. Little Rule Britannia made a gallant appearance at the head of a train of beauties, among whom were the divine H———, who looked very inviting, and little Taylor, who looked still more so.

Britannia was gorgeously dressed in a queer kind of hat of stiff purple and silver stuff, that had marvellously the appearance of copper, and made us suppose she had procured the real Mambrino's helmet. Her dress was trimmed with what we simply mistook for scalps, and supposed it was in honor of the nation ; but we blushed at our ignorance on discovering that it was a gorgeous trimming of marten tips—would that some eminent furrier had been there to wonder and admire!

The little Taylor was as amusing and fascinating as ever. She is an arrant little tory, and entertained me exceedingly with her sly jokes upon our navy. She looks uncommonly well, and is as plump as a partridge.

Our winter does not promise to be as gay even as the last ; neither do I feel as much disposition to enter into dissipation. Mrs. Renwick's family is in mourning for the death of Dr. Kemp ; of course, they do not go abroad so much, and their fireside is more quiet and pleasant. . . . .

The Gracies are likewise in mourning for the death of old Mrs. Rogers, Mrs. Gracie's mother. Mr. Gracie has moved into his new house, and I find a very warm reception at the fireside. Their country-seat was one of my strongholds last summer, as I lived in its vicinity. It is a charming, warm-hearted family, and the old gentleman has the soul of a prince.

. . . . This war has completely changed the face of things here. You would scarcely recognize our old peaceful city. Nothing is talked of but armies, navies, battles, etc. Men who had loitered about, the hangers on and incumbrances of society, have all at once risen to importance and been the only useful men of the day. Had not the miserable accounts from our frontiers dampened in some measure the public zeal, I believe half our young men would have been military mad. As it is, if this war continue, and a regular army be raised, instead of depending on volunteers and militia, I believe we shall have the commissions sought after with avidity by young gentlemen of education and good-breeding, and our army will be infinitely more respectable, and infinitely more successful.

I hope this letter may find you on the eve of your departure for this country. I do long most earnestly to see you here again. I suppose my brother will remain longer in Europe ; and much as I wish to see him home once more, I feel content that he should stay until he can return with money in both pockets, and the whole of us be able to live after our own hearts for the rest of our lives.

God bless you, my dear fellow.

Yours ever,

W. I.

Mr. HENRY BREVOORT, Jr.

The vessel being detained, he adds in a postscript of January 12th :—

Get my brother Peter to have his likeness taken by some good painter, and bring it out with you—*do not neglect this.*[1] Look for scarce and odd books, and make up a collection of quaint and curious works. When at London visit the Talbot Inn Burrough, High Street, Southwark. It is the ancient Tabard Inn where your old friend Geoffrey Chaucer and his pilgrims lodged on their journey to Canterbury, 1383 ; and they pretend to show you the chamber where he supped—vide *Gentleman's Magazine* for September, 1812. I happened to lay my hands on the passage this morning.

---

[1] Peter, though not ill-favored, would not consent then, or ever, to have his likeness taken.

CHAPTER XVII.

FROM Edinburgh, where Brevoort was busily employed in various studies, which were enlivened by the kind attentions of a most intelligent circle of acquaintances, he writes to Washington, December 9, 1812 :—

I have just written to my friend Sherbette in Paris to use his utmost endeavors in procuring and forwarding to New York the different periodical journals of France, as well as those of note published on the continent, such, for instance, as Kotzebue's, etc. All these are intended for the benefit of *The Independent Columbian Review*, which I am happy to learn, is soon to issue from Mulberry Street under the fostering care of Seth Handaside, Esq., already so advantageously known to the reading world for his spirited efforts in the cause of letters.

The work here playfully mentioned as *The Independent Columbian Review*, was the *Select Reviews*, a monthly periodical established in Philadelphia, to which allusion has been made in former letters. The name was changed to the *Analectic Magazine* when Mr. Irving assumed the editorial charge. His contributions, extending through the years 1813 and 1814, consisted of a review of the works of Robert Treat Paine, then dead ; a review of odes, naval songs, and other occasional poems by Edwin C. Holland of Charleston ; a notice of Paulding's " Lay of the Scottish Fiddle " ; of Lord Byron ; " Traits of Indian Character," and " Philip of Pokanoket," afterward incorporated in the " Sketch-Book " ; and biographies of Captain James Lawrence, Lieutenant William Burrows, Commodore Oliver Perry, and Captain David Porter.

There was also a biographical sketch of Thomas Campbell, the poet, revised, corrected, and materially altered from the former, published in the March number of 1815.

In addition to these productions from his own pen, he received occasional articles from Paulding and Verplanck, which are designated by their respective initials, P. and V.

The conduct of this magazine, which he had hoped to find a mere pastime, proved to be an irksome business. He had a great repugnance to periodical labor of every description, and to one branch of it, criticism, his aversion was pointed, for he wished to be just, and could not bear to be severe. He shrunk from the idea of inflicting pain. " I do not profess," he says in one of his articles, " the art and mystery of reviewing, and am not ambitious of being wise or facetious at the expense of others." The naval biographies afforded a more agreeable occupation. It was a proud satisfaction to record the triumphs, to quote the strong language of a letter to his brother William, " of that choice band of gallant spirits who had borne up the drowning honor of their country by the very locks," and he hoped by these hasty and imperfect sketches " not merely to render a small tribute of gratitude to these intrepid champions of his country's honor," but to assist in promoting a higher tone of national feeling.

It was about this period that Mr. Irving received from his friend Brevoort the letter of Scott already given, speaking in such cordial praise of his " History of New York " :—

Before I left Edinburgh (he writes from London, June 24th), I presented Walter Scott with a copy of the second edition of " Knickerbocker " in return for some very rare books that he gave me, respecting the early history of New England. I enclose you a letter that I received from him since. You must understand his words literally, for he is too honest and too sincere a man to compliment any person.

In the same letter, after giving a sketch of Sir James Mackintosh and other luminaries whom he had met, Brevoort adds :—

And now, having made you slightly acquainted with these eminent personages, let me have a higher gratification in making you personally known to one of the most distinguished literary ornaments of this country. I mean Francis Jeffrey, Esq., of Edinburgh, the conductor of the *Review.*

He is to embark from Liverpool in the ship *Hercules* by the 5th of next month for Boston, accompanied by his brother, Mr. John Jeffrey, for the purpose of settling some domestic concerns. I am deeply indebted to him, both for his hospitality to me in Edinburgh, as well as for the letters he gave me to persons in London. I have endeavored to repay him by giving him a letter to you, one to Mr. Hoffman, one to our friend Mrs. Renwick (who is his namesake), and another to Judge Van Ness, besides many others to different parts of America.

I enjoin it upon you all to receive him in the most friendly manner, so that I may make some returns to him.

I really cannot fix upon any man in this country whose acquaintance is better worth cultivating than Mr. J. You will find him full of the most precise as well as universal knowledge of men and things on this side of the water, which he will delight to communicate as copiously as you please. You will do well to see as much of him as you can ; he will be glad to make friends with you, and after you have become reconciled to somewhat of an artificial manner, you will find him one of the most sprightly and best-tempered men imaginable.

As his introductory letters will be chiefly to persons connected with the Federal party, I wish you to make him known to both sides. It is essential that Jeffrey may imbibe a just estimate of the United States and its inhabitants ; he goes out strongly biassed in our favor, and the influence of his good opinion upon his return to this country, would go far to efface the calumnies and the absurdities that have been laid to our charge by ignorant travellers. Persuade him to visit Washington, and by all means to see the Falls of Niagara : the obstacles which the war may oppose may be easily overcome, and at all events he may see them without ever crossing into Canada.

As his business is wholly of a private nature, neither political nor commercial, I hope Government will not limit his motions.

Your brother has also given Mr. J. a letter to you.

Mr. Irving could not be indifferent to the pleasure of a meeting with this celebrated personage ; but whether he obeyed the injunction of his friend and saw as much of him as he could, I cannot say. I have heard him recall a dinner at Mr. Gracie's, in which he was particularly brilliant, and he always spoke of him as one of the celebrities that did not disappoint you, whose conversation was as eloquent as his reviews.

In the autumn of this year Peter Irving had interested himself most warmly in behalf of Thomas Campbell, the poet, who was in great need of an American friend to secure for him the copyright of a work which he meant to publish contemporaneously in England and the United States. Campbell says to him in a letter, dated September 17, 1813 : " I look back to the day we had to ourselves at Sydenham as one which I shall never forget "; and in another, a month later (October 19th), in return for a copying-machine which Peter had sent him, he writes : " It is really like a friend and most warm-hearted on your part to take such an interest in my new work. Your present shall be beside me, and my constant friend and memorial of you, as long as I continue to scribble prose or verse." December 15th he invites him to Sydenham to meet Mrs. Siddons ; and here is Peter's hasty account of the visit in a letter to Washington :—

LONDON, Dec. 18, 1813.

MY DEAR BROTHER :—

I this instant learn that a vessel is to sail from Liverpool, but that I must write this day, and the hour of limitation is nearly at hand. . . . .

The day before yesterday I passed delightfully with Campbell, the poet, in his retreat at Sydenham. I had also the further treat of meeting Mrs. Siddons there, and having considerable conversation with her during dinner. It was a rich gratification to see the Queen of Tragedy thus out of her robes. Yet her manner even at the social board still partakes of the state and gravity of tragedy. Not that there is an unwillingness to unbend, but that there is a difficulty in throwing aside the solemnity of long-acquired habit. She reminded me of Walter Scott's knights "who carved the meal with their gloves of steel, and drank the red wine through their helmets barred." There was, however, entirely the disposition to be gracious, and to play her part like herself in conversation. She, therefore, exchanged anecdote and incident, in the course of which she detailed her feelings and reflections while wandering among the sublime and romantic scenery of North Wales and on the summit of Pennmanmawr. As she did this, her eye kindled and her features beamed, and in her countenance, which is indeed a volume where one may read strange matters, you might trace the varying emotions of her soul. I was surprised to find her face, even at the near approach of sitting by her side, absolutely handsome, and unmarked with any of those wrinkles which generally attend advanced life. Her form is at present becoming unwieldy, but not shapeless, and is full of dignity. Her gestures and movements are eminently graceful. Mr. and Mrs. Campbell say that I was quite fortunate, and might flatter myself on her being so conversable, for that she is very apt to be on the reserve toward strangers. The circumstance of being from another quarter of the world has given her an interest in the conversation she would not otherwise have felt.

Campbell is just completing a work in three pretty thick octavo volumes. The subject is to be characters of the principal poets, with specimens of their writing. From the passages he read to me from the account of Sir William Jones and some others, it will be a most eloquent and interesting work. He will wish you to dispose of the copyright in America, or make such arrangements as may be best for his interest. And as he intends the publication to be contemporaneous in both countries, and contemplates to publish here about in June, it may be advisable for you instantly to take preparatory steps. The manuscript will be sent in a few weeks. This opportunity is so excessively sudden, that I am unable to give further particulars. But lose no time and do every thing the best in your power, as I have a warm friendship for him. Give my love to mother and to all.

Your affectionate brother,

P. I.

Washington, however, had no opportunity of supporting the interest of Campbell, as his brother urged, for there was greater delay than the poet anticipated in the preparation of his work; and in March, 1814, he informs Peter he had come to an arrangement with Murray not to deliver his MSS. until September, and that he would not publish before December, 1814, or January, 1815 ; and he was anxious, if possible, to sell the copyright in the United States for as much as it would fetch, instead of waiting the slow return of profits by editions. "Of that sort of profit," he says, "I have had too sad experience on this side of the Atlantic."

On his return to New York, Brevoort resumed his quarters with Irving at Mrs. Ryckman's, No. 16 Broadway, but they soon after changed to Mrs. Bradish's, a choice house kept on the most liberal scale at the corner of Greenwich and Rector streets. Here they had, as before, a parlor in common. Among the occasional inmates in 1814 were that "second Sindbad, Captain Porter," of whom Mr. Irving prepared a biographical sketch for the *Analectic*, and Commodore Decatur and his wife.

CHAPTER XVIII.

M R. IRVING had deeply regretted that the difficulties between England and the United States had reached the
lamentable extremity of war, but, hostilities once commenced, his
sympathies were all on the side of his country.   In his biographical
sketch of Perry, published in the *Analectic Magazine*, he writes :

> Whatever we may think of the expediency or inexpediency of the
> present war, we cannot feel indifferent to its operations.   Whenever our
> arms come in competition with those of the enemy, jealousy for our coun-
> try's honor will swallow up every other consideration—our feelings will
> ever accompany the flag of our country to battle, rejoicing in its glory,
> lamenting over its defeat.   For there is no such thing as releasing our-
> selves from the consequences of the contest.   He who fancies he can stand
> aloof in interest, and by condemning the present war, can exonerate him-
> self from the shame of its disasters, is wofully mistaken.   Other nations
> will not trouble themselves about our internal wranglings and party ques-
> tions ; they will not ask who among us fought, or why we fought, but *how*
> we fought.   The disgrace of defeat will not be confined to the contrivers
> of the war, or the party in power, or the conductors of the battle ; but will
> extend to the whole nation, and come home to every individual.   If the
> name of American is to be rendered honorable in the fight, we shall each
> participate in the honor ; if otherwise, we must inevitably support our
> share of the ignominy.

With such sentiments, watching with mingled pride and sorrow the alternations of defeat and success, it may be imagined with
what a feeling of outraged patriotism he heard of the triumphant

entry of the British into Washington, and the acts of uncivilized hostility which followed.

He was descending the Hudson in a steamboat when the tidings first reached him. It was night, and the passengers had betaken themselves to their settees to rest, when a person came on board at Poughkeepsie with the news of the inglorious triumph, and proceeded in the darkness of the cabin to relate the particulars : the destruction of the President's house, the Treasury, War, and Navy offices ; the Capitol, the depository of the national library and public records. There was a momentary pause after the speaker had ceased, when some paltry spirit lifted his head from his settee, and in a tone of complacent derision " wondered what *Jimmy* Madison would say now." " Sir," said Mr. Irving, glad of an escape to his swelling indignation, " do you seize on such a disaster only for a sneer ? Let me tell you, sir, it is not now a question about *Jimmy* Madison, or *Jimmy* Armstrong.[1] The pride and honor of the nation are wounded ; the country is insulted and disgraced by this barbarous success, and every loyal citizen would feel the ignominy and be earnest to avenge it." " I could not see the fellow," said Mr. Irving, when he related the anecdote to me, "but I let fly at him in the dark." A murmur of approbation followed the outburst, and then every ear was listening for the reply, but the energy of the rebuke had cowed the spokesman, for he did not again raise his voice.

The spirit shown in this rebuke did not evaporate in words. On his arrival in New York he repaired immediately to Governor Tompkins with an offer of his services. The latter showed no backwardness in securing the new recruit, and at once made him his aide and military secretary with the rank of colonel. The letters addressed to him at this period bear this martial designation : " Washington Irving, Esquire " being transformed into " Colonel Washington Irving." A general order of the commander-in-chief, of September 2, 1814, bears the signature of " Washington Irving, Aide-de-Camp."

---

[1] The Secretary of War.

This destruction of Washington kindled a flame of patriotic energy throughout the country. The citizens of New York had before been busy in making preparations to repel a threatened invasion, but this urged them to the completion of their works of defence with redoubled spirit. The city was alive with the zeal of its inhabitants. Persons exempt from military service enrolled themselves anew; all trades and professions took their tour of duty at the line of fortifications, raised night and day on the heights of Brooklyn and Harlem; even clergymen with their parishioners sometimes volunteered in these measures of defence; and teachers with their juvenile scholars also turned out for a day's duty. The victorious outrage was well stigmatized in the House of Parliament as an "enterprise which most exasperated the people and least weakened the Government of any recorded in the annals of war." Scarcely two weeks had elapsed before the disgrace was wiped out in the death of the invading general, the repulse of the British at Baltimore, the defeat of England's veterans at Plattsburg, and the overthrow and surrender of her fleet on Lake Champlain. If Mr. Irving entered upon his military functions at a disastrous period, it was not long before he had cause for rejoicing.

He had been two or three weeks on the staff of the governor when it became necessary for the latter to proceed to Albany to attend an extraordinary session of the Legislature, which he had convened to meet on the 26th of September.

From Albany he writes to Brevoort, at Burlington, on Lake Champlain, September 26, 1814 :—

I have been incessantly occupied since I saw you by the duties of my station; and feel more pleased than ever with it. I am very anxious to hear how matters go with you. I think there is no prospect of immediate peace, and am of opinion that, should the British wait the results of the present campaign, they will rather be disposed to continue hostilities, to wipe out the stains of late defeats. This scourging campaign has on the whole been thus far a degrading one to them, and the victory on Champlain will be a pill not easily swallowed. I wish you would treasure up all the striking particulars you may hear concerning it, as I must give McDonough a dash.

Shortly after his arrival at Albany, it was rumored that Sackett's Harbor was threatened with an attack by land and water; and eager to share in the excitement, the secretary requested from the governor some mission to the lines. He was accordingly sent to Sackett's Harbor with discretionary powers to consult with the commanding officers stationed there; and, if necessary, to order out more militia.

I leave this (he writes from Albany to his brother Ebenezer, September 28th) at four o'clock in the morning for Sackett's Harbor. Affairs, I am afraid, are about to look squally on our Canada frontier. Drummond has fallen back to Fort George, and Brown is not in sufficient force to pursue him. Izard has landed at Genesee River; and by the time he forms a junction with Brown, or advances on Fort George, Drummond, I apprehend, will be able to get to the head of the lake, so that I think he has escaped from our clutches. In the meanwhile, we hear that Chauncey is at Sackett's Harbor. If the enemy takes the lake with his large ship, Chauncey is dished; he dare not come out, and may be attacked in the harbor by land and sea. It is said he does not mean to remain in the harbor, but to put out again immediately. As there is no regular force there of any consequence, I shall be empowered, if on consulting the officers there it is deemed necessary, to order out a requisite militia force. Should matters be safe there, and the lake be unmolested by the enemy, I think it probable I shall sail to the upper part of it, and visit Brown's army; having powers to transact business there, if necessary.

The travelling, at present, is rough; but the expedition will be a very interesting one.

He proceeded to Utica in the stage, and at that point took horse for Sackett's Harbor, which with all diligence he could not reach under three days, for the roads were exceedingly heavy, and the journey rough and toilsome, though not without interest. A great part of his lonely ride lay through the track which he had traversed with the Hoffmans and Ogdens in 1803; but eleven years had made great changes in the face of the country.

At the close of an account of this forest ride, left among his papers, he says:—

After toiling along this rough road, amidst the most lonely and savage scenery, I at length came to where the country suddenly opened;

Sackett's Harbor lay before me—a town which had recently sprung up in the bosom of this wilderness; beyond it the lake spread its vast waters like an ocean, no opposing shore being visible; while a few miles from land rode a squadron of ships of war at anchor on the calm bosom of the lake, and looking as if they were balanced in the air.

The next day he writes :—

[*To Ebenezer Irving.*]

SACKETT'S HARBOR, Oct. 3, 1814.

DEAR BROTHER:—

I arrived here this morning after incessant travelling through the mire for four or five days—the last three on horseback. The British have completed their large ship, and she has dropped down to Snake Island, where she lies under the batteries.' Chauncey lies at anchor about six miles off the harbor. It is expected the British will immediately take the lake, and Chauncey be obliged to come in. Preparations are making to resist an attack by land and sea, which is expected. Breastworks are throwing up and pickets erected, which will enclose the whole place, and form protection for the militia. I have been constantly employed at the general's quarters all day, so that I have not been able to look about me. In compliance with the instructions of the governor, I have ordered out a large reinforcement of militia, and hope they may come in time; but there is a sad deficiency of arms and military munitions. I write in great haste, as the mail is on the point of departing. Give my love to mother and the family; I am in excellent health, and feel all the better for hard travelling. Should there be no business to detain me here, I shall leave this place in a day or two. I wish first to visit Chauncey's fleet, and should like to witness an action were there a prospect of an immediate one.

The first wish was gratified the next day. In a letter to his brother William he says :—

The *Lady of the Lake* happening to come into the harbor, I went out in her to the fleet, which lay at anchor off Stony Island, about eleven miles distant, and remained aboard with Chauncey for part of two days; during which time he took me round the little fleet, and I had a fine opportunity of witnessing their admirable order and equipment. It is a gallant little squadron, and I could not but regret continually that it should be doomed to rot in a fresh-water pond. The *Superior* is by great odds the finest frigate I was ever on board of. Her gun-deck shows a

---

' A mistake. She had not dropped down. This large ship was the *St. Lawrence*, of 90 guns.

tremendous battery. I was in hopes of having an opportunity of looking into Kingston Harbor and getting a peep at that *big ship*, which is the bugbear of these seas; the *Lady of the Lake*, however, was not sent on a reconnoitring expedition while I was in the fleet, and I did not think proper to make any request.

Nothing could exceed the surprise of Chauncey on receiving Mr. Irving on board of his ship in these remote solitudes. " You here ? " he exclaimed, in extending his hand; " I should as soon have thought of seeing my wife."

As there was no immediate prospect of any thing at Sackett's Harbor, the aide set off on the 7th of October, for Albany, in company with a commissary.

As they were wending their way toward Utica they were constantly meeting with squads of militia from Herkimer, Oneida, and the Black River counties, trudging toward Sackett's Harbor to reinforce the inadequate defence for that place, who would hail him as they passed with " What news of the Big Ship ? " then jeer him for going the wrong way, and banter him to face about, little dreaming that it was to him they were indebted for the summons to turn out.

On the 12th of October he was again in New York, having every reason to be delighted with his position on the governor's staff. In a letter to his brother William, at Washington, he says (October 14th) :—

I feel more and more satisfied with my situation. It gives me a charming opportunity of seeing all that is going on, and Tompkins is absolutely one of the worthiest men I ever knew. I find him honest, candid, prompt, indefatigable, with a greater stock of practical good-sense and ready talent than I had any idea he possessed, and of nerve to put into immediate execution any measure that he is satisfied is correct. I expect he will have the command here in a few days, in which case my situation will be every thing I could wish.

A letter of the 27th October, to the same brother, says :—

The governor arrived in town yesterday, and this day will take command. I expect and hope he will keep his staff stirring, and have been endeavoring, as much as the little leisure I have would permit, to prepare myself for the duties of my situation.

These duties were sufficiently agreeable, but he used frequently to be annoyed by the good-humored facility of Tompkins in giving audience to the hosts of danglers that beset a man in office, when his time was too precious for such courtesy, even if his personal dignity had not required a more chary demeanor. " Let me," he would sometimes say in a spirit of friendly expostulation, " receive their messages, and if it be important for you to see them, I will admit them one at a time. Some degree of form and etiquette is indispensable." Tompkins would consent, but soon his good-nature would get the better of his dignity, and he would sally forth to meet some importunate demand from without, when his attention would be instantly claimed by a multitude of other spirits in waiting. " I had constantly to go out," said once the quondam aide to me, "and dig him out of the crowd."

While Washington was on the staff, his brother William was representing his native city in Congress. This brother, like himself, lacked confidence for a public speaker, and was too apt to become embarrassed and break down under any formal attempt to deliver his views ; while in conversation, he spoke with an animation and fluency that once elicited from the distinguished Lowndes, of South Carolina, the exclamation, grasping him at the same time by the hand, " Why in the name of God, will you not speak in this way in the House ? " He could not, however, command his nerves, and lost heart whenever he attempted to speak ; so that during the seven years he was in Congress, though an efficient and popular member, he rarely rose to his feet. The following extract from a letter of Washington, dated December 20, 1814, and which I quote in illustration of the writer's sensitive patriotism, has reference to one of the few occasions on which he broke silence. It was on a bill to authorize a draft of militia from the several States. His speech took strong ground in favor of a vigorous prosecution of the war, and reprobated the mistaken economy which, by withholding what was necessary, rendered useless what was bestowed. The bill, as introduced, provided for eighteen months' service, but was reduced to twelve.

As to the bill on which you spoke (writes Washington), I consider it another of those skeleton measures, which, after having been stripped of flesh, and blood, and muscles, is sent forth to mock the country with a mere shaking of dry bones. We shall now have men for six months to drill and make soldiers of, and six months to feed and support in winter-quarters. If it had been eighteen months we might have had two campaigns out of them, or if six months, we could have one and no after-trouble and expense of keeping them through a long winter: I think you were right, however, to support any show of defence, though I regret that you were not able to effect any thing more substantially efficient. I am really heartsick at the present wretched state of public affairs, and loathe that make-shift policy that has only aimed at scuffling through present embarrassments, and maintaining present popularity at the risk, or rather certainty, of future confusion and disaster.

A few days after this, Governor Tompkins repaired to Albany to attend the session of the Legislature, leaving General Boyd in command of the station. Mr. Irving's connection with the staff was consequently dissolved without any thing having occurred to give prominence to his brief military career of four months, or test his martial accomplishments. He used jokingly to speak of an equestrian mischance of the governor as the only event of his campaign. Tompkins was about to visit a fort on Brooklyn Heights, manned by marines. It was surrounded by a deep trench, over which you passed into the fort by a somewhat narrow cause-way. The governor, who was not over-firm in the stirrups, had a rather mettlesome steed, and, fearing the effect of the customary salute, sent his aide in advance to have it dispensed with. The marines would not be balked in this way. They were annoyed at being disappointed of their salute, and, determined upon some ceremonial of respect, when the governor was making his exit, by a preconcerted movement they jumped upon the cannon, and made the welkin ring with their cheers. Never was a popular demonstration so ill-timed. The governor was just crossing the causeway, when, startled with the stentorian chorus, the horse gave a pirouette, and the next thing I saw, said his aide, was Tompkins lying in the ditch and his steed bounding madly away. The aide hastened to the rescue of his dismounted chief, and was glad to perceive that he had received no greater injury than a sprained thumb and a sudden sickness of the stomach; but ever afterward—on such perilous occasions—the governor was apt to give his steed to him and borrow for the nonce his "Archy." This was a little bay of which he once wrote: "I never had occasion to lay the whip on his back, and, indeed, would almost as soon have had it laid on my own."[1]

Of a piece with this military history was his jesting advice to Samuel Swartwout, the Major of the Iron Greys, a choice corps of volunteers to which his friend Brevoort belonged. The Major was very fussy about their equipments: first this thing was wrong, then that; now their guns were too light, then they were too heavy. "Put two men to a gun, Sam," was the remedy advised under the last annoyance.

Soon after his retirement from the staff, Washington made a jaunt to Philadelphia, and had thoughts of proceeding to the seat of government to apply for a commission in the regular army, but was prevented in the way detailed in the following letter to his brother William.

PHILADELPHIA, January 15, 1815.

DEAR BROTHER:—

On arriving in Philadelphia I find that Bradford and Inskeep have failed and ruined poor Moses Thomas, the bookseller, who publishes the *Analectic.* This will detain me here some time to arrange my affairs with him and settle about the future fate of the magazine. This circumstance, and the vileness of the roads, etc., have induced me to give up my intention of visiting Washington for the present. I shall therefore return to New York in about a week.

He "signed off what was owing to him," and being anxious that the magazine should not fall through, effected an arrangement by which it was continued, though he never resumed the editorship.

Before he returned from Philadelphia, where his stay was prolonged to the beginning of February, came the news of the victory of New Orleans and the tidings of peace.

---

[1] A letter to his brother Ebenezer furnishes this other characteristic token of affection for the animal: "When you next visit little Archy's stall, pat him on the sides for me."

During his absence his friend Decatur had put to sea in the frigate *President* and been captured by a British squadron. Having been released, he got back to the city in time to witness the illumination which announced the rejoicing of the citizens at the return of peace ; but he had scarcely arrived when an act passed the two Houses of Congress, announcing the existence of a state of war between the United States and Algiers. The Dey of Algiers had taken advantage of the war with England to prey upon the commerce of the United States in the Mediterranean, and several citizens had been confined in prisons and large sums refused for their ransom. Two squadrons were accordingly fitted out to obtain redress. The command of the first was offered to Decatur, and of the second to Bainbridge. This last was to follow the first, and on its arrival in the Mediterranean the commander of the first was to return in a single vessel, and leave the two squadrons in charge of Bainbridge. The command of the first had been offered to Decatur by the Government in token of their undiminished confidence ; yet he hesitated about accepting it, and consulted Irving on the subject. The latter was his fellow-boarder at Mrs. Bradish's, whence Decatur had started on his unfortunate cruise, leaving his wife behind, who was miserable during his absence, and would sometimes walk her room whole nights, incapable of sleep. Mr. Irving strongly urged his acceptance, insisting that he should by no means lose the opportunity of emerging from the cloud which had come over his celebrity by the loss of the *President;* that here was a chance for a brilliant dash ; that he could precede Bainbridge, who was fitting out at Boston, and, as he expressed it to me, "whip off the cream of the enterprise." The distress of his wife at the idea of this renewed separation so soon after his return caused Decatur to hesitate, but at length he decided to go, and, turning suddenly to Mr. Irving, he proposed that he should accompany him, offering as an inducement the attraction of a cruise in the Mediterranean, and a promise to land him wherever he wished.

The project was too captivating to be resisted. Mr. Irving took but half an hour to consult with his brother Ebenezer, his partner, and decided to go. His trunks were soon packed and on board of the frigate, the *Guerrière*. Just at this time, when on the eve of departure, came news of Bonaparte's return from Elba, and it was deemed prudent by the Government to delay the expedition for a while under this new turn of affairs.   Meanwhile, Mr. Irving thought he perceived some little wavering on the part of the Commodore, and unwilling to embarrass his decision, should he incline to relinquish the command, he had his trunks brought ashore.   But as he was now fully bent on a voyage to Europe, had made all his preparations, and was sure, as he thought himself, of fortune's favors from the success of the commercial establishment into which he had been admitted, he determined to embark, and mingle for a while in the exciting scenes that seemed to be opening on that side of the Atlantic.

The fleet weighed anchor on the 20th of May, and if Mr. Irving had accompanied Decatur, as he was so near doing, he would have been on board of his vessel in her brilliant action with the *Mazouda*, which took place in less than a month after the gallant hero had sailed, and in which the Algerine frigate was captured, and Hammida, her famous Rais or Admiral, killed.

It was on the 25th of May, only five days after the departure of Decatur, that he bade adieu to his aged mother, his brothers, and friends, and embarked on board of the ship *Mexico* for Liverpool, looking forward to a pleasant voyage, but little dreaming that the ocean he was to cross would roll its waters for seventeen years between him and his home.

CHAPTER XIX.

Pride of the Village.

R. IRVING had led a very listless life for a month or two before he left New York, and was building, at his departure, large anticipations upon the exciting scenes that would follow the return of Bonaparte from Elba. The curtain, however, had already fallen upon this brief interlude when he landed at Liverpool. The first spectacle which met his eye was the mail-coaches coming in, decked in laurel and dashing proudly through the streets, with the tidings of the battle of Waterloo and the flight of Napoleon. From this time he was all alive to watch the progress of Bonaparte's disastrous career, though his letters are somewhat sparing of remark on the astounding catastrophe. In writing to Brevoort, July 5th, he observes :—

I have forborne making any comments on the wonderful events that are taking place in the political world. They are too vast and astonishing to be grasped in the narrow compass of a familiar letter, and, indeed, as yet I can do nothing but look in stupid amazement, wondering with vacant conjecture "what will take place next." I am determined, however, to get a near view of the actors in this great drama.

In pursuit of this purpose in part he went up to London for a few days before Parliament rose, and on his return to Birmingham he thus records his impressions of the prince and people most deeply interested in these momentous events :—

Since I wrote you last (to Ebenezer, July 21st) I have made a short visit to London, where I was much gratified by seeing the House of Lords in full session, and the Prince Regent on the throne, on the proroguing of Parliament. The spirits of this nation, as you may suppose, are wonderfully elated by their successes on the continent, and English pride is inflated to its full distension by the idea of having Paris at the mercy of Wellington and his army. The only thing that annoys the honest mob is that old Louis will not cut throats and lop off heads, and that Wellington will not blow up bridges and monuments, and plunder palaces and galleries. As to Bonaparte, they have disposed of him in a thousand ways; every fat-sided John Bull has him dished up in a way to please his own palate, excepting that as yet they have not observed the first direction in the famous receipt to cook a turbot—" first catch your turbot."

In a postscript he adds :—

The bells are ringing, and this moment news is brought that poor Boney is a prisoner at Plymouth. *John has caught the Turbot!*

I am extremely sorry (he writes to his brother William the same day) that his career has terminated so lamely; it's a thousand pities he had not fallen like a hero at the battle of Waterloo.

And soon after, announcing to Brevoort that Bonaparte had at length left the coast for St. Helena, he says, with a strong feeling of sympathy for his fallen fortunes and the dreary exile to which he was devoted :—

I must say I think the Cabinet has acted with littleness toward him. In spite of all his misdeeds, he is a noble fellow, and I am confident will eclipse, in the eyes of posterity, all the crowned wiseacres that have crushed him by their overwhelming confederacy.

If any thing could place the Prince Regent in a more ridiculous light, it is Bonaparte suing for his magnanimous protection. Every compliment paid to this bloated sensualist, this inflation of sack and sugar, turns to the keenest sarcasm ; and nothing shows more completely the caprices of Fortune, and how truly she delights in reversing the relative situations of persons, and baffling the flights of intellect and enterprise—than that, of all the monarchs of Europe, *Bonaparte* should be brought to the feet of the *Prince Regent*.

> " An eagle towering in his pride of place
> Was by a mousing owl hawked at and killed."

And now, having been led away for a moment to trace the tone of his allusion to the vast events that came breaking upon him at his arrival on the shores of Europe, I return to more domestic details.

Nearly seven years had passed since his parting with Peter, " a fearful lapse of time to gentlemen of a certain age "; yet he found him in manner and conversation so much like old times that it soon seemed, he says, as if they had parted but yesterday. " I found him," is his language to Ebenezer, " very comfortably situated, having handsome furnished rooms, and keeping a horse, gig, and servant, but not indulging in any extravagance or dash. He lives like a man of sense, who knows he can but enjoy his money while he is alive, and would not be a whit the better though he were buried under a mountain of it when dead." Peter was at this time confined to the house by an indisposition, which, though apparently yielding to strict regimen and medical prescription, ultimately lengthened into a most tedious illness, driving him in September to Harrowgate for the benefit of the waters, and thence, almost a cripple from rheumatism, to his sister's house in Birmingham, where he lingered, an uncomplaining invalid, to the middle of May.

Washington spent a week with Peter at Liverpool, and then took leave of him, seemingly recruiting rapidly in health, " for the redoubtable castle of Van Tromp," as he playfully styles the residence of his brother-in-law, Henry Van Wart, in the vicinity of Birmingham.

From Birmingham he went, for a few days, to London, and made an excursion thence to Sydenham, to visit Campbell, who, unfortunately, was not at home.

I spent an hour (he writes) in conversation with Mrs. Campbell, who is a most engaging and interesting woman. Campbell was still engaged in getting his critical work through the press; and as he is a rigid censor of his own works, correcting is as laborious as composition to him.   He alters and amends until the last moment.   I am in hopes when he has this work off his hands, he will attempt another poem.   Mrs. Campbell gave me some anecdotes of Scott, but none so remarkable as to dwell in my memory.   He has lost much by the failure of the Ballantynes, but is as merry and unconcerned to all appearance as ever; one of the happiest fellows that ever wrote poetry.   I find it is very much doubted whether he is the author of " Waverley " and " Guy Mannering."   Brown, one of the publishers, positively says he is not.

It was in this interview with the poet's wife, that the conversation took place of which he has given an account in the introduction to the American reprint of Beattie's " Life of Campbell."

I had considered (he says) the early productions of Campbell as brilliant indications of a genius yet to be developed ; and trusted that, during the long interval which had elapsed, he had been preparing something to fulfil the public expectation.   I was greatly disappointed, therefore, to find that, as yet, he had contemplated no great and sustained effort.   [He expressed to Mrs. Campbell his regret " that her husband did not attempt something on a grand scale."]   " It is unfortunate for Campbell," said she, " that he lives in the same age with Scott and Byron." I asked why.   " Oh ! " said she, " they write so much and so rapidly.   Now Campbell writes slowly, and it takes him some time to get under way ; and just as he has fairly begun, out comes one of their poems, that sets the world agog, and quite daunts him, so that he throws by his pen in despair."   I pointed out the essential difference in their kinds of poetry, and the qualities which ensured perpetuity to that of her husband.   " You can't persuade Campbell of that," said she.   " He is apt to undervalue his own works, and to consider his own little lights put out whenever they come blazing out with their great torches."

I repeated the conversation to Scott (continues Mr. Irving) some time afterward, and it drew forth a characteristic comment.

" Pooh ! " said he, good-humoredly, " how can Campbell mistake the matter so much.   Poetry goes by quality, not by bulk.   My poems are mere cairngorms, wrought up, perhaps, with a cunning hand, and may pass well in the market as long as cairngorms are the fashion ; but they are mere Scotch pebbles, after all ; now Tom Campbell's are real diamonds, and diamonds of the first water."

From London Mr. Irving returned to his " English home," the domestic circle at Birmingham, and made an excursion thence

to Kenilworth, Warwick, and Stratford-on-Avon with James Renwick.

After pausing a few days at Birmingham, on their return, he and Renwick set out again on a tour by the way of Bath and Bristol through South and North Wales to Liverpool, where he joined his brother Peter about the middle of August. "I found Renwick," he writes, "an excellent travelling companion, and from his uncommon memory an exceeding good book of reference, so as to save me a vast deal of trouble in consulting my travelling books." He gives no particulars of his "delightful tour," but his pencil memoranda abound with sketches taken on his route, and record in language that cannot clearly be deciphered that he clambered up to the tower of the cathedral which commands a noble view of the valley in which Gloucester stands, and was locked up by the old sexton while he accompanied other visitors round the church, fearful he might give him the slip.

Soon after Washington got to Liverpool, Peter left for Harrowgate, and his indisposition continuing, his absence was prolonged through more than eight months.

Washington had now to take charge of the establishment, which, as he was very inexperienced, was a sufficient employment for all his faculties. The confused manner in which the business had been conducted in consequence of Peter's illness and the death of his principal clerk, obliged him to examine every thing thoroughly, and by that means to acquaint himself with every detail. Averse as he was to business, he now gave himself up to it entirely, and he had a faculty of applying himself thoroughly to a subject until he had mastered it. "I am leading a solitary bachelor's life in Peter's lodgings," he writes to his mother, September 21st, "and perhaps should feel a little lonesome were I not kept so busy." September 24th he was instituting an examination into the accounts of the concern, and having the books brought up, for which purpose he had studied book-keeping.

During this interval, though his letters to Brevoort might savor of pleasantry, the sordid cares of the counting-house took up his whole time and completely occupied his mind, "so that at present," he writes in October, " I am as dull, commonplace a fellow as ever figured upon 'Change." At this time he had begun to apprehend that Peter, following too many others at that period, had purchased too deeply for their capital, and he had become very anxious and apprehensive about their fall payments, and how he was to meet the great demands for funds which began to press upon them.

His constant injunction to his brother Ebenezer, who, meanwhile, was straining every nerve to do it, was to remit continually until all the goods were paid for; not to flag, nor think, because he had done well, he could afford for a time to do nothing.

I could not help smiling (says he) at a passage in one of brother William's letters to Van Wart, wherein he intimates that they should have to stop to take breath from remitting; but in the meantime he must wait patiently and do his best. This was something like the Irishman calling to his companion, whom he was hoisting out of the well, to hold on below while he spit on his hands.

On the 10th of November Mr. Irving was able to "emerge from the mud of Liverpool, and shake off the sordid cares of the counting-house," and join " the little family circle at Birmingham," where Peter was now confined in helpless inactivity. From Birmingham he made a three weeks' visit to London, returning in time to eat his Christmas dinner with his relatives, and to learn how cruelly circumstances had operated against their fall business ; the goods that had been shipped for New York failing, through adverse winds, to reach that market in season, and having to lie over for the spring. Notwithstanding this great discouragement, Ebenezer wrote in a cheerful and resolute spirit, but it was easy to foresee how much their difficulties must be increased from this source, and what a taste they were likely to have of the anxieties, embarrassments, and disadvantages of an overstrained business.

I close the year 1815 with the following letter to Brevoort, which touches upon his visit to London, and his theatrical experiences :—

BIRMINGHAM, December 28, 1815.

DEAR BREVOORT:—

It is a long while since I have heard from you; and since your last we have been very uneasy, in consequence of hearing of your being dangerously ill. Subsequent accounts, however, have again put you on your legs, and relieved us from our anxiety. I have lately been on a short visit to London; merely to see sights, and visit public places. Our worthy friend Johnson, and his brother, arrived in town while I was there, and we were frequently together. The Governor enjoyed the amusements of London with high zest, and, like myself, was a great frequenter of the theatres— particularly when Miss O'Neil performed. We were both agreed that were you in England, you would infallibly fall in love with this "divine perfection of a woman." She is, to my eyes, the most soul-subduing actress I ever saw. I do not mean from her personal charms, which are great, but from the truth, force, and pathos of her acting. I never have been so completely melted, moved, and overcome at a theatre as by her performances. I do not think much of the other novelties of the day. Mrs. Mardyn, about whom much has been said and written, is vulgar without humor, and hoydenish without real whim and vivacity; she is pretty, but a very bad actress. Kean—the prodigy—is cried up as a second Garrick— as a reformer of the stage, etc., etc.; it may be so. He may be right, and all the actors wrong; this is certain, he is either very good or very bad— I think decidedly the latter; and I find no medium opinions concerning him.

I am delighted with Young, who acts with great judgment, discrimination, and feeling. I think him much the best actor at present on the English stage. His Hamlet is a very fine performance, as is likewise his Stranger, Pierre, Chamont, etc. I have not seen his Macbeth, which I should not suppose could equal Cooper's. In fact, in certain characters, such as may be classed with Macbeth, I do not thing that Cooper has his equal in England. Young is the only actor I have seen that can be compared with him. I cannot help thinking that if Cooper had a fair chance, and the public were to see him in his principal characters, he would take the lead at once of the London theatres. But there is so much party work, managerial influence, and such a widely spread and elaborate system of falsehood and misrepresentation connected with the London theatres, that a stranger who is not peculiarly favored by the managers, or assisted by the prepossessions of the public, stands no chance. I shall never forget Cooper's acting in Macbeth last spring, when he was stimulated to exertion by the presence of a number of British officers. I have seen nothing equal to it in England. Cooper requires excitement to arouse him from a monotonous, commonplace manner he is apt to fall into, in consequence of acting so often before indifferent houses. I presume the crowded audiences, which I am told have filled our theatres this season, must bring him out in full splendor.

While at London I saw Campbell, who is busily employed printing his long-promised work. The publisher has been extremely dilatory; and has kept poor Campbell lingering over the pages of this work for months longer than was necessary. He will in a little while get through with the printing of it; but it will not be published before spring. As usual, he is busy correcting, altering, and adding to it, to the last, and cannot turn his mind to any thing else, until this is out of hand.

Later in life, after fuller opportunity of seeing him, Mr. Irving wrote to Brevoort of Kean as follows :—

Kean is a strange compound of merits and defects. His excellence consists in sudden and brilliant touches—in vivid exhibitions of passion and emotion. I do not think him a *discriminating* actor, or critical either at understanding or delineating *character ;* but he produces effects which no other actor does. He has completely bothered the multitude ; and is praised without being understood. I have seen him guilty of the grossest and coarsest pieces of false acting, and most " tyrannically clapped " withal ; while some of his most exquisite touches passed unnoticed.

Miss O'Neill, of whom he writes with such enthusiasm in the letter just given, afterward played a round of her most effective parts at Birmingham ; and Mr. Irving was so completely carried away by his admiration of her acting, that when offered to be introduced to her he declined, unwilling to take the risk of a possible disenchantment. She had lost herself so completely in the characters she represented that he feared to have the illusion broken. " Well," said Scott, when he afterward told him of his reasons for this avoidance, " that was very complimentary to her as an actress, but I am not so sure that it was as a woman."

CHAPTER XX.

I HAVE no intention for the present of visiting the continent. I wish to see business on a regular footing before I travel for pleasure. I should otherwise have a constant load of anxiety on my mind.

So wrote Washington to his brother Ebenezer at the close of 1815. Yielding to a roving propensity, " the offspring of idleness of mind and a want of something to fix the feelings," he had pulled up anchor in New York seven months before to drift about Europe in search of novelty and excitement, ready, as he expresses it, " to spread his sails wherever any vagrant breeze might carry him," and now, for weary months, he is detained in Liverpool by irksome and unexpected employment, and we find him at the opening of another year renouncing every project he had in view when he embarked, and sighing for the easy, unconcerned days and tranquil nights he had enjoyed before he left.

Peter still continued an invalid at Birmingham. Washington, therefore, went to Liverpool after New Year to put business in train for the next month's payments, and then start for London, " to endeavor to make some financial arrangements." Expecting little from remittances for some time to come, he wished to make matters easy ahead as much as possible. " I would not again," he writes from Liverpool, January 9, 1816, " experience the anxious days and sleepless nights which have been my lot since I have taken hold of business to possess the wealth of Crœsus." The next evening he left that city for Birmingham, where he spent a few hours on the morrow, and then proceeded to London, in which city he remained two months. I give some extracts from a letter to

Brevoort, dated at Birmingham, March 15, 1816, after his return from that city.

MY DEAR BREVOORT :—

I have received your most kind letter of February 18th, and also the magazines and newspapers, forwarded by Mr. Sheldon. I believe 1 am still in your debt for your letters of the 1st January ; but, indeed, I have been so completely driven out of my usual track of thought and feeling by "stress of weather" in business, that I have not been able to pen a single line on any subject that was not connected with traffic. . . . . We have, in common with most American houses here, had a hard winter of it in money matters, owing to the cross-purposes of last fall's business, and have been harassed to death to meet our engagements. I have never passed so anxious a time in my life ; my rest has been broken, and my health and spirits almost prostrated ; but, thank Heaven! we have weathered the storm, and got into smooth water, and I begin to feel myself again. Brom [1] has done wonders, and proved himself an able financier ; and though a small man, a perfect giant in business. I cannot help mentioning that James Renwick has behaved in the most gratifying manner. At a time when we were exceedingly straitened, I wrote to him begging to know if he could in any way assist us to a part of the amount we were deficient. He immediately opened a credit for us to the full amount, guaranteeing the payment of it, and asking no security from us than our bare words. But the manner in which this was done heightened the merit of it, from the contrast it formed to the extreme distrust and tenfold caution that universally prevailed throughout the commercial world of England, in the present distressed times. . . . .

I have had much gratification from the epistles of that worthy little tar, Jack Nicholson, who, I find, still sighs in the bottom of his heart for the fair ——, though he declares that his hopes do not aspire to such perfection. Why did not the varlet bring home the head of Rais Hammida, and lay it at her feet ; that would have been a chivalric exploit few ladies could have withstood ; and if Paulding had only dished him up in full *length* (if I may be allowed the word), in a wood-cut in the *Naval Chronicle*, like little David of yore, with the head of Goliah in his fist, I think his suit would have been irresistible.[2]

. . . . I wish you would send to me the numbers of the *Analectic Magazine* that have the Traits of Indian Character and the story of King

---

[1] A nickname for his brother Ebenezer.

[2] The *American Naval Chronicle* formed a department of the *Analectic Magazine*, to which Paulding was contributing the biographies.

Philip; likewise a copy of the "History of New York"; send them by the first opportunity.

He was probably meditating at this time a revised edition of "Knickerbocker," with illustrations by Allston and Leslie, whom he had met in London.

At the date of this letter Mr. Irving hoped that they had now got through their difficulties, and that future business would not merely be profitable, but easy and pleasant ; and with such feelings he returned to Liverpool, leaving Peter still at Birmingham, not yet "able to trust his rheumatic limbs out of the house." He was destined, however, to find "everybody dismal," from the hard times, and to continue to lead an anxious life.

May 9th he writes to Brevoort :—

I was in hopes of hearing from you by the *Rosalie*, but was disappointed. A letter from you is like a gleam of sunshine through the darkness that seems to lower upon my mind. I am here alone, attending to business; and the times are so hard, that they sicken my very soul. Good God! what would I give to be once more with you, and all this mortal coil shuffled off my heart !

About this time Peter returned to Liverpool reëstablished in health, and his presence enabled Washington once more to repair to Birmingham. But he had been "so harassed and hag-ridden by the cares and anxieties of business," and had been so long "brooding over the hardships of the disordered times," that it was in vain that he attempted to divert his thoughts into other channels and employ himself with his pen. "My mind is in a sickly state," he writes July 16th, "and my imagination so blighted that it cannot put forth a blossom or even a green leaf. Time and circumstances must restore them to their proper tone."

The sunny spot in this gloomy year was a little excursion into Derbyshire which he concerted with Peter, when a suspension for a while of dismal letters from New York left him a disposition for a ramble among the scenes described by "old Izaak Walton." This excursion was made about the beginning of August. The rest of the year was spent under his sister's roof at Birmingham, in a vain attempt to revive the literary feeling.

On the 23d of February in the following year he went back to Liverpool, feeling that his company was important to keep up Peter's spirits.

About this time Mr. Irving was preparing a new edition of his " History of New York," for which Allston and Leslie were making designs.   In a letter from the former, dated London, April 15th, he remarks :—

I have made a design for your " Knickerbocker," but I shall say nothing about it, as I hope you will soon be here to see it.

He then speaks of having "added four new incidents to the first three acts of the play" he was intending to offer to the theatres, and adds in a postscript : "I have completed a sketch, and am making other preparations for a large picture; but more of this when I see you.   I promise myself much advantage as well as pleasure from your society the ensuing summer."

This expectation, however, was put to flight by a sudden resolution of Mr. Irving to return home, which gives occasion to the following interesting letter from Allston, in which he unfolds the design of his large picture, and of his sketch for " Knickerbocker " :—

LONDON, May 9, 1817,
8 Buckingham Place, Fitzroy Sq.

DEAR IRVING :

Your sudden resolution of embarking for America has quite thrown me, to use a sea-phrase, all aback ; I have so many things to tell you of— to consult you about, etc., and am such a sad correspondent, that before I can bring my pen to do its office 't is a hundred to one but the occasions for which your advice would be wished will have passed and gone.   One of these subjects (and the most important) is the large picture I talked of soon beginning: The prophet Daniel interpreting the *handwriting on the wall* before Belshazzar.   I have made a highly finished sketch of it, and I wished much to have your remarks on it.   But as your sudden departure will deprive me of this advantage, I must beg, should any hints on the subject occur to you during your voyage, that you will favor me with them, at the same time you let me know that you are again safe in our good country.   I think the composition the best I ever made.   It contains a multitude of figures, and (if I may be allowed to say it) they are without confusion. Don't you think it a fine subject? I know not any that so happily unites the magnificent and the awful: a mighty sovereign, surrounded by his whole court, intoxicated with his own state, in the midst of his revellings palsied in a moment under the spell of a preternatural hand suddenly tracing his doom on the wall before him; his powerless limbs, like a wounded spider's shrunk up to his body, while his heart, *compressed to a point*, is only kept from vanishing by the terrific suspense that animates it during the interpretation of his mysterious sentence; his less guilty, but scarcely less agitated, queen, the panic-struck courtiers and concubines, the splendid and deserted banquet-table, the half-arrogant, half-astounded magicians, the holy vessels of the temple (shining, as it were, in triumph through the gloom), and the calm, solemn contrast of the prophet, standing like an animated pillar in the midst, breathing forth the oracular destruction of the empire! The picture will be twelve feet high by seventeen feet long. Should I succeed in it even to my wishes I know not what may be its fate. But I leave the future to Providence. Perhaps I may send it to America. Agreeably to your request I send, by the coach, the design for " Knickerbocker." The subject is Wouter Van Twiller's decision in the case of Wandle Schoonhoven and Barent Bleecker. I think the astonished constable the best figure. Indeed, that relating to him appeared to me the dryest part of the joke. Let me know how you like it. If you don't like it—mind —I sha'n't be offended. 'T is a sad bore to be obliged to laugh through complaisance; so I won't take it amiss even though you should be grave upon it. By the bye, I should like to know whether that lawsuit satirizes any *living* persons. If so, I should be sorry, for though they may cheerfully join in the laugh themselves at a ridiculous description, they would not so well bear a pictured personal caricature. Do let me know, and I will make a design from another part of the book that shall hurt nobody. Now, don't laugh at me. I would only be a harmless creature. I send at the same time a design by Leslie. The subject is the Dutch courtship. It is really a very beautiful drawing. If you mean to have them engraved, I think they had better be done here. They could not engrave them well in America. Here they would be well done, and much cheaper. If you think so too, and will leave them with your brother to be sent to me, I will see that they are properly done. You will probably see in New York a little picture of " Rebecca at the Well " which I painted last summer for my friend Van Schaick. My friends here thought it one of my best pictures. I hope he likes it. I have not heard. I shall not regret that I have written so much about myself if it induce you, in return, to favor me with some of your plans and projects.

Wishing you a prosperous voyage, and happy meeting with your friends,

I remain truly your friend,

WASHINGTON ALLSTON.

Campbell, also, under the impression that he was about returning to America, had sent him the printed sheets of the greater part of the first two volumes of his new work, wishing him to try if something could not be procured for it.

In the conclusion of his letter, dated May 26th, he remarks :—

I congratulate you on the happiness of returning to your native land. Alas! you leave us in sad times. I have been just telling Ogilvie that if things get worse here I shall expect to finish my days teaching Greek in America. I fear our political horizon is brewing a storm that will not soon be allayed. I see no termination of our difficulties. God knows I love my country, and my heart would bleed to leave it, but if there be a consummation such as may be feared I look to taking up my abode in the only other land of liberty, and you may behold me perhaps flogging your little Spartans of Kentucky into a true sense and feeling of the beauties of Homer !

Mr. Irving sent the sheets to his friend Brevoort, with an earnest request that he would do what he could to promote the poet's interest, and in the conclusion of his letter gives this explanation of his change of purpose :—

I received some time since your kind letter urging my return. I had even come to the resolution to do so immediately, but the news of my dear mother's death put an end to one strong inducement that was continually tugging at my heart, and other reasons have compelled me to relinquish the idea for the present.

What the " other reasons " were, does not appear.

The death of his mother, which was the main cause of his postponement, took place on the 9th of April. When he parted from her in New York he had expected to return after a short absence and settle down beside her for the rest of her life. She was near seventy-nine when she died.

I now follow with the reply to Allston's letter.

[*To Washington Allston.*]

BIRMINGHAM, May 21, 1817.

MY DEAR ALLSTON:—

Your letter of the 9th instant, and likewise the parcel containing the pictures, came safely to hand, and should have been acknowledged sooner, but I have been much discomposed since last I wrote to you, by intelligence of the death of my mother. Her extreme age made such an event constantly probable, but I had hoped to have seen her once more before she died, and was anxious to return home soon on that account. That hope is now at an end, and with it my immediate wish to return; so that I think it probable I shall linger some time longer in Europe.

I have been very much struck with your conception of the warning of Belshazzar. It is grand and poetical, affording scope for all the beauties and glories of the pencil; and if it is but executed in the spirit in which it is conceived, I am confident will ensure you both profit and renown.

As to its future fate, however, never let that occupy your mind, unless it be to stimulate you to exertion. As to sending it to America, I would only observe that, unless I got very advantageous offers for my paintings, I would rather do so, as it is infinitely preferable to stand foremost as one of the founders of a school of painting in an immense and growing country like America—in fact to be an object of national pride and affection—than to fall into the ranks in the crowded galleries of Europe, or perhaps be regarded with an eye of national prejudice, as the production of an American pencil is likely to be in England. I will not pretend at this moment to discuss the merits of your design for the proposed painting; I do not feel in the vein; but if, at a more cheerful moment, any idea suggests itself that I may think worth communicating, I will write to you.

I cannot express to you how much I have been pleased with the two designs for "Knickerbocker." The characters are admirably discriminated, the humor rich but chaste, and the expression peculiarly natural and appropriate. I scarcely know which figure in your picture to prefer; the constable is evidently drawn *con amore*, and derives additional spirit from standing in high relief opposed to the ineffable phlegm of old Wouter. Still, however, the leering exultation of the fortunate party is given to the very life, and is evident from top to toe—the bend of the knee, the play of the elbows, the swaying of the body, are all eloquent; and are finely contrasted with the attitude and look of little Schoonhoven. By the way, I must say the last figure has tickled me as much as any in the picture. But each has its peculiar merits, and is the *best* in its turn. The sketch by

Leslie is beautiful. The Dutch girl is managed with great sweetness and naïveté. The expression of her chin and mouth shows that she is not likely to break her lover's heart. The devoted leer of the lover's eye and the phlegmatic character of the lower part of his countenance, form a whimsical combination. The very cat is an important figure in the group, and touched off with proper expression ; a delicate humor pervades the whole ; the composition is graceful, and there is a rural air about it that is peculiarly pleasing.

I dwell on these little sketches because they give me quite a new train of ideas in respect to my work ; and I only wish I had it now to write, as I am sure I should conceive the scenes in a much purer style, having these pictures before me as correctives of the *grossièreté* into which the writer of a work of humor is apt to run. At any rate, it is an exquisite gratification to find that any thing I have written can present such pleasing images to imaginations like yours and Leslie's ; and I shall regard the work with more complacency, as having in a measure formed a link of association between our minds.

The lawsuit was an entirely imaginary incident, without any personal allusion, though by a whimsical coincidence there was a Barent Bleecker at Albany who had been comptroller ; and his family at first suspected an intention to asperse his official character. The suspicion, however, was but transient, and is forgotten ; so that the picture will awaken no hostility.

I had no idea, when I began this letter, that I should have filled the sheet ; but words beget words ; I shall write to you again before long, and will then endeavor to direct my attention to topics more immediately interesting to you. In the meanwhile give my most friendly remembrances to Leslie, and believe me truly yours,

WASHINGTON IRVING.

July 11th he writes to Brevoort, who kept urging his return :—

I have no intention of returning home for a year at least. I am waiting to extricate myself from the ruins of our unfortunate concern, after which I shall turn my back upon this scene of care and distress, and shall pass a considerable part of my time in London. I have a plan, which, with very little trouble, will yield me for the present a scanty but sufficient means of support, and leave me leisure to look around for something better. I cannot at present explain to you what it is. You would probably consider it precarious, and inadequate to my subsistence, but a small matter will float a drowning man.

The plan here hinted at was to make some arrangements with booksellers for the republication in America of choice English works, and to throw them into the hands of Moses Thomas, the Philadelphia publisher, at a stipulated compensation. It was a plan which could give him present subsistence, and enable him, in the meanwhile, to employ his pen, to which his thoughts now began to turn, though he kept it a secret even from Brevoort.

At this period of gloom and disaster he received from one whose name will recur hereafter the following animating and almost prophetic epistle. The writer had made the acquaintance of Mr. Irving in the United States, which he visited about the time of the completion of " Salmagundi," as a lecturer on eloquence and criticism, introducing a style of reading and speaking, traces of which, I have been told, remain to this day. He was the son of Dr. Ogilvie, the Scottish poet.

LONDON, July 22, 1817.

The intelligence, my dear Irving, of the misfortune you have sustained, has reached me, and as it may affect the prosperity and happiness of persons near and most dear to you, all my sympathy with your feelings was awakened.

So far, however, as you are individually concerned, I should deem the language of condolence a sort of mockery.

I am perfectly confident that even in two years you will look back on this seeming disaster as the most fortunate incident that has befallen you.

Yet in the flower of youth, in possession of higher literary reputation than any of your countrymen have hitherto claimed, esteemed and beloved by all to whom you are intimately or even casually known, you want nothing but a stimulus strong enough to overcome that indolence which, in a greater or less degree, besets every human being. This seemingly unfortunate incident will supply this stimulus—you will return with renovated ardor to the arena you have for a season abandoned, and in twelve months win trophies, for which, but for this incident, you would not even have contended.

At this moment, in your secret soul, you feel aspirations and reachings, which presage and guarantee the completion of all and more than all to which I look forward. . . . .

Believe me to be,

Yours most affectionately,

JAMES OGILVIE.

Soon after the receipt of this letter, Mr. Irving left Liverpool for London, where he arrived about the first of August, and spent three weeks during the summer heats. It was in this interval, as his memoranda show, that he made that ramble of observation, depicted in the " Sketch-Book," in which he was so sorely buffeted against the current of population setting through Fleet Street, and, in a movement of desperation, tore his way through the throng and plunged into a little narrow by-way, which led him through several nooks and angles, until he found himself in a court of the Temple. Of this period we have some further particulars of interest in the following passages of a letter to Brevoort, dated August 28th :—

I was in London for about three weeks, when the town was quite deserted. I found, however, sufficient objects of curiosity and interest to keep me in a worry; and amused myself by exploring various parts of the city, which in the dirt and gloom of winter would be almost inaccessible.

I passed a day with Campbell at Sydenham. He is still simmering over his biographical and critical labors, and has promised to forward more letter-press to you. He says he will bring it out the coming autumn. He has now been teasing his brain with this cursed work about seven years—a most lamentable waste of time and poetic talent.

Campbell seems to have an inclination to pay America a visit, having a great desire to see the country, and to visit his brother, whom he has not seen for many years. The expense, however, is a complete obstacle. I think he might easily be induced to cross the seas; and his visit made a very advantageous one to our country. He has twelve lectures written out on poetry and belles-lettres, which he has delivered with great applause to the most brilliant London audiences. I believe you have heard one or two of them. They are highly spoken of by the best judges. Now, could not subscription lists be set on foot in New York and Philadelphia, among the first classes of people, for a course of lectures in each city; and when a sufficient number of names is procured to make it an object, the lists sent to Campbell with an invitation to come over and deliver the lectures? It would be highly complimentary to him—would at once remove all pecuniary difficulties ; and, if he accepted the invitation, his lectures would have a great effect in giving an impulse to American literature, and a proper direction to the public taste. Say the subscription was ten dollars for the course of lectures. I should think it an easy matter to fill up a large list at that rate ; for how many are there in New York, who would give that sum to hear a course of lectures on belles-lettres, from one of the first poets of Great Britain! I sounded Campbell on the subject, and have no doubt that he would accept such an invitation. Speak to Renwick on the subject, and if you will take it in hand I am sure it will succeed. Charles King would, no doubt, promote a thing of the kind; and Dr. Hosack would be delighted to give his assistance, and would be a most efficient aid. . . . . I saw two or three of the Lions of the *Quarterly Review* in Murray's Den; but almost all of the literary people are out of town; and those that have not the means of travelling, lurk in their garrets, and affect to be in the country; for you know these poor devils have a great desire to be thought fashionable.

The proposition here suggested in Campbell's behalf was taken up in America, but afterward discouraged by himself, he pleading that he was too old.

The following letter gives an account of a dinner at Murray's, and has allusion to his project of procuring works for republication in America, with glimpses of Scott, Campbell, and D'Israeli, the author of the "Curiosities of Literature" and other works which had a great currency in the United States. "King Stephen" is Stephen Price, the manager of the Park Theatre in New York, and the "Dusky Davy" is Longworth, the publisher of "Salmagundi," and who at this time aspired to a monopoly in the publication of plays. "Mishter Miller" is the London bookseller who preceded Murray in the publication of the "Sketch-Book."

[*To Peter Irving, Esq.*]

LONDON, August 19, 1817.

MY DEAR BROTHER:—

I have yours of the 17th. I received likewise the parcel, which contained a letter from Brevoort and one from Mrs. Bradish. I enclose Brevoort's to you.

I had a very pleasant dinner at Murray's. I met there with D'Israeli, and an artist, just returned from Italy with an immense number of beautiful sketches of Italian scenery and architecture.

D'Israeli's wife and daughter came in, in the course of the evening, and we did not adjourn until twelve o'clock. I had a long tête-à-tête with old D'Israeli in a corner. He is a very pleasant, cheerful old fellow; curious about America, and evidently tickled at the circulation his works have had there ; though, like most authors just now, he groans at not being able to participate in the profits.   Murray was very merry and loquacious.   He showed me a long letter from Lord Byron, who is in Italy.   It is written with some flippancy, and is an odd jumble.   His lordship has written 104 stanzas of the 4th canto.   He says it will be less metaphysical than the last canto, but thinks it will be at least equal to either of the preceding.   Murray left town yesterday for some watering-place, so that I had no further talk with him ; but am to keep my eye on his advertisements, and write to him when any thing offers that I may think worth republishing in America.   I shall find him a most valuable acquaintance on my return to London.

I called at Longman & Co.'s, according to appointment, and saw Mr. Orme.   They are not disposed, however, to make any arrangement.   They have been repeatedly disappointed in experiments of the kind, and are determined not to trouble their thoughts any more on the subject.   They had just received letters from America on the subject of Moore's poem, " Lalla Rookh," which they had sent out either in MSS. or sheets ; but there were two or three rival editions in the market, which would prevent any profits of consequence.

They intimated that they would be willing to give an advantage in respect to the republication of new works, for any moderate price in cash ; but they would not perplex and worry themselves with any further arrangements, which were only troublesome and profitless.   They intimated, for instance, a disposition to sell an early copy of " Rob Roy " for a small sum in hand.   But as I knew they had not yet received the MSS. of that work, I did not make any offer.   It will be time enough by and by.   I find it is pretty generally believed that Scott is the author of those novels, and Verplanck[1] tells me he is now travelling about, collecting materials for " Rob Roy."   I see that there will be a great advantage in being here on the spot during the literary seasons, with funds to make purchases from either authors or booksellers.   They consider the chance of participation in American republication so very slender and contingent, that they will accept any sum in hand, as so much money found.   I have written to Thomas, advising him to remit funds to me for the purpose ; if he does so, I will be able to throw many choice works into his hands.

Mishter Miller is full of the project of going out to New York, to set up an establishment there.   He thinks he will have an advantage in publishing plays, from his interest with the theatres here, which will enable him to get MSS. copies, and the countenance of King Stephen, which has

---

[1] Gulian C. Verplanck, who was then travelling in Europe.

been promised him. He talks of embarking in September or October, should he be able to make his arrangements in time. He must beware the "Dusky Davy."

In some notes of this dinner at Murray's, which came off August 16th, I find this record : " Lord Byron told Murray that he was much happier after breaking with Lady Byron—he hated this still quiet life."

CHAPTER XXI.

THE following letter from Mr. Irving is dated Edinburgh,
August 26, 1817; to which place he had gone, as well for
pleasure as with some views to future plans. After giving to his
brother Peter, to whom it is addressed, some account of his fellow-
passengers on board the smack *Lively* for Berwick, in which he
had embarked, he proceeds :—

The first two days of our voyage were unfavorable ; we had rain and
head wind, and had to anchor whenever the tide turned. But Saturday,
though calm, was beautiful, with a bright sunny afternoon and a bright
moon at night. On Sunday we had a glorious breeze, and dashed bravely
through the water. I have always fine health and fine spirits at sea, and
enjoyed the latter part of this little voyage excessively. On Monday
morning we came in sight of the coast of Northumberland, which at first
was wrapped in mist ; but as it cleared away, we saw Dunstanborough
Castle at a distance ; and some time after, we passed in full view of
Bamborough Castle, which stands in bleak and savage grandeur on the sea-
coast. You may recollect these places, mentioned in the course of the
Abbess of Hilda's voyage in " Marmion " :—

> " And next they crossed themselves to hear
> The whitening breakers sound so near,
> Where boiling through the rocks they roar
> On Dunstanborough's caverned shore.
> Thy tower, proud Bamborough, marked they there ;
> King Ida's castle, huge and square,
> From its tall rock look grimly down
> And on the swelling ocean frown."

We next skirted the Holy Isle, which was the scene of Constance de Beverly's trial, and where the remains of the Monastery of St. Cuthbert are still visible, though apparently converted into some humbler purposes, as a residence of people that attend the beacons. To make a long story short, however, about twelve o'clock I landed at Berwick. I had intended proceeding from thence to Kelso, and so to Melrose, etc.; but I found there would be no coach in that direction until Wednesday; so I determined to come to Edinburgh direct, and visit Melrose from thence. After walking about Berwick, therefore, and surveying its old bridge, walls, etc., I mounted a coach and rattled off through the rich scenes of Lothian to this place, where I arrived late last night.

I got the parcel from you this morning; but neither Mrs. Fletcher nor Mr. Erskine are in town. I left a card for Jeffrey, whose family is three miles out of town. His brother called on me about an hour afterward, but I was not at home. Edinburgh is perfectly deserted, so that I shall merely have to look at the buildings, streets, etc., and then be off. I am enchanted with the general appearance of the place. It far surpasses all my expectations; and, except Naples, is, I think, the most picturesque place I have ever seen.

I dined to-day with Mr. Jeffrey, Mrs. Renwick's brother. He informs me that Mrs. Fletcher is in Selkirkshire, but that the family is rather secluded, having lost one of the young ladies about three months since by a typhus fever. I did not learn which it was. Mrs. Grant is likewise in the Highlands.

Walter Scott is at Abbotsford; busy, it is supposed, about "Rob Roy," having lately been travelling for scenery, etc. They told me at Constable's that it will be out in October, though others say not until toward Christmas. As it will probably be some days before Preston reaches here, I do not know but I shall make excursion to Melrose, and make an attempt on Walter Scott's quarters, so as to be back in time to accompany Preston to the Highlands. I have a very particular letter to Scott from Campbell. . . . .

August 27th.—A gloomy morning, with a steady, pitiless rain. What a contrast to the splendor of yesterday, which was a warm day, with now and then a very light shower, and an atmosphere loaded with rich clouds through which the sunshine fell in broad masses; giving an endless diversity of light and shadow to the grand romantic features of this town. It seemed as if the rock and castle assumed a new aspect every time I looked at them; and Arthur's Seat was perfect witchcraft. I don't wonder that any one residing in Edinburgh should write poetically; I rambled about the bridges and on Calton height yesterday, in a perfect intoxication of the mind. I did not visit a single public building, but merely gazed and revelled on the romantic scenery around me. The enjoyment of yesterday alone would be a sufficient compensation for the whole journey.

There is nobody in Edinburgh, and I shall merely remain here as a headquarters whence to make two or three excursions about the neighborhood. I think it probable I shall leave this by the 4th of next month.

Your affectionate Brother,

W. I.

Half-past one.—Jeffrey has just called on me. I am to dine with him to-day *en famille*, and also to-morrow, when I shall meet Dugald Stewart and Madame La Voissier, whilom the Countess De Rumford. Jeffrey tells me I am lucky in meeting with Dugald Stewart, as he does not come to Edinburgh above once in a month.

P. S.—As I was too late for the mail yesterday, I have reopened this letter, merely to add a word or two more.

I walked out to Jeffrey's castle yesterday with his brother, John Jeffrey, and had a very pleasant dinner. I found Jeffrey extremely friendly and agreeable; indeed, I could not have wished a more cordial reception and treatment. He has taken an ancient castellated mansion on a lease of thirty-two years, and made some alterations and additions, so that it is quite comfortable and even elegant within, and is highly picturesque without. Jeffrey inquired particularly after you. He offered me a letter to Scott; but as Campbell's is very particular, I thought it would be sufficient. He is to mark out a route for me in the Highlands. I expect to be much gratified by my dinner there to-day. I find in addition to the persons already mentioned, we are to have Sir Humphrey Davy's lady, who was formerly Miss Aprecce, and a *belle esprit.* . . . .

The weather is still sulky and threatening. If it is fine to-morrow, I shall probably be off for Melrose.

[*To Peter Irving.*]

ABBOTSFORD, September 1, 1817.

MY DEAR BROTHER :—

I have barely time to scrawl a line before the *gossoon* goes off with the letters to the neighboring post-office.

I was disappointed in my expectation of meeting with Dugald Stewart at Mr. Jeffrey's; some circumstance prevented his coming, though we had Mrs. and Miss Stewart. The party, however, was very agreeable and interesting. Lady Davy was in excellent spirits, and talked like an angel. In the evening, when we collected in the drawing-room, she held forth for upward of an hour; the company drew round her and seemed to listen in

mute pleasure; even Jeffrey seemed to keep his colloquial powers in check to give her full chance. She reminded me of the picture of the Minister Bird with all the birds of the forest perched on the surrounding branches in listening attitudes. I met there with Lord Webb Seymour, brother to the Duke of Somerset. He is almost a constant resident of Edinburgh. He was very attentive to me; wrote down a route for me in the Highlands, and called on me the next morning, when he detailed the route more particularly. I have promised to see him when I return to Edinburgh, which promise I shall keep, as I like him much.

On Friday, in spite of sullen, gloomy weather, I mounted the top of the mail-coach, and rattled off to Selkirk. It rained heavily in the course of the afternoon, and drove me inside. On Saturday morning early I took chaise for Melrose; and on the way stopped at the gate of Abbotsford, and sent in my letter of introduction, with a request to know whether it would be agreeable for Mr Scott to receive a visit from me in the course of the day. The glorious old minstrel himself came limping to the gate, took me by the hand in a way that made me feel as if we were old friends; in a moment I was seated at his hospitable board among his charming little family, and here have I been ever since. I had intended certainly being back to Edinburgh to-day (Monday), but Mr. Scott wishes me to stay until Wednesday, that we may make excursions to Dryburgh Abbey, Yarrow, etc., as the weather has held up and the sun begins to shine. I cannot tell you how truly I have enjoyed the hours I have passed here. They fly by too quick, yet each is loaded with story, incident, or song; and when I consider the world of ideas, images, and impressions that have been crowded upon my mind since I have been here, it seems incredible that I should only have been two days at Abbotsford. I have rambled about the hills with Scott; visited the haunts of Thomas the Rhymer, and other spots rendered classic by border tale and witching song, and have been in a kind of dream or delirium.

As to Scott, I cannot express my delight at his character and manners. He is a sterling golden-hearted old worthy, full of the joyousness of youth, with an imagination continually furnishing forth picture, and a charming simplicity of manner that puts you at ease with him in a moment. It has been a constant source of pleasure to me to remark his deportment toward his family, his neighbors, his domestics, his very dogs and cats; every thing that comes within his influence seems to catch a beam of that sunshine that plays round his heart; but I shall say more of him hereafter, for he is a theme on which I shall love to dwell.

Before I left Edinburgh I saw Blackwood in his shop. It was accidental—my conversing with him. He found out who I was; is extremely anxious to make an American arrangement; wishes to get me to write for his magazine (the *Edinburgh Monthly*). Wishes to introduce me to Mackenzie, Wilson, etc. Constable called on me just before I left town. He had been in the country and just returned. He was very friendly in his manner. Lord Webb Seymour's coming in interrupted us, and Constable took leave. I promised to see him on my return to Edinburgh. He is about regenerating the old *Edinburgh Magazine*, and has got Blackwood's editors away from him in consequence of some feud they had with him. . . . .

Commend me to Hamilton. I hope to hear from him soon, and shall write to him again.

Your affectionate brother,

W. I.

P. S.—This morning we ride to Dryburgh Abbey, and see also the old Earl of Buchan—who, you know, is a queer one.

[*To the same.*]

EDINBURGH, September 6, 1817.

MY DEAR BROTHER:—

. . . . I left Abbotsford on Wednesday morning, and never left any place with more regret. The few days that I passed there were among the most delightful of my life, and worth as many years of ordinary existence. We made a charming excursion to Dryburgh Abbey, but were prevented making our visit to Yarrow by company. I was with Scott from morning to night; rambling about the hills and streams, every one of which would bring to his mind some old tale or picturesque remark. I was charmed with his family. He has two sons and two daughters. Sophie Scott, the eldest, is between seventeen and eighteen, a fine little mountain lassie, with a great deal of her father's character; and the most engaging frankness and naïveté. Ann, the second daughter, is about sixteen; a pleasing girl, but her manner is not so formed as her sister. The oldest lad, Walter, is about fifteen; but surprisingly tall of his age, having the appearance of nineteen. He is quite a sportsman. Scott says he has taught him to ride, to shoot, and to tell the truth. The younger boy, Charles, however, is the inheritor of his father's genius; he is about twelve, and an uncommonly sprightly amusing little fellow. It is a perfect picture to see Scott and his household assembled of an evening—the dogs stretched before the fire; the cat perched on a chair; Mrs. Scott and the girls sewing; and Scott either reading out of some old romance, or telling border stories. Our amusements were occasionally diversified by a border song from Sophia, who is as well versed in border minstrelsy as her father.

I am in too great a hurry, however, to make details. I took the most friendly farewell of them all on Wednesday morning, and had a cordial invitation from Scott to give him another visit on my return from the Highlands; which, I think it probable, I shall do.

I found Preston here on my arrival; he had been in Edinburgh for three days. We shall set off for the Highlands to-morrow. Scott has given me a letter to Hector Macdonald Buchanan of Ross Priory, Loch Lomond, with a request for him to give me a day on the lake. This Macdonald is a fine fellow, I understand, and a particular friend of Scott. He took Scott up the lake lately in his barge, when Scott visited Loch Lomond, so I shall be able to trace Scott in his Rob Roy scenery.

We dined yesterday with Constable, and met Professor Leslie there; with whom I was somewhat pleased, and more amused.

I have arranged with Constable, greatly to my satisfaction in respect to books, etc., and shall be enabled to forward " Rob Roy " in time to secure the first publication to Thomas.

I have also made an arrangement with Blackwood.

I shall return to Edinburgh after my visit to the Highlands, and stop here a day or two ; so you may address letters to me here—MacGregor's.

I received a very pleasant letter from Hamilton, for which give him my thanks, and assure him I will answer it the first leisure moment.

Affectionately your brother,

W. I.

[*To the same.*]

EDINBURGH, September 20, 1817.

MY DEAR BROTHER :—

I arrived here late last evening after one of the most delightful excursions I ever made. We have had continual good weather, and weather of the most remarkable kind for the season—warm, genial, serene sunshine. We have journeyed in every variety of mode—by chaise, by coach, by gig, by boat, on foot, and in a cart ; and have visited some of the most remarkable and beautiful scenes in Scotland. The journey has been a complete trial of Preston's indolent habits. I had at first to tow him along by main strength, for he has as much alacrity at coming to anchor, and is as slow getting under way, as a Dutch lugger. The grand difficulty was to get him up in the morning ; however, by dint of perseverance, I at last succeeded in rousing him from his lair at six o'clock, and making him pad the hoof often, from morning till night. The early part of the route he complained sadly, and fretted occasionally; but as he proceeded, he grew into condition and spirits, went through the latter part in fine style, and I brought him into Edinburgh in perfect order for the turf. . . . . .

I must hasten to conclude this letter; this is Saturday, and I wish to arrange what I have to do in this place this morning, that I may leave it, if possible, on Monday morning. I intend to pay another visit to Abbotsford; I could not leave Scotland with a quiet conscience, if I did not have one more *crack* with the prince of minstrels, and pass a few more happy hours with his charming family. I want to set out another evening there; Scott reading, occasionally, from " Prince Arthur"; telling border stories or characteristic anecdotes; Sophy Scott singing with charming naïveté a little border song; the rest of the family disposed in listening groups, while greyhounds, spaniels, and cats bask in unbounded indulgence before the fire. Every thing around Scott is perfect character and picture.

On my return to Edinburgh, I found a most friendly note from Jeffrey, dated some time back, inviting me to dinner on the day after, to meet again Lady Davy and Sir Humphrey; or three days after to meet Dr. Mason of New York. I am too late for either party.

In a note in his " Life of Scott," Lockhart gives the minstrel's impression of his American visitor, which I quote :—

There is in my hand a letter from Scott to his friend John Richardson, dated 22d September, 1817, in which he says: "When you see Tom Campbell, tell him with my best love, that I have to thank him for making me known to Mr. Washington Irving, who is one of the best and pleasantest acquaintances I have made this many a day."

Though William had failed to obtain for Washington the Secretaryship of Legation, his situation continued to engage his mind ; for early in December I find him writing to Ebenezer, from the seat of government :—

I have not been inattentive to the situation of brothers Washington and Peter. I have had two conversations with Clay on the subject. He stands ready to aid in any thing that can be suggested. . . . . You may rest assured that I will do my best. I need no pressing on that head, for my mind is full of the subject. I think on it night and day.

The author, however, was shaping his course for himself; and we have, in the following extract of a letter to his brother William, the first indistinct intimation of his intention to make a business of literature.

LIVERPOOL., December 23, 1817.

. . . . Ebenezer tells me you have been exerting yourself to get me appointed to the Secretaryship of Legation at the Court of St. James, but without success ; but that you hoped to get some other appointment for me. I feel in this as in many other things deeply indebted to your affectionate care for my interests ; but I do not anticipate any favors from government, which has so many zealous and active partisans to serve ; and I should not like to have my name hackneyed about among the office-seekers and office-givers at Washington.

For my own part, I require very little for my support, and hope to be able to make that little by my own exertions. I have led comparatively such a lonely life for the greater part of the time that I have been in England, that my habits and notions are very much changed. For a long while past, I have lived almost entirely at home ; sometimes not leaving the house for two or three days, and yet I have not had an hour pass heavily ; so that if I could but see my brothers around me prospering, and be relieved from this cloud that hangs over us all, I feel as if I would be contented to give up all the gayeties of life. I certainly think that no hope of gain, however flattering, would tempt me again into the cares and sordid concerns of traffic. . . . .

I have been urged by several of my friends to return home immediately ; their advice is given on vague and general ideas that it would be to my advantage. My mind is made up to remain a little longer in Europe, for definite, and, I trust, advantageous purposes, and such as ultimately point to my return to America, where all my views and wishes, my ambition and my affections are centred. I give you this general assurance, which, I trust, will be received with confidence, and save the necessity of particular explanations, which it would be irksome for me to make. I feel that my future career must depend very much upon myself, and therefore every step I take at present is done with proper consideration. In protracting my stay in Europe I certainly do not contemplate pleasure, for I look forward to a life of loneliness and of parsimonious and almost painful economy.

CHAPTER XXII.

Bankruptcy.—Studies German.—Letter from Allston, Giving Account of his New Subject for "Knickerbocker."—His "Angel Uriel."—Leslie's Opinion of it.—Letter from Allston.—Lord Egremont's Purchase of his "Jacob's Dream."—Letter to Leslie.—Goes up to London to Try his Pen.— Parting with Allston.—Letter to Ebenezer about New Edition of "Knickerbocker."—No Intention of Publishing in England.—Declines an Offer of a Place under Government.

One of Hendrick Hudson's Crew.

IN the beginning of the year 1818, after vain and harassing attempts to compromise with their creditors, Peter and Washington made up their minds, as the surest mode of perfect extrication, to take the benefit of the Bankrupt Act. It was a humiliating ordeal to go through for two proud-spirited men ; and especially for Washington, who was a mere nominal party in the concern. Their first meeting before the Commissioners of Bankruptcy took place on the 27th of January, and their last on the 14th of March. At this time Washington had shut himself up from society and was studying German, day and night, in the double hope that it would be of service to him, and tend to keep off uncomfortable thoughts. Three days after he received from Allston the following letter, which gives the artist's own notion of a new comic subject he had chosen for illustration, designed for a third edition of Knickerbocker's "History of New York," with other particulars of interest respecting himself :—

190

LONDON, March 13, 1818.

MY DEAR IRVING:—

I received yours of the 5th, and have the pleasure to inform you that the drawing is finished, and now in the hands of the engraver; to whom I gave it (since you were so good as to rely on my judgment) as soon as it was finished. I gave up the subject which Leslie mentioned, and chose another with which I am much better pleased, namely, a Schepen doing *duty* to a Burgomaster's joke.

Leslie agrees with me in thinking it superior to the lawsuit. Indeed, so far as I can judge of my own work, it is one of my happiest comic efforts, if not the best. It contains six figures. I think no one could fail to see that the Burgomaster is bringing forth a joke; for the action is so contrived as to leave no doubt of it. The Schepen, who sits opposite to him, is laughing with all his might and main; while the rest of the company, who have nothing to gain by a laugh, are impenetrably and most Dutchly grave. But I think I had better not describe it. Descriptions of pictures are generally flat. Besides, their impression is always better, at least truer, when they come upon us without preparation. So the less said the better.

The plate after Leslie's [1] is finished, and I think you will be very much pleased with it. It makes a very beautiful print; is extremely well engraved: but what particularly pleases me in it, is the close rendering of the characters, which is the most important part in subjects of this kind. If the engraver preserves mine as well, I shall be amply satisfied. I hope the time the engraver demands for graving my drawing will not inconveniently affect your plans. His engagements, he says, are so pressing, just at this time, that he could not possibly promise it sooner than four months hence.

The price, also, is considerably higher than for Leslie's, [2] being from thirty-five to forty guineas. If he can do it for thirty-five, he says, he will: but he will not limit himself to less than forty, nor be bound to five-and-thirty.

The reason he gives for demanding so much more is the greater number of the figures and the quantity of detail. I was a little at a stand when I heard this; but knowing no other engraver of his abilities that works so cheap, I concluded it must be done by him even at this rate. Do let me know by return of post if you approve of what I have done.

Since my return from Paris I have painted two pictures, in order to have something in the present exhibition at the British Gallery; the subjects: the angel Uriel in the sun, and Elijah in the wilderness. " Uriel "

[1] The allusion is to Leslie's sketch of the Dutch courtship.
[2] Leslie's was twenty-five guineas.

was immediately purchased (at the price I asked, one hundred and fifty guineas) by the Marquis of Stafford, and the Directors of the British Institution, moreover, presented me a *donation* of a hundred and fifty pounds, "as a mark of their *approbation* of the talent evinced," etc. The manner in which this was done was highly complimentary; and I can only say that it was full as gratifying as it was unexpected. As both these pictures together cost me but ten weeks, I do not regret having deducted that time from the "Belshazzar," to whom I have since returned with redoubled vigor.

I am almost sorry I did not exhibit "Jacob's Dream." If I had dreamt of this success, I certainly would have sent it there.

I hope your affairs are being settled to your mind, and that we shall see you here soon.

Yours affectionately,

WASHINGTON ALLSTON.

Ogilvie has returned full of health and spirits from his success in Scotland. He has overcome his formidable enemy laudanum, and looks like another being. Leslie begs to be remembered.

Of the picture which received this emphatic approbation from the Directors of the British Institution, Leslie had before written to Mr. Irving this opinion :—

Allston has just finished a very grand and poetical figure of the angel Uriel sitting in the sun. The figure is colossal, the attitude and air very noble, and the form heroic without being overcharged. In the color he has been equally successful, and with a very rich and glowing tone he has avoided *positive* colors, which would have made him too material. There is neither red, blue, nor yellow in the picture, and yet it possesses a harmony equal to the best pictures of Paul Veronese.

Mr. Irving was at Birmingham when he received from Allston the following reply to a letter on the subject of a plate for the "Knickerbocker" engraving. It is the last letter of Allston which I find among his papers, and concludes with the saddening announcement to his correspondent that he had taken his passage for America.

LONDON, July 24, 1818.

MY DEAR IRVING :—

You are so accustomed to my apologies for epistolary delinquency that they must be to you like old stories; so I had better say nothing about it. Leslie, I believe, has already written to you on the subject of the plate. I called on the engraver soon after the receipt of your letter, and was more grieved than surprised that it was not already finished; for I know the press of his engagements, and remembered the difficulty he had in fixing on the time of its completion, when I first put it into his hands. I would have strained a point to scold about it, if I had thought that would have mended the matter. But as it would not, I could only urge the importance of its speedy termination in the strongest way, and leave the rest to the engraver, who then promised to finish it as soon as it was in his power, and he has since engaged to produce a proof in the course of the next week. He begged that I would not insist on seeing the plate, as he never liked to show his works in an unfinished state. As that is also the case with myself, I did not urge it. But I have no doubt, from the ability he has shown in other works, that it will be well done. If it is equal to that he did from Leslie's drawing, I shall be more than satisfied. As soon as I see a proof I will write you.

Now that you are your own master again, your Muse, I suppose, has already paid you a visit. Pray do not turn your back upon her, for I have it on the testimony of thousands that she has not a greater favorite than yourself in all Parnassus. Do tell me what you are doing, or mean to do. Your imagination has been so long fallow that I anticipate a most luxurious harvest when you again cultivate it.

Leslie tells me he has informed you of the sale of "Jacob's Dream." I do not remember if you have seen it. The manner in which Lord Egremont bought it was particularly gratifying—to say nothing of the price, which is no trifle to me at present. But Leslie having told you all about it, I will not repeat it. Indeed, by the account he gives me of his letter to you, he seems to have puffed me off in grand style. Well, you know I don't bribe him to do it. And "if they will buckle praise upon my back," why, I can't help it.

Leslie has just finished a very beautiful little picture of Anne Page inviting Master Slender into the house. Anne is exquisite; soft and feminine, yet arch and playful,—she is all she should be. Slender, also, is very happy; he is a good parody on Milton's "linked sweetness long drawn out." Falstaff and Shallow are seen through a window in the background. The whole scene is very picturesque, and beautifully painted. 'T is his best picture. You must not think this praise the "return in kind." I give it because I really admire the picture, and I have not the smallest doubt that he will do great things when he is once freed from the necessity of painting portraits.

Believe me affectionately yours,

W. ALLSTON.

I suppose Leslie has told you that the price of printing your plates would be five pounds a thousand—and that on French paper, which is the best; this includes paper. As I shall leave my lodgings in a short time, pray direct to me to " the care of Samuel Williams, Esq., No. 13 Finsbury Square." Lord Egremont has invited me to his seat at Petworth, and I shall go down there next week. I have taken my passage in the *Galen* from this port. Shall not I see you here before I go? She sails about the 10th of August.

A few days after the receipt of this letter, Mr. Irving writes as follows to Leslie :—

BIRMINGHAM, July 29, 1818.

MY DEAR SIR :—

I thank you for your letter and for the information it contains. I have since received one from Allston; but as he will probably be out of town about this time, I must trouble you instead of him. I wish the plates put in the printer's hands as soon as possible, and to be executed on the best paper. *Two thousand of each.* I should like, also, to have three hundred proof impressions of each struck off in such a manner that they would do to frame should any persons like to have them in that manner; if not they can hereafter be cut down to the size of the volume. You and Allston will have as many struck off for yourselves as you please. Let me know the whole expense, and I will send the money immediately. I have had my trunk packed to come to London, and should have attended to all this myself, but one circumstance or other occurs to baffle my plans, and I am at this moment in a little uncertainty when I shall get there. I shall try hard to see Allston before he sails; had he been going to embark at Liverpool the thing would have been certain. I regret exceedingly that he goes to America, now that his prospects are opening so promisingly in this country; but perhaps it is all for the best. His " Jacob's Dream " was a particular favorite of mine. I have gazed on it again and again, and the more I gazed the more I was delighted with it. I believe if I was a painter I could at this moment take a pencil and delineate the whole with the attitude and expression of every figure.

Allston gives me a charming account of your picture of Anne Page and Master Slender. I hope you will take frequent opportunities to steal away from the painting of portraits to give full scope to your taste and imagination.

About the middle of August Mr. Irving went up to London and cast himself upon the world, determined to seek support from his pen.   He had brought with him some unfinished sketches upon which he had been engaged, and which he had hoped to work up, but the very foreboding of his mind seemed to unfit it for composition.

He had been but two weeks in London when he was called to the hard trial of parting with Allston.   On first arriving in London he heard from Leslie that Allston was dining with Coleridge at High-gate, and he went out there to meet him, and tried in vain to dissuade him from returning by urging he could do better where he was.   Until informed of his intention to embark for America he had been looking forward with delight to a meeting with him and Leslie, and to an exchange of the hard and painful life he had been leading for one of intercourse with them.   " As he drove off in the stage and waved his hand to me," said Mr. Irving, in adverting to his parting, " my heart sank within me, and I returned gloomy and dispirited to my lodgings."   At another time he said of Allston to me :—

He was the most delightful, the most lovable being I ever knew ; a man I would like to have had always at my side—to have gone through life with ; his nature was so refined, so intellectual, so genial, so pure.

But though he felt deeply the departure of Allston, he could still hope for sympathy and companionship from Leslie and Newton. Leslie he had known as a boy, when he was attracting attention at Philadelphia by his likeness of Cooke, the actor, and he had met him since during his transient visits to London ; but their intimacy dates from the period of his present sojourning in the English capital.   Leslie writes to him more than two years afterward :—

You came to London just when I was losing Allston, and I stood in need of an intimate friend of similar tastes with my own.   I not only owe to you some of the happiest social hours of my life, but you opened to me a new range of observation in my art, and a perception of qualities and characters of things which painters do not always imbibe from each other.

Stuart Newton he now met for the first time.   He was the nephew of Gilbert Stuart, so well known for his celebrated portrait of Washington, and Leslie had met him the preceding year at Paris on his way from Italy to London.

About two months after he came up to London, October 13th, he writes to Ebenezer :—

> I have forwarded to your care a parcel containing plates for the new edition of the " History of New York," which I will thank you to forward safely and without delay to Mr. Thomas, as I wish the work to be printed as soon as possible. There are but two plates, one for each volume; but they are charming little things by Allston and Leslie, and are engraved in the best style. The engraving and printing of them have cost me about one hundred pounds sterling.

He had no purpose, as will be seen from this extract, of publishing the " History of New York " in England ; nor had he any views of that kind in preparing the " Sketch-Book," upon which he was now engaged. The postscript to the letter would seem to be in reply to some inquiry of his brother, and has a melancholy significance.

> As to the sealed packet, which I left with you, it may be destroyed. I have nothing now to leave my brothers but a blessing, and that they have whenever I think of them.

It was at this period that he received a letter from his brother William, informing him that his old friend, Decatur, was keeping a place open for him in the Navy Board ; that it was then in waiting for his answer, and would make him as independent and comfortable as he could wish.

> Commodore Decatur informs me (says the letter of October 24th) that he had made such arrangements, and such steps would further be made by the Navy Board, as that you will be able to obtain the office of first clerk in the Navy Department, which is similar to that of under-secretary in England. The salary is equal to $2,400 per annum, which, as the Commodore says, is sufficient to enable you to live in Washington like a prince. The Secretary of the Navy has resigned, and as harmony in that department is wished, the President desires that the new one may meet with their approbation. They have been looking round for a suitable person, and they are resolved to make it a *sine qua non* with him, whoever he may be, that the present chief clerk, who has rendered himself peculiarly obnoxious to all the fine spirits of the Navy, shall be dismissed ; and they have determined to secure the berth for you, until your answer can be

obtained. It is a berth highly respectable—very comfortable in its income, light in its duties, and will afford you a very ample leisure to pursue the bent of your literary inclination. It may also be a mere stepping-stone to higher station, or may be considered at any rate permanent.

To the great chagrin of his brothers, William and Ebenezer, and contrary to their expectations, Washington declined this offer.

Flattering as the prospect undoubtedly is which your letters hold out (he writes to Ebenezer), I have concluded to decline it for various reasons, some of which I have stated to William. [This letter never came to hand, or has been lost.] The principal one is, that I do not wish to undertake any situation that must involve me in such a routine of duties as to prevent my attending to literary pursuits.

It was not without many misgivings that he brought himself to decline a certainty on such vague grounds ; and I have heard him say, that he was so disturbed by the responsibility he had taken in refusing such a situation, and trusting to the uncertain chances of literary success, that for two months he could scarcely write a line.

His declining was a sad disappointment to his brother William, especially as Peter had also made up his mind to remain abroad, and, as he expressed it, " battle the watch for himself." " Home," writes this brother to Ebenezer, " has lost its charms to both the Doctor and Washington. It is as well to accommodate the heart to its loss, and to consider them, as to all but epistolary correspond-ence, dead to us." So far as William was concerned, this sentence was indeed prophetic. His health was already failing ; but he lived long enough to witness, with the deepest emotions of pride and delight, the brilliant success of the " Sketch-Book."

CHAPTER XXIII.

IN the beginning of this year Washington was joined by Peter, who had been detained at Liverpool and Birmingham, and who left soon after for Bordeaux on confidential business for a house of high standing in London, while William was pressing him at home for an appointment of importance and handsome emolument under the treaty with Spain for settling claims. Meanwhile, Washington was preparing to launch the first number of the " Sketch-Book."

The letter in which he transmits the manuscript to his brother Ebenezer, and the contents of which he requests him to keep to himself as " babblings only fit for a brother's eye," is characteristic and full of interest. It bears date London, March 3, 1819.

I have sent (he writes) by Capt. Merry of the *Rosalie* the first number of a work which I hope to be able to continue from time to time. I send it more for the purpose of showing you what I am about, as I find my declining the situation at Washington has given you chagrin. The fact is, that situation would have given me barely a genteel subsistence. It would have led to no higher situations, for I am quite unfitted for political life.

My talents are merely literary, and all my habits of thinking, reading, etc., have been in a different direction from that required for the active politician. It is a mistake also to suppose I would fill an office there, and devote myself at the same time to literature. I require much leisure and a mind entirely abstracted from other cares and occupations, if I would write much or write well. I should therefore at Washington be completely out of my element, and instead of adding to my reputation, stand a chance of impairing that which I already possess. If I ever get any solid credit with the public, it must be in the quiet and assiduous operations of my pen, under the mere guidance of fancy or feeling.

I have been for some time past nursing my mind up for literary operations, and collecting materials for the purpose. I shall be able, I trust, now to produce articles from time to time that will be sufficient for my present support, and form a stock of copyright property that may be a little capital for me hereafter. To carry this into better effect it is important for me to remain a little longer in Europe, where there is so much food for observation, and objects of taste on which to meditate and improve. I feel myself completely committed in literary reputation by what I have already written ; and I feel by no means satisfied to rest my reputation on my preceding writings. I have suffered several precious years of youth and lively imagination to pass by unimproved, and it behooves me to make the most of what is left. If I indeed have the means within me of establishing a legitimate literary reputation, this is the very period of life most auspicious for it, and I am resolved to devote a few years exclusively to the attempt. Should I succeed, besides the literary property I shall amass in copyright, I trust it will not be difficult to obtain some official situation of a moderate, unpretending kind, in which I may make my bread. But as to reputation, I can only look for it through the exertions of my pen. . . . .

In fact, I consider myself at present as making a literary experiment, in the course of which I only care to be kept in bread and cheese. Should it not succeed—should my writings not acquire critical applause, I am content to throw up the pen and take to any commonplace employment. But if they should succeed, it would repay me for a world of care and privation to be placed among the estalished authors of my country, and to win the affections of my countrymen.

. . . . I have but one thing to add. I have now given you the leading motive of my actions—it may be a weak one, but it has full possession of me, and therefore the attainment of it is necessary to my comfort. I now wish to be left for a little while entirely to the bent of my own inclination, and not agitated by new plans for subsistence, or by entreaties to come home. My spirits are very unequal, and my mind depends upon them ; and I am easily thrown into such a state of perplexity and such depression as to incapacitate me for any mental exertion. Do not, I beseech you, impute my lingering in Europe to any indifference to my own country or my friends. My greatest desire is to make myself worthy of the good-will of my country, and my greatest anticipation of happiness is the return to my friends. I am living here in a retired and solitary way, and partaking in little of the gayety of life, but I am determined not to return home until I have sent some writings before me that shall, if they have merit, make me return to the smiles, rather than skulk back to the pity, of my friends.

In this letter he had requested his brother Ebenezer to send the manuscript to ——— for publication, but getting a communication from Brevoort just after he had concluded it, informing him of this bookseller's delay in paying a draft for books purchased for him, and of which he (Brevoort) had advanced the amount, he now determines to place the manuscript in charge of Brevoort, and draw upon him when in want of money, against the probable profits of his new writings.

I give his letter to Brevoort, which introduces his request to his friend to assume the management of his literary interests, and brings them together in a new and interesting relation.

LONDON, March 3, 1819.

MY DEAR BREVOORT :—

I have this moment received your letter of February 2d, which came most opportunely, as it showed the impossibility of my relying further on ——— in literary matters, and I was on the point of commencing further operations with him. He is a worthy, honest fellow, but apt to entangle himself. Were I a rich man I would give him my writings for nothing; as I am a very poor one I must take care of myself.

I have just sent to my brother Ebenezer MS. for the first number of a work which, if successful, I hope to continue occasionally. I had wished him to send it to ——— for publication, but I now must have it published by some one else. Will you, as you are a literary man and a man of leisure, take it under your care. I wish the copyright secured for me, and the work printed and then sold to one or more booksellers, who will take the whole impression at a fair discount, and give cash or good notes for it. This makes short work of it, and is more profitable to the author than selling the copyright. I should like Thomas to have the first offer, as he has been and is a true friend to me, and I wish him to have any advantage that may arise from the publication of it.

If the work is printed in New York, will you correct the proof-sheets, as I fear the MS. will be obscure, and you are well acquainted with my handwriting.

I feel great diffidence about this reappearance in literature. I am conscious of my imperfections, and my mind has been for a long time past so preyed upon and agitated by various cares and anxieties that I fear it has lost much of its cheerfulness and some of its activity.

I have attempted no lofty theme, nor sought to look wise and learned, which appears to be very much the fashion among our American writers at present. I have preferred addressing myself to the feeling and fancy of the reader more than to his judgment. My writings, therefore, may appear light and trifling in our country of philosophers and politicians; but if they possess merit in the class of literature to which they belong, it is all to which I aspire in the work. I seek only to blow a flute accompaniment in the national concert, and leave others to play the fiddle and French horn.

I shall endeavor to follow this first number by a second, as soon as possible; but some time may intervene, for my writing moods are very precarious.

God bless you, my dear Brevoort,

Your friend,   W. I.

In a postscript to this letter, he adds :—

Do not press poor ——— about the draft, if still unpaid—let him have time. I fear I shall be sadly disappointed in the receipt of funds from the new edition of the " History of New York." I had depended upon it for current expenses, but must now look forward to the future exertions of my pen.

The first number of the " Sketch-Book of Geoffrey Crayon, Gent.," the title chosen for the series, was printed, as were the others, in New York, by C. S. Van Winkle, and consisted of " The Prospectus," " The Author's Account of Himself," " The Voyage," " Roscoe," " The Wife," and " Rip Van Winkle "; making ninety-three pages of octavo of large type and copious margin.

The first edition consisted of two thousand copies. The number was got up in beautiful style for that day, and the price was

made to conform to it, being seventy-five cents.   In "The Prospectus," not to be found in the late editions of the work, he thus
introduces himself anew to the public :—

The following writings are published on experiment; should they
please they may be followed by others.   The writer will have to contend
with some disadvantages.   He is unsettled in his abode, subject to inter-
ruptions, and has his share of cares and vicissitudes.   He cannot, therefore,
promise a regular plan, nor regular periods of publication.   Should he be
encouraged to proceed, much time may elapse between the appearance of
his numbers; and their size will depend on the materials he may have on
hand.   His writings will partake of the fluctuations of his own thoughts
and feelings—sometimes treating of scenes before him, sometimes of others
purely imaginary, and sometimes wandering back with his recollections to
his native country.   He will not be able to give them that tranquil attention necessary to finished composition; and as they must be transmitted
across the Atlantic for publication, he will have to trust to others to correct the frequent errors of the press.   Should his writings, however, with
all their imperfections, be well received, he cannot conceal that it would
be a source of the purest gratification; for though he does not aspire to
those high honors which are the rewards of loftier intellects, yet it is the
dearest wish of his heart to have a secure and cherished, though humble,
corner in the good opinions and kind feelings of his countrymen.

This number was published simultaneously in New York,
Boston, Philadelphia, and Baltimore ; it was deposited for copyright
on May 15, 1819, and its appearance took place shortly after.
It was soon evident, from the sensation it produced, how warmly
the public were disposed to welcome an old acquaintance.

When the first number of this beautiful work was announced (says a
contemporaneous notice), it was sufficient to induce an immediate and
importunate demand, that the name of Mr. Irving was attached to it in the
popular mind.   With his name so much of the honor of our national
literature is associated, that our pride as well as our better feelings is interested in accumulating the gifts of his genius.   We had begun to reproach
him with something like parsimony; to tell him that he was in debt to us;
that the wealth and magnitude of his endowments were the patrimony of
his country—a part of our inheritance.

Of the different papers of this number, " Rip Van Winkle "
was the favorite ; and the popularity which it seized at the outset

it has ever retained. " His stories of 'Rip Van Winkle' and 'Sleepy Hollow'" (says Chambers's "Cyclopædia of English Literature," more than twenty years after the appearance of the " Sketch-Book " in Great Britain) " are perhaps the finest pieces of original fictitious writing that this century has produced next to the works of Scott."

It was just as he had finished the story of " Rip Van Winkle," as he has before told us, that he received a copy of the discourse of Verplanck before the New York Historical Society, in which he administers his reproof of the " Knickerbocker " travesty. As this story purported to be a posthumous production of Diedrich, he took occasion in the introduction to allude to the misdeeds of the departed sage.

The old gentleman (he remarks) was apt to ride his hobby his own way ; and though it did now and then kick up the dust a little in the eyes of his neighbors, and grieve the spirit of some friends for whom he felt the truest deference and affection, yet his errors and follies are remembered "more in sorrow than in anger," and it begins to be suspected that he never intended to injure or offend.

The *Analectic Magazine* for July of this year had a notice of the first number of the " Sketch-Book," from the classic pen of Verplanck, which, under the circumstances, has a peculiar interest. I quote the kindly opening :—

We believe that the public law of literature has entirely exempted periodical publications from the jurisdiction of the ordinary critical tribunals : and we therefore notice the first number of this work with-out any intention of formal criticism, but simply for the purpose of announcing its appearance, and of congratulating the American public that one of their choicest favorites has, after a long interval, again resumed the pen. It will be needless to inform any who have read the book, that it is from the pen of Mr. Irving. His rich, and sometimes extravagant humor, his gay and graceful fancy, his peculiar choice and felicity of original expression, as well as the pure and fine moral feeling which imper-ceptibly pervades every thought and image, without being anywhere ostentatious or dogmatic, betray the author in every page ; even without the aid of those minor peculiarities of style, taste, and local allusions, which at once identify the travelled Geoffrey Crayon with the venerable Knicker-bocker.

On the 1st of April, 1819, the author writes to Brevoort :—

I send a second number of the "Sketch-Book." It is not so large as the first, but I have not been able to get more matter ready for publication; and, indeed, I am not particular about the work being regular in any way. The price of this number, of course, must be less than the first. . . . .

I hope you have been able to make arrangements with Thomas for the publication of my writings. I should greatly prefer its being published by him.

The number here transmitted across the Atlantic consisted of four articles : " English Writers on America "; " Rural Life in England"; " The Broken Heart"; and "The Art of Book-making." The size was not so large as the first, but the same price was put upon it, though he had intimated in his letters it must be less.

A notice of this number at that day remarks : " When we read the description of English scenery, we are apt to think the descriptive is Mr. Irving's forte, but ' The Broken Heart ' convinces us that his prevailing power is in natural and sweet pathos."

This story was undoubtedly the general favorite. The particulars had been given to Mr. Irving by a young Liverpool friend, Mr. Andrew Hamilton, long since dead, who had himself seen the heroine, the daughter of Curran, the celebrated Irish barrister, " at a masquerade "—the scene in which she is introduced by the author.

But though this story won the palm of popularity, there were not wanting many with whom the first was most commended, while the essay on " Rural Life in England " was considered by others as exhibiting most of the peculiar talents of the author. In this light it seems to have struck one of the most eminent names in American literature, Richard H. Dana, who, in his notice of the first two numbers of the " Sketch-Book " in the *North American Review*, after some rather critical animadversions on "The Broken Heart," thus speaks of this essay :—

We came from reading " Rural Life in England " as much restored and as cheerful as if we had been passing an hour or two in the very fields and woods themselves. Mr. Irving's scenery is so true, so full of little beautiful particulars, so varied yet so connected in character, that the

distant is brought nigh to us, and the whole is seen and felt like a delightful reality. It is all gentleness and sunshine; the bright influences of
nature fall on us, and our disturbed and lowering spirits are made clear
and tranquil—turned all to beauty like clouds shone on by the moon.

This beautiful tribute exhibits the mellow charm of that essay
upon an American mind. I follow it with an extract from a letter
of the distinguished author of "Caleb Williams," in which we have
his verdict on a copy of the second number, which had been
transmitted to London from New York, and in which he singles
out the essay on "Rural Life in England" for special commenda-
tion. This letter from such a source and so long in advance of the
London publication of the "Sketch-Book," has a marked literary
interest. I found it among Mr. Irving's papers, to whom it had
been given by his friend Ogilvie, who had two years before
predicted his successful return to the literary arena.

[*To James Ogilvie.*]

SKINNER STREET, September 15, 1819.

DEAR SIR :—

You desire me to write to you my sentiments on reading the "Sketch-
Book," No. II., and I most willingly comply with your request.

Everywhere I find in it the marks of a mind of the utmost elegance
and refinement, a thing, as you know, that I was not exactly prepared to
look for in an American. . . . . Each of the essays is entitled to its
appropriate praise, and the whole is such as I scarcely know an Englishman that could have written. The author powerfully conciliates to
himself our kindness and affection. But the essay on "Rural Life in
England" is incomparably the best. It is, I believe, all true ; and one
wonders, while reading, that nobody ever said this before. There is
wonderful sweetness in it. . . . .

Very truly yours,

W. GODWIN.

I have anticipated a little in giving this letter. On the 13th
of May, four months before its date, Mr. Irving writes to Brevoort :—

By the ship which brings this, I forward a third number of the
"Sketch-Book"; and if you have interested yourself in the fate of the

preceding, I will thank you to extend your kindness to this also. I am extremely anxious to hear from you what you think of the first number, and am looking anxiously for the arrival of the next ship from New York. My fate hangs on it, for I am now at the end of my *fortune.*

It was not, however, until July that his suspense was relieved, and he received the letter which gave Brevoort's opinion. It was still later before he heard of the encouraging reception of his work and the run it was having. It would seem from an intimation in a letter of Ogilvie, that the author was painfully depressed during this interval. " I am impatient," writes that gentleman, "for the arrival of the first number of your ' Sketch-Book ' ; because I feel assured that nothing else is wanting to restore the equipoise of your mind, the steadiness of your intellectual exertions, and to prevent those occasional fits of depression which I can never witness or even think of without feelings of sincere and even painful sympathy."

The following letters to Brevoort also give glimpses of this state of feeling :—

LONDON, July 10, 1819.

MY DEAR BREVOORT:—

I received a few days since your letter of the 9th June, and a day or two afterward yours of the 2d and 8th May, which had been detained in Liverpool. This last gave me your opinion of my first number. I had felt extremely anxious to ascertain it, and your apparent silence had discouraged me.

I am not sorry for the delay that has taken place in the publication, as it will give me more time to prepare my next number. Various circumstances have concurred to render me very nervous and subject to fits of depression that incapacitate me for literary exertion. All that I do at present is in transient gleams of sunshine which are soon overclouded, and I have to struggle against continual damps and chills. I hold on patiently to my purpose, however, in hopes of more genial weather hereafter, when I will be able to exert myself more effectively.

It is a long time since I have heard from my brother William, and I am apt to attribute his silence to dissatisfaction at my not accepting the situation at Washington : a circumstance which I apprehend has disappointed others of my friends. In these matters, however, just weight should be given to a man's tastes and inclinations. The value of a situation is only as it contributes to a man's happiness, and I should have been perfectly out of my element and uncomfortable in Washington. The place could merely have supported me, and instead of rising, as my friends appeared to anticipate, I should have sunk even in my own opinion. My mode of life has unfortunately been such as to render me unfit for almost any useful purpose. I have not the kind of knowledge or the habits that are necessary for business or regular official duty. My acquirements, tastes, and habits are just such as to adapt me for the kind of literary exertions I contemplate. It is only in this way I have any chance of acquiring real reputation, and I am desirous of giving it a fair trial.

I feel perfectly satisfied with your arrangements respecting the work, and more than ever indebted to you for these offices of friendship. I have delayed drawing on you until I should hear further about the work, but shall have to do so soon. . . . .

Give my sincere regards to Mrs. Brevoort, and speak a good word for me now and then to your little boy, whom I hope some day or other to have for a playmate.

Remember me to the rest of your domestic circle, and believe me as ever,

Affectionately yours,   W. I.

[*To Henry Brevoort, Esq.*]

LONDON, July 28, 1819.

MY DEAR BREVOORT :—

As usual, I have but a few moments left to scribble a line before this opportunity departs by which I write. I have seen a copy of the first number of the " Sketch-Book," which was sent out to a gentleman of my acquaintance. I cannot but express how much more than ever I feel myself indebted to you for the manner in which you have attended to my concerns. The work is got up in a beautiful style. I should scarcely have ventured to have made so elegant an *entrée* had it been left to myself, for I had lost confidence in my writings. I have not discovered an error in the printing, and indeed have felt delighted at my genteel appearance in print. I would observe that the work appears to be a little too *highly pointed*. I don't know whether my manuscript was so, or whether it is the scrupulous precision of the printer. High pointing is apt to injure the fluency of the style if the reader attends to all the stops.

I am quite pleased that the work has experienced delay, as it gives me time to get up materials to keep the series going. I have been rather *aflat* for a considerable time past, and able to do nothing with my pen. I was fearful of a great *hiatus* in the early part of my work, which would have been a disadvantage. My spirits have revived recently, and I trust, if I receive favorable accounts of the work's taking in America, that I shall be able to go on with more animation.

I had intended to despatch a number by this ship. It is all written out and stitched up, but as I find you will not stand in immediate need of it, I will keep it by me for a few days, as there is some trivial finishing necessary. You may calculate upon receiving it, however, by one of the first ships that sails after this.

I do not wish any given time to elapse between the numbers, but that they should appear irregularly; indeed, the precariousness and inequality of my own fits of composition will prevent that. . . . .

I look anxiously for your letter by the packet, which must come to hand in a few days; and trust at the same time to hear something of the reception of my work: until then I shall continue a little nervous. . . . .

Most affectionately yours,

W. I.

The following is Brevoort's reply to the two foregoing letters :—

BLOOMINGDALE, September 9, 1819.

MY DEAR IRVING :—

Just as I was preparing to answer your letter of the 10th July, I had the pleasure to receive by the *Amity* your letter of the 28th July.

I hope we shall soon receive the 4th number, which you state was nearly completed. The 3d number will be published on Monday, the 13th. We were retarded a few days by not getting the paper from Mr. Thomas. The orders for Boston, Philadelphia, and Baltimore were forwarded this day, in order that the publication may be contemporaneous—a point very much insisted on by the craft. The edition of the 1st number has all been sold ; of the 2d number only 150 copies remain unsold. The demand rises in every quarter.

Your corrections shall be carefully inserted, and the punctuation somewhat diminished. It was not owing to your MS., but to the scrupulousness of Van Winkle. The 2d edition of No. 1 will be sent to press in a few days. The 2d edition of No. 2 will also follow that of No. 1, as soon as possible. . . . . It is a point universally agreed upon that your work is an honor to American literature, as well as an example to those who aspire to a correct and elegant style of composition.

By the *James Monroe* I have forwarded to Richards five copies of No. 3. . . . .

I think you are mistaken in supposing your brother William dissatisfied respecting the Washington affair. I had a long talk with him a day or two since, in the course of which he adverted to that business, and seemed rather to have yielded to the justness of your objections. He expressed great remorse at his long silence to you, and resolved to take pen in hand and write you a long epistle, by way of atonement. He retains his old habit of burdening himself with a world of unnecessary cares and vexations. In walking the street he seems literally bent downward with at least a dozen gratuitous years ; yet his heart is as mellow and his sensibilities just as acute as ever.

The third number, which was published on the 13th of September, consisted of four articles : " A Royal Poet " ; " The Country Church " ; " The Widow and her Son " ; and " The Boar's Head Tavern, Eastcheap—a Shakespearian Research." The fourth number, which Brevoort was expecting at the date of his letter, was forwarded on the 2d August, as will be seen by the following epistle :—

[*To Henry Brevoort, Esq.*]

LONDON, August 2, 1819.

MY DEAR BREVOORT:—

I forward " Sketch-Book," No. 4, to my brother E. Irving. . . . . I send the present number with reluctance, for it has grown exceedingly stale with me ; part of it lay by me during a time that I was out of spirits and could not complete it.

So much time has elapsed, however, that I dare not delay any longer. I shall endeavor to get up another number immediately, having part of the materials prepared. Should you at any time think any article so indifferent as to be likely to affect the reputation of the work, you may use your discretion in omitting it, and delaying the number until the arrival of my next number, out of which you can take an article to supply the deficiency.

I write in great haste, and am as ever,

Affectionately yours,

W. I.

The number here transmitted consisted of three articles : " The Mutability of Literature," " The Spectre Bridegroom," and " John Bull " ; but this last was afterward reserved for the sixth, and the essay on " Rural Funerals " was substituted for it.

[*To Henry Brevoort, Esq.*]

LONDON, August 12, 1819.

MY DEAR BREVOORT :—

I have received your letter of July 9th, which has given me infinite gratification; but I have not time to reply to it as I could wish. I wrote to you lately, expressing how much I was delighted by the manner in which you got up my work; the favorable reception it has met with is extremely encouraging, and repays me for much doubt and anxiety.

I am glad to hear from you and my brother Ebenezer, that you think my second number better than the first. The manner in which you have spoken of several of the articles is also very serviceable; it lets me know where I make a right hit, and will serve to govern future exertions.

I regret that you did not send me at least half a dozen copies of the work; I am sadly tantalized, having but barely the single copy. I have not made any determination about republishing in this country, and shall ask advice, if I can meet with any one here who can give it me: but my literary acquaintance is very limited at present. I wish you would inquire, and let me know how the "History of New York" sells, as Thomas is rather negligent in giving me information about it. Let him have his own time in settling for it.

. . . .

You observe that the public complain of the price of my work; this is the disadvantage of coming in competition with republished English works, for which the booksellers have not to pay any thing to the authors. If the American public wish to have a literature of their own, they must consent to pay for the support of authors. A work of the same size, and got up in the same way as my first number, would sell for *more* in England, and the cost of printing, etc., would be less. . . . .

I drew on you lately, in favor of Mr. Samuel Williams, at thirty days' sight, for $1,000. General Boyd bought the draft, and I have the money.

. . . .

I feel very much obliged by Verplanck's notice of my work in the *Analectic;* and very much encouraged to find it meets with his approbation. I know no one's taste to whom I would more thoroughly defer.

You suppose me to be on the continent, but I shall not go for some time yet; and you may presume on letters, etc., finding me in England.

. . . .

Four days after the date of this letter, in which he had forwarded a correction for " John Bull," he sends his essay on " Rural Funerals," to be substituted for that article; a rapid effusion, to which he had been stimulated by Brevoort's and Ebenezer's letters, communicating the favorable reception of his first number, their opinion of the superiority of the second, and the popularity of the pathetic element in his compositions.

[*To Brevoort.*]

LONDON, August 16, 1819.

DEAR BREVOORT :—

In great haste I enclose you an essay, which I have just scribbled, and which I wish inserted in the fourth number in place of one of the articles, as I am afraid the number has too great a predominance of the humorous. You may insert it in place of " John Bull," and keep that article for the fifth number. I have not had time to give this article a proper finishing, and wish you to look sharp that there are not blunders and tautologies in it. It has been scribbled off hastily, and part of it actually in a church-yard in a recent ramble into the country.

The unnamed essay here sent was " Rural Funerals." He had forwarded a correction for " John Bull " on the 12th of August, and on the 16th he is putting that aside for this, which must have been prepared in the interim. Part of it, the letter informs us, was written in a church-yard, on a ramble into the country ; and part, I have heard from his own lips, was written at Miller's, where he stopped in at early dawn, feverish and excited, after having been all night at a dance, and borrowed pen and paper to jot down his " thick-coming fancies," some of which no doubt were brought from memories of the past.

In your sketch of " Rural Funerals " (writes Mrs. Hoffman to him), I recognized a scene which you have related in a very touching manner. It surprises me to see that your memory is as tenacious as mine—some things are so deeply fixed there, which passed without striking others nearly interested. I should think your mind would be relieved by writing off these melancholy feelings.

About three weeks after he had despatched this essay, he receives two parcels from America, containing copies of the first and second numbers of the " Sketch-Book," and a letter from Brevoort, enclosing commendatory notices of the press. I give his touching and characteristic reply :—

LONDON, September 9, 1819.

MY DEAR BREVOORT:—

I have received this morning a parcel from Liverpool, containing two parcels from you—one of four of the first number, and the other, five of the second number of the " Sketch-Book," with your letter per courier. The second number is got up still more beautifully than the first. I cannot express to you how much I am delighted with the very tasteful manner in which it is executed. You may tell Mr. Van Winkle that it does him great credit, and has been much admired here as a specimen of American typography; and among the admirers is Murray, the " prince of booksellers," so famous for his elegant publications. Indeed, the manner in which you have managed the whole matter gives me infinite gratification. You have put my writings into circulation, and arranged the pecuniary concerns in such a way as to save future trouble and petty chafferings about accounts, and to give the whole an independent and gentlemanlike air. I would rather sacrifice fifty per cent. than have to keep accounts, and dun booksellers for payment.

The manner in which the work has been received, and the eulogiums that have been passed upon it in the American papers and periodical works, have completely overwhelmed me. They go far, *far* beyond my most sanguine expectations ; and, indeed, are expressed with such peculiar warmth and kindness, as to affect me in the tenderest manner. The receipt of your letter, and the reading of some of those criticisms this morning, have rendered me nervous for the whole day. I feel almost appalled by such success, and fearful that it cannot be real, or that it is not fully merited, or that I shall not act up to the expectations that may be formed. We are whimsically constituted beings. I had got out of conceit of all that I had written, and considered it very questionable stuff; and now that it is so extravagantly be-praised, I begin to feel afraid that I shall not do as well again. However, we shall see as we get on. As yet I am extremely irregular and precarious in my fits of composition. The least thing puts me out of the vein, and even applause flurries me, and prevents my writing; though, of course, it will ultimately be a stimulus.

I hope you will not attribute all this sensibility to the kind reception I have met with to an author's vanity. I am sure it proceeds from very different sources. Vanity could not bring the tears into my eyes, as they have been brought by the kindness of my countrymen. I have felt cast down, blighted, and broken-spirited, and these sudden rays of sunshine agitate even more than they revive me.

I hope—I hope I may yet do something more worthy of the approbation lavished on me. . . . .

Give my best regards to your wife, and remember me heartily to the little circle of our peculiar intimacy.

I am, my dear Brevoort,

Yours affectionately,

W. I.

It was probably under the influence of this encouraging news that he wrote, four days after, the following familiar and playful letter to Leslie, then on a visit to some Quaker friends in Wales. They had been living near together and meeting almost every day; and this letter is pleasantly indicative of the perfect cordiality and freedom that existed between them. Newton cuts quite a figure in it. The others who are mentioned belonged to an American circle in London, in which Irving, Leslie, and Newton seem to have mingled in easy familiarity.

LONDON, September 13, 1819.

You Leslie!—What is the reason you have not let us hear from you since you set out on your travels? We have been in great anxiety lest you should have started from London on some other route of that six-inch square map of the world which you consulted, and through the mistake of a hair's-breadth may have wandered, the Lord knows where.

Here have been sad evolutions and revolutions since you left us. Newton had his three shirts and six collars packed up in half of a saddle-bag for several days, with the intention of accompanying Lyman, Everett, and Charles Williams to Liverpool, and returning with the latter through Wales, in which case they intended beating up your quarters, and endeavoring to surprise you with your mall stick turned into a shepherd's crook, sighing at the feet of Miss Maine. Newton did nothing, for two or three days, but scamper up and down between Finsbury Square and Sloane Street, like a cat in a panic, taking leave of everybody in the morning, and calling upon them again in the evening, when to his astonishment he found Charles Williams had the private intention of embarking for America. Charles had actually sailed, and Newton, instead of his Welsh tour, accompanied me on a tour to Deptford and Eltham. He has now resumed his station at the head of Sloane Street. Jones has taken possession of the bottom, and between them both I expect they will tie the two ends of the street into a true lover's knot. For my part I have been almost good for nothing since your departure, and would not pass another summer in London if they would make me Lord Mayor.

I have received the second number of the "Sketch-Book," and shall be quite satisfied if I deserve half the praise they give me in the American journals; but they always overdo these matters in America. I am glad to find the second number pleases more than the first. The sale is very rapid, and, altogether, the success exceeds my most sanguine expectation. Now you suppose I am all on the alert, and full of spirit and excitement. No such thing. I am just as good-for-nothing as ever I was; and, indeed, have been flurried and put out of my way by these puffings. I feel something as I suppose you did when your picture met with success—anxious to do something better, and at a loss what to do.

But enough of egotism. Let me know how you find yourself; how you like Wales; what you are doing; and, especially, when you intend to return. I hope you will not remain away much longer. Newton's manikin has at length arrived, and he is to have it home in a few days, when it is to be hoped he will give up rambling abroad, and stay at home, drink tea, and play the flute to the lady. William Macdougall means to give her a tea-party, and it is expected she will be introduced into company with as much éclat as Peregrine Pickle's protégée. I have now fairly filled my sheet with nonsense, and craving a speedy reply,

I am yours,

W. I.

It must have been about the date of this letter that Mr. Irving's sympathizing friend, Ogilvie, left with Godwin for his critical opinion one of the copies of No. II. of the "Sketch-Book," which, as we have seen, the author had received a few days before from New York. I have already given Godwin's letter, which may be taken as the first sound of that cheering voice which was soon to greet him from the English public.

Ten days after Godwin had written his critical approbation of No. II., the *London Literary Gazette*, a weekly periodical, commenced a republication of the sketches from No. I., which was continued through two successive issues. A copy of the third number also reached England, and it was said that a London bookseller was about to have these separate portions printed in a collective form. It had not been the intention of the author to publish them in England, conscious that much of their contents could be interesting only to American readers, and having a distrust of their being able to stand the severity of British criticism;

but he now determined to revise and bring them forward himself, that they might at least come correctly before the public. The rest shall be told in his own words, as given in his preface to the revised edition of the " Sketch-Book " of 1848 :—

I accordingly took the printed numbers which I had received from the United States, to Mr. John Murray, the eminent publisher, from whom I had already received friendly attentions, and left them with him for examination, informing him that should he be inclined to bring them before the public, I had materials enough on hand for a second volume. Several days having elapsed without any communication from Mr. Murray, I addressed a note to him, in which I construed his silence into a tacit rejection of my work, and begged that the numbers I had left with him might be returned to me. The following was his reply :—

My DEAR SIR :—

I entreat you to believe that I feel truly obliged by your kind intentions toward me, and that I entertain the most unfeigned respect for your most tasteful talents. My house is completely filled with work-people at this time, and I have only an office to transact business in; and yesterday I was wholly occupied, or I should have done myself the pleasure of seeing you.

If it would not suit me to engage in the publication of your present work, it is only because I do not see that scope in the nature of it which would enable me to make those satisfactory accounts between us, without which I really feel no satisfaction in engaging ; but I will do all that I can to promote their circulation, and shall be most ready to attend to any future plan of yours. With much regard, I remain, dear sir,

Your faithful servant,

JOHN MURRAY.

The letter here given is now before me ; it is without date by Murray, but is marked in the author's handwriting, October 27, 1819. It bears also this later endorsement by him, made probably in 1848 at the time he transcribed it for the preface to his revised edition of the " Sketch-Book,"—" Letter from Murray declining the publication of the ' Sketch-Book,' after I had sent him the first three or four numbers of the American edition in print, comprising the first volume." It is manifest from this endorsement that the author was a little at fault as to the precise contents submitted to Murray's inspection, and if none but printed numbers of the American edition were handed to the great bibliopolist, the fourth number could not have been included, for that was not published in America until November 10th, a fortnight after his declension, and did not, in fact, reach England until the beginning of January, more than two months later. It is not a point, however, upon which I lay any stress.

Mr. Irving intimates in his preface, that after this he might have been deterred from any further prosecution of the matter, had the question of republication in Great Britain rested entirely with him : but he apprehended the appearance of a spurious edition. I find no trace in his letters of discouragement under the disheartening decision, for only four days later he writes to his brother Ebenezer: "I intend republishing in this country, the work having been favorably received by such as have seen it here, and extracts having been made from it with encomiums in some of the periodical works." And now, recalling the cordial reception he had experienced from Scott at Abbotsford, the impression made upon him by his manners and conversation, and the favorable opinion he had expressed of his " Knickerbocker," he turned to him in his perplexity, and sent him the printed numbers of the "Sketch-Book," with a letter in which he observed that since he had the pleasure of partaking of his hospitality, a reverse had taken place in his affairs which made the exercise of his pen important to him. He begged him, therefore, to look over the literary articles he had forwarded to him, and if he thought they would bear European publication, to ascertain whether Mr. Constable would be inclined to be the publisher.

"The parcel containing my work," says the preface, " went by coach to Scott's address in Edinburgh ; the letter went by mail to his residence in the country. By the very first post I received a reply."

This reply, of which the preface contains some extracts, I transcribe in full :—

November 17, 1819.

My Dear Sir :—

I was down at Kelso when your letter reached Abbotsford. I am now on my way to town, and will converse with Constable and do all in my power to forward your views; I assure you nothing will give me more pleasure.

I am now to mention a subject in which I take a most sincere interest. You have not only the talents necessary for making a figure in literature, but also the power of applying them readily and easily, and want nothing but a sphere of action in which to exercise them. Let me put the question to you without hesitation : Would you have any objection to superintend an Anti-Jacobin periodical publication which will appear weekly in Edinburgh, supported by the most respectable talent, and amply furnished with all the necessary information? The appointment of the editor (for which ample funds are provided) will be £500 a year certain, with the reasonable prospect of further advantages. I foresee this may be involving you in a warfare you care not to meddle with, or that your view of politics may not suit the tone it is desired to adopt ; yet I risk the question, because I know no man so well qualified for this important task, and perhaps because it will necessarily bring you to Edinburgh. If my proposal does not suit, you need only keep the matter secret and there is no harm done ; "and for my love I pray you wrong me not." If, on the contrary, you think it could be made to suit you, let me know as soon as possible, addressing Castle St., Edinburgh.

I have not yet got your parcel. I fancy I shall find it in Edinburgh. I wish I were as sure of seeing you there with the resolution of taking a lift of this same journal. One thing I may hint, that some of your coadjutors, being young though clever men, may need a bridle rather than a spur, and in this I have the greatest reliance on your prudence. I myself have no more interest in the matter than I have in the *Quarterly Review*, which I aided in setting afloat.

Excuse this confidential scrawl, which was written in great haste when I understood the appointment was still open, and believe me,

Most truly yours,

WALTER SCOTT.

This is dated Abbotsford, Monday. In a postscript dated Edinburgh, Tuesday, he adds :—

I am just come here and have glanced over the "Sketch-Book"; it is positively beautiful, and increases my desire to *crimp* you if it be possible. Some difficulties there always are in managing such a matter, especially at the outset. But we will obviate them as much as we possibly can.

I find among the author's papers the "imperfect draft" of his reply, to which he alludes in the preface as having undergone some modifications in the copy sent; and as I have given the whole of Scott's letter, I copy this too in full.

My Dear Sir:—

I cannot express how much I am gratified by your letter. I had begun to feel as if I had taken an unwarrantable liberty, but somehow or other there is a genial sunshine about you that warms every creeping thing into heart and confidence. Your literary proposal both surprises and flatters me, as it evinces a much higher opinion of my talents than I have myself. I am peculiarly unfitted for the post proposed. I have no strong political prejudices; for though born and brought up a republican, and convinced that it is the best form of government for my own country, yet I feel my poetical associations vividly aroused by the old institutions of this country, and should feel as sorry to see them injured or subverted as I would to see Windsor Castle or Westminster Abbey demolished to make way for brick tenements.

But I have a general dislike to politics. I have always shunned them in my own country, and have lately declined a lucrative post under my own government, and one that opened the door to promotion, merely because I was averse to political life, and to being subjected to regular application and local confinement.

My whole course of life has been desultory, and I am unfitted for any periodically recurring task, or any stipulated labor of body or mind. I have no command of my talents such as they are, and have to watch the varyings of my mind as I would a weathercock. Practice and training may bring me more into rule; but at present I am as useless for regular service as one of my own country Indians or a Don Cossack.

I must, therefore, keep on pretty much as I have begun—writing when I can, not when I would. I shall occasionally shift my residence, and write whatever is suggested by objects before me, or whatever runs in my imagination; and hope to write better and more copiously by and by.

I am playing the egotist, but I know no better way of answering your proposal but by showing what a very good-for-nothing kind of being I am. Should Mr. Constable feel inclined to make a bargain for the wares I at present have on hand, he will encourage me to further enterprise; and it will be something like bargaining with a gypsy, who may one time have but a wooden bowl to sell, and at another a silver tankard.

The following is Scott's considerate reply, in which he enters into a detail of the various terms upon which books were published, that his correspondent might take his choice of them :—

EDINBURGH, December 4, 1819.

MY DEAR SIR :—

I am sorry but not surprised that you do not find yourself inclined to engage in the troublesome duty in which I would have been well contented to engage you. I have very little doubt that Constable would most willingly be your publisher, and I think I could show him how his interest is most strongly concerned in it. But I do not exactly feel empowered to state any thing to him on the subject except very generally. There are, you know, various modes of settling with a publisher. Sometimes he gives a sum of money for the copyright. But more frequently he relieves the author of all expense, and divides what he calls the free profit on the editions as they arise. There is something fair in this, and advantageous for both parties; for the author receives a share of profit exactly in proportion to the popularity of his work, and the bookseller is relieved of the risk which always attends a purchase of copyright, and has more rapid returns of his capital. In general, however, he contrives to take the lion's share of the booty; for, first, he is always desirous to delay settlement till the edition sells off, and if disposed to be unfair (which I never found Constable) he can contrive that there be such a reserve of the edition as shall put off the term of accounting, to him the *quart d' heure* de Rabelais au Græcas Kalendas ; 2dly, the half profits are thus accounted for: Print, paper, and advertising are usually made to amount to about one-third of the whole price of the edition, and one-third is deducted as allowance to the retail trade. The bookseller usually renders something about the remaining third as divisible profit betwixt the author and himself; so that upon a guinea volume the author receives three and six-pence. In cases where a rapid sale is expected, booksellers will give better terms; for example, they will grant bills for the author's share of profit at perhaps nine or twelve months' date, and thus insure him against delay of settlements. They have also been made to lower or altogether abandon the charge of advertising, which in fact is a stump charge which booksellers make against the author, of which they never lay out one-sixth part, because they advertise all their productions in one advertisement, and charge the expense of doing so against every separate work though there may be twenty of them, from which you can easily see he must be a great gainer. Now this is all I know of bookselling as practised by the most respectable of the trade, and I am certain that under the system of half profits in one of its modifications Constable will be happy to publish for you. I am certain the "Sketch-Book" could be published here with great advantage; it is a delightful work. "Knickerbocker" and "Salma-gundi" are more exclusively American, and may not be quite so well suited for our meridian. But they are so excellent in their way, that if the public attention could be once turned on them I am confident that they would become popular; but there is the previous objection to over-come. Now you see, my dear sir, the ground on which you stand. I therefore did no more than open trenches with Constable, but I am sure, if you will take the trouble to write to him, you will find him disposed to treat your overture with every degree of attention. Or if you think it of consequence in the first place to see me, I shall be in London in the course of a month, and whatever my experience can command is most heartily at your service. But I can add little to what I have said above, excepting my earnest recommendation to Constable to enter into the negotiation.

In my hurry I have not thanked you in Sophia's name for the kind attention which furnished her with the American volumes.[1] I am not quite sure I can add my own, since you have made her acquainted with much more of papa's folly than she would ever otherwise have learned, for I had taken special care they should never see any of these things during their earlier years. I think I told you that Walter is sweeping the firmament with a feather like a May-pole, and indenting the pavement with a sword like a scythe; in other words, he is become a whiskered hussar in the 18th dragoons. Trusting to see you soon, I am always, my dear sir,   Most truly yours,

WALTER SCOTT.

"Before the receipt of this most obliging letter," says Mr. Irving in his preface, "I had determined to look to no leading bookseller for a launch, but to throw my work before the public at my own risk, and let it sink or swim according to its merits." But though he had come to this resolution before the receipt of Scott's letter, it was not until the 9th of the succeeding month that his contract with Miller took a written form and the latter undertook to proceed with the publication. "I have just made arrangements to have a volume of the 'Sketch-Book' published here," he writes to his brother Ebenezer from London, January 13th. "I expect the first proof-sheet to-day, and the volume will be published in about a month. If the experiment succeeds I shall follow it up by another volume."

[1] An American edition of his own poems.

CHAPTER XXIV.

Christmas in England.

AVING anticipated a little in giving the letters of Scott in the preceding chapter, I now go back in my narrative to a period just succeeding the author's receipt of the great publisher's "civil note" of refusal, when Brevoort was writing to him : " I wish you would *permit* Murray to publish your work." At this time Brevoort was about to leave for Charleston, where he was to spend the winter, and had written to Mr. Irving : " After distributing the fourth number I shall settle accounts with the purchasers as well as with the printer, and advise you of the balance in your favor, which will be payable within ninety days. Your brother Ebenezer will then take charge of No. V. and the second edition. I shall give him every sort of information as to the manner of managing the work."

Ebenezer, upon whom this novel guardianship now devolves, writes : " Brothers William and John T. will assist me in the correction of proofs."

The day after Murray's non-acceptance, and about a fortnight prior to the publication of No. IV. in America, he transmits No. V. to his brother Ebenezer, consisting of " Christmas." " Whether No. V. will please or not," he writes, " I cannot say, but it has cost me more trouble and more odd research than any of the others."

This number did not exactly hit the taste of his brother. He missed the pathetic element which had been so attractive a feature in the former numbers, and allowed himself, on a first perusal, to remark upon its length, and to lament the absence of the usual variety. In reply to these remarks, Washington writes :—

The article you object to, about Christmas, is written for peculiar tastes—those who are fond of what is quaint in literature and customs. The scenes there depicted are formed upon humors and customs peculiar to the English, and illustrative of their greatest holiday. The old rhymes which are interspersed are but selections from many which I found among old works in the British Museum, little read even by Englishmen, and which will have a value with some literary men who relish these morsels of antiquated humor. When an article is studied out in this manner, it cannot have that free-flowing spirit and humor that one written off-hand has ; but then it compensates to some peculiar minds by the points of character or manners which it illustrates. Had I not thought so, I certainly would not have taken the trouble which the article cost me. If it possesses the kind of merit I mention, and pleases the peculiar, though perhaps few, tastes to which I have alluded, my purpose in writing the article is satisfied, and it will go to keep up the variety which is essential to a work of the kind.

On the 29th of December, he transmits to New York No. VI., consisting of " The Pride of the Village," and " The Legend of Sleepy Hollow,"—" John Bull," which formed one of the articles, being already there.

I send you MS. for No. VI. (he writes to Ebenezer). There is a Knickerbocker story which may please from its representation of American scenes. It is a random thing, suggested by recollections of scenes and stories about Tarrytown. The story is a mere whimsical band to connect descriptions of scenery, customs, manners, etc.

The outline of this story had been sketched more than a year before at Birmingham, after a conversation with his brother-in-law, Van Wart, who had been dwelling upon some recollections of his early years at Tarrytown, and had touched upon a waggish fiction of one Brom Bones, a wild blade, who professed to fear nothing, and boasted of his having once met the devil on a return from a nocturnal frolic, and run a race with him for a bowl of milk-punch. The imagination of the author suddenly kindled over the recital, and in a few hours he had scribbled off the frame-work of his renowned story, and was reading it to his sister and her husband. He then threw it by until he went up to London, where it was expanded into the present legend.

In the interval between the transmission of the sixth and seventh numbers to New York, a volume of the " Sketch-Book" was published in England. February 24, 1820, Washington writes to Ebenezer :—

The volume containing the first four numbers of the " Sketch-Book" was published on Monday last by John Miller, Burlington Arcades. I shall not publish any more, and should not have done this, had there not been a likelihood of these works being republished here from incorrect American numbers.

On the publication of this volume, Miller urged Mr. Irving to send copies to the different periodicals ; but he declined, being unwilling to do what might appear like a desire to propitiate their favor.

It was put to press (as he says in his preface) without any of the usual arts by which a work is trumpeted into notice. All he permitted himself was an appeal, not to the indulgence but the candor of the critics in his advertisement to the edition. The following desultory papers (he says) are part of a series written in this country, but published in America. The author is aware of the austerity with which the writings of his country-men have hitherto been treated by British critics ; he is conscious, too, that much of the contents of his papers can be interesting only in the eyes of

American readers. It was not his intention, therefore, to have them reprinted in this country. He has, however, observed several of them from time to time inserted in periodical works of merit, and has understood that it was probable they would be republished in a collective form. He has been induced, therefore, to revise and bring them forward himself, that they may at least come correctly before the public. Should they be deemed of sufficient importance to attract the attention of critics, he solicits for them that courtesy and candor which a stranger has some right to claim, who presents himself at the threshold of a hospitable nation.

February, 1820.

Before this he had written to Scott, who had not come to London at the time proposed in his letter, informing him of the arrangement he had made with Miller, by the terms of which the publication was to consist of one thousand copies, and the author took upon himself the entire expense of paper, printing, and advertisements, and the risk of sale. The following is Scott's reply :—

EDINBURGH, March 1, 1820.

MY DEAR SIR :—

I was some time since favored with your kind remembrance of the 9th, and observe with pleasure that you are going to come forth in Britain. It is certainly not the very best way to publish on one's own account, for the booksellers set their faces against the circulation of such works as do not pay an amazing toll to themselves. But they have lost the art of altogether damming up the road in such cases between the author and the public, which they were once able to do as effectually as Diabolus, in John Bunyan's " Holy War," closed up the windows of my Lord Understanding's mansion. I am sure of one thing, that you have only to be known to the British public to be admired by them ; and I would not say so unless I really was of that opinion. If you ever see a witty but rather local publication called *Blackwood's Edinburgh Magazine*, you will find some notice of your works in the last number. The author is a friend of mine to whom I have introduced you in your literary capacity. His name is Lockhart—a young man of very considerable talent, and who will soon be intimately connected with my family. My faithful friend " Knickerbocker " is to be next examined and illustrated. Constable was extremely willing to enter into consideration of a treaty for your works, but I foresee will be still more so when

" Your name is up and may go
From Toledo to Madrid."

And that will be soon the case.

Scott came to London about the middle of March, for the purpose of receiving his baronetcy, at which time Mr. Irving was on a visit to his brother-in-law, Van Wart, at Birmingham, not having seen the family for more than a year and a half, during which interval he had been leading a solitary life in London. He had returned on the 27th of March, and on the 9th of April Leslie wrote to his sister :—

Walter Scott (now Sir Walter) is in London ; and I am to have the honor, and I am sure it will be the very great pleasure, of breakfasting with him at his lodgings on Friday next. Irving, whom I suspect of being a very great favorite of Scott's, is to introduce me. It is what I did not venture to ask of him ; but Irving, knowing how much such an introduction would gratify me, proposed it himself. I believe we are to meet Crabbe, the poet, there. Scott is one of those men of genius who delights in the genius of others, and is not for having it all to himself. He has expressed the highest opinion of Irving's productions, and perhaps there is not another man in this country whose good opinion is so valuable. You will be glad to hear that there is every prospect of Irving's writings speedily becoming as popular here as they are in America. An edition of the first volume of the " Sketch-Book " is very nearly sold off here already. One of the stories, "The Wife," has been translated into French ; and many of the articles have been extracted for the magazines and newspapers. Scott was very much delighted with the sixth number, particularly with the story of " Brom Bones."

This allusion to the sixth number of the " Sketch-Book," which was not yet printed in England, would imply that an American number had been shown to Scott, or a duplicate in manuscript. But while Leslie was penning this account of the success of his friend, the volume he had put to press in England was destined to an untoward mischance. His bookseller failed, and the sale of the work, which was just getting into fair circulation, was interrupted, and his hopes of profit, if he had been sanguine of any, dashed to the ground. At this juncture Scott interposed his good offices.

I called to him for help (writes Mr. Irving in the preface to the revised edition of the " Sketch-Book ") as I was sticking in the mire ; and more propitious than Hercules, he put his own shoulder to the wheel. Through his favorable representations, Murray was quickly induced to undertake the future publications of the work which he had previously declined. A further edition of the first volume was struck off, and the second volume was put to press, and from that time Murray became my publisher; conducting himself in all his dealings with that fair, open, and liberal spirit which had obtained for him the well-merited appellation of the Prince of Booksellers.

The following letter to Brevoort will now be in place :—

LONDON, May 13, 1820.

MY DEAR BREVOORT :—

I send this letter by my friend Delafield, whom, I presume, you know ; if not, you ought to know him, for he is a right worthy fellow. He has in charge a portrait of me, painted by Newton, the nephew of Mr. Stuart. It is considered an excellent likeness, and I am willing it should be thought so—though, between ourselves, I think myself a much better-looking fellow on canvas than in the looking-glass. I beg you to accept it as a testimony of my affection; and my deep sense of your truly brotherly kindness toward me on all occasions. . . . .

The " Sketch-Book " is doing very well here. It has been checked for a time by the failure of Miller ; but Murray has taken it in hand, and it will now have a fair chance. I shall put a complete edition to press next week, in two volumes ; and at the same time print a separate edition of the second volume, to match the editions of the first already published. I have received very flattering compliments from several of the literati, and find my circle of acquaintance extending faster than I could wish. Murray's drawing-room is now a frequent resort of mine, where I have been introduced to several interesting characters, and have been most courteously received by Gifford. Old D'Israeli is a staunch friend of mine also ; and I have met with some very interesting people at his house. This evening I go to the Countess of Besborough's, where there is to be quite a collection of characters, among whom I shall see Lord Wellington, whom I have never yet had the good luck to meet with. . . . .

I shall not send any more manuscript to America, until I put it to press here, as the second volume might be delayed, and the number come out here from America. The manner in which the work has been received here, instead of giving me spirit to write, has rather daunted me for the time. I feel uneasy about the second volume, and cannot write any fresh matter for it. . . . .

The following letter to James K. Paulding, written twelve days later, is in answer to one from him, dated at Washington, where he now held a post under Government, and of which Mr. Irving says in a letter to Brevoort : " It brought so many recollections of early times, and scenes, and companions, and pursuits to my memory, that my heart was filled to overflowing." In the allusion to Decatur, it will be recollected that he had on the 22d of March previous fallen in a duel with Commodore Barron, induced by some animadversions of his on the conduct of the latter in the affair of the *Leopard* and the *Chesapeake*.

LONDON, May 27, 1820.

MY DEAR JAMES :—

It is some time since I received your very interesting and gratifying letter of January 20th, and I have ever since been on the point of answering it, but been prevented by those thousand petty obstacles that are always in the way of letter-writing.

As I am launched upon the literary world here, I find my opportunities of observation extending. Murray's drawing-room is a great resort of first-rate literary characters ; whenever I have a leisure hour I go there, and seldom fail to meet with some interesting personages. The hours of access are from two to five. It is understood to be a matter of privilege, and that you must have a general invitation from Murray. Here I frequently meet with such personages as Gifford, Campbell, Foscolo, Hallam (author of a work on the Middle Ages), Southey, Milman, Scott, Belzoni, etc., etc. The visitors are men of different politics, though most frequently ministerialists. Gifford, of whom, as an old adversary, you may be curious to know something, is a small, shrivelled, deformed man of about sixty, with something of a humped back, eyes that diverge, and a large mouth. He is generally reclining on one of the sofas, and supporting himself by the cushions, being very much debilitated. He is mild and courteous in his manners, without any of the petulance that you would be apt to expect, and is quite simple, unaffected, and unassuming. Murray tells me that Gifford does not write any full articles for the *Review*, but revises, modifies, prunes, and prepares whatever is offered ; and is very apt to extract the sting from articles that are rather virulent. Scott, or Sir Walter Scott, as he is now called, passed some few weeks in town lately, on coming up for his baronetcy. I saw him repeatedly, having formed an acquaintance with him two or three years since at his country retreat on the Tweed. He is a man that, if you knew, you would love; a right honest-hearted, generous-spirited being; without vanity, affectation, or assumption of any kind. He enters into every passing scene or passing pleasure with the interest and simple enjoyment of a child ; nothing seems too high or remote for the grasp of his mind, and nothing too trivial or low for the kindness and pleasantry of his spirit. When I was in want of literary counsel and assistance, Scott was the only literary man to whom I felt that I could talk about myself and my petty concerns with the confidence and freedom that I would to an old friend. Nor was I deceived; from the first moment that I mentioned my work to him in a letter, he took a decided and effective interest in it, and has been to me an invaluable friend. It is only astonishing how he finds time, with such ample exercise of the pen, to attend so much to the interests and concerns of others ; but no one ever applied to Scott for any aid, counsel, or service that would cost time and trouble, that was not most cheerfully and thoroughly assisted. Life passes away with him in a round of good offices and social enjoyments. Literature seems his sport rather than his labor or his ambition, and I never met with an author so completely void of all the petulance, egotism, and peculiarities of the craft ; but I am running into prolixity about Scott, who I confess has completely won my heart, even more as a man than as an author ; so, praying God to bless him, we will change the subject.

Your picture of domestic enjoyment indeed raises my envy. With all my wandering habits, which are the result of circumstances rather than of disposition, I think I was formed for an honest, domestic, uxorious man, and I cannot hear of my old cronies snugly nestled down with good wives and fine children round them, but I feel for the moment desolate and forlorn. Heavens! what a hap-hazard, schemeless life mine has been, that here I should be, at this time of life, youth slipping away, and scribbling month after month and year after year, far from home, without any means or prospect of entering into matrimony, which I absolutely believe indispensable to the happiness and even comfort of the after-part of existence. When I fell into misfortunes and saw all the means of domestic establishment pass away like a dream, I used to comfort myself with the idea that if I was indeed doomed to remain single, you and Brevoort and Gouv. Kemble would also do the same, and that we should form a knot of queer, rum old bachelors, at some future day, to meet at the corner of Wall Street or walk the sunny side of Broadway and kill time together. But you and Brevoort have given me the slip, and now that Gouv. has turned Vulcan and is forging thunder-bolts so successfully in the Highlands, I expect nothing more than to hear of his conveying some blooming bride up to the smithy. But Heaven prosper you all, and grant that I may find you all thriving and happy when I return.

I cannot close my letter without adverting to the sad story of our gallant friend Decatur; though my heart rises to my throat the moment his idea comes across my mind. He was a friend "faithful and just" to me, and I have gone through such scenes of life as make a man feel the value of friendship. I can never forget how generously he stepped forth in my behalf, when I felt beaten down and broken-spirited; I can never forget him as the companion of some of my happiest hours, and as mingled with some of the last scenes of home and its enjoyments; these recollections bring him closer to my feelings than all the brilliancy of his public career. But he has lived through a life of animation and enjoyment, and died in the fulness of fame and prosperity; his cup was always full to the brim, and he has not lingered to drain it to the dregs and taste of the bitterness. I feel most for her he has left behind, and from all that I recollect of her devoted affection, her disconsolateness even during his temporary absence and jeopardy, I shrink from picturing to myself what must now be her absolute wretchedness. If she is still near you give her my most affectionate remembrances; to speak of sympathy to her would be intrusion.

And now, my dear James, with a full heart I take my leave of you. Let me hear from you just when it is convenient; no matter how long or how short the letter, nor think any apologies necessary for delays, only let me hear from you. I may suffer time to elapse myself, being unsettled, and often perplexed and occupied; but believe me always the same in my feelings, however irregular in my conduct, and that no new acquaintances that a traveller makes in his casual sojournings are apt to wear out the deep recollections of his early friends. Give my love to Gertrude, who I have no doubt is a perfect pattern for wives, and when your boy grows large enough to understand tough stories, tell him some of our early frolics, that he may have some kind of an acquaintance with me against we meet.

Affectionately your friend,   W. IRVING.

On the 28th of June, after the printers had commenced upon the English edition of the second volume of the "Sketch-Book," Mr. Irving transmitted to his brother Ebenezer the sheets for the seventh number, to be made up of "Westminster Abbey," "Stratford-on-Avon," "Little Britain," and "The Angler."

Of the last article he writes :—

It is a sketch drawn almost entirely from the life; and, therefore, if it has no other merit, it has that of truth and nature.

It is not likely (he adds) that I shall publish another number soon. I have had so much muddling work with the "Sketch-Book" from publishing in both countries, that I have grown tired of it, and have lost all excitement.   I shall feel relieved from a cloud, when I get this volume printed and out of my sight. . . . .

The seventh number, published September 13, 1820, terminated the series in America; but the second volume of the English "Sketch-Book" included two additional articles, previously contributed by Mr. Irving to the *Analectic Magazine*, namely : " Traits of Indian Character," and " Philip of Pokanoket." These articles were subsequently incorporated in the American volumes.

The following letters to his brother Ebenezer and Brevoort were written on the eve of his departure for the continent on that long-talked-of excursion, to which he was looking forward when he embarked from America ; but which circumstances had so conspired to delay.

[*To Ebenezer Irving.*]

LONDON, August 15, 1820.

. . . . The "Sketch-Book" has been very successful in England. The first volume is out of print, which is doing very well, considering that it is but four or five months since it was published ; that it has had to make its own way, against many disadvantages, being written by an author the public knew nothing of, and published by a bookseller who was going to ruin.   The second volume, of which a thousand were printed, is going off briskly ; and Murray proposes putting to press immediately a uniform edition of the two volumes at his own expense.   I have offered, however, to dispose of the work to him entirely, and am to know his answer to-morrow.[1]   He wishes likewise to publish an edition of " Knickerbocker," which has been repeatedly spoken well of in the British publications, and particularly in *Blackwooa's Magazine*, in which I have received the highest eulogium that has ever been passed upon me.   It is written by Lockhart, author of " Peter's Letters to his Kinsfolk," and son-in-law to Sir Walter Scott.   You will perceive that I have dedicated my second volume to Scott ; but this dedication had not been seen by Lockhart at the time he wrote the eulogium.   Should a new and complete edition of the work be published in America, I wish the dedication to be placed in the first volume. I cannot sufficiently express how sensible I feel of the warm and affectionate

---

[1] Murray bought the copyright for two hundred pounds.

interest which Scott has taken in me and my writings. My second volume has been noticed by two or three periodical publications, and in the same favorable way with the first. I have received abundance of private marks of approbation from literary people here; and, upon the whole, have reason to be highly gratified with the success of my literary enterprise in this country. After all, I value success here chiefly as tending to confirm my standing in my own country; for it is to popularity at home that I look as the sweetest source of enjoyment.

LONDON, August 15, 1820.

MY DEAR BREVOORT :—

I am now in all the hurry and bustle of breaking up my encampment, and moving off for the continent. After remaining so long in one place it is painful to cast loose again and turn one's self adrift; but I do not wish to remain long enough in any place in Europe to make it a home.

Since I have published with Murray, I have had continual opportunities of seeing something of the literary world, and have formed some very agreeable acquaintances. . . . .

There have been some literary coteries set on foot lately, by some Blue-Stockings of fashion, at which I have been much amused. Lady Caroline Lamb is a great promoter of them. You may have read some of her writings, particularly her " Glenarvon," in which she has woven many anecdotes of fashionable life and fashionable characters; and hinted at particulars of her own story, and that of Lord Byron. She is a strange being, a compound of contradictions, with much to admire, much to stare at, and much to condemn. . . . .

I have been very much pleased also with Belzoni, the traveller, who is just bringing out a personal narrative of his researches, illustrated with very extraordinary plates. There is the interior of a temple, excavated in a hill, which he discovered and opened; which had the effect on me of an Arabian tale. There are rows of gigantic statues, thirty feet high, cut out of the calcareous rock, in perfect preservation. I have been as much delighted in conversing with him, and getting from him an account of his adventures and feelings, as was ever one of Sindbad's auditors. Belzoni is about six feet four or five inches high; of a large frame, but a small, and, I think, a very fine head; and a countenance which, at times, is very expressive and intelligent. . . . .

I have also frequently met with Mr. Hallam, whose able and interesting work on the Middle Ages you have no doubt seen, and most probably have in your library. Like all other men of real talent and unquestionable merit, he is affable and unpretending. He is a copious talker, and you are sure, when he is present, to have conversation briskly kept up. But it is useless merely to mention names in this manner; and is too much like entertaining one with a description of a banquet, by merely naming the dishes. One thing I have found invariably, that the greater the merit, the less has been the pretension ; and that there is no being so modest, natural, unaffected, and unassuming as a first-rate genius.

I am delighted to hear that our worthy Patroon is doing well with his foundry. God bless and prosper him, and make him as rich and as happy as he deserves to be. I believe I told you in my last of a long letter, which I received from James Paulding—it was a most gratifying one to me ; and it gave me a picture of quiet prosperity and domestic enjoyment, which it is delightful for a wandering, unsettled being like myself to contemplate. Oh! my dear Brevoort, how my heart warms toward you all, when I get talking and thinking of past times and past scenes! What would I not give for a few days among the Highlands of the Hudson, with the little knot that once assembled there! But I shall return home and find all changed, and shall be made sensible how much I have changed myself. It is this idea which continually comes across my mind, when I think of home ; and I am continually picturing to myself the dreary state of a poor devil like myself, who, after wandering about the world among strangers, returns to find himself a still greater stranger in his native place.

. . . . And now, my dear fellow, I must take my leave, for it is midnight, and I am wearied with packing trunks and making other preparations for my departure. The next you will hear from me will be from France ; and after passing five years in England among genuine John Bulls, it will be like entering into a new world to cross the channel.

CHAPTER XXV.

THE two brothers left London for Paris on the 17th of August. I ought to have mentioned before, that they had occupied the same lodgings in London for about a year, during which Peter gave anonymously to the world a Venetian tale, taken from the French, entitled "Giovanni Sbogarro," which he had written at Birmingham. It was published in London and in New York, but belonging as it did to a school of fiction that was passing away under the brilliant advent of Scott, its pecuniary success was not very encouraging.

Mr. Irving took lodgings at Paris, at No. 4 Rue Mont Thabor, in the vicinity of the Tuileries ; but he had become so unsettled in mind by shifting his quarters to new scenes, that it was some time before he was able to resume his pen.

I have been about a month in Paris (he writes to William, September 22d), and begin to feel a little more at home. Mr. Gallatin[1] has been extremely attentive to me. I have dined with him repeatedly. Either Paris or myself has changed very much since I was here before. It is by no means so gay as formerly ; that is to say, the populace have a more grave and triste appearance. You see but little of the sprightliness and gayety of manner for which the French are proverbial. However, as I have been here but a little time I will not begin to give opinions ; and as

---

[1] Albert Gallatin, the American Minister.

I wish my letter to go safe, I will not interlard it with any speculations on national character or concerns.

Meanwhile the "Sketch-Book" was making a fame for him in England. The *Edinburgh Review*, in an article written by Jeffrey, contained a handsome tribute to his talents, and perhaps not the least flattering circumstance connected with its publication, in the eyes of Mr. Irving, was a rumor which ascribed its parentage to Sir Walter Scott.

This fact was brought to his knowledge in a most gratifying manner in a letter from Mr. Richard Rush, our minister at the court of St. James, transmitting one from the accomplished Lady Lyttleton, the daughter of Earl Spencer. As it forms a curious and interesting anecdote, I give the correspondence ; a portion of it being from copies retained by Mr. Irving.

[*From the Hon. Richard Rush to Washington Irving.*]

LONDON, October 20, 1820,
11 Blenheim Street.

MY DEAR SIR :—

I value the enclosed letter very highly, and would not trust it out of my own hands but to pass it to yours, and almost tremble at risking it to Paris. Pray, therefore, do not fail to return it, and I must say the sooner the better, as I shall wait impatiently for your answer before returning a final one to my fair correspondent.

She is Lady Lyttleton, the daughter of Earl Spencer, and is among the most accomplished and lovely women of England; worthy, as I think, of another monody from Hayley, should fate ever snatch her from her almost equally estimable husband. If you do not write to me soon all that you have to say upon her letter, I shall certainly give her to understand, and perhaps under my official seal, that *you* are the author of "Waverley," "Rob Roy," and some two or three more of the Shakespearian novels; for as Sir Walter Scott is to have the credit of the "Sketch-Book," I can see no good reason why a portion of his laurels should not be transferred to you by way of indemnification. . . . .

[*From Lady Lyttleton to Mr. Rush.*]

DEAR SIR :—

I hope your Excellency will not think that I am presuming too far upon your goodness in taking the liberty of making an inquiry which relates to a subject of some interest, I think to yourself as well as to me. A report has lately prevailed in the literary world, I do not exactly know upon what grounds, that the "Sketch-Book," which you first procured us the very great pleasure of reading, was written, not as it professes to be, by a countryman of yours, but by Sir Walter Scott, whose very numerous disguises and whose well-known fondness for literary masquerading seem to have gained him the advantage of being suspected as the author of every distinguished work that is published. It appears to me that the merits of the "Sketch-Book" are so very unlike those of Scott, and that the style and nature of the work are so new and peculiar, that it puts me out of all patience to hear the surmise, and I could not rest till I had applied to your Excellency for *some proof* of its falsehood. I am told that nobody has yet *actually seen* a copy of the book printed in America; that Sir Walter Scott, a great friend, as he calls himself, of the pretended author, inadvertently asserted one day that Mr. Washington Irving had resided in *London* all the time he was in England; he *could* not, therefore, it was inferred, have written the admirably just descriptions of English *rural* life ; and upon my appearing obstinately incredulous, I was assured that if Sir Walter Scott did not write the whole, he at least revised the language, and had all the merit of the style. Let me entreat your Excellency to send me a *triumphant* proof that all this is groundless, and that the very prettiest and *most amiable* book we have read for a long time has not the defect of being a trick upon readers. . . . .

[*From Washington Irving to Mr. Rush.*]

PARIS, October 28, 1820, }
4 Rue Mont Thabor. }

MY DEAR SIR :—

I feel very much obliged by your letter of the 20th, and am highly flattered by the letter of Lady Lyttleton, which you were so good as to enclose, and which I herewith return. It is indeed delightful to receive applause from such a quarter. As her ladyship seems desirous of full and explicit information as to the authorship of the "Sketch-Book," you may assure her that it was entirely written by myself; that the revisions and corrections were my own, and that I have had no literary assistance either in the beginning or the finishing of it. I speak fully to this point, not from any anxiety of authorship, but because the doubts which her ladyship has heard on the subject seem to have arisen from the old notion that it is impossible for an *American to write decent English.* If I have indeed been fortunate enough to do any thing, however trifling, to stagger this prejudice, I am too good a patriot to give up even the little ground I have

gained. As to the article on " Rural Life in England," which appears to
have pleased her ladyship, it may give it some additional interest in her
eyes to know that though the result of general impressions received in
various excursions about the country, yet it was sketched in the vicinity of
Hagley,[1] just after I had been rambling about its grounds, and whilst its
beautiful scenery, with that of the neighborhood, was fresh in my recollection.

I cannot help smiling at the idea that any thing I have written should
be deemed worthy of being attributed to Sir Walter Scott, and that I
should be called upon to vindicate my weak pen from the honor of such a
parentage. He could tenant half a hundred scribblers like myself on the
mere skirts of his literary reputation. He never saw my writings until in
print; but though he has not assisted me with his pen, yet the interest
which he took in my success; the praises which he bestowed on some of
the first American numbers forwarded to him; the encouragement he gave
to me to go on and do more, and the countenance he gave to the first
volume when republished in England have, perhaps, been more effectually
serviceable than if he had revised and corrected my work page by page.
He has always been to me a frank, generous, warm-hearted friend, and it
is one of my greatest gratifications to be able to call him such. Indeed,
it is the delight of his noble and liberal nature to do good and to dispense
happiness; those who only know him through his writings know not a
tithe of his excellence.[2]

Present my sincere remembrances to Mrs. Rush, and believe me,
dear sir.

With very great respect,

Yours faithfully,

WASHINGTON IRVING.

The information contained in this letter, or perhaps the letter
itself, was communicated by Mr. Rush to Lady Lyttleton, and was
succeeded by a message from Lord and Lady Spencer, her parents,
expressing an earnest desire to become acquainted with the author
of the " Sketch-Book," and inviting him to spend the approaching
Christmas at their place. The invitation was conveyed through Mr.
Rush, in a note from Mr. Lyttleton. The following is Mr. Irving's
reply, which I give from a copy preserved among his papers.

---

[1] The seat of Lord Lyttleton, where the old customs were kept up, as related
by Geoffrey Crayon in his " Christmas Eve and Christmas Dinner."

[2] From a draft of Mr. Irving's reply.

[*To the Hon. Richard Rush.*]

PARIS, December 6, 1820.

MY DEAR SIR:—

I feel very much indebted to you for your letter of the 27th, and hardly know how to express myself as to the very flattering communication from Mr. Lyttleton. It is enough to excite the vanity of a soberer man than myself. Nothing would give me greater gratification than to avail myself of the hospitable invitation of Lord and Lady Spencer, but at present it is out of my power to leave Paris, and would be deranging all my plans to return immediately to England. Will you be kind enough to convey to Mr. Lyttleton my sincere acknowledgments of his politeness, and also of the honor done me by Lord and Lady Spencer; but above all, my heart-felt sense of the interest evinced in my behalf by Lady Lyttleton, which I frankly declare is one of the most gratifying circumstances that has befallen me in the whole course of my literary errantry.

Excuse all this trouble which circumstances oblige me to give your Excellency, and believe me, with my best remembrances to Mrs. Rush,

Yours very faithfully,

WASHINGTON IRVING.

Some weeks prior to the date of this letter (October 26th), Mr. Murray informed the author that his volumes had succeeded so much beyond his mercantile estimate, that he begged he would do him the favor to draw on him at sixty-five days for one hundred guineas, in addition to the terms agreed upon.

He had also been encouraged to publish the "History of New York."

I did not know you [he writes] as I ought and might have known you until I read "Knickerbocker," of which I am equally happy and proud to have been, though tardily, the publisher. After all, it is at present, and only at present I trust, your opus magnum; it is the Don Quixote or Hudibras of your country, and, connected with your age at the time it was written, displays most certain marks of genius. It is very generally liked here; and if so, how much more it must be felt, and therefore much more enjoyed, by your own countrymen. I am quite delighted with the novelty of character and scenery, which you have so admirably dramatized, and so vividly painted. I have printed it in one octavo volume to range with the "Sketch-Book"; but I think this is not the form most appropriate to it, and I now propose to reprint it in four or five small volumes like Lord Byron's works, and denominated foolscap octavo.

In the same letter, Mr. Murray informs him that he had been very much struck with the exquisite humor and correct taste of Leslie's first design, and had engaged him to look over the volume and see if he could make eight or twelve designs equally happy with the first. He also urges him no longer to conceal his name from the world, but to accept openly the wreath the public had in store for him, give his name to the works, and write a simple preface announcing it.

At this time Murray had already reprinted the second volume of the " Sketch-Book," and was preparing a new and uniform edition of both volumes in a smaller size.

In another part of his letter he says : " By the way, Lord Byron says in his pithy manner, in a letter received to-day, of date October 8th, 'Crayon is [very] good,' interlined as I have written it."[1]

It is very evident, if Mr. Murray had placed too low an estimate upon Mr. Irving at first, he was fully alive to his merits now. " I am convinced," he says, " I did not half know you, and esteeming you highly as I did, certainly my esteem is doubled by my better knowledge of you." It was something of a triumph to receive such a letter from the bookseller who had first declined being his publisher.

On the receipt of this letter he writes to Leslie :—

---

[1] In a manuscript account of a visit to Byron at Ravenna, in June, 1821, now before me, by a young American, whom Byron describes as "intelligent, very handsome," "a little romantic," the poet, after a high encomium upon the Knickerbocker history, thus breaks off about the "Sketch-Book": "His Crayon —I know it by heart, at least there is not a passage that I cannot refer to immediately."

In alluding to this American visitor, Mr. Coolidge of Boston, Byron says in a letter to Moore : " I talked with him much of Irving, whose writings are my delight. But I suspect that he did not take quite so much to me, from his having expected to meet a misanthropical gentleman, in wolf-skin breeches, and answering in fierce monosyllables, instead of a man of this world. I can never get people to understand that poetry is the expression of *excited passion*, and that there is no such thing as a life of passion any more than a continuous earthquake, or an eternal fever."

I have just received a very long and friendly letter from Mr. Murray, who in fact has overwhelmed me with eulogiums. It appears that my writings are selling well, and he is multiplying editions. I am very glad to find that he has made your acquaintance, and still more that he has taken a great liking to you. He speaks of you in the most gratifying terms. He has it in his power to be of service to you, and I trust he will be. He tells me he has requested you to look over " Knickerbocker " for subjects for eight or ten sketches, and the " Sketch-Book " for a couple, and he wishes me to assist you with my opinion on the subject. I will look over the books and write to you in a day or two. Murray is going to make me so fine in print that I shall hardly know myself. Could not Allston's design be reduced without losing the characteristic humor of it ? I am delighted to think that your labors are to be thus interwoven with mine, so that we shall have a kind of joint interest and pride in every volume.

My dear boy, it is a grievous thing to be separated from you, and I feel it more and more. I wish to Heaven this world were not so wide, and that we could manage to keep more together in it ; this continual separating from those we like is one of the curses of an unsettled life, and with all my vagrant habits I cannot get accustomed to it.

. . . . Mr. Tappan, who bears this letter, told me that it was the wish of Fairman and yourself that an engraving should be made from the likeness you have of me. It is a matter I do not feel so much objection to as I did formerly, having been so much upon the town lately as to have lost much of my modesty. And as I understand that there has been some spurious print of my phiz in America, I do not care if another is made to push it out of sight. You will only be careful to finish the picture so as not to give it too fixed and precise a fashion of dress. I preferred the costume of Newton's likeness of me, which was trimmed with fur. These modern dresses are apt to give a paltry, commonplace air.

This caution to Leslie about the costume proved the occasion of a piece of waggery on the part of a facetious friend, Peter Powell, one of his little circle of intimates in London, consisting of Leslie, Newton, the " Childe," as he was nicknamed, and Willis, an Irish landscape-painter, more frequently spoken of in his letters as Father Luke. In writing to him, Powell informed him that he understood the world was soon to be gratified by an engraving of his physiognomy, to grace the next edition of his works. " Leslie's picture is very much like you," he writes, " but I think plain, unsophisticated people will be monstrously puzzled to know why you should be drawn in the habiliments of a Venetian nobleman of the sixteenth century, though as far as effect goes it is *picturesque* enough."

This supposed change in Leslie's portrait of him called out the following sensitive comment in a letter to the artist, of December 19th.

I received a letter from Peter Powell, in which he speaks of my portrait being in the engraver's hands, and that it is painted in the old Venetian costume. I hope you have not misunderstood my meaning when I spoke about the costume in which I should like to be painted. I believe I spoke something about the costume of Newton's portrait. I meant Newton's portrait of *me*, not of *himself*. If you recollect, he painted me as if in some kind of an overcoat with a fur cape ; a dress that had nothing in it remarkable, but which merely avoided any present fashion that might in a few years appear stupid. The Venetian dress which Newton painted himself in would have a fantastic appearance, and savor of affectation. If it is not too late, I should like to have the thing altered. Let the costume be simple and picturesque, but such a one as a gentleman might be supposed to wear occasionally at the present day. I only wanted you to avoid the edges, and corners, and angles with which a modern coat is so oddly and formally clipped out at the present day.

I received yesterday yours of the 19th (writes Leslie in reply), and hasten to relieve your mind from any apprehensions you may entertain with regard to the costume of your portrait, which is still in my room exactly in the state in which you last saw it. I shall finish it in a day or two strictly according to your wishes. The Venetian dress was only a phantom of Peter Powell's imagination, conjured up to disturb your evening dreams.

The whimsical personage who had thus amused himself at the expense of the author, I have heard Mr. Irving characterize as a fine, honorable little fellow, with a fund of humor and a special gift for mimicry. One of his performances was a burlesque of the opera of " Moses in Egypt" ; another, an oratorio in which he began by handing in his imaginary female singers ; and Leslie hints at a third, in an allusion to his " gallanting that imaginary flock of geese." It was a great treat to his friends to witness these comic exhibitions, but in all his travesties, said Mr. Irving, in attempting an exemplification of one of them, there was nothing overdone. He made his acquaintance when preparing the first number of the "Sketch-Book," and introduced him afterward to Leslie and Newton, with the first of whom he became a great crony.

November 30, 1820, he writes to Leslie :—

I hear that you are going on with the sketches for "Knickerbocker," and that you have executed one on the same subject Allston once chose, namely, "Peter Stuyvesant rebuking the cobbler." I wish you would drop me a line and let me know what subjects you execute, and how you and Murray make out together. I hear that you have taken the "Childe" to Murray's; you have only to make him acquainted with Willis and Peter Powell, and he will then be able to make one at your tea-kettle debauches.

"The Childe" had just written to him that Willis had sent them home at four in the morning, "reeling with Bohea."

The letter proceeds :—

I have just made a brief but very pleasant excursion into Lower Normandy in company with Mr. Ritchie. I must refer you to a letter scribbled to Peter Powell for a full and faithful narrative of this tour.

I have not this letter; but some pencil memoranda of the tour show that he started on the 8th November, and that his travels extended to Honfleur, at the mouth of the Seine, the scene of his story of " Annette Delarbre " in " Bracebridge Hall."

In his answer, dated December 3d, Leslie says :—

The subjects I have chosen are a Dutch fireside, with an old negro telling stories to the children ; William the Testy suspending a vagrant by the heels on his patent gallows ; Peter Stuyvesant confuting the cobbler ; and Anthony Van Corlear taking leave of the young vrows. All of them I have finished except the last, and Mr. Murray appears to be highly pleased with them.

He is delighted with Allston's picture of " Wouter Van Twiller," which will be engraved with the rest. He talks a great deal about you, whenever I see him, in terms of the highest praise and friendship. The " Sketch-Book " is entirely out of print.

I like all the subjects that you have chosen for the designs [writes the author in reply], except that of William the Testy suspending the vagabond by the breeches. The circumstance is not of sufficient point or character in the history to be illustrated.

Leslie, in explanation, assigns as a reason for the selection, that Murray wished one design at least from the reign of each governor, and he was puzzled in finding one that could be brought within a small compass from that part of the book. " I was somewhat fearful of it myself," he adds, " but Newton thinks you would like it."

Meanwhile the new candidate for fame was steadily gaining in reputation in England. " I think you are a most fortunate fellow of an author," writes Peter Powell, December 3d, " in regard to your debut amongst us in this critical age, for I have not heard of your having so much as a *nose* or a member of any kind cut up by the anatomists of literature ; on the contrary, there seems to be almost a *conspiracy* to hoist you over the heads of your contemporaries." And Leslie writes, December 24th : " Miller says Geoffrey Crayon is the most fashionable fellow of the day. I am very much inclined to think if you were here just now, 'company would be the spoil of you.'" Then, begging to be remembered to his brother Peter, he concludes : " All the lads join in wishing you both a merry Christmas and happy New Year. I intend appropriating a part of to-morrow to reading your Christmas article. I shall stick up your portrait before my face, and bury myself in an enormous elbow-chair I have got, over which 'Murphy often sheds his puppies,' relying on the book I shall hold in my hand to act as a charm against the seductions of the seat. These associations are the best means by which I can console myself for your absence."

CHAPTER XXVI.

Makes the Acquaintance of Thomas Moore, the Poet.—Visit to the Prison of Marie Antoinette.—Letter to Brevoort.—Reasons for Remaining Abroad.—Moore.—Canning.—John Howard Payne.—Talma.—His Performance of Hamlet.—Letter to Leslie.—Kenney, Author of " Raising the Wind," etc.—Luttrel.—Introduced to the Hollands.—Murray Begs his Acceptance of an Additional One Hundred Pounds for the " Sketch-Book."—The Author's Letter Thereupon.—Reads Manuscript to Moore. —Bancroft.—Sets off for England July 11th, Hoping to have Something Ready for the Press by Autumn.

IT was at the close of this year that Mr. Irving made the acquaintance of one of the most brilliant and delightful of his contemporaries, Thomas Moore, the Irish poet, then an absentee in Paris, on account of some pending liabilities of government against him, arising out of the defalcation of his deputy at Bermuda, which he was hoping to adjust. Moore has this entry on the subject in his diary :—

December 21, 1820.—Dined with McKay at the *table d' hôte* at Meurice's for the purpose of being made known to Mr. Washington Irving, the author of the work which has lately had success, the " Sketch-Book "; a good-looking and intelligent-mannered man.

McKay, who brought the two authors together, was an Irish gentleman who had come to the French capital from England on a mission to inspect the prisons ; and two days after (December 23d), he, Lord John Russell, Moore, and Mr. Irving were visiting in company the room in which the ill-fated Marie Antoinette was confined.

I find loose among his papers this brief record of the visit to a place seldom open to a stranger's inspection.

I have just returned from the prison of Marie Antoinette. Under the palace of Justice is a range of cavernous dungeons, called the Conciergerie, the last prison in which criminals are confined previous to execution. We were admitted through grated doors, and conducted along damp, dark passages, lighted in some places by dim windows, in others by lamps. On these passages opened the grates of several dungeons in which victims were thrown during the revolution, to indulge in the horrible anticipation of certain death. My flesh crept on my bones as I passed through these regions of despair, and fancied these dens peopled with their wretched inhabitants. I fancied their worn and wasted faces glaring through the grates, to catch, if possible, some ray of hope or mitigation of horror, but seeing nothing except the sentinel pacing up and down the passage, or perhaps some predecessor in misery dragged along to execution. In this were confined the victims of Robespierre, and finally Robespierre himself.

From this corridor we were led through a small chapel into what at present forms the sacristy, but which was once the dungeon of the unhappy Queen of France. It is low and arched; the walls of prodigious thickness, lighted dimly by a small window. The walls have been plastered and altered, and the whole is fitted up with an air of decency; nothing remains of the old dungeon but the pavement. In one part is a monument placed by Louis XVIII., and around the dungeon are paintings illustrating some of the latest prison scenes of her unhappy life. The place is shown where her bed stood, divided simply by a screen from the rest of the dungeon in which a guard of soldiers was constantly stationed; beside this dungeon is the black hole—I can give it no better term—in which the Princess Elizabeth was thrust a few hours prior to her execution.

Never have I felt my heart melting with pity more than in beholding this last abode of wretchedness. What a place for a queen, and such a queen! one brought up so delicately, fostered, admired, adored.

The acquaintance with Moore thus commenced grew speedily into intimacy, as will be seen by the following letter to Brevoort, in answer to one urging his return to New York.

PARIS, March 10, 1821.

DEAR BREVOORT:—

. . . . You urge me to return to New York, and say, many ask whether I mean to renounce my country. For this last question I have no reply to make, and yet I will make a reply. As far as my precarious and imperfect abilities enable me, I am endeavoring to serve my country. Whatever I have written has been written with the feelings and published as the writing of an American. Is that renouncing my country? How else am I to serve my country? by coming home and begging an office of it; which I should not have the kind of talent or the business habits requisite to fill ? If I can do any good in this world it is with my pen. I feel that even with that I can do very little, but if I do that little and do it as an American, I think my exertions ought to guarantee me from so unkind a question as that which you say is generally made.

As to coming home, I should at this moment be abandoning my literary plans, such as they are. I should lose my labor in various literary materials which I have in hand, and to work up which I must be among the scenes where they were conceived. I should arrive at home at a time when my slender finances require an immediate exercise of my talents, but should be so agitated and discomposed in my feelings by the meetings with my friends, the revival of many distressing circumstances and trains of thought, and should be so hurried by the mere attentions of society, that months would elapse before I could take pen in hand, and then I would have to strike out some entirely new plan and begin *ab ovo*. As to the idea you hold out of being provided for *sooner or later* in our *fortunate* city, I can only say that I see no way in which I could be provided for, not being a man of business, a man of science, or, in fact, any thing but a mere belles-lettres writer. And as to the fortunate character of our city ; to me and mine it has been a very disastrous one. I have written on this point at some length, as I wish to have done with it. My return home must depend upon circumstances, not upon inclinations. I have by patient and persevering labor of my most uncertain pen, and by catching the gleams of sunshine in my cloudy mind, managed to open to myself an avenue to some degree of profit and reputation. I value it the more highly because it is entirely independent and self-created ; and I must use my best endeavors to turn it to account. In remaining, therefore, abroad, I do it with the idea that I can best exert my talents, for the present, where I am ; and, that I trust, will be admitted as a sufficient reply from a man who has but his talents to feed and clothe him.

I have become very intimate with Anacreon Moore, who is living here with his family. Scarce a day passes without our seeing each other, and he has made me acquainted with many of his friends here. He is a charming, joyous fellow ; full of frank, generous, manly feeling. I am happy to say he expresses himself in the fullest and strongest manner on the subject of his writings in America, which he pronounces the great sin of his early life. He is busy upon the life of Sheridan and upon a poem. His acquaintance is one of the most gratifying things I have met with for some time, as he takes the warm interest of an old friend in me and my concerns.

Canning is likewise here with his family, and has been very polite in his attentions to me. He has expressed a very flattering opinion of my writings both here and in England, and his opinion is of great weight and value in the critical world. I had a very agreeable dinner at his house a few days since, at which I met Moore, Sir Sidney Smith, and several other interesting characters.

" You keep excellent company in Paris," Brevoort answers. " Anacreon Moore and Mr. Canning ; these are names that set one's blood in motion." Brevoort would have been glad if he had enriched his letters with more particulars of the interesting characters he was meeting, but his friend used jestingly to say that he was now living by his pen, and must save up all his anecdotes and good things for his publishers.

A few loose leaves of an imperfect journal of the author, found among his papers after his death, give an interesting account of his first meeting with Talma, the great French tragedian, in company with John Howard Payne, the young American Roscius of former days. Payne was a fellow townsman of Mr. Irving, who had appeared with great éclat at the Park Theatre in New York in his sixteenth year, in the character of young Norval. He had outgrown all tragic symmetry after leaving his country in 1813 to try his success in England, and from being an actor, had assumed at one time the management of Sadler's Wells ; had failed in this and got in debt. He afterward brought out " Junius Brutus," a tragedy which he had manufactured out of two or three plays. It had a great run, and Mr. Irving called on him in London to congratulate him on his success : but alas ! its success had proved his ruin. It brought his creditors down upon him, and he was thrown into prison. Here he wrote " Teresa, or the Orphan of Geneva," which was successful and extricated him. Then he escaped to Paris, where Mr. Irving met him. Payne was a fluent writer, and for a while a successful performer ; but he is most favorably known at the present day as the author of " Home, Sweet Home," a popular song which he introduced in his opera of " Clari, or the Maid of Milan." The profits arising from it, realized by the manager and not by Payne, have been stated to have amounted to two thousand guineas in two years.

Paris, April 25, 1821.—Breakfasted this morning with John Howard Payne. He has the first floor of a small house, in a garden No. 16 Petit Rue de St. Petre, Pont aux Choux. The morning was fine and the air soft and spring-like. His casements were thrown open, and the breezes that blew in were extremely grateful. He has a couple of canary birds, with a little perch ornamented with moss. He stands it in the window, and they fly about the garden and return to their perch for food and to rest at night.

Payne is full of dramatic projects, and some that are very feasible.

After breakfast we strolled along the Boulevards, gossiping, staring at groups and sights and signs, and looking over booksellers' stalls. He proposed to me to call on Talma, who had just returned to Paris. He has a suite of apartments in a hotel, No. —— Rue des Petites Augustines. He has a seat in the country about — miles from Paris, of which he is extremely fond, and is continually altering and improving, though he can seldom get there above once a week. He is about to build a town residence, and at present lives in lodgings. I got Payne to mount before me, as I did not wish to call on Talma so unceremoniously. Payne found him changing his linen. He requested him immediately to bring me up. On entering he received me in a very friendly, frank way, and turning to Payne, said : " Why, he is quite a young man"; it seems he had expected to see an old one: his room was full of furniture, and books, etc., rather confused. I remarked a colored engraving of John Kemble.

Talma is about 5 feet 7 or 7½ inches English, rather inclined to fat, with large face and thick neck. His eyes are bluish, and have a peculiar cast in them at times. He speaks English well, and is very frank, animated, and natural in conversation; a fine, hearty simplicity of manner. Asked me if this was my first visit to Paris; told him that I had been here once before—about fourteen years since. " Ah! that was in the time of the Emperor," said he. He remarked that Paris was very much changed; thinks the French character greatly changed; more grave. "You see the young men from the colleges," said he; "how grave they are; they walk together, conversing incessantly on politics and other grave subjects"; says the nation has become as grave as the English.

We spoke of the French play of " Hamlet." I asked if other of Shakespeare's plays were adopting for the French stage. He believed not. He thinks there is likely to be great changes in French drama. The public feel greater interest in scenes that come home to common life and people in ordinary situations, than in the distresses of heroic personages of classic literature. Hence they never come to the Théâtre Français except to see a few great actors, but they crowd to the minor theatres to see the representation of ordinary life. He says the revolution has made so many strong and vivid scenes of real life pass before their eyes, that they can no longer be affected by mere declamation and fine language; they require character, incident, passion, life.

Says if there should be another revolution it would be a bloody one. The nation (*i. e.*, the younger part, children of the revolution) have such a hatred of the priests and noblesse, that they would fly upon them like sheep. Mentions the manner in which certain parts of plays have been applauded lately at Rouen ; one part which said: " Usurpers are not always tyrants." When we were coming away he followed us to the door of his antechamber ; in passing through the latter I saw children's swords and soldiers' caps lying on the table, and said: " Your children, I see, have swords for playthings." He replied, with animation, that all the amusements of the children were military ; that they would have nothing to play with but swords, guns, trumpets, drums, etc.

It was after this interview that Mr. Irving saw Talma's performance of Hamlet, and I find among his papers this allusion to the tragedy and the actor.

The successful performance of a translation of " Hamlet " has been an era in the French drama. It is true the play has been sadly mutilated ; it has been stripped of its most natural and characteristic beauties, and an attempt has been made to reduce it to the naked stateliness of one of their own dramas ; but it still retains enough of the wild magnificence of Shakespeare's imagination to give it an individual character on the French stage. Though the ghost of Hamlet's father does not actually tread the boards, yet he hovers in idea about his son, and the powerful acting of Talma gives an idea of this portentous visitation far more awful and mysterious than could be presented by any spectral representation. The effect of this play on the French audiences is astonishing. The doors of the theatre are besieged at an early hour on the evening of its representation ; the houses are crowded to overflowing ; the audience continually passes from intervals of breathless attention to bursts of ungovernable applause. I have seen a lady carried fainting from the boxes, overcome by the acting of Talma in the scene with his mother, where he fancies he sees the spectre of his father.

Newton had at this time acquired a good deal of distinction from a picture, " Le Fâcheux," which had got one of the best places at the exhibition, between Wilkie and Jackson. It had made quite a sensation in the papers, and had been purchased by Thomas Hope, the author of " Anastasius." He could hardly have been more fortunate in the character of the purchaser or the gallery to which it was destined, Hope having the finest collection in London. " I have something of your feeling," he writes to the author of the " Sketch-Book," February 10, 1821, " on occasion of this distinction, and am terribly nervous lest I should not get as good a subject for my next."

At the date of the leaf or fragment which follows, and which, like the note of his visit to Talma, I gleaned from some literary rubbish of the author, Moore had changed his quarters for a cottage in the neighborhood of St. Cloud ; and Kenney, the delineator of " Jeremy Diddler," had found a nestling place in the elbow of an old royal castle on the crest of a hill opposite.

May 16, 1821.—I took an early dinner at four o'clock, and rode out afterward to see Moore. Took a place in a cuckoo to St. Cloud. It was a lovely afternoon, and the walk through the park of St. Cloud was delightful ; views of the Seine, with boats drifting down it ; bridges crossing it. Found Moore at his cottage in the park of Mr. Villamil's seat, La Butte ; a very pretty cottage ; magnificent scenery all about it. It stands on the side of the hill that rises above Sèvres. To the left is St. Cloud and its grand park. The Seine winds at the foot of the hill, and the great plain of Neuilly lies before you, with the Bois de Boulogne and Paris in the distance ; glorious effect of sunset on Moore's balcony ; the gilded dome of Invalides flaming in the sunshine.

Accompanied Mr. and Mrs. Moore, and the Villamils to Mr. Kenney's, author of " Raising the Wind," etc. He married the widow of Holcroft, who had several children ; her stock and his own make eight children. They have apartments in one of the wings, or rather the offices of the old chateau of Bellevue, built by Louis XV., where he and Madame Pompadour lived. The old chateau is a picture of grandeur in decay ; the windows broken ; the clock shattered ; the court-yards grass-grown ; apartments in a ruined and dilapidated state. Kenney's establishment squalid ; remains of magnificent furniture ; old sofa, with griffin-head arms ; old stools, which had doubtless been for the courtiers in the royal apartments.

Kenney a very worthy and a very pleasant fellow ; a thin, pale man, with a gentleness of demeanor and manner, and very nervous. He gave some descriptions of scenes in London with admirable truth and character. Moore told me that he was once giving Kenney an account of his misfortunes ; the heavy blow he sustained in consequence of the default of his agent in Bermuda. Kenney expressed the strongest sympathy. "Gad, sir, it 's well you were a poet; a philosopher never would have borne it."

June 21st, we have this mention in Moore's diary of a dinner at his cottage, in which Lord John Russell, Luttrel, the author of " Advice to Julia," then newly arrived, and Irving, were his guests. " In speaking of my abuse of the Americans, Irving said it was unlucky that some of my best verses were upon that subject ; ' put them in his *strongest* pickle,' said Luttrel."

Luttrel was noted for the grace and delicacy of his wit, and I have heard Mr. Irving express admiration of an impromptu specimen which occurred about this time in his presence.

Moore, Luttrel, and himself were walking together, when Moore alluded to the uncertain fate of a female aëronaut who took her flight into the empyrean and continued to ascend in her " airy ship," until she was lost to view, and, added the poet, " never heard of more." " Handed out by Enoch and Elijah," was Luttrel's immediate and happy response.

In Moore's diary we have this further glimpse of his friend at Paris.

July 2, 1821.—Took Irving to present him to the Hollands; my lady very gracious to him.

Mr. Irving was at this time so anxious to get on with his literary pursuits, that he rather avoided the gay world.

I have advances made me by society [he writes to Brevoort not long before], that were I a mere seeker of society, would be invaluable ; but I dread so much being put out in my pursuits and distracted by the mere hurry of fashionable engagements, that I keep aloof and neglect opportunities which I may perhaps at some future day look back to with regret.

About this time he received from his London publisher the following concise authority to draw on him for a hundred pounds, a second gratuitous contribution for the "Sketch-Book," of which, writes Newton, " Murray says its success, considering all things, is unparalleled."

LONDON, June 20, 1821.

MY DEAR IRVING:—

Draw upon me for a hundred pounds, of which I beg thy acceptance, and pray tell me how you are and what you are about; and above all, pardon my short letter. Believe me ever,

Thy faithful friend,

JOHN MURRAY.

There is a review of the "Sketch-Book" in the *Quarterly* which you will like.

The following is the author's reply :—

[*To John Murray.*]

PARIS, July 6, 1821.

MY DEAR SIR:—

I write in very great haste to acknowledge the receipt of your letter of the 29th ult. I am extremely happy to hear that the "Sketch-Book" has been favorably noticed in the *Quarterly.* I have not seen the *Review,* but I doubt whether any criticism in it can be so emphatic as that in your letter. You were certainly intended for a critic. I never knew any one to convey so much meaning in so concise and agreeable a manner. In compliance with your request, I have drawn on you for a hundred pounds in favor of Mr. Samuel Williams of London. The supply came opportunely. I am on the point of leaving Paris for Brussels, and where I shall go from thence is at present undetermined; but I shall write to you from the Netherlands, should I make any stop there.

I have been leading a "miscellaneous" kind of life at Paris, if I may use a literary phrase. I have been rather distracted by engagements, in spite of all my efforts to keep out of society. Anacreon Moore is living here, and has made me a gayer fellow than I could have wished; but I found it impossible to resist the charm of his society. Paris is like an English watering-place, with the advantage of the best kind of amusements, and excellent society.

I have scribbled at intervals, and have a mass of writings by me ; rather desultory, as must be the case when one is so much interrupted; but I hope, in the fulness of time, to get them into some order.

I write in extreme haste, having to pack up and make other preparations for departure.

With my best regards to Mrs. Murray and the rest of your family, I am, my dear sir,

Very faithfully yours,

WASHINGTON IRVING.

In this letter, the author is " on the point of leaving Paris for Brussels"; but a sudden change of purpose comes over him, and he determines to start for London at once, to be in time for the approaching coronation of George IV.; hoping also to get something ready for the press by autumn.   One of his last acts in Paris is to read to Moore a portion of the manuscript of " Buckthorne and his Friends," originally designed for " Bracebridge Hall," his next work, but forming part of the contents of " The Tales of a Traveller," which succeeded it.   He had already read a portion of it to the poet, " sitting on the grass in the walk up the Rocher."

July 9th.—Moore has the following: Irving came to breakfast for the purpose of taking leave (being about to set off for England), and of reading to me some more of his new work; some of it much livelier than the first he read.   He has given the description of the booksellers' dinner so exactly like what I told him of one of the Longmans (the carving partner, the partner to laugh at the popular author's jokes, the twelve-edition writers treated with claret, etc.), that I very much fear my friends in Paternoster Row will know themselves in the picture.

Subsequently, he affords the author an opportunity to improve the picture by personal observation, a part of his record of May 22, 1822, in London, being : " Introduced Irving to the Longmans, and dined with him there."

It is no disparagement of the poet, however, to say, as has been said by a critical authority, that the picture " owed every thing to Irving's handling."

It must have been about this time, also, that Mr. Irving read to our distinguished historian George Bancroft, then fresh from two years' study at Göttingen, a portion of the work he was preparing for the press.   " During a summer in Paris," says that gentleman in his commemorative remarks before the New York Historical Society, " I formed with him that relation of friendly intimacy, which grew in strength to the last.   Time has in a measure effaced the relative difference in our years, but then he was almost twice as old as I. . . . .   One evening, after we had been many hours together, he took me to his room, and read to me what he had written at one sitting. . . . .   I remember it to this day : it

was his 'St. Mark's Eve,' from the words 'I am now alone in my chamber,' to the end."

The last glimpse we have in Moore's Diary, of Irving at Paris, is the following :—

July 10*th.*—Went in to dine at Lord Holland's. Company: Lord John, Fazakerly, Irving, Allen. . . . . Kenney and Irving set off for England to-morrow.

The poet does not mention what I have heard Mr. Irving speak of as an impressive recollection of the occasion, that Talma came in after dinner with the news of the death of Napoleon.

The next day he set off for England, accompanied by Kenney, who, by the way, was the personage alluded to in his " Life of Goldsmith," as the author whom he had seen with his back to a tree and his foot to a stone, trying to bother out a scene in a farce which he could not manage to his satisfaction.

CHAPTER XXVII.

The Coronation of George IV.—Meeting with Scott.—Detained in London about a Play of Payne.—Literary Concerns.—Excursion to Birmingham with Leslie.—" The Stout Gentleman."—Its Moral.—Kept at Birmingham by Illness.—Newton's Introduction to La Butte by Himself.—Leslie and Powell's Joint Account of their Housekeeping in Buckingham Place.—Letter to Leslie.—Death of his Brother William.—Moore.

William the Testy.

MR. IRVING arrived in London the day before the coronation, and the next morning got a stand on the outside of Westminster Abbey, with Newton and Leslie, to see the procession pass. The following day he called on Scott, who congratulated him in his hearty manner on his success, and asked him if he had seen the coronation. He told him he had seen the procession on the outside. "Oh, you should have been inside." "Why, I only came over the day before, and I did not know how to manage it." "Hut, man," said Scott, "you should have told them who you were, and you would have got in anywhere." At parting, Scott expressed his regret that he would not probably see any thing more of him in London, as he was *engaged up to the hub.*

Mr. Irving had not meditated any stay in London, but was kept there some time in a fruitless attempt to bring upon the stage a petite comedy of John Howard Payne, entitled "The Borrower," which he had sent him from Paris. The circumstances of Payne were such as to call for prompt action in the matter, and as England was not open to him by reason of his debts, he had availed himself of Mr. Irving's kindness to send him the manuscript. He wrote, July 14th, apprising him of its transmission, but the letter would seem not to have taken a very direct course, and to have kept Mr. Irving in London waiting its receipt some time after he had hoped to have joined his sister in Birmingham. Payne laments, in a letter of August 12th, that his kind dispositions toward him should have been the source of any derangement of his plans.

In a letter to Peter, dated London, September 6th, he says:—

I have a variety of writings in hand, some I think superior to what I have already published ; my only anxiety is to get them into shape and order. . . . .

I have fagged hard to get another work under way, as I felt that a great deal depended upon it, both as to reputation and profit. I feel my system a little affected now and then by these sedentary fits to which, until two or three years past, I have not been accustomed. When I get my present manuscript finished and off of hands, I think I will give myself holiday.

Mr. Irving brought with him to London the manuscript of the chief part of "Bracebridge Hall," in the rough, intending or hoping to make arrangements for its publication in the autumn. On reading to Leslie "Buckthorne," the part of his "writings in hand" which he had in view in the letter to Peter just quoted, as in his judgment "superior to what" he had "already published," the artist suggested that he should retain that as the groundwork of a novel, and substitute something else. He accordingly threw it by, and replaced it with the "Student of Salamanca"; an ill-judged change, as he afterward regarded it, but he was prone to yield too readily to the suggestions of others.

It was about the 9th of September that Mr. Irving and Leslie started on the excursion to Birmingham, of which the latter speaks in the extract given below. Irving had been previously suggesting to Leslie for his pencil, the subject of Shakespeare brought up for deer-stealing, having a picture in his own mind, which the artist, after repeated efforts, could not make out.   He caught at the idea at first, however, and was in pursuit of materials, when they started off together, intending to bring up at the residence of Mr. Van Wart, Irving's brother-in-law.

In the account of the expedition which follows, Leslie touches upon the origin of " The Stout Gentleman," the gem of " Brace-bridge Hall."   I transcribe from his Autobiography :—

Toward the close of the summer of 1821 I made a delightful excursion with Washington Irving to Birmingham and thence into Derbyshire. We mounted to the top of one of the Oxford coaches at three o'clock in the afternoon, intending only to go as far as Henley that night ; but the evening was so fine, and the fields filled with laborers gathering in the corn by the light of a full moon presented so animated an appearance, that although we had not dined, we determined to proceed to Oxford, which we reached about eleven o'clock, and then sat down to a hot supper.

The next day it rained unceasingly, and we were confined to the inn, like the nervous traveller whom Irving has described as spending a day in endeavoring to penetrate the mystery of " the stout gentleman." This wet Sunday at Oxford did in fact suggest to him that capital story, if story it can be called. That next morning, as we mounted the coach, I said something about a *stout gentleman* who had come from London with us the day before, and Irving remarked that " The Stout Gentleman " would not be a bad title for a tale ; as soon as the coach stopped, he began writing with his pencil, and went on at every like opportunity. We visited Stratford-on-Avon, strolled about Charlecot Park and other places in the neighborhood, and while I was sketching, Irving, mounted on a stile or seated on a stone, was busily engaged with " The Stout Gentleman." He wrote with the greatest rapidity, often laughing to himself, and from time to time reading the manuscript to me. We loitered some days in this classic neighborhood, visiting Warwick and Kenilworth ; and by the time we arrived at Birmingham, the outline of " The Stout Gentleman " was completed.   The amusing account of " The Modern Knights-Errant," he added at Birmingham, and the inimitable picture of the inn-yard on a rainy day, was taken from an inn where we were afterward quartered at Derby.

If I may venture to add any thing to this delightful sketch by Leslie, which harmonizes with all that Mr. Irving has told me relative to the composition of that story, one of the few things he had written, of which from the first, as I have heard him say, he had never doubted, it is that he gave the concluding touch to it, sitting on a gravestone in Lillington church-yard close by Leamington, while Leslie was sketching a view of Warwick Castle, which the yard commanded.

Another anecdote rises to my memory, connected with that light and frolicsome specimen of his pen.

I was once reading aloud in his presence a very flattering review of his works, which had been sent him by the critic in 1848, and smiled as I came to this sentence : " His most comical pieces have always a serious end in view." " You laugh," said he, with that air of whimsical significance so natural to him, " but it is true. I have kept that to myself hitherto, but that man has found me out. He has detected the moral of ' The Stout Gentleman.' "

Mr. Irving had intended but a short visit to the residence of his sister at Birmingham, but was detained there nearly four months by illness, most of the time confined to the house.

I have been upward of two months in England [he writes to his brother Ebenezer, September 28th]. I came over in hopes of getting some manuscript ready for the press this autumn, but ever since my arrival in England I have been so much out of health as to prevent my doing any thing of consequence with my pen. I have been troubled with bilious attacks, to which I had never before been subject. It is the consequence of being too much within doors, and not taking exercise enough. I am now dieting myself and taking medicine, and I trust I shall, with a little care and attention, get myself in fine order again. I am very anxious to get something into print, but find it next to impossible, in my present state of health, to do any thing material. Murray is also extremely desirous ; and indeed the success of my former writings would insure a run to any thing I should now bring forward. . . . .

You have wished for an additional number of the " Sketch-Book," but I have not been able to prepare one, being occupied with other writings. If you could clear off the stock of odd numbers that remain, even though it should be at considerable sacrifice, I wish you would do it. We could then publish a complete and corrected edition in two volumes.

The following letter to Leslie is written eleven days later from his sister's house, which he designates, with characteristic playfulness, Edgbaston *Castle*, as he had styled her husband, Van Wart, on a former occasion, Baron Von Tromp, and his residence the *Castle* of the Von Tromps.

EDGBASTON CASTLE, October 9, 1821.

MY DEAR LESLIE:—

I have been looking for a letter from you every day. Why don't you drop me a line? It would be particularly cheering just now. I have not been out of the house since you left here; having been much indisposed by a cold, I am at the mercy of every breath of air that blows. I have had pains in my head, my face swollen, and yesterday passed the greater part of the day in bed, which is a very extraordinary thing for me. To-day I feel better; but I am sadly out of order; and what especially annoys me is, that I see day after day and week after week passing away without being able to do any thing. . . . . Have you begun any new picture yet, or have you any immediately in contemplation? I received a letter from Newton, which I presume was forwarded by your direction. Why did you not open it? It was dated the 15th September. He had arrived but two or three days; had sailed up the Seine from Havre to Rouen with my brother in the steamboat. He had dined with Moore, had passed a day in the Louvre, where he met Wilkie, and strolled the gallery with him. He speaks in raptures of the Louvre. He says it strikes him in quite a different way from what it did when he was there before. He intended to go to work a day or two afterward, and expected to pass the greater part of his time there.

Have you seen Murray? when you see him you need not say where I am. I want the quiet, and not to be bothered in any way. Tell him I am in a country doctor's hands at Edgbaston somewhere in Warwickshire. I think that will puzzle any one, as Edgbaston has been built only within a year or two. Get me all the pleasant news you can, and then sit down in the evening and scribble a letter without minding points or fine terms. My sister is very anxious to hear of you. You have quite won her heart, not so much by your merits as by your attention to the children. By the way, the little girls have become very fond of the pencil since you were here, and are continually taking their dolls' likenesses.

Ever yours,   W. I.

In a postscript, dated the 17th, of Newton's letter here alluded to, the artist mentions his dining with Moore the day preceding, and in the body of the letter he gives this account of his introduction to La Butte :—

I was presented last night at La Butte in a most characteristic manner. As Mr. Moore leaves town in a day or two, Mr. Story thought no time should be lost to introduce me, so set off for that purpose after dark and in the rain, which, as you know the place, will of itself give you an idea of the enterprise. I, of course, was ignorant of the situation, or I should have opposed it, as it was undertaken on my account. As it was, figure to yourself Mrs. Story equipped with an old gentleman's shoes (who sat in a carriage the while), and me with a lanthorn and umbrella, slipping about, drabbled, and sometimes lost in those mazes of which I have only still a sort of nightmare recollection. I was extremely mortified at being the cause of so much disaster, but they did not seem to think it so much out of the way, and as we came off happily, I was on the whole glad of the oddity of the adventure. This and some other little traits amused me extremely, as corresponding with the idea you had given me of this coterie.

October 22d, Leslie writes him :—

Powell and I commenced housekeeping a week ago. It is probable that nothing will more astonish you on your return than the metamorphosis at Buckingham Place. Not to speak of window curtains, a pianoforte, *small knives* and plates at breakfast, you will be surprised to find an *academy* established on the principle of mutual education in various branches of learning and the fine arts. During breakfast, Powell gives me a lesson in French. At five we both study carving. After tea I teach him to draw the figures, and at odd times he instructs himself in German and the piano-forte, and once a week he unfolds to me the mysteries of political economy according to Cobbett. Instruction is even extended beyond our walls, as far indeed as Sloane Street, where Powell delivers a weekly lecture on perspective. In this way we pass the time ; and I am quite sure that if I get through the winter as I have passed the last week, and with you and Newton here, it will be the most agreeable one I shall have spent in London. I was glad to hear of Newton from you. I did not see his letter or I should have opened it. I am at present painting the portraits of two little girls, and making a drawing from the " Royal Poet," the incident of the dove flying into the window. Powell has promised to fill up the sheet. I must therefore bid you good-by.

Powell fills up the sheet after this burlesque fashion :—

I am beginning to be ashamed of the prejudices I had imbibed about Buckingham Place. All prejudices are hateful, and people ought to live in every spot they do not like, in order to ascertain whether their opinions are well or ill-founded. There are many charms about this place, the enjoyment of which I never contemplated. While I am now writing, in addition to the enjoyment of my tea and rolls, a sort of troubadour is warbling beneath my window, together with the partner of his bosom, and a little natural production between both, equally regardless of fame and weather, and seemingly smitten only by the love of half-pence; the pleasure of getting which in this neighborhood must, I suppose, like that of angling, be greatly increased by the rarity of the bite. Those things about us here, that to the common view appear disagreeable, tend to increase our happiness. The repose and quiet of our evening talk or studies is rendered still more so by its contrast with a matrimonial squabble in the street, or the undisguised acknowledgment of pain in the vociferations of a whipped urchin up the court.

We are also much more pastoral here than you would imagine.

We have a share in a *cow*, which makes its appearance twice a day in a blue and white cream-jug. We eat our own dinners, and *generally* have enough. Yesterday, to be sure, we came a little short, in consequence of Leslie, who acts as maitre d' hôtel, having ordered a sumptuous hash to be made from a cold shoulder of lamb, the meat of which had been previously stripped from it with surgical dexterity by our host himself during the three preceding days. There have been a great many disputes in all ages about the real situation of Paradise. I have not, to be sure, read all the arguments upon the subject; but if I were to go entirely by my own judgment, I should guess it to be somewhere near the corner of Cambridge Court, Fitzroy Square.

Adieu, and increased health to you.

Yours, etc., etc., etc.,

P. P.

The following is the author's reply to Leslie, the address to his " friend Peter " being missing.

EDGBASTON, October 25, 1821.

MY DEAR LESLIE :—

I thank you a thousand times for your letter. I had intended to have answered your preceding one before, but I am not in mood or condition to write, and had nothing to say worth writing. I am still in the hands of the physician. I have taken draughts and pills enough to kill a horse, yet I can not determine whether I am not rather worse off than when I began.

I cannot at this moment suggest any thing for your Christmas piece. I do not know your general plan. Is it to be a daylight piece, or an evening round a hall fire? Is there no news of Newton? If I had thought he would remain so long at Paris, I would have written to him.

I am glad to hear that you are so snugly fixed with friend Powell for the winter, though I should have been much better pleased to have heard that you were turned neck and heels into the street. Reconcile it to yourself as you may, I shall ever look upon your present residence as a most serious detriment to you; and were you to lose six or even twelve months in looking for another, I should think you a gainer upon the whole.

What prospects are there of the plates being finished for " Knickerbocker " and the " Sketch-Book "? When do you begin a large picture, and what subject do you attack first? It is time you had something under way. I must leave a space to reply to friend Peter; so farewell for the present,

Yours, ever,

W. I.

Two days after the date of this letter, Mr. Irving received one from Ebenezer, informing him that his brother William was gradually growing weaker under a seated consumption. He died November 9, 1821.

In alluding to the loss of this brother, whom he describes as having been " a kind of father to them all," he speaks of him in a later letter as " a man full of worth and talents, beloved in private and honored in public life." Paulding has also recorded his appreciation of him as "a man of wit and genius." William died at the age of fifty-five. His disease was thought to have been hastened by over-anxiety in business. He had been about retiring at the close of the war with a handsome fortune, when a cloud came over the commercial world, and though not involved in the embarrassments of his brothers, he found himself a serious sufferer from the times, and obliged to continue a life of exertion when his health required entire repose.

About this time Mr. Irving received from Newton a letter, which gives the following tidings of Moore.

Moore's affairs are settled, and he is coming to live in England; he goes to France on Monday next; he is sitting to me. He desires his best regards to you, and had he known you were in Birmingham would have stopped there.

Moore had come over *incog.* from Paris some three weeks before the date of this letter; had settled his affairs—that is, the

Bermuda difficulty, with the money arising from the sale to Murray of the " Memoirs of Byron," which the poet had given him in Italy some two years previous, to make what use of them he pleased, though with the understanding that they could not be published during his life.   He was now about to return to Paris, where he remained nearly four months after Mr. Irving had gone up to London.   He had passed through Birmingham twice during his incognito, without being aware of Mr. Irving's presence in that city. The last time was October 21st, on his way from Ireland to London. His diary gives the following record for the next day :—

October 22d.—Arrived in London at *7 incog.* . . . . Was preparing, as usual, to sneak out in a hackney-coach, when Rees arrived with the important and joyful intelligence that the agent has accepted the £1,000, and that I am now a free man again.   Walked boldly out into the sunshine, and showed myself up St. James Street and Bond Street.

Moore had returned to Paris on the 11th of November, and when he visited London again in April, he rescinded his bargain with Murray for the " Memoirs of Byron," making himself a debtor to the publisher for the two thousand guineas advanced, and leaving the manuscript in his hands as security for its repayment.   These memoirs, which were not destined to see the light, Mr. Irving had read while in Paris with Moore.

CHAPTER XXVIII.

*Return to London.—Transmits First Volume of " Bracebridge Hall."—
Moses Thomas.—Cooper and " The Spy."—Sends off Volume II.
" Bracebridge Hall."—Makes Contract with Murray for Publication in
England.—John Randolph.—Mrs. Siddons.—Visit to Wimbledon, one
of the Country-Seats of Earl Spencer.—Meeting with Rogers.—Visit to
the Country-Seat of Thomas Hope.—Lines Written in the Deep Dene
Album.—Rogers.—Mathews, the Comedian.—Preparing for an Excur-
sion into Germany.*

MR. IRVING returned to London on the 26th of December,
and four weeks thereafter transmitted across the Atlantic
the first volume of " Bracebridge Hall," which he had hoped to
have had ready for the press the preceding autumn, but which had
been retarded by indisposition, depression, and the fact that when
he had got it nearly complete he was induced, as has been before
stated, to subtract from it a large portion, which would form the
foundation of a work by itself, and task himself in the height of his
illness to supply its place.

[*To Ebenezer Irving.*]

LONDON, January 29, 1822.

MY DEAR BROTHER :—

By the packet from Liverpool which brings this letter I forward you a
parcel, containing the first volume of " Bracebridge Hall, or the Humor-
ists," a medley in two volumes. I had hoped to have sent both volumes,
but I have not been able to get the second volume ready in time for this
opportunity, though I have tried until the last moment. You will receive
it, however, by the next opportunity, and very probably before you can
have made the necessary arrangements for printing. At any rate, put the
first volume to press *immediately* and publish it *as soon as possible*, with or
without the second volume. As it is not like a novel, but rather a
connected series of tales and essays, it is of no great importance that they
should be published together ; but it is of the greatest importance that
some part of the work should appear as early as possible, to give me

some chance of securing copyright. I shall have to put it to press here in a very short time, as the season is advancing, and my publisher is very impatient; besides, the public has been expecting something from me for some time past, and it will not do to let expectation get too high. If the work is not got out, therefore, very soon in America, there will be a chance of an English copy getting out beforehand, and thus throwing me at the mercy of American publishers. Should the number of copies make any material difference in the time of getting out the work, you had better let the first edition be rather small; and put another to press the moment I furnish you with proof-sheets of the English edition, in which there will doubtless be many alterations, as I have not had time to revise some parts of the work sufficiently, and am apt to make alterations to the last moment.

The work had better be printed in duodecimo, and to save time in binding, let the volumes be put up in lettered covers like the "Sketch-Book." The second edition can be got up in better style. The first volume runs, as near as I can guess, between 340 and 350 pages of the American edition of the "Sketch-Book." The second volume will be about the same size. You can make your estimates accordingly. Put what price you think proper. I do not care about its being a very high one. *I wish, expressly, Moses Thomas to have the preference over every other publisher.* I impress this upon you, and beg you to attend to it as earnestly as if I had written three sheets full on the subject. Whatever may have been his embarrassments and consequent want of punctuality, he is one who showed a disposition to serve me, and who did serve me in the time of my necessity, and I should despise myself could I for a moment forget it. Let him have the work on better terms than other publishers, and do not be deterred by the risk of loss.

My health is still unrestored. This work has kept me from getting well, and my indisposition on the other hand has retarded the work. I have now been about five weeks in London, and have only once been out of doors, about a month since, and that made me worse.

From what Mr. Irving has told me, I infer he must have left his sick-chamber this " once " to confer with Murray respecting the publication of " The Spy," the first of Cooper's novels which created his reputation and laid the foundation of his claim to enduring literary distinction. Wiley, his American publisher, had sent the printed volume to Murray, accompanied by a letter from Cooper, referring him to Mr. Irving for terms. Mr. Wiley at the same time

wrote to Mr. Irving, apprising him of this proceeding, and requesting him, should Murray decline to make such an offer for the work
as in his opinion it might be worth, " to call on some other
respectable house." Murray retained the work until Mr. Irving
grew impatient for an answer, and then declined its publication, as
he had formerly done in the case of the " Sketch-Book." Meanwhile, it found its way to the English public through another
channel. Mr. Irving reported its fate in a letter to Wiley not in
my possession, if it be still in existence, and it is that communication which led to this direct epistle from Cooper, prior to his
adoption, as will be seen from the signature, of his middle name of
Fenimore.

DEAR SIR :—

The friendly interest you have taken in the success of my books
demands of me a direct acknowledgment of your kindness. I was not
very sanguine as to the success of " The Spy " in England, nor was I at
all surprised, when I learned that the book was referred to Mr. Gifford,
that Mr. Murray declined publishing it. If the latter is made sensible of
the evil guidance that he has been subjected to, one good purpose, at
least, will follow the success which you are so good as to communicate.
Mr. Benjamin W. Coles, of this city, is now in Europe, and has been so
kind as to take charge of my new work, " The Pioneers " ; I should be
pleased to have him aided by your experience. If you meet he will
probably call on you, and you will find him a gentleman of acquirements,
and modest, pleasing manners.

By a Mr. Halleck, the admirable Croaker, I have sent to Mr. Coles
the first hundred pages of the work in print. I shall take proper caution
to secure the copyright in both countries, if it can be done.

I desire, sir, to thank you again for your attention to my interests,
and the advice for my future government.

Very respectfully,

Your servant,

JAMES COOPER.

NEW YORK, July 30, 1822.

Fitz-Greene Halleck, mentioned above, who shared with
Joseph Rodman Drake the authorship of the satirical effusions first
published in the New York *Evening Post*, under the signatures of

"Croaker" and "Croaker and Co.," was soon destined to a wider and more exalted celebrity in the front rank of American poets. Drake, whose genius gave promise of a brilliant career, died at the early age of twenty-five, leaving behind him in manuscript that exquisite creation of fancy, "The Culprit Fay."

Mr. Irving was in Germany when this letter of Cooper was received, and did not return to London for some time, so that he had no opportunity of conferring with Murray respecting "The Pioneers," of which he [Murray] became the publisher.

The second volume of "Bracebridge Hall" was despatched to New York the last of February, a month after the other, but reached its destination within eight days of it, the first having a passage of sixty days. They were received in April, and hurried through the press by Ebenezer for fear of being anticipated by the copy on the English side. The work was printed in the style of the "Sketch-Book," and for want of time only a thousand copies were printed in the first edition ; "it would have been more profitable," says Ebenezer, "to have made the edition larger, but it would not do to venture on it." It appeared May 21, 1822. Soon after Mr. Irving had sent the second volume to America, and thus given it a fair start, he proceeded to make a contract with Murray for its publication in England.

When the author came up from Birmingham to London with the MS. of "Bracebridge Hall," Colburn called on him, introduced by Campbell the poet, and offered him a thousand guineas for it, but he would not entertain a proposition to leave Murray. The latter had been very anxious to have something from him, as the season was advancing, and when Mr. Irving went to him, at the instance of his friends, who probably knew his too easy acquiescence in any sum that might be offered, he was induced to name his own price, which was fifteen hundred guineas. This staggered Murray, who, after a moment's hesitation, began : "If you had said a thousand guineas,"—"You shall have it for a thousand guineas," said Mr. Irving, breaking in. Murray was taken aback by this. He had probably been prepared to divide the difference, and go the length of twelve hundred and fifty guineas. When he found

Mr. Irving respond so promptly to the lesser sum, he sat down at once, and drew out the notes for the amount, and gave them to him, although he did not receive the manuscript until nearly two weeks afterward. He also threw in a handsome donation of books, which the author sent to his sister at Birmingham.

After all, as his brother Peter writes him on hearing of the bargain with Murray, " a thousand guineas has a golden sound."

Mr. Irving sent the last proof of " Bracebridge Hall " to press in London, May 11, 1822. He had made great alterations and additions as the work was printing, so that the first English edition differed considerably from the first American one. The two editions were published within two days of each other, the American appearing on the 21st, and the English on the 23d of May.

Some time before the appearance of "Bracebridge Hall " in London, Mr. Irving found himself getting the better of the tormenting malady in his ankles, which had troubled him at Birmingham, and confined him to the house since his arrival in London. He had been at a grievous expense with doctors to but little purpose, and he finally determined to undertake his own cure ; " for I fancy," he says, " I understand the complaint as well as any of them." His first step was to go out and take exercise every day. Finding his health improving under this regimen, he began to pay visits, and was soon in a constant hurry of engagements, in the midst of which Moore came over to London from Paris for a brief sojourn, arriving April 16th, and leaving May 7th. During this interval his diary, for Mr. Irving kept none at this period, gives us a few glimpses of the author, of which I select the following :—

May 2d.—Went with Irving to breakfast at Holland House. The Duke of Bedford came in after breakfast, fresh from his duel with the Duke of Buckingham.

May 5th.—Irving walked about with me ; called together at Lady Blessington's, who is growing very absurd. " I have felt very melancholy and ill all this day," she said. " Why is that?" I asked. " Don't you know ?" " No." " It is the anniversary of my poor Napoleon's death."

In the following extract from a letter to Brevoort, dated London, June 11th, we find mention of John Randolph and Mrs. Siddons :—

John Randolph is here, and has attracted much attention. He has been sought after by people of the first distinction. I have met him repeatedly in company, and his eccentricity of appearance and manner makes him the more current and interesting; for in high life here, they are always eager after any thing strange and peculiar. There is a vast deal, too, of the old school in Randolph's manner, the turn of his thoughts, and the style of his conversation, which seems to please very much.

Among other interesting acquaintances that I have made is Mrs. Siddons. She is now near seventy, and yet a magnificent-looking woman. It is surprising how little time has been able to impair the dignity of her carriage, or the noble expression of her countenance. I heard her read the part of Constance at her own house one evening, and I think it the greatest dramatic treat I have had for a long time past.

Four days after the date of this letter, Mr. Irving received an invitation from Lady Spencer to dine with her at Wimbledon, one of the country-seats of Lord Spencer, about twelve miles from London. This was the lady whose Christmas invitation he had not been able to accept. At this dinner he first met the poet Rogers, who had lately returned from the continent; and who, though a stranger, received him with the hearty cordiality of an old friend. Irving at this time was overrun with invitations from many of whom he knew nothing. Rogers cautioned him to be on his guard, or the commonplace would hunt him down. "Show me your list of invitations," said he, "and let me give you a hint or two. This accept," to one; "that decline," to another, to a third, "this man avoid by all means; oh, he's a direful bore!" Mr. Irving was quite amused at this worldly advice of the poet, and especially at the decided emphasis of the last sentence. Who the individual was, so impressively complimented, he did not specify when the anecdote fell from him.

I have heard Mr. Irving relate the following curious incident, as occurring at Wimbledon, where it appears he passed the night. He was reading, as was his custom through life, in bed. His door suddenly opened cautiously, and in stalked a grim apparition in the shape of a man with a lantern, who quietly walked up to his light, and, with some muttered sentence which escaped him, extinguished it, and then walked out, shutting the door after him, and leaving

Geoffrey in a maze at the mysterious intrusion. Lady Spencer laughed heartily when he mentioned the incident the next morning at breakfast. "Oh," said she, "that was my fireman ; we once lost a country-seat by fire, and ever since he has had orders to walk the corridors at night, and when he detects a light from under the door, to extinguish it."

The next trace of him is June 21st, when he is passing a few days at the country-seat of Mr. Thomas Hope, author of "Anastasius"; from which he writes to his sister Catharine :—

I am now writing from a country-seat in a beautiful part of the country where I am passing a few days. It is the residence of Mr. Thomas Hope, one of the richest and most extraordinary men in England, not more famous for his wealth and magnificence than for being the author of "Anastasius," a work of great merit and curious character. His wife, the Hon. Mrs. Hope, is one of the loveliest women in the kingdom, and one of the reigning deities of fashion. Their country-seat is furnished in a style of taste and magnificence of which I can give you no idea. With all this, they are delightfully frank, simple, and unpretending in their manners, especially in their country retreat ; which is the true place to see English people to advantage. There are several persons on a visit here, besides myself, and time passes away very pleasantly.

The following contribution to the Album at Deep Dene, the country-seat above mentioned, I take from the *Cornhill Magazine* of May, 1860, in which it appeared after Mr. Irving's death.

WRITTEN IN THE DEEP DENE ALBUM.

June 24, 1822.

Thou record of the votive throng
    That fondly seek this fairy shrine,
And pay the tribute of a song
    Where worth and loveliness combine—

What boots that I, a vagrant wight
    From clime to clime still wandering on,
Upon thy friendly page should write—
    Who 'll think of me when I am gone ?

> Go plough the wave, and sow the sand ;
>   Throw seed to every wind that blows;
> Along the highway strew thy hand
>   And fatten on the crop that grows.
>
> For even thus the man that roams
>   On heedless hearts his feeling spends ;
> Strange tenant of a thousand homes,
>   And friendless, with ten thousand friends.
>
> Yet here for once I 'll leave a trace,
>   To ask in after-times a thought ;
> To say that here a resting-place
>   My wayworn heart has fondly sought.
>
> So the poor pilgrim heedless strays,
>   Unmoved, through many a region fair ;
> But at some shrine his tribute pays,
>   To tell that he has worshipped there.
>   WASHINGTON IRVING.

June 30th, he writes to Brevoort from London :—

Rogers, the poet, returned not long since from the continent, and I
breakfast occasionally with him, and meet Crabbe and others of his literary
friends. He has one of the completest and most elegant little bachelor
establishments that I have ever seen. It is as neat, and elegant, and
finished, and small, as his own principal poem.

Mathews, the comedian, is coming out to make a tour in America, which
I have no doubt will be a successful one. His powers of entertainment are
wonderful. By his talents at imitation, he in a manner raises the dead, and
makes them walk and talk for your amusement ; for his specimens of Tate
Wilkinson, Macklin, Wilkes, etc., etc., are among the best of his imitations.
He is a very correct, gentlemanlike man in private life, and at times the
life of a dinner-table by his specimens of characters of the day. I shall
give him letters to America, and among others to yourself.

When Mr. Irving returned from Deep Dene to his lodgings
in London, he found his table covered with invitations which had
accumulated during his absence.

I have been leading a sad life lately [he writes to his brother Peter,
June 30th], burning the candle at both ends, and seeing the fashionable

world through one of its seasons.   The success of my writings gave me an opportunity, and I thought it worth while to embrace it if it were only for curiosity's sake.   I have therefore been tossed about " hither and thither and whither I would not " ; have been at the levee and the drawing-room, been at routs, and balls, and dinners, and country-seats ; been hand-and-glove with nobility and mobility, until, like Trim, I have satisfied the sentiment, and am now preparing to make my escape from all this splendid confusion.

He was intending to make the best of his way to Aix-la-Chapelle, for the benefit of the baths and waters.

CHAPTER XXIX.

Mayence.—Introduction to the " Tales of a Traveller."—Heidelberg.— Letter from Moore.—Munich.—Eugène Beauharnais.—Vienna.—The Young Napoleon.

THE restless life which the author had been leading in London had thrown him back in his recovery, and when he started for Aix-la-Chapelle, he was still rather lame from the lingerings of his complaint.

From this "little old ghost-ridden city," as he terms Aix-la-Chapelle in his notes, he ascended the Rhine to Wiesbaden, and proceeded thence to Mayence, where he remained about three weeks.

It was from the Hotel de Darmstadt at Mayence, that the introduction to the "Tales of a Traveller" is dated. The author was thrown back in his recovery after his arrival at Mayence, and was detained there some time by indisposition, as stated in that introduction, nor was Katrina, the pretty daughter of mine host, under whose tuition he conjugated *ich liebe*, a fiction, but the tales really were written partly in Paris and partly in England. As, however, he tells Peter, he was in hopes to have something under way for spring publication, it is probable he attempted some scribbling under the roof of the jolly publican, John Ardnot, from which the fancy took him to date his lucubrations from that hotel. From Mayence, which he left on the 13th of September, he proceeded to Frankfort and thence through Darmstadt to Heidelberg.

With all my ailments and my lameness [he writes to a sister from this place], I never have enjoyed travelling more than through these lovely countries. I do not know whether it is the peculiar fineness of the season, or the general character of the climate, but I never was more sensible to the delicious effect of atmosphere : perhaps my very malady has made me more susceptible to influences of the kind. I feel a kind of intoxication of the heart, as I draw in the pure air of the mountains; and the clear, transparent atmosphere, the steady, serene, golden sunshine, seems to enter into my very soul.

Awaiting his arrival at Heidelberg, which he had expected to reach much earlier, when he set out on his tour, Mr. Irving found the following letter :—

[*From Thomas Moore.*]

August 5, 1822.

MY DEAR IRVING :—

I have been so deplorably lazy about writing to you, that I fear I am now too late to catch you at Heidelberg, and lest it should be the fate of my letter to die in the Dead-Letter office of a German town (" la plus morte mort " as Montaigne calls it, that I can imagine), I will only venture two or three hasty lines, to tell you that we are all quite well, and full of delight at the idea of seeing you here in autumn. I have taken up a subject for a poem since I came to Passy, and nearly finished it—only about twelve or thirteen hundred lines in all, which I shall publish singly. Bessy has been for some weeks (with that " John Bull," as Tom now calls himself) at Montmorenci, drinking the waters. I will just give you an extract from a letter I received from her yesterday, because I think it is about as good criticism as is to be had (for *love* at least, whatever there may be for *money*) nowadays. " I have just finished ' Bracebridge Hall,' and am more than ever delighted with the author. How often he touches the heart ! at least mine." I think you will agree with me that the modesty of this last limitation is such as critics would do well to imitate oftener. " Parlez pour vous " would dispel the illusions of the plurality exceedingly.

I want you very much here, and often express my wants aloud, though I have not Mrs. Story to give her gentle echo to them. She complains in her last letter to Bessy, that she has no longer any traces of your existence in the world. I could scribble a good deal more, now I have begun, but having the fear of that epistolary death at Heidelberg before my eyes, I must stop short, and am, my dear Irving,

Ever faithfully yours,

THOMAS MOORE.

At the receipt of this letter Mr. Irving was undetermined whether to return to Paris, or to strike into the interior of Germany and pass his winter in Dresden. He left Heidelberg on the 30th of September, with his mind made up to the latter course, though at Strasburg, as he records, he had to resist " several strong tugs of feeling that pulled him toward Paris." He reached Ulm on the 5th of October, continued along the Danube the next day to visit the field of Blenheim, the famous battle-ground, and the day following arrived at Munich, the capital of Bavaria, where " a grand fête on the king's birthday " gave him a fine opportunity of seeing both the court and the populace.

> I had a good view also [he writes] of Eugène Beauharnais, the stepson of Bonaparte. He married a daughter of the King of Bavaria, and is one of the most fortunate of Bonaparte's relatives and followers; for he has ever maintained a character for honor and bravery, and now lives in opulence and ease, with a superb palace, a charming wife and family, beloved by his father-in-law, the old king, and esteemed by the public.

On the 17th of October he left Munich for Salzburg, which he pronounces " one of the most romantic places, as to its situation and scenery, he had ever beheld." Here he remained two or three days and then resumed his journey for Vienna, where he was occupied " in looking about for nearly a month." In a letter to his sister from this city, dated November 10th, he gives this glimpse of the young Napoleon :—

> The Emperor is at present in Italy, attending the Congress at Verona. I have seen the other members of the Imperial family several times at the theatre, where they appear in the Imperial box without any show, nor any sensation on the part of the audience, as it seems quite a common occurrence. The most interesting member of the family, however, was the young Napoleon, son of poor Boney. His mother, now called the Archduchess Marie Louise, was, as you may recollect, daughter of the Emperor of Austria. She is now at Verona. The young Napoleon, or the Duke of Reichstadt, as he is called, is a very fine boy, full of life and spirit, of most engaging manners and appearance, and universally popular. He has something of Bonaparte in the shape of his head and the lower part of his countenance; his eyes are like his mother's. I have seen him once in an open carriage, with his tutor. Every one took off his hat as the little fellow passed. I have since seen him at the theatre, where he appeared to enjoy the play with boyish delight; laughing out loud, and continually turning to speak to his more phlegmatic uncles, the other young princes.

CHAPTER XXX.

*From Vienna to Dresden.—Intimacy with an English Family.—Mrs. Ful-
ler's Impressions of the Author.—Letter to Mrs. Van Wart.—Letter to
Peter.—Private Theatricals.—The Conspiracy.—Plays Sir Charles
Rackett in "Three Weeks After Marriage."—Letter to Leslie.—Boar
Hunt.—Extracts from Note-Book.—Leaves Dresden for Paris.*

Brom Bones.

EFORE he left Vienna the author
visited the Imperial library, where
he saw the MSS. of Tasso's " Jeru-
salem." He has this note on
the subject : " I thought I saw a
similarity between his handwriting
and Lord Byron's ; many alterations in MSS." He left Vienna
on the 18th of November, and
passing a few days at Prague on
the way, arrived at Dresden on the
28th.

In this little capital, where his
stay was prolonged through several
months, the author was destined
to find a delightful residence.

He met an old acquaintance
here in Morier, the British Minister, whom he had known as Chargé
at Washington, in 1811, and through him he soon found himself
mingling familiarly with the diplomatic corps, who formed a sort of
social brotherhood. Here he also met, for the first time, an English
family by the name of Foster, with whom he became extremely
intimate, and to whom allusion is made in the notes and letters which
are to follow. Mrs. Foster had been for some time residing in

Dresden for the education of her children, two daughters now grown up, and two younger sons. Her house soon became a home to him. One of the daughters, in a letter addressed to him long years afterward, says of this period: "You formed a part of our daily life." I transcribe a letter from another daughter, which gives her impression of his character, as exhibited at this period of familiar intercourse. The letter, it will be seen, bears date after the author's death, and was addressed to me in reply to an application for his correspondence with the family.

> THORNHAUGH RECTORY, WANSFORD, }
> NORTHAMPTONSHIRE, March 10, 1860. }

DEAR SIR:—

I have sent a few extracts from Mr. Irving's letters that I thought were characteristic, or might be generally interesting, but only a few, for he expressed so strong a desire that his correspondence should be strictly private, that I have only chosen those that I think he would not have disliked being made public, or I should feel as if I had violated the sacred confidence of a friendship so valued. The passages I have sent give an idea of his life in Dresden. Sought after by all in the best society, and mingling much in the gay life of a foreign city, and a court where the royal family were themselves sufficiently intellectual to appreciate genius; but really intimate with ourselves only, and to such a degree that it gives me a right to judge of some points in his character. He was thoroughly a gentleman, not merely externally in manners and look, but to the innermost fibres and core of his heart. Sweet-tempered, gentle, fastidious, sensitive, and gifted with the warmest affections, the most delightful and invariably interesting companion, gay and full of humor, even in spite of occasional fits of melancholy, which he was however seldom subject to when with those he liked—a gift of conversation that flowed like a full river in sunshine, bright, easy, and abundant. He stayed at Dresden till we left, and then accompanied us on our return home, even into the packet-boat, and left us in the channel. That was not, happily, our last parting; he visited us in England, and I saw a good deal of him in London afterward; but the farewell in that open boat, with the looks of regret on all sides, seemed the real farewell, and left the deepest impression. The picture he received in Paris was the little miniature you mention.

> I am, dear sir,
> Yours very truly,
> EMILY FULLER.

You are quite welcome to make any use of my letter that you please. It is a very faint testimony of a real friendship.

The "picture" referred to at the close of this tribute to the departed, was a miniature copy of the "Head of Herodias," painted by Miss Foster, from the Dresden gallery, and which has been for years suspended from the walls of Sunnyside. "I treasure it," says the author in a letter to her a few years before his death, "as a precious memorial of those pleasant days." It was received by Mr. Irving at Paris four or five months after his parting with the family on their return to England in July, 1823. One of the records of his diary at Paris, under date of December 15, 1823, is as follows :—

Return home, and find parcel from Mrs. Foster, with German books, and miniature painted by Emily.

The following letters, written after he had been more than three months in Dresden, give some pleasant glimpses of his mode of life in that city :—

[*To Mrs. Sarah Van Wart.*]

DRESDEN, March 7, 1823.

MY DEAR SISTER:—

. . . . My winter in Dresden has been extremely agreeable. I have become quite at home among the good people, and am invited to every thing that is going on in the world of fashion and gayety. The old court has particularly pleased me from its stiff old-fashioned formalities, and buckram ceremonies. I have been treated uniformly with the most marked attention, by all the members of the royal family, and am in great favor with the old queen. There is a singular mixture of state and familiarity in some of the court fêtes. There have been, for instance, several court balls given by the royal family. At those given by the king the common people are admitted as spectators, and rows of seats are erected for them on each side of the great saloon in which the company dance. Here then you see the nobility and visitors of the court, in full court-dresses, dancing in the centre of the saloon, while on each side are long banks of burly faces wedged together, men, women, and children, and gazing, and courtesying as at a theatre. As the court dances are not always the most dignified, one would think this opportunity of seeing royalty cutting capers, would be enough to destroy the illusion with which it is surrounded. There is one romping dance called "The Grandfather," something in the style of *Sir Roger de Coverly*, which generally winds up the balls, and of which the princes and princesses are extremely fond. In this I have seen the courtiers of all ages capering up and down the saloon to the infinite amusement of the populace, and in conformity to the vagaries of the dance, I have been obliged to romp about with one of the princesses as if she had been a boarding-school girl. . . . .

I wish I could give you a good account of my literary labors, but I have nothing to report. I am merely seeing and hearing, and my mind seems in too crowded and confused a state to produce any thing. I am getting very familiar with the German language; and there is a lady here who is so kind as to give me lessons every day in Italian [Mrs. Foster], which language I had nearly forgotten, but which I am fast regaining. Another lady is superintending my French [Miss Emily Foster], so that if I am not acquiring ideas, I am at least acquiring a variety of modes of expressing them when they do come. . . . .

[*To Peter Irving.*]

DRESDEN, March 10, 1823.

MY DEAR BROTHER :—

What a time have I suffered to pass by without writing to you! I can give no excuse for it but the wretched and unsatisfactory one of continual procrastination, and too much distraction and dissipation of mind; but I know you to be indulgent in these cases, and not to consider a casual career of dissipation among the *crying* sins. I have been passing a very agreeable, a very idle, but I trust after all, a very profitable winter in Dresden; for though I have done nothing with my pen, and have been tossed about on the stream of society, yet I console myself with the idea that I have *lived into* a great deal of amusing and characteristic information; which, after all, is perhaps the best way of studying the world. I have been most hospitably received and even caressed in this little capital, and have experienced nothing but the most marked kindness from the king downward. My reception, indeed, at court has been peculiarly flattering, and every branch of the royal family has taken occasion to show me particular attention, whenever I made my appearance. I wish you were here with me to study this little court; it is just the thing that would delight you. It is one of the most formal and ceremonious in Europe, keeping up all the old observances that have been laid aside in other courts. The king is an excellent old gentleman, between seventy and eighty, but a stanch stickler for the old school. He has two brothers, Prince Max and Prince Antoine, and the trio are such figures as you see in the prints of Frederick the Great. Prince Max is one of the most amiable old gentlemen I have ever met with; his countenance and manners peculiarly benevolent ; he has two sons, Frederick and John (the former will one day inherit the throne), and two daughters, the youngest of whom is the present Queen of Spain.   Prince Antoine, the other brother of the king, is a brisk, lively little gentleman ; very religious, but withal as great a hunter as Nimrod, and as fond of dancing as King David.   He married a sister of the Emperor of Austria, an old lady who is a complete picture of the dames of the old school.   Prince Antoine has always shown a great fancy for me, and I believe I owe much of my standing in the old gentleman's favor to dancing French quadrilles.   I have dined with the king, and been at a number of balls and soirées given by the different members of the royal family.   As at these balls every one must be in uniform or court-dress, they are very showy.

Among the other amusements of the winter, we have had a little attempt at private theatricals.   These have been at the house of Mrs. Foster, an English lady of rank, who has been residing here for a couple of years.   She has two daughters, most accomplished and charming girls. They occupy part of a palace, and in a large saloon a little theatre was fitted up, the scenery being hired from a small theatre and the dresses from a masquerade warehouse.   It was very prettily arranged, I assure you.   We first tried "Tom Thumb," which, however, went no farther than a dress rehearsal, in which I played the part of King Arthur, to Mrs. Foster's Dollalolla ; and the other parts were supported by some of the English who were wintering in Dresden.   There was then an attempt to get up a little opera, altered from the French by Colonel Livius, a cousin of Mrs. Foster, and some such a character as I have described in Master Simon in my last work.   The colonel, however, who is a green-room veteran, and has written for the London theatres, was so much of a martinet in his managerial discipline, that the piece absolutely fell through from being too much managed.   In the meantime a few of the colonel's theatrical subjects conspired to play him a trick, and get up a piece without his knowledge.   We pitched upon the little comedy of "Three Weeks after Marriage," which I altered and arranged so as to leave out two or three superfluous characters.   I played the part of Sir Charles Rackett ; Miss Foster, Lady Rackett ; Miss Flora Foster, Dimity ; Mrs. Foster, Mrs. Druggett ; and a young officer by the name of Corkran, the part of Mr. Druggett.   You cannot imagine the amusement this little theatrical plot furnished us.   We rehearsed in Mrs. Foster's drawing-room, and as the whole was to be kept a profound secret, and as Mrs. Foster's drawing-room is a great place of resort, and as especially our dramatic sovereign, Colonel Livius, was almost an inmate of the family, we were in continual risk of discovery, and had to gather together like a set of conspirators.

We, however, carried our plot into execution more successfully than commonly falls to the lot of conspirators. The colonel had ordered a dress rehearsal of his little opera; the scenery was all prepared, the theatre lighted up, a few amateurs admitted; the colonel took his seat before the curtain, to direct the rehearsal. The curtain rose, and out walked Mr. and Mrs. Druggett in proper costume. The little colonel was perfectly astonished, and did not recover himself before the first act was finished; it was a perfect explosion to him. We afterward performed the little comedy before a full audience of the English resident in Dresden, and of several of the nobility that understood English, and it went off with great spirit and success. We are now on the point of playing "The Wonder," which I have altered and shortened to suit the strength of the company, and to prune off objectionable parts. In this, I play the part of Don Felix, to Miss Foster's Violante; she plays charmingly. The part of Colonel Briton I have had to alter into a British captain of a man-of-war, to adapt it to the turn of the actor who is to play it, namely, Captain Morier, of the navy, brother of the British Minister. I have dwelt rather long on this subject because I know you relish matters of the kind.

[*To C. R. Leslie.*]

DRESDEN, March 15, 1823.

I have just been seized with a fit of letter-writing, after having nearly forgotten how to use my pen, so I take the earliest stage of the complaint to scribble to you. I had hoped to receive a gratuitous letter from you before this, but you are one of those close codgers who never pay more than the law compels them.

How often I have wished for you and Newton during the last eight or nine months, in the course of which I have been continually mingling in scenes full of character and picture.

The place where I am now passing my time is a complete study. The court of this little kingdom of Saxony is, perhaps, the most ceremonious and old-fashioned in Europe, and one finds here customs and observances in full vigor that have long since faded away in other courts.

The king is a capital character himself,—a complete old gentleman of the ancient school, and very tenacious in keeping up the old style. He has treated me with the most marked kindness, and every member of the royal family has shown me great civility. What would greatly delight you is the royal hunting establishment, which the king maintains at a vast expense, being his hobby. He has vast forests stocked with game, and a complete forest police, forest masters, chasseurs, piqueurs, jägers, etc., etc. The charm of the thing is, that all this is kept up in the old style; and to go out hunting with him, you might fancy yourself in one of those scenes of old times which we read of in poetry and romance. I have followed him thrice to the boar hunt. The last we had extremely good sport. The boar gave us a chase of upward of two hours, and was not overpowered until it had killed one dog, and desperately wounded several others. It was a very cold winter day, with much snow on the ground ; but as the hunting was in a thick pine forest and the day was sunny, we did not feel the cold. The king and all his hunting retinue were clad in an old-fashioned hunting uniform of green, with green caps. The sight of the old monarch and his retinue galloping through the alleys of the forest ; the jägers dashing singly about in all directions, cheering the hounds ; the shouts ; the blast of horns ; the cry of hounds ringing through the forest, altogether made one of the most animating scenes I ever beheld.

I have become very intimate with one of the king's forest masters, who lives in a picturesque old hunting lodge with towers, formerly a convent, and who has undertaken to show me all the economy of the hunting establishment. What glorious groupings, and what admirable studies for figures and faces I have seen among these hunters !

I have done nothing with my pen since I left you, absolutely *nothing !* I have been gazing about, rather idly perhaps, but yet among fine scenes of striking character, and I can only hope that some of them may stick to my mind, and furnish me with materials in some future fit of scribbling.

I have been fighting my way into the German language, and am regaining my Italian, and for want of more profitable employment have turned *play-actor.*

We have been getting up private theatricals here at the house of an English lady. I have already enacted Sir Charles Rackett in " Three Weeks After Marriage," with great applause ; and I am on the point of playing Don Felix in "The Wonder." I had no idea of this fund of dramatic talent lurking within me ; and I now console myself that if the worst comes to the worst I can turn stroller, and pick up a decent maintenance among the barns in England. I verily believe nature intended me to be a vagabond.

I continue the sketch of his life at Dresden, with some extracts from his note-book, beginning some days after the date of the letter to Leslie, just given.

April 1st.—Write letters all the morning—little Madame de Bergh [1] makes an April fool of me. *2d.*—In evening, dressed rehearsal of " The

---

[1] Wife of the Danish Minister.

Wonder" at Mrs. Foster's.   3*d*.   [*Thursday*]—My birthday—at one o'clock drive into the country with the Fosters and Colonel Livius; . . . . return before dark.   In the evening a small party at Mrs. Foster's to keep my birthday.   The Misses Foster prepare a surprise by getting up tableaux of scenes in the "Sketch-Book" and "Bracebridge Hall" and "Knickerbocker."   The picture by Leslie of Dutch courtship admirably represented by Madame de Bergh and Captain Morier.   Annette Delarbre by the young Countess Hernenbern, Madame Foster, and Captain Morier.   Boar's Head Tavern, Eastcheap, by Mrs. Foster, Miss Flora Foster, and Captain Morier.—Conclude the evening by waltzing.

April 10*th*.—.   .   .   .   Go to Ponic to hear decision about my having fired a pistol out of my window.   The legal penalty twenty dollars and forfeiture.   I am let off for two dollars eight groschen fine, and two dollars some groschen cost, and the pistol returned to me.   Very lenient on the part of Mr. Rarow the President.

[The pistol was a small one, borrowed of Colonel Livius, to be used in playing Don Felix in " The Wonder," in the mock drunken scene.   Finding it loaded, he opened a window and fired it off, making himself unconsciously amenable to the law.]

Sunday, April 27*th*.—Go to Mrs. F.—read Italian till two—dine there early, as there is a court ball at six—return home to dress—at six go to ball given by Prince Max in Prince Frederick's apartments—the King and Queen of Bavaria and of Saxony there—dance with E. and F. Foster. —Queen of Saxony sent the master of ceremonies to bring me to her—said she had not seen me for a century—that she had just received my works from Paris, and made many compliments on it—said she expected I would write something about Dresden, etc., and about the *chasse* [a purpose entertained by him, but never fulfilled].—King of Bavaria told me he knew Franklin in Paris, and after Franklin's departure he had bought a horse and cabriolet which belonged to him—returned home about ten or half past.

May 14*th*.—Walked out to Preussnitz in morning—saw Cockburn, who agreed to accompany me in tour to the Riesen Gebirge—went to Foster's in evening—spent a very pleasant evening chatting.

On the 20th of May, in company with the young English officer just named, Mr. John Cockburn of the artillery, Mr. Irving set out on a tour he had been some time contemplating to the Riesen Gebirge, or Giant Mountains, a chain of mountains that separate Silesia from Bohemia. He revisited Prague seven days after his departure, and in this picturesque old city his stay was prolonged by the illness of his companion to the 24th of June. He returned to Dresden on the 26th of June, after an absence of five weeks. Here he remained until the 12th of July, when he took his final departure for Paris, travelling part of the way in company with his friends, the Fosters, who were on their return to England.

They had made their house absolutely a home to me [he writes to Peter] during my residence in Dresden. I travelled in an open carriage with Mrs. Foster; the two Misses Foster and her two little boys followed on in a post-chaise with their German tutor.

The commencement of our tour was most auspicious, but after leaving Leipsic, as we approached the Hartz regions, we met with one of the most tremendous squalls of wind, dust, rain, hail, thunder and lightning I ever experienced.

I extract the particulars of this travelling incident from some scarcely legible pencilled memoranda.

Mrs. Foster gets on the box with me—fine and warm—country begins to grow more varied—see a storm gathering ahead—it advances rapidly— I see that it is a thunder-gust and likely to be a severe one—get Mrs. Foster into carriage—make the carriage all fast and ready—mount the dicky with box-coat and a fur-mantle about my legs, and umbrella—gust comes on with a hurricane of wind, raising clouds of dust—the earth seems thrown up into the air—the clouds brown with dust—the whole atmosphere thick-ened and darkened—gust comes more and more terrible—horses can hardly draw on the carriage—begins to rain—rain driven with incredible violence—hail—large as hazel-nuts—storm increases—one horrible blast of wind succeeds another—umbrella breaks and is whirled off into a neigh-boring field—mantle flies after it—horses get frightened—I descend from coach-box—fear the carriage will be blown over—the two leaders become unmanageable—postilion jumps off and tries to hold them—they turn round and go down a bank—try to keep them quiet—they continue restive—drag carriage after them down a steep bank into a ditch—pole breaks—carriage overturns—rush to the place and get the ladies out— none hurt materially—bruised a little—drenched to the skin in an instant —leave them there and run to a house about half a mile off—find a smith's shop with a small country inn beside it—send workmen to look after the carriage, and order rooms to be prepared for ladies—run back to carriage

--the storm is already over—find them all drenched to the skin, but in good spirits and unhurt—they walk to the inn—the carriage is with much trouble righted and dragged up the bank backward by two horses and six or eight men—get safe to the inn—a new pole is made—we all change our clothes, and after a repast of cold tongue and wine, set off in good spirits —the ladies give their hats, which were quite wet, to a pretty maid-servant at the inn—and likewise a shawl—she will be the belle of the neighborhood.

This storm was "the overture to a long series of bad weather" [he writes to Peter] that lasted during our tour. Still there were intervals of beautiful sunshine which we enjoyed the more from contrast. We accomplished a tour through the Hartz Mountains, which surpassed my expectations; not from their height, but from the magnificence of the forest scenery, which reminded me of our American forests. We then passed through the *Golden Acre* or Golden Meadow, which lies between the Hartz and the Kyffhauser mountains, and continued on to Hesse. I was delighted with the beauty of this last country, of which, somehow or other, I had no expectation. In about ten days from our leaving Dresden, we arrived at the beautiful little city of Cassel, the capital of Hesse, where we remained a couple of days to repose from the fatigues of travelling, and to have a little pleasant time together before we parted, as I had intended making the best of my way for Paris from that place. When it came to the last evening, however, it seemed hard to part thus in the midst of a tour, so the next morning I resumed my seat in the carriage, determined to see my fair companions safely on board the steamboat at Rotterdam. We had better weather during the remaining part of the journey and passed through some lovely country; a part of what was formerly Westphalia. At Rotterdam the Fosters embarked. I accompanied them down to the Brille, and then bade them adieu as if I had been taking leave of my own family; for they had been for nearly eight months past more like relatives than friends to me.

I now made the best of my way for Paris, travelling day and night, excepting a short stay of a night and part of a day at Antwerp. I arrived here the day before yesterday [August 3d], and have been taking lodgings in the *Hotel de Yorck, Boulevard Montmartre.* I shall now put myself *en train* for literary occupation, as it is high time for me to do something, having been so long unsettled.

END OF VOLUME I.

www.ingramcontent.com/pod-product-compliance
Lightning Source LLC
Chambersburg PA
CBHW020932030726
47496CB00005B/1151